THE DEVIL &
THE DETAILS

KELLY R. NELSON

Cover design by Zoetic Arts.

Edited and formatted by Dr. Mekhala Spencer at All The Proof Editing.

Library of Congress Cataloging-in-Publication Data has been applied for.

ISBN 979-8-9993111-0-8 (paperback)
ISBN 979-8-9993111-1-5 (eBook)

First Edition: September 2025

CONTENTS

— • —

DEDICATION

For my book girlies who love it complicated, a little chaotic, and downright filthy.
You came for the plot—but stayed for the pleasure.
Clutch your pearls, turn the page, and don't you dare hide that cover in public.
Let them wonder why you're blushing.

—•—

ACKNOWLEDGMENTS

Robert, thank you for your patience and quiet support while I poured myself into this book.

To my two Ks—you kept the spice hot and the feedback honest. I couldn't have done it without you.

And to the Women of Word's Book Club—my fierce Beta Readers—thank you for showing up for this story and for me.

To every reader who dared to dive in: this book is yours now.

1

BLOOD & CONCRETE

BETHANY

The room was a cell. Bare. Cold. Its silence thick enough to smother. A dull bulb hung overhead; its weak glow died before it reached the corners, leaving the rest to the shadows. A stained mattress lay on the floor, surrounded by nothing but concrete walls and a rusted bucket in the corner—a reminder that I had no dignity left here. There were no windows, no sense of time. Only stillness, and the faint metallic tang of blood.

I looked down at Kevin's body sprawled beside me. His blue jeans were soaked. His white shirt clung to his chest, already blooming dark crimson. Once, I loved him. Once, he'd been everything. That love had led me here, his blood on my hands and clothes, seeping into my skin like a curse. My heart barely beat. I could feel it slowing, the weight of what I had done pressing down until I could barely breathe.

Kneeling beside him, I reached out and touched his face. His eyes were closed, as if he were only asleep. I leaned in, pressing my lips to his cold mouth—a final goodbye to the man I loved and lost. My voice was barely a whisper. "Why did you make me do this, Kevin? Why?"

I swallowed the scream clawing at my throat and forced my blurred vision to focus. Numb fingers searched his pockets. Left side. Nothing. Right side. Nothing. Panic scratched at my ribs. I rolled his heavy body, fumbling, desperate. Where is it? Where's the key?

A hollow ache sank beyond bone, buried in my core. A guttural sound ripped loose as I pounded his chest. "Where did you put the key?" The demand ricocheted off concrete, the only living thing in this tomb. I was trapped in the prison he made, and no one knew. No one would come.

I crawled to the wall, knees to chest, and rocked in silence. A broken lullaby slipped out—the same one he forced me to sing, the one that always reminded me of just how alone I was.

"He's got the whole world...in His hands...

He's got the whole world...in His hands...

He's got the whole world...in His hands...

He's got you and me, sister...in His hands..."

2

INHERITANCE OF GHOSTS

BETHANY

I never wanted to set foot in this godforsaken town again. As I climbed out of my rental car, the stench of manure and wet grass clung to my clothes and lungs. I was here to settle my father's affairs, to tie up whatever loose ends he left behind. I hadn't spoken to him in nearly five years—not since I left with nothing but a bus ticket and the clothes in my backpack. But his sudden heart attack dragged me back, forcing me to confront the ghosts I thought I'd escaped.

Pastor Julius Martin. To the town, a righteous leader. To me, just Father—distant, rigid, judgmental. A man who loved his congregation more than his own blood. Now I was his sole heir, left to clean up his legacy. Even his title weighed on me as I stood outside the church that had been both a second home and a prison.

My mother left on a Sunday afternoon while I was at church with him. She said she wasn't feeling well and waved us off from the front door. I remember the worry sitting in my chest, the slight frown on my father's face as we drove away. The sermon was long that day, but even as he preached, I kept glancing at the back doors, hoping to see her standing there. But when the service ended, she was gone.

We walked into silence.

A note sat on the kitchen table, addressed to me with a single word: Sorry.

For years, I tried to understand why she left, how she could walk away from her only child. I was her mirror image—everyone said so. Golden blonde hair, piercing blue eyes, and the beauty mark on my right cheek. A younger version of her. A living reminder of her youth. And still, she left me. Abandoned me to my father's strict, suffocating control.

3

Two years later, I found the divorce papers in his desk. Alongside them, a signed form surrendering her rights to be my mother. She was gone for good—erased from my life by her hand and his. I clenched my fists. I had a plan—quick and clean.

The mortuary was going to Mayor Lawrence Spellman for $75,000. It was worth more, but I didn't care. It meant nothing. I'd arranged everything over the phone from Santa Monica—the place I now called home after years of wandering. This town was a skeleton of memories. Belle's Diner still wore its faded pink awning. John Hill's hardware store stood at Elm and Cedar, now run by his grandson. Even the cracks in the sidewalks hadn't changed.

My black dress was stiff, shapeless, hanging to mid-calf. High neck, long sleeves, thick stockings—just the way he liked it. I loathed it. The fabric scratched, a reminder of everything he forced on me. I wore it—not out of grief, but obligation.

"Hideous," I muttered, barely holding back a sneer as I looked up at the church doors. I knew this place by heart—every warped floorboard, every worn Bible. I'd walked through those doors for twenty-one years. Until the day I finally found the courage to leave. Now, standing here, my legs felt like lead, as if my body knew I didn't belong anymore.

"Bethany, you've got to do this," I whispered, trying to calm myself. "The service starts in ten minutes." I took a deep breath and fumbled with the clasp of my purse. I found the small bag of gummies I'd packed. Their strawberry scent hit like a flash of comfort in the middle of the nightmare. I popped one into my mouth, letting the sweet-sour taste ground me.

Moving towards the church, each step dragged me back to the life I left behind. The building loomed above me, casting its shadow, just as it always had. Inside, they'd be waiting. The congregation. Ready to mourn their beloved Pastor. Ready to mourn the man they idolized. The man they also called Father.

I was the outsider now. The prodigal daughter they'd all but forgotten. The door creaked as I pushed it open, stepping into the familiar scent of old wood and candle wax. Faces turned. Whispers floated like shadows, reminding me I'd never escape this place.

3

SHADOWS IN THE PULPIT

BETHANY

The moment I stepped through the heavy church doors, Pastor Campbell was waiting. His face split into a wide smile, and he pulled me into a fatherly hug. "Bethy! It's been far too long." I stiffened at the name. Bethy yanked me back to the girl who left on a Greyhound years ago.

Forcing a polite smile, I said, "Pastor Campbell, it's nice to see you again." The words felt tight in my mouth.

He released me with a sigh. "I just hate that it has to be under such difficult circumstances. Your father always hoped you'd come back, Bethy. He never gave up."

A chill skittered down my spine. The last time I spoke to him, I'd snarled, "No way in hell," and slammed the phone down—yet here I was, dragged back by death. Pastor Campbell seemed to read my discomfort. He placed a hand on my shoulder and glanced at his watch.

"The service starts in five minutes. Let me take you to him so you can have a moment alone." He didn't wait for an answer. Each step down the sanctuary aisle felt like a rewind. Halfway there, I slowed.

"I thought I made it clear this was to be a closed-casket service," I murmured.

He stopped, guilt flickering across his face. "Yes...Sister Margaret mentioned it, but I felt it wasn't right. Your father was this town's beloved Pastor. The congregation deserves a chance to say goodbye." Anger flared, then died. To them, he was a saint. The rest wasn't theirs to know. I followed each step, heavier than the last. Alone now, I faced the casket. I closed my eyes, searching for grief, anger, anything that made sense. Then I looked.

He lay still, dressed in his Sunday best. His hair, once thick and brown, had faded to washed-out gray; the mortician had shaped it into the familiar half-smile he wore when pleased with himself. A silver cross rested between folded hands: a man who had lived and died for his faith. For a heartbeat, I was eight again, an obedient child of an iron-fisted shepherd. But that girl was gone. The gummies kept me numb. I turned and walked away.

The service dragged. Two stifling hours later, my dress felt like a wool cage, sweat trickling down my spine while the broken air conditioner wheezed. My high faded. I had the urge to bolt with each testimonial. Pastor Campbell stood at the pulpit, calling one parishioner after another. I sat rigid in the front pew, nodding as they told me how blessed I'd been to have such a father. I swallowed the truth and played the dutiful daughter.

At last, Pastor Campbell returned to the podium. My shoulders eased—then stiffened—as his attention zeroed in on me. "Now, before our final goodbyes, there's one more blessing we'd love." His tone turned coaxing. "Bethy, would you come up and sing your father's favorite song? It's been so long since you blessed us with that voice."

My stomach dropped. I'd told Sister Margaret just last night that I wouldn't sing. Pastor Campbell turned back to the congregation, beaming. "Come on, give Bethy a hand. God has gifted her with a powerful voice. I know her father would appreciate it."

Applause thundered. Praise as manipulation. Exactly why I left, I rose, set my purse down, and walked toward the front. Expectations pressed against me like lead. I held the microphone and closed my eyes. A breath, then the words surfaced through resentment and sorrow.

"He's got the whole world...in His hands..."

My voice rolled through the sanctuary. The crowd joined in, their voices merging with mine, binding me to this place whether I wanted it or not.

"He's got the whole world...in His hands..."

I kept singing, each note a tether.

"He's got the whole world...in His hands...

He's got you and me, sister...in His hands..."

The last note lingered, and then silence settled like a final goodbye.

4

ESCAPE VELOCITY

BETHANY

I couldn't leave that town fast enough. The scent of incense still clung to my skin—a bitter reminder of what I'd just escaped. Mayor Spellman followed my instructions to the letter, handing over the cashier's check and a thick stack of documents in the church's cramped back office. His attempt at small talk was met with my polite but pointed insistence that I had a flight to catch. To my surprise, he took the hint.

Six hours later, I touched down at LAX. I sank back in the seat, scrolling through Instagram, just trying to feel normal again. My phone buzzed, snapping me out of my daze. It was my roommate, Katie. I picked up, her bubbly voice instantly filling the line. "Yay, you're back home! I missed you so much!" Her giggle somehow managed to pull me out of the shadows, even on my darkest days.

"Thank goodness," I muttered, feeling the tension drain from my shoulders. "I hated going back there."

"How far are you from the apartment?" she asked. Before I could answer, she chirped, "Wait, never mind—I see you're twenty minutes away." Katie made me share my location. "We're young single ladies in this city full of wolves," she always said.

Katie and I met working at a thrift store off Pico, a tiny place filled with secondhand treasures and half-buried memories. Normally, I kept my distance from everyone, especially the people I worked with. But she wasn't easy to overlook. She was 5'1" but carried herself like someone twice her size: quick, curious, always in motion. Her chestnut-brown hair was cut into a bob that suited her no-nonsense energy, and her bright brown eyes missed nothing. There was a dimple in her left cheek that showed up whenever she smiled, usually at something inappropriate. She had this old-school charm, like someone who could talk her way into or out of anything, and people naturally gravitated toward her without really knowing why. We were complete opposites. Maybe that's what made it easy to let my guard down.

Katie, it turned out, was from a small town too, just as eager to escape her own history. She'd moved here with dreams of studying cybersecurity at Santa Monica Community College, determined to make something of herself in this sprawling city. Despite being three years younger, she had a strange worldliness—a knack for understanding people and navigating life's chaos with ease.

One afternoon, after I'd been at the thrift store for about a month, she leaned over the counter and announced, "You should let me dye your hair. You'd look amazing as a dirty blonde. It would really make those blue eyes of yours pop."

I was caught off guard, both shocked and intrigued by her boldness. No one had ever spoken to me like that—like they knew me well enough to make that kind of suggestion. From that moment, we were inseparable. She coaxed me into letting her do the dye job, and when I walked into work the next day, the compliments poured in. She was this lively, slightly reckless presence who brought color and mayhem into my otherwise controlled world. She convinced me to get my nose pierced with her. Eventually, we found a rent-controlled apartment and moved in. But tonight, her enthusiasm wore thin.

"Katie, no," I said. "I'm exhausted. All I want is a shower and my bed."

"Oh, come on," she whined. "You're in a pissy mood, and I won't let you stay in this funk. It's your last weekend before the nine-to-five grind. We have to go out."

"I don't have anything to wear," I protested.

"I knew you'd say that!" she sang, triumphant. "So, I've already picked something out for you." I rolled my eyes. "Katie, what could I possibly wear of yours? I'm four inches taller than you!"

"Trust me." She buzzed with excitement. "It'll fit perfectly, and you're going to look amazing. I'll see you in twenty—and I'm not taking no for an answer." She hung up before I could argue.

An hour later, I was at the mirror, trying not to murder her. The dress she'd chosen was tight enough to turn heads the moment I walked in. It was dark blue, clinging to every curve, hugging my hips and dipping low enough to make me feel scandalous. It barely reached the tops of my thighs, making my legs look impossibly long as I perched on our table at the Scarlet Lady, a dimly lit bar known for its karaoke nights.

At 5'5", I usually didn't feel tall, but in this dress, my legs seemed to go on forever. My blonde hair fell in loose waves around my shoulders. I felt exposed, but even I had to admit—Katie had a knack for making me look sexy. I tugged at the neckline, trying to cover more of my chest. Katie slapped my hand away, grinning mischievously. "Stop that! You'll just draw more attention."

I shot her a glare as she handed me a shot of tequila. "Katie, I told you—I'm not drinking tonight. The last time, I was puking my guts out the next day."

"Do you trust me?" she asked, her eyes serious. I sighed. "Yes, I do."

"Then drink," she said, pressing the shot into my hand. "It'll help you relax. You're up next."

I froze. "You signed me up?" I hadn't planned on singing tonight, especially after the week I'd had.

Katie's expression softened. She squeezed my hand. "I know you don't want to talk about your dad, and I won't push. And I know what it's like to lose someone, especially when the relationship isn't perfect. You're grieving, even if you don't want to admit it. Just...sing one song. For him. To say goodbye." Her words hit a nerve, and I felt something inside me crack, the tension loosening.

"Okay," I whispered, a faint tremor in my voice.

As the current singer finished up, I thought about what I wanted to sing. Only one song felt right, echoing the emotions tangled inside me. When the DJ called my name, I stood, the tequila humming through my veins as I walked to the front, aware of every eye on me. Taking a deep breath, I closed my eyes as the first chords played. I started slow, the sound barely more than a breath, but it was enough to fill the space. I hadn't sung this melody in years. Each line brushed a wound that never fully closed. The lyrics told the story of giving everything and being left with less. Feelings I'd avoided for years—quiet, unexpected, too real to ignore.

The crowd fell silent, each word pulling them in as I sang with my whole soul. The familiar ache welled up, and I felt myself letting go, surrendering to the melody that had been buried inside me for years. When I opened my eyes, I caught a glimpse of him. Across the room, his stare pinned me—eyes as steely gray as a storm, piercing right through me.

A slow heat crept in, catching me off guard. He looked dangerously delicious. Black hair pushed back like he ran his hands through it. Dark facial hair traced his jawline and mouth, just enough to make me wonder what it'd feel like against my skin. Even sitting, he took up more space than he should—broad shoulders straining beneath a worn leather jacket that looked like it was made for him. And that damn jacket—hugging him like it knew what it was doing. But it wasn't just the way he looked. It was the way he watched me—like I was the only thing that mattered.

My heart stuttered. My pulse jumped, and suddenly, it was just the two of us, everything else fading away. I sang to him, my voice unwavering, pouring out every bit of pain and longing, the words reaching across the room like a confession. His eyes held mine. I couldn't look away. The bar disappeared. For those minutes, it felt like he was the only one listening, like he saw straight through the walls I'd built.

5

—•—

THE LAST GOODBYE

BETHANY

As I stepped off the stage, I barely heard the sound of the standing ovation. Standing ovations weren't new, but this one felt different. The room buzzed with energy, but my focus was elsewhere—it was on him. The man with steel-gray eyes who had been watching me like I was the only person in the room.

I weaved through the bar, offering polite smiles to strangers who stopped to compliment me. He wasn't there anymore.

"How do you feel now?" Katie asked, grinning like a Cheshire cat.

"You were right, as usual," I admitted, trying to suppress a smile.

"I know." She threw her arms around my neck and kissed my cheek. The song didn't just reach me—it exposed a part I didn't know was still hurting.

"Maybe we should go," I suggested, hoping she'd be agreeable for once.

"Absolutely not," she laughed, tossing back the last of her beer and turning back to the guy whispering in her ear. She wasn't leaving anytime soon. Resigned, I grabbed my jacket.

"I'll be back. I need to vape."

Katie waved me off without looking. "Go on, but don't take too long."

I stepped out, the crisp night brushing against my skin like a balm. Leaning against the wall, I pulled out my vape and took a long inhale, savoring the strawberry flavor as it filled my lungs. I exhaled, watching the smoke curl into the night sky.

"That's unexpected," a deep voice rumbled from behind me.

I jumped, turning so fast I nearly lost my balance. Gray eyes met mine, and my heart skipped. It was him. I stumbled, but his hands shot out, catching me by the waist. He pulled me close, bracing me against him.

"I've got you," he said, his voice low and gravelly, sending a shiver down my spine. His hands locked around my waist, radiating heat as they kept me in place. My mind scrambled, but all I could focus on was the heat of his body and the scent of leather and cedar clinging to him. "Strawberry?" he asked, his lips quirking into a slow, teasing smile as he sniffed the air. Then, to my shock, he licked his bottom lip, like he was tasting the word itself.

I blinked, my breath catching. "I—uh—" I placed my hands on his forearms to balance myself. His muscles flexed under my touch, solid and unyielding.

"Are you okay?" he asked, his eyes searching mine.

"I think so," I managed, my voice barely above a whisper. He didn't release me immediately. His hands lingered at my waist, the space between us charged with an energy that made my skin prickle. When he finally let go, I felt the loss of his touch like a cold wind cutting through me.

"You scared me," I said, laughing nervously as I leaned back against the wall.

"Sorry about that," he replied, running a hand through his dark hair. The way he moved drew my eyes to his mouth—that smirk, confident and dangerous, awakened something hungry in me. Everything about him screamed danger, but I couldn't look away. "You sang beautifully," he said after a moment. "I imagine you hear that all the time."

I hesitated, lowering my face. "Not really."

"That's hard to believe." He stepped closer, closing the gap between us again. "You have a gift. It's not just your voice—it's the way you feel every word." His words made me blush; it stirred something in me.

"Thanks." I took another drag from my vape.

"That song," he continued, "when Sheryl Crow sings The First Cut is the Deepest, it's about heartbreak. Losing a love so deep it leaves a scar, makes you wonder if you'll ever really heal."

I nodded. "It's about losing something that changes you," I said quietly.

He tilted his head, studying me with a focus that made me feel seen and exposed. "But that's not why you sang it." My breath hitched as his gray eyes bore into mine,

13

cutting through every defense I thought I had. He reached out, brushing a strand of hair from my face and tucking it behind my ear. His fingers grazed my cheek, slow and careful. "You weren't singing about love lost," he said softly. "You were singing about losing someone...someone who hurt you." A shiver ran through me. My walls started to crumble.

"Yes," I admitted, my voice barely audible.

"Who?"

I closed my eyes, swallowing hard. "My father." The words hung between us, heavy with unspoken pain. Without hesitation, he stepped closer and pulled me into his arms. His embrace was strong, unyielding, and yet impossibly comforting. I stiffened at first, caught off guard, but then the feel of him melted the tension in my body.

"It's okay," he murmured against my ear. "Let it out." The tears came fast, hot, and unchecked. I cried into his chest, embarrassed but unable to stop. His hand moved to the back of my head, his fingers threading gently through my hair as he held me tighter. For those few moments, the rest of the world ceased to exist. When the tears finally slowed, I pulled back, my cheeks flushed.

"Thank you," I said softly, avoiding his eyes. "You can let go now."

"Are you sure?" His voice stayed low, close. Before I could answer, he took my phone from my hand, his movements so confident I didn't think of stopping him. He typed something in and handed it back to me. "Get home safe," he said, stepping back. He didn't wait for a response, turning and walking toward a sleek, dark blue motorcycle parked at the curb. I watched as he swung a leg over the seat, the leather of his jacket catching the glow of the streetlight. He slid on a helmet, revved the engine, and sped off into the night. I stood there, the sound of the bike fading into the distance, my heart still racing.

Later, after a long, hot shower, I crawled into bed, hoping the night would fade with the steam. My phone buzzed on the nightstand; I reached for it, frowning at the unknown number.

Unknown Person: Did you make it home safely?

I gasped, my stomach flipping. It was him.

Me: Yes. Thank you for checking.

His response came almost immediately.

Him: Are you okay now?

I stared at the screen, my fingers hesitating. The truth felt too painful to admit, but something about him—his arms, his voice—made me feel safe enough to say it.

Me: Not really, but I'll be fine. Thank you again.

I wondered if I'd said too much. His reply appeared.

Him: You will be. Tonight, you carried something heavy and let it go. That's not easy, but you did it. You're stronger than you realize.

I bit my lip, butterflies stirring low in my stomach as I reread his words. There was a tenderness there, like he saw the part of me I tried hardest to hide.

Me: I don't feel very strong right now.

Him: That's the thing about strength—it's not about how you feel in the moment. It's what you do. And tonight, you were brave.

Heat crept into my cheeks, his words clinging to me like a cozy blanket. His kindness had a quiet strength. It wasn't overbearing—it felt like he understood me, like I didn't need to keep my walls up with him.

Me: You're very good at this.

Him: At what?

Me: Making me feel better.

Him: Maybe it's because you make it easy.

I laughed softly, shaking my head.

Me: You don't even know me.

Him: Not yet.

I paused, staring at the screen. His confidence was disarming, but it wasn't arrogant. It was like he'd already decided he wanted to know me. Before I could stop myself, I typed:

Me: What's your name?

He replied almost instantly, but his response made my heart skip.

Him: I'll tell you if you tell me yours first.

I smiled, my fingers hovering over the keyboard.

Me: Bethany.

Him: Bethany. It suits you.

I rolled my eyes, unable to suppress the grin spreading across my face.

Me: You're stalling. What's yours?

Him: Good night, Bethany. Sweet dreams.

I looked at the screen, a soft flutter rising in my chest as his words settled over me. Sweet dreams. I smiled, letting the words linger in my mind. Just as I was about to set my phone down, a realization hit me. I quickly typed:

Me: What's your name?

Him: Kevin.

I whispered it, testing the name. "Kevin." As I set my phone down and sank into the pillows, his name echoed in my mind. I fell asleep with a faint smile, the memory of his arms lulling me into dreams.

6

CRACKS IN THE ARMOR

BETHANY

The knocks were loud and relentless, but it was the singsong voice that made me groan. "Bethany! I know you're awake! Let me in, or I'll pick the lock again!" I rolled over, burying my face into the pillow, willing her to go away. My head throbbed from last night, my mouth like sandpaper. I didn't have the energy for Katie. The door creaked open anyway. She wasn't bluffing about the lock-picking.

"You're the worst," I muttered.

Katie bounced in, her energy as loud as her sunflower-covered pajamas. "Good morning, sunshine!" she chirped, clapping her hands like she was waking a classroom of kindergarteners. "Rise and shine! We're alive, and it's a beautiful day!"

I groaned again, dragging the comforter over my head. "Go away, Katie." She yanked the blanket off in one swift motion, her grin impossibly wide.

"Nope. It's ten a.m., and you're not wasting this gorgeous day sulking in bed. Come on! Brunch won't eat itself!"

I sat up slowly, glaring at her through blurry eyes. "Katie, I'm not sulking. I'm recovering. Unless brunch is in this room and made of black coffee, I'm not interested." Katie plopped onto the bed, crossing her legs underneath her.

"Black coffee? Who hurt you?" She reached out to playfully ruffle my already disheveled hair. "What you need is a triple-shot caramel macchiato with whipped cream and a side of bacon."

I swatted her hand away. "What I need is silence. And caffeine. Strong, black caffeine." She gasped, placing a dramatic hand over her heart.

KELLY R. NELSON

"Bethany Martin, are you hungover? Did I finally corrupt you?" I let out a heavy sigh, rubbing my temples.

"You didn't corrupt me. You bullied me into going out last night, and now I'm paying the price." Katie's grin didn't falter.

"Oh, please. You had fun. Admit it. That song? The crowd loved you. I mean, standing ovation? And that guy—"

I held up a hand to stop her. "Not now, Katie. Not before coffee." She jumped up, throwing her hands up.

"Fine! Coffee first. But you're telling me everything. Especially about him." I froze for a moment, but she was already halfway to the kitchen, humming a cheery tune. My heart fluttered at the thought of him. Kevin. His name circled my mind like a forbidden melody, and the memory of his arms started to unravel into something else. I let myself sink, recalling the way his hands had felt on my waist—strong, commanding, as though they belonged there. My hand moved instinctively down to my panties as I imagined his hands sliding lower, tracing the curve of my hips, pulling me closer until there was no space left between us.

The scent of leather and cedar clung to him, intoxicating. I pictured his mouth near mine, the way his lips would graze my skin, his breath hot against my neck. My heart raced as my fingers moved inside me, the fantasy pulling me deeper. His hands would be strong, rough in the best way, skimming over my bare skin, leaving trails of fire in their wake.

The heat spread through me like a slow burn. My thighs opened wider, my breath shallow as the image of him came into focus. His lips on my collarbone, moving lower, his voice a low murmur that sent chills down my spine. I let out a soft gasp, my body arching involuntarily, my mind racing. The way his muscles had flexed under my touch—it wasn't just strength; it was control, the promise of being utterly consumed. My other hand clutched at the sheets as a wave of heat surged through me, teetering on the brink—so close, so tantalizingly close—

"Bethany!" Katie's voice shattered the moment, her yell cutting through my thoughts like a bucket of ice water. I jerked upright, my face flushing so hot I thought it might catch fire. My breath came in quick, shallow gasps as I blinked at the door, disoriented. "Get dressed, you heathen!" Katie's head popped back in. "You've got five minutes before I drag you out of here in your pajamas. Don't test me."

I stared at her, the heat still simmering in my chest, quickly replaced by mortification. "What the hell, Katie?" I snapped.

She smirked. "I don't know what you're up to in here, but you'd better hurry up. Brunch waits for no one." She skipped off, leaving me flustered and frustrated. I pressed a hand to my face, trying to shake him off, what he almost made me feel.

"Get a grip," I muttered, throwing the covers aside and stumbling out of bed. Katie's chaos was better than this dangerous rabbit hole I was sliding into. At least, that's what I told myself.

The bar wasn't my idea. Katie had dragged me here with promises of fun and freedom, but all I wanted was to slip into the shadows and disappear. The music was loud, the bass thrumming in my chest as I sat in the corner nursing a whiskey I barely wanted. I tapped the glass, condensation dampening my skin as I tried not to think about last night. Or him. Kevin. I shifted in my chair, the memory of his eyes making my stomach twist. No one had ever looked at me like that before, like I was something they couldn't look away from. The thought made me flush—not just with nerves, but with something gentler. Something I didn't want to name.

"Stop it," I muttered, taking another sip. But as I stared into the amber liquid, the room seemed to fade, and for just a moment, I let myself wonder what it would feel like to let go. To let someone like him in. Then I felt it again—that pull. That awareness. When I looked up, he was there. Kevin leaned against the bar, a drink in hand, his eyes scanning the room until they landed on me. My heart stuttered. I froze, torn between bolting and staying put.

He wasn't supposed to be here. This was my safe space. My escape from the drama in my head. But with him here, everything felt too close. Too real. He didn't move immediately. Instead, he raised his glass in a silent acknowledgment, his lips curving into the faintest of smiles. My cheeks burned, and I quickly looked away, pulse pounding.

When I glanced back, he was already walking toward me, his movements smooth, almost lazy, like he had all the time in the world. I clenched my glass like it tethered me.

"Fancy seeing you here," he said, sliding into the chair across from me. "Or should I say lucky?"

I raised an eyebrow, forcing myself to look him in the eye. "Lucky for who?" His smile widened, but he didn't answer. Instead, he leaned forward, elbows on the table.

"I was here with someone," he said casually, voice smooth as silk. "They left. I was just about to do the same...until I saw you. So I guess that would mean—lucky for me."

I hated the way my heart fluttered. Hated the way his presence seeped into my bones, making it impossible to think. "Well," I said, keeping my voice even, "don't let me keep you."

His eyes sparkled. "Maybe I don't want to leave...now." The pull between us tightened. I inched back, but his presence was magnetic. Consuming.

"You're staring," I said, harsher than I intended.

"I know," he replied without apology. "It's hard not to."

I looked away, frustration and desire tangling. "You don't even know me."

"Not yet," he said softly. "But I'd like to." His words cracked something open, and that terrified me. I stood, the chair scraping the floor.

"I need air," I muttered, bolting for the door. Coolness bit at my skin the second I stepped out. I didn't stop until I was halfway down the block. I needed distance. Each step didn't feel far enough. I called it a night and texted Katie that I was heading home. Kevin was dangerous—not in the way my father warned, but in a way that was harder to resist. He didn't force anything. He was just there, pulling me in like a moth to a flame. By the time I got home, my thoughts were a mess, and the silence made it worse. I kicked off my shoes, collapsing onto my bed as my mind drifted.

I was fifteen, hunched over a desk in the church's computer lab, the monitor's glow on my face. My heart pounded as I created a Facebook account, a small act of rebellion in a world where everything was controlled. Favorite books. Dream vacation. Name: Beth. Just Beth. For the first time, I felt like more than Pastor Martin's daughter. Then a shadow fell over me.

"What is this?" my father said, voice cold. I didn't have time to close the screen before he yanked me out of the chair. "You dare to bring this filth into God's house?"

I tried to explain, but his anger was a storm. He shoved a Bible into my hands.

"Ten thousand times," he thundered. "'Do not love the world or the things in the world.' 1 John 2:15. And you will learn." By day three, my fingers bled. The words blurred. He didn't care. He stood there until my will broke.

I jerked back to the present, breath shallow, chest tight. I pressed my hand to my face, trying to forget. But Kevin slipped in—his voice, his eyes, the way he made me feel. Wanted. Without thinking, I grabbed my phone. Opened a new message.

Me: Breakfast tomorrow?

I hit send before I could talk myself out of it. When the reply came, fast and simple, I smiled.

Kevin: Yes.

7

A STRANGER'S PROMISE

BETHANY

I sat across from Kevin, trying to focus on his words, but my mind wouldn't cooperate. My eyes drifted to his lips, full and inviting, moving with words I couldn't quite process. What was I doing? Sitting in an IHOP with the most attractive man I'd met in years? An anxious flutter stirred beneath my ribs. This wasn't me. I didn't do this. I didn't go on dates—not since...well, it didn't matter.

Kevin leaned back, his white T-shirt stretching across his chest, making my cheeks flush. His gray denim jeans were tight in all the right places, and God help me, I was suddenly dying to know what was underneath. When I met him outside earlier, my first instinct had been to turn around and run. I nearly did. But then he'd smiled—a slow, knowing, heart-stopping smile—and I was utterly doomed. That smile stirred things I'd worked hard to bury.

Before I left, Katie had been relentless, practically shoving me out the door. "Oh wow! I didn't know you had it in you," she'd teased when I spilled every detail about seeing Kevin again, her eyes sparkling mischievously.

"Me either," I grumbled, sifting through my closet. "I'm seriously thinking about canceling. I mean, what's the point?"

"Absolutely not!" Katie snatched my phone before I could text him. "Bethany, this is sad. You deserve a little fun—and maybe a hot guy to finally rock your world. You've been acting like a hermit for too long." I rolled my eyes as she rummaged through my clothes, eventually holding up a black flowy dress with purple and white flowers. "Wear this."

"You know I hate dressing girly," I groaned, crossing my arms.

"Which is why I'm giving you your favorite Docs." She tossed the boots at me. "See? Comfort for your brooding soul and a hint of style for the guy who's clearly into you. Win-win." Katie paused, softening. "Bethany, I love you. I just want to see you happy. One breakfast won't kill you. And who knows? Maybe this guy is exactly what you need." She winked, then held up my pink vibrator with a smirk. "Because this"—she shook it at me—"Is not cutting it."

I hurled a pillow at her and shouted, "Get out!" Her laughter echoed as she left, and despite my protests, I knew she was right. Now I was pretending to listen while wondering what he looked like naked.

"Bethany?" His voice pulled me from my thoughts. I blinked, heat creeping up my neck. "Yeah, sorry. What were you saying?"

"I was asking if you're from California."

"No, I'm from a small town in Indiana. Willow Creek," I replied, tucking a strand of hair behind my ear. Kevin raised an eyebrow, a teasing smile playing on his lips.

"Willow Creek, huh? Sounds like the kind of place with more cows than people."

"Pretty much," I said, chuckling. "Population: 200 on a good day." He leaned forward, eyes sparkling with amusement.

"How does a small-town girl like you end up here in the big city, eating pancakes with me?" I laughed softly, a strange flutter dancing in my stomach.

"I ask myself the same thing."

"Maybe it's fate," he said, his voice dropping slightly, making my pulse jump.

"Fate?" I scoffed. "That your go-to line?"

"Only when it works," he shot back with a grin.

I shook my head, biting back a smile. "You're ridiculous."

"And you're intriguing," he countered smoothly. "Which is why I think we should do this again—somewhere a little less...geriatric." He nodded toward the tables around us, filled with elderly diners.

I laughed. "What's wrong with IHOP?"

"Nothing, but I'd like to see you somewhere that doesn't serve 'a cuppa Joe.'" His stare lingered, and I dropped my eyes, chewing my bottom lip, his words still hanging there. Maybe Katie was right. Maybe letting my past dictate my future wasn't the best idea. Kevin was charming, maybe too much, but his eyes held a sincerity that made me want to try.

"Okay," I said, my eyes finally meeting his. "A real date. Just let me know when." Kevin's grin widened, and for the first time in a long time, I felt a flicker of something I'd lost—hope.

As we stepped outside, the morning sun greeted us, soft against my skin. Kevin, ever the gentleman, held the door open, his arm brushing lightly against mine. I tried not to think about how his touch thrilled me. I was still buzzing from the way his eyes had lingered on mine like I was the only person in the room.

"Want me to give you a ride home?" he asked, nodding toward the parking lot. My eyes followed his gesture to a sleek blue motorcycle. My heart skipped, but not in a good way.

"Uh, no," I said quickly. "Absolutely not."

Kevin chuckled. "What? You don't trust me?"

"It's not you," I said, crossing my arms. "It's the bike. And the lack of doors. Or a roof."

He grinned. "You're missing out, Bethany. Nothing beats the feeling of wind in your hair."

"Hard pass," I replied, stepping back.

"All right, suit yourself." He shrugged with mock defeat, but that mischievous glint was still in his eyes. "I'll just have to save the thrill ride for another time." Before I could respond, he stepped forward, arms outstretched. "Hug goodbye?" My brain short-circuited. A hug? I panicked, throwing my hand up like a shield.

"Handshake's fine," I blurted. Kevin blinked at my hand, lips twitching into a slow, amused smile.

"A handshake? Classy."

Heat rushed to my face as he clasped my hand and held it a beat too long. His thumb brushed lightly over my knuckles before he let go. He stepped back, studying me with a smirk.

"You really are something else," he said softly. I flushed, hating how his words burrowed under my skin.

"Thanks, I guess?" I mumbled. He laughed again, that rich, genuine sound that made my stomach flip.

"Don't mention it, Bethany. I'm intrigued, that's all."

I couldn't tell if he meant to flatter or disarm me, but either way, I felt exposed. I glanced at my phone, pretending to check the time, really counting the minutes until my Uber arrived. Kevin leaned casually against the lamppost. He didn't say much, and the silence between us felt unbearably loud. When my Uber finally pulled up, I exhaled.

"Well, this is me," I said, waving toward the car. Kevin straightened, flashing that same easy smile.

"Guess I'll see you around?"

"Yeah," I said, softer than I meant to. "See you."

I slid into the backseat and peeked back—Kevin still stood there, smiling like he knew something I didn't. Was I ready for this?

8

— • —

THROUGH THE WIND

BETHANY

All week, Kevin and I texted. At first, I kept it light. Short bursts. But even then, he slipped past my defenses, like he could read between the lines. It felt like talking to an old friend—if that friend made my pulse race. A spark simmered beneath the surface, and no matter how I tried to ignore it, I couldn't. Kevin flirted easily, never trying too hard—until one night, when he did.

Kevin: What are you wearing right now?

I stared at the message, stomach flipping like I'd just stepped off a roller coaster. Bold, unexpected, way out of my comfort zone. But I didn't brush it off—I kind of...liked it. Okay, more than liked it. My mind raced, scrambling for something flirty that didn't make me sound like an idiot. The truth? I was curled up in bed in an old concert tee from a festival years ago. Soft, comfortable, and not remotely sexy. Still, I felt the need to meet his energy—to show I could keep up. I typed a response, erased it, and then tried again. Everything sounded ridiculous until I settled on something that felt close enough.

Me: Oh, you know...just something light and breezy. Black, sheer, with a little lace. Perfect for lounging.

The second I hit send, I winced. Light and breezy? I sounded like I was describing curtains. My heart raced as I waited, bracing for him to call me out. But then, his message popped up. *You're adorable.* Stop overthinking it. Adorable. Not what I'd expected. Not sexy. Not hot. Just...adorable. Not exactly the word every girl wants to hear, right? Still, the way he said it made me smile. He wasn't brushing me off or laughing at me. It was like he saw right through me—past the nervousness, past the awkwardness—and liked what he saw anyway. On Thursday, he threw another curveball.

Friday night. Be ready at seven. Wear jeans, your Docs, and whatever top you feel like.

No explanation. No clue about what we were doing. Just instructions—as if I wasn't going to spend the next twenty-four hours overanalyzing every detail. Of course, I pushed back, asking where we were going, what we were doing. All he sent back was a winking emoji and two words:

Kevin: Trust me.

Trust him? That wasn't exactly my strong suit. I'd spent years building a shell, convincing everyone—even myself—I was fine alone. That I don't need anyone to take care of me. But something about Kevin makes me want to let my guard down, just a little. Maybe it's the way he doesn't push too hard, or the way he seems to like me as I am, awkwardness and all.

Friday couldn't come fast enough. I was both nervous and excited—torn between wanting to know and savoring the anticipation. Whatever this was, it was new territory. And even though it scared me, it made me feel alive.

Now it was Friday, and I stood at the curb in my combat boots and high-rise black jeans, my white cropped T-shirt suddenly feeling inadequate. I kept tugging at the hem, wondering if it was too short, too plain, too everything. I crossed my arms, trying to keep the nerves in. Second-guessing was my full-time hobby, and tonight was no exception. What was I doing? I barely knew Kevin, and here I was—waiting to be whisked off to who-knows-where. The longer I stood there, the louder the doubts grew.

The low, distinct hum of an engine shattered my spiraling thoughts. I froze, the sound curling around me, thick and intoxicating. My eyes snapped to the end of the block, where Kevin rolled into view on a motorcycle that demanded attention. Midnight-blue paint shimmered under the streetlights, its sleek, dangerous lines promising thrills and reckless abandon. It was magnetic, like the man riding it.

Kevin pulled up, engine low and rumbling. My eyes dragged up from his jeans. The white T-shirt clinging to his chest did me in—stretched just enough to show muscle and dry my mouth. The leather jacket? The final nail. Moist in places I didn't think a look could reach. God, he was danger and allure in human form, and I hated how much my breath hitched. He pulled off his helmet with a practiced motion, shaking out slightly tousled hair that begged for my fingers. That grin—crooked, confident, and laced with just enough mischief—hit me like a physical force. My mouth went dry; I had to remind myself to breathe.

"Tell me that's not what we're riding. What kind of bike is that?" I asked, trying to sound confident, even as my eyes kept flicking between him and the machine.

Kevin stepped off, slow and smooth, like he had all the time in the world. There was something electric in how he moved—controlled, unrushed, like he knew exactly how to get under my skin. He held up a second helmet.

"Kawasaki Ninja 400," he said. "Sleek. Fast. Dangerous—if you don't trust the driver."

I glanced at the bike, its polished curves catching the light. "Dangerous is exactly the word I'd use," I shot back, though my pulse betrayed me. Kevin stepped closer, closing the distance like he belonged there.

"Dangerous can be good," he murmured, voice a secret meant only for me. "It's about control. Precision. This bike isn't reckless—it's an experience. Not too big, not too small. Just the right balance of power and finesse." His grin turned wicked. "Kind of like me." Heat flushed through me. I swallowed hard, trying to muster something clever, but the way he looked at me, like he already knew my thoughts. I snorted, masking the flip in my stomach.

"You're impossible."

"And yet, here you are," he countered smoothly, holding out the helmet. "So, what do you say? Ready to stop overthinking and let me show you how to really live?" I hesitated, heart pounding. The thought of pressing up against Kevin, arms tight around him, sent a shiver of dread and exhilaration through me.

"I've never been on a motorcycle before," I admitted.

"I figured," he said. "That's why I'm here. You'll be safe—I'll keep it slow...unless you're into something faster." He gave me a playful wink. His fingers grazed mine, a jolt shooting through me. Tension sparked between us, hot and magnetic. This wasn't just butterflies—yearning coiled low, spreading. I clenched my jaw, resisting his pull, but my hand still reached for the helmet.

"Fine," I said, feigning nonchalance. "But if I die, I'm haunting you." His rich, low laugh was impossible to resist.

"Deal," he said, stepping closer. "Though I've got a feeling you'll thank me by the end of the night."

When he secured the helmet, his fingers brushed my cheek, lingering a moment too long. My breath hitched, the slow burn flaring into open flame. He swung onto the bike with easy grace, then offered his hand. The moment our fingers touched, a spark leapt—lighting.

"Come on," he said, his voice laced with something deeper than encouragement, like he knew how perfectly we fit. I took his hand, climbed on behind him, the world shrinking to the feel of his body and the deep vibration of the engine. Arms around his waist, I hesitated, unsure how tight to hold. Kevin glanced back, eyes glinting, and pulled my hands tighter. "Hold on like you mean it," he said with a wicked grin. "Unless you feel like flying solo tonight." My heart slammed as the bike roared to life. Fear and anticipation tangled, leaving me breathless. One thing was certain: this was a ride I'd never forget.

The city blurred into streaks of light. At first, my hold was iron-tight, nerves sparking with every turn. My heart pounded—fear or thrill, I couldn't tell. But as the ride went on, fear melted, replaced by freedom. Wind whipped past, carrying doubts and worries away in the bike's wake. Kevin kept the ride smooth, the bike gliding along open roads. Now and then, he tapped my arm, pointing out the skyline or lights on the water. Each small gesture sent a pang through me—a soft counterpoint to the ride's wild energy.

We rolled into the lot of a plain industrial building. Beige, featureless, with a weathered logo. Ordinary—but knowing Kevin, I should've expected anything but. He cut the engine, and I turned toward him, tugging at my helmet strap.

"What is this place?" Kevin swung off the bike, pulled off his helmet, and shook out his hair. His grin—wide and unrepentant—made me question my judgment.

"Your next adventure."

I groaned. "You're full of surprises, aren't you?" I muttered, slipping off the bike and yanking off my helmet. My hair tumbled around my face in a wild mess. Before I could fix it, Kevin stepped closer, sliding his fingers through the curls like he had every right. I didn't move—unsure whether to push him away or lean in. His touch was gentle, focused on untangling a few strands, but it made my pulse skip. He didn't seem to notice—or maybe he didn't care that this was an intimate move.

"You're good," he said, stepping back like it was nothing. I exhaled slowly.

"Come on," he added. "You'll love it."

Inside, the sound hit me first: a steady hum of wind tunnels, bursts of laughter echoing off high ceilings. The air smelled faintly of rubber and machinery. People milled around in brightly colored jumpsuits beneath towering glass walls that enclosed vertical wind tunnels. I watched someone twist midair, balancing against the wind. My jaw dropped.

"You're kidding," I said, turning to him. "You brought me here to jump into a giant fan?"

"It's indoor skydiving," he replied, annoyingly casual. "Safer than it looks. But don't worry—I'll go first. You can just watch and chicken out if you want."

"I'm not a chicken," I snapped.

"That's the spirit," he said, clearly amused. "Let's suit up." As he led me toward the gear counter, I couldn't help but smile. I liked how he pushed me just enough, like he believed I could handle anything. I wasn't sure if I'd live up to that, but I wasn't about to let him see me hesitate. Kevin went first, striding in with confidence, clearly knowing what he was doing. The instructor gave him a nod, and then the air roared to life. Kevin lifted off the ground, twisting in a smooth arc. He moved with practiced ease. He was showing off—no question about it—but I couldn't look away. He spotted me through the glass and blew me a dramatic, over-the-top kiss. My cheeks burned. He was ridiculous, bold, and completely sure of himself. And damn, I loved it.

When my turn came, I stopped at the doorway. The space was still and quiet, but my heart wasn't. It pounded in my throat. My feet stayed planted. Every fear clawed its way up, each one louder than the last, begging me to back out. What if I lose control? I'd spent my life avoiding loss of control. My father drilled it in early: Control your emotions. Your actions. Lose control, lose everything. His words settled bitter in my gut. The urge to step away, to retreat, grew stronger. But just as I started to turn, I felt Kevin's hand on my arm.

"Hey," he said, his voice cutting through the whirlwind of doubt in my head. "You've got this. I'm right here. I promise." His hand on my arm said more than words ever could. I just looked at him. There was no teasing this time, no smugness—just quiet encouragement. And it was enough to remind me of something I'd almost forgotten: This is my life now. No one else gets to dictate what I can or can't do.

Taking a deep breath, I nodded and stepped into the tunnel. The fan roared, and the wind hit me. Before I could second-guess myself, it lifted me into the air. A startled laugh burst from my lips as I felt my feet leave the ground. It was overwhelming and exhilarating. The wind pressed against me as I floated higher. My heart raced—not from fear, but something lighter. Freer.

I glanced toward the glass and saw Kevin watching me, his grin wide and triumphant. He gave me a thumbs-up, and I couldn't help but smile back—this time without hesitation. The higher I went, the more everything else faded: doubts, rules, the walls I'd built. They fell away, carried by the wind. The higher I floated, the less afraid I was to let go. I tilted, letting the wind guide me into a spin. Laughter bubbled up—unrestrained and real. It wasn't just the tunnel—it was me, breaking free. Floating there—weightless, alive—I realized I wasn't just flying. I was learning to live.

As I stepped out of the tunnel, still feeling the exhilarating rush of weightlessness, Kevin was already chatting with someone near the front desk. The man looked older—maybe in his fifties—with a tanned face that suggested he spent more time outdoors than in. His gray hair was slicked back, and his smile was easy and genuine, with an ease that made you feel instantly welcome.

They exchanged a few words, their tones low but friendly. The man reached into his pocket and pulled out a small set of keys, handing them to Kevin with a knowing nod. Curiosity bubbled as Kevin turned, keys glinting, that infuriating grin saying he had the best-kept secret.

He walked toward me with easy confidence, his eyes practically daring me to question what he was up to. Without a word, he took my hand, sending a faint spark through my fingers. Guiding me past the bustling main area, Kevin led me to a nondescript door tucked into the side of the building. I glanced up, trying to read his expression, but his face gave nothing away; that unreadable smirk only deepened my curiosity.

When he pushed the door open, candlelight spilled into the dim hallway, catching me off guard. The room was small but cozy, a laid-back escape from the buzz outside. I slowed, taking it in. A small table stood in the center, two candles flickering softly. The room was thick with the scent of melted wax, bubbling pizza, and roasted vegetables. Beside it, a bucket of beer sweated onto the table, next to a simple salad stacked with greens and tomatoes. But the star was the pizza—golden crust, bright toppings—exactly how I liked it. Quiet, save for the crackle of candles and the low hum of ventilation. It wasn't lavish—nothing about Kevin was—but it was perfectly thoughtful. I'd once texted him about loving veggie pizza. He'd scoffed—insisted pizza needed meat. Yet here it was—a small gesture that landed deeper than I wanted to admit.

I turned to him, a smile tugging at my lips. "You remembered." He shrugged, leaning on the doorframe.

"Yeah, well," he said, grin turning sheepish, "figured you deserved something good tonight—even if it's not real pizza." I laughed, a rush of gratitude swelling in my chest—not from the food, but from the effort. He'd noticed. He cared enough to act.

"You're impossible," I said, shaking my head, gratitude clear in my voice.

We sat and dug in—salad crisp, pizza warm and cheesy. Kevin cracked open two beers, sliding one to me.

A few bites in, he asked, "So," he began, tone casual but gray eyes probing, "how did you end up in Santa Monica?"

The question caught me off guard. I considered deflecting, but something in the way he looked at me made me pause. I set my beer down, tracing the rim.

"A bad breakup," I said quietly. "It pushed me to move. I needed a change—a fresh start."

He nodded. "Sometimes you need a reset."

The truth was messier but that wasn't for tonight. I forced a small smile. "I'll tell you more someday, when I'm ready."

"Whenever you're ready," he said, sincerity settling something inside me.

I tilted my head. "So, are you originally from California?"

He set his beer down, thoughtful. "No. I'm from Tacoma, Washington. My brother and I lived there until we were thirteen—our parents died in a car accident."

"Kevin..." I whispered, unsure what to say.

He shook his head, a wistful smile crossing his face. "It's okay. It was a long time ago. After that, we moved to Denver to live with our aunt and uncle. They were great, but mostly my brother and I leaned on each other." He spoke calmly, almost detached. I couldn't tell if he'd healed or just learned to hide it.

"And after high school, you came here?"

"Yeah," he said. "We headed to California for a fresh start. I enrolled at the Musicians Institute in Hollywood—studied audio engineering."

"Audio engineering?" I echoed, intrigued. "That's amazing."

Pride lit his face. "It's been a good fit. I freelance now, mostly with musicians and studios. Busy, but I love it. Music's always been my thing." He hesitated, eyes locking on mine. "It's part of what drew me to you, you know."

"Me?" I blinked. He shifted forward, resting his forearms on the table.

"Your voice, Bethany. That night at karaoke, you're not just good; you have real talent. Have you ever thought about pursuing it?"

I laughed. "That's...complicated."

"How so?" he asked, tone gentle. I paused, the question hanging heavy.

"It's complicated," I repeated with a small smile. "Not something I can explain right now—maybe someday."

Kevin studied me, reading between the lines. After a beat, he nodded, backing off. "Fair enough," he said lightly, shifting focus back to the pizza. "For what it's worth, you've got a gift."

I grabbed another slice, grateful he didn't press. The room lit up. Soon we were laughing about bad karaoke and arguing over pineapple on pizza. Stepping out of the building a little while later, my cheeks ached from smiling, the night still buzzing in my veins.

"Okay," I said, glancing at Kevin, who walked beside me with that smug grin. "I'll admit it—that was...incredible."

"Told you. And look at that—you didn't even have to haunt me." I laughed, light and carefree, almost not recognizing my own voice.

"You're lucky." We reached his bike, and he handed me the helmet, his fingers brushing mine. Without a word, I climbed behind him, settling into the now-familiar seat. As the engine roared to life and we pulled onto the street, I leaned into him, resting my head against his back. The constant thrum of the bike beneath us matched the rhythm of my breathing, and for the first time in what felt like forever, I let my guard down completely. I closed my eyes, listening to the city rush past—the distant hum of traffic, an occasional bark of a dog, the soft murmur of life happening all around us. It was calming, almost hypnotic, and with Kevin so close, I felt safe in a way I hadn't in years.

When we reached my house, Kevin cut the engine and swung off the bike before turning to help me down. His hands slid to my waist, holding me just long enough to make my breath catch. The touch sent a wave of nerves through me, and I couldn't meet his gaze as I fumbled with the helmet strap.

"So," he said, voice softer now, "how was your first ride?"

I looked up at him, my heart fluttering. It wasn't the ride I was thinking about—it was him, and how he made me feel.

"Terrifying," I admitted, a small smile breaking through, "but worth it." His smile spread slowly, almost tenderly, and the look in his eyes made my pulse race.

"Good. Because I'd like to do this again—soon."

I didn't overthink. "Yeah," I said, my voice steadier than I felt. "I'd like that, too."

As he stood there, something dawned on me: I really liked this guy—more than I wanted to admit. The thought hit me like a freight train, and before I could stop myself, I kissed him. I didn't ease in or second-guess—I grabbed his collar and kissed him. The woodsy scent of his cologne enveloped me, sending my pulse racing. Kevin froze, then kissed me back—his hands sliding to my waist, fingers skimming the skin under my shirt. He pulled me in like he couldn't get close enough, like he needed me as badly as I needed him.

The kiss deepened, and my heart pounded as his lips moved with mine, slow and measured at first, then more urgent. His fingers dug into my waist, drifted down to my ass, paused just long enough to leave me breathless, then traced up my spine. Heat rippled through me, and as his fingers splayed across my back, the kiss grew wilder, more consuming.

His tongue brushed mine—tentative, then bolder—igniting a fire that spread through every inch of me. It was magnetic, wild, and unexpected, like stepping off a ledge and realizing you could fly. My head spun from the rush of it. Our tongues moved together in a rhythm that felt natural, like we'd been building to this moment forever, each second intensifying the connection until everything else faded away. Just as I was about to spiral, I pulled back, breathless and reeling. My lips tingled, and my hands trembled slightly as I stepped away. Kevin looked stunned, then a slow, amused smile crept across his face.

"Goodnight, Kevin," I said, voice flat despite the storm inside me. I turned and walked toward my door before he could respond. I couldn't believe I'd done that—me, kissing him first. So unlike me. And for the first time in forever, I didn't regret a thing. Inside, the lock clicked into place. I exhaled, lips tingling, heart racing. A sly smile crept across my face as I replayed the kiss. My phone dinged. I already knew who it was.

Kevin: Tonight wasn't enough. I want more of you—and I won't pretend otherwise.

His words lit a spark low in my stomach, spreading everywhere. Bold. Unapologetic. Maddeningly irresistible. I stared at the message a moment longer, fingers hovering over the keyboard while a thousand replies flooded my mind. I sank back against the door, biting back a grin.

"Damn," I whispered, the heat refusing to fade. Kevin had upped the stakes—and I wasn't sure I cared.

9

ECHOES OF DEFIANCE

BETHANY

That night, all I could see were Kevin's gray eyes: chaos and calm, storm and stillness. Hunger lived there. Not just for me, but something deeper. The way he looked at me, like he saw every part I tried to hide. And that kiss...God, that kiss. It looped in my mind like a song I didn't want to forget. I kept touching my lips. The kiss lingered, a promise. A claim. The way my body melted into his shimmered under my skin. Need bloomed low. I crossed my legs, startled by how much he still affected me.

Kevin made me feel bold, reckless, like freedom with a pulse. To laugh out loud, choose what I wanted, take risks without apology. I smiled, remembering his look after the kiss—those gray eyes daring me into the unknown. I wanted to. God, I still did. But the feeling shifted. Sweet turned uneasy. Kevin wasn't the first to make me feel that way. The thought struck—like ice water on my skin.

I rolled onto my side as memories of Danny crept in. My secret. My first escape from my father's hold—the one who saw me not as the pastor's daughter. I tried to shake the doubts, but they clung, heavy and suffocating, stealing the joy I wanted to feel.

I was eighteen when I recorded my first video, and the memory still feels vivid. The house was unnervingly quiet—a rare moment of peace. My father was out visiting a church member, and for once, I had the space to myself. Even in silence, his absence felt strange—like a shadow lingered in every corner. I knew he wasn't home, but I still locked the door with shaking fingers. My heart pounded as I peeked through the curtains, scanning the driveway for his truck. Only when I was sure did I exhale.

My bedroom reflected my life: clean, plain, devoid of anything personal. The faded pink wallpaper hadn't changed since I was six. A discoloration on the nightstand marked where a Bible had sat for years. It could've belonged to any child in a conservative home, exactly how my father liked it. No posters, no books beyond church texts, no hint of individuality. I was an adult, but everything felt frozen in time. I didn't look eighteen. With blonde hair and wide blue eyes, I could still pass for fourteen.

Sitting on my bed, I stared at my brand-new iPhone—the one gift my father had reluctantly given me for my birthday. My fingers trembled as I opened the camera and switched to video. The reflection staring back looked pale and nervous, unsure if she was brave enough to do this. But beneath the fear was a spark, a need to do something for me, not my father or the church.

I propped the phone against a stack of books on my desk and adjusted it until the frame was right. My heart pounded in my ears. I took a breath and hit record. The first notes of *Ocean Eyes* by Billie Eilish left my lips shakily, my voice trembling. Nerves threatened to take over, but I let the melody pull me in. Eyes closed, fear faded as I got lost in the song. Each lyric became a confession—emotions bottled up for years.

My voice grew stronger, vibrating through me, filling the still room. The ache in the song mirrored mine—the longing for more, the frustration of being trapped in a life I hadn't chosen. I moved instinctively, letting the music flow. I wasn't performing for anyone but myself. The words were my truth. By the final note, my chest heaved. I opened my eyes, adrenaline buzzing. For the first time, I felt like me, not the obedient servant of rigid rules. Just Bethany.

I hovered over the delete button, hesitating. If my father found out, the consequences would be unbearable—but deleting it felt just as wrong. I shut off the screen and set the phone down—decision clear. That recording wasn't just a song—it was proof that I could be something else if I found the courage to be free. It didn't take long for that first video to spark something—a fire I hadn't known was waiting to burn.

A week later, I sat at my desk, supposedly working on lesson plans for Children's Bible Study, but my mind was far from church. My fingers rested over the keyboard as an idea took root.

I knew what YouTube was; I'd been sneaking onto it for years, secretly watching what my father called "the devil's music" whenever he was away. It had been my gateway to artists who felt like kindred spirits—Sheryl Crow's unapologetic strength, Billie Eilish's raw vulnerability, Fiona Apple's haunting intensity, Lana Del Rey's bittersweet melodies, and Florence + The Machine's ethereal power. Their songs made me feel understood. I'd learned early to cover my tracks, deleting my browser history with a precision born of necessity ever since I got caught creating a Facebook account at fifteen. This was different. Creating my own channel meant stepping into the world I'd only dreamed of—even if it had to be under a fake name. Riley Waters. I typed it into the account registration. The name felt like a version of me outside my father's control: bold, fearless, untouchable.

I uploaded the *Ocean Eyes* video and watched the progress bar crawl forward, my heart racing. When "Publish" appeared, I hesitated. What if someone I knew found it? What if my father discovered it? Fear twisted in my stomach, but it wasn't enough to stop me. I clicked the button, hand shaking. The video went live. Exhilaration caught my breath. For once, I'd done something entirely for me. No approval. No permission. Mine. The freedom of that moment filled me with a giddy lightness; I covered my mouth to stifle a laugh. I checked the channel obsessively. Likes trickled in—then poured. Comments followed, most encouraging. One stood out: "Your voice is just as hot as you look." The username was Sk8erDanny.

At first, I didn't know how to respond. I blushed, rereading his words. Flirtatious, yes, but they felt genuine. We started chatting in the comment section; his replies were easy and fun, like he didn't take himself too seriously. He asked if I had a way to chat privately. Letting someone into my secret world was terrifying. But Danny felt different. He saw me, like he understood what it meant to want more. I told him the truth—my father monitored everything, and privacy didn't exist in my house. Danny offered a solution: Telegram. "It's an app with secret chats," he explained in a video message, voice smooth and confident. "No one can see what you're doing. Trust me, Bethany. I'll show you."

He taught me to set self-destruct timers and hide the app behind a generic icon so my father wouldn't suspect a thing. It felt like a lifeline—a door to a part of me I'd never explored. The next day, he sent a picture of himself. His hair looked like he barely touched it, and his grin—stupid-cute—could make you forget your name. But it was his green eyes, sparkling with mischief, that drew me in. Danny was everything my life wasn't—freedom, adventure, possibility. I started to believe I could belong there too.

For three years, I lived a double life. By day, I was Bethany—the obedient pastor's daughter. I taught Sunday School, sang in the choir, recited scripture with practiced grace. My father's eyes reminded me that perfection wasn't just expected—it was required. By night, I was Riley Waters—singer, dreamer, untethered. Riley didn't ask for permission. She spoke her mind, sang like no one was listening, and refused to shrink.

Danny became part of that secret life. Four years older, he lived in New York City, worlds away from me. He rattled off obscure bands, listed the best coffee shops in Brooklyn, and talked about Central Park like it was his backyard. His life felt free, and it drew me in. At first, we were just friends—he teased my small-town stories, I rolled my eyes at his city-slicker tales. Our conversations deepened as we talked about music, dreams, fears, and expectations. Danny never judged my father's rules; he urged me to imagine life beyond them. "Bethany," he'd say, voice soft through the phone, "you don't belong there. You belong where your voice is heard—where you can live."

Two years in, Danny confessed his feelings: "I think I'm falling for you, Bethany. I want us to be something more." My heart fluttered. I'd been falling too—slowly, quietly—a secret I hadn't dared to admit. That night, I told him the truth—I felt the same. Our relationship shifted; Danny became my confidant, my escape, my possibility. He spoke of a future together—of me coming to New York to pursue singing.

"You could make it here," he insisted. "I know people—gigs, maybe a record deal. You're too talented to stay stuck."

His words filled me with longing and fear. "I can't leave," I whispered. "My father would never allow it."

"You're an adult," he reminded me. "You make your own decisions." But my father's rules felt like iron bars. He'd find me, I thought. He'd drag me back. The idea of defying him seemed impossible. Our relationship became a painful dance of longing and restraint. Danny begged me to visit; I always had excuses. The double life drained me—perfect daughter by day, soul-baring music and late-night calls by night. I was trapped between two selves—neither felt like home. The pressure built like a dam. Two months before my twenty-first birthday, it burst.

I was sitting on my bed, a book in my hands, letting the words pull me into a world far from my own. Late-afternoon light filtered through the curtains, casting a soft veil on the faded pink wallpaper. I felt a sliver of peace. Then, like thunder, my father's voice boomed from the hallway.

"Bethany!" Before I could process the sound, my bedroom door flew open and slammed against the wall. I flinched, dropping my book as he stormed inside—face red, jaw clenched, eyes blazing. His phone was in his hand like a weapon, and, even before he spoke, I knew why. My heart plummeted.

"What is this?!" he roared, holding up the screen. My stomach churned, throat dry. I shrank against the headboard, heart pounding so loud I could barely hear. "Your YouTube channel!" He thrust the phone toward me, shaking it like proof of my sins.

"I can explain—" I started, voice trembling.

"You will not speak!" His words exploded in the room, shaking the air. Suddenly, I wasn't twenty anymore—I was six, crying in the kitchen while he yelled about a broken plate. I lowered my eyes, trying to keep my breath from shaking, but my chest felt tight. He paced, footsteps heavy, anger radiating in waves.

"You deceived me! Lied to me! Singing for strangers? Do you know what kind of evil you invited into this house?"

"It's just music," I whispered.

"Just music?" He spun, glare pinning me. "It's the devil's music! That industry is run by corrupt, sinful people who will destroy you. You brought shame upon this family—upon the Lord!" Tears blurred my vision.

"Dad, I'm good at it. I want to be a singer. This is my dream."

His face twisted, veins bulging. "Your dream?" He pointed a shaking finger, voice dripping contempt. "Your dream is rebellion! 'The heart is deceitful above all things.' Sin has taken root in your heart!" He stepped closer, towering over me. I couldn't breathe. My hands clutched the blanket. He grabbed my phone from the nightstand and slammed it onto the desk. "Deactivate the account. Right now."

"Please, Dad, just listen—"

"Do it!" he roared, voice cracking with rage. "Honor your father, Bethany, or face the consequences!"

Hands shaking, I picked up the phone as tears spilled onto the screen. Each tap chipped away at the fragile freedom I'd claimed. The screen blurred; I blinked rapidly. With one last click, it was done. My channel was gone. He loomed over me, breathing hard. His voice dropped—low, cold, still cutting.

"From now on, you go nowhere without my permission. No calls, no texts unless I approve them. You will spend every free moment in prayer, asking God to forgive your disobedience. The only singing you'll do is in the choir on Sunday." He turned on his heel and slammed the door; the walls rattled.

Silence swallowed the room. I stared at the phone in my shaking hands. Then the dam broke—I collapsed, face buried in the pillow as sobs tore through me. My chest burned. His control felt like a cage. I cried until I trembled. When the tears stopped, I stared at the ceiling. That's when it hit me: I would leave after my twenty-first birthday. Danny had promised a place to stay. Connections. A chance to live the life I dreamed of. Because if I stayed under my father's thumb, one thing was certain—I'd never truly live.

10

—•—

BENEATH THE SURFACE

BETHANY

I woke with a gasp, sunlight slicing through the blackout curtains. But it wasn't the day ahead that stirred me. It was Kevin. His name sparked a tight rush in my stomach, a feeling I hadn't had in years. s. Those steely-gray eyes, filled with desire, saw every mask I wore. That look made me forget how to think. I stretched under the covers, trying to shake the restless energy building inside me, but it was no use. His face crystallized: the curve of his jaw, stubble against my skin, the quiet strength he carried, Kevin wasn't just attractive—he was irresistible. The way he slipped past my defenses? Unfair.

My lips tingled at the memory of his kiss, slow and teasing. His tongue traced mine with a confidence that made me melt, like he knew exactly what he was doing. A soft moan escaped as the thought pulled me under. My fingers drifted beneath my shirt. I closed my eyes, giving in. His hands—rough, mapping every inch. The scent of his leather jacket clung to me, mixed with something uniquely his: addictive and all-consuming. His body, hard and unyielding, had pressed against mine, and for the first time in forever, I let myself fall. No walls, no pretense. Just him.

His text replayed in my mind: Tonight wasn't enough—I want more of you, and I won't pretend otherwise. The words burned. Paired with that look—like I was the only thing that mattered—it was too much. My hand moved lower, chasing the phantom of his touch. But shame crept in like a shadow. I froze, heart pounding, and yanked my hand away.

"God, Bethany." I raked a hand through my hair. "What are you doing?"

I stared at the wall, thoughts spinning. This wasn't who I wanted to be anymore. Yet Kevin broke through everything I thought I had under control, and that terrified me. I

42

threw off the covers and stood. Legs shaky, skin flushed. I needed air. I needed to run. Most of all, I needed to understand how Kevin had gotten under my skin so fast. Because no matter how much I tried to fight it, I wanted more of him, too—and that scared the hell out of me.

I rubbed my face, groaning. It had been over a year since I'd sworn off sex, relationships, everything. After Danny and New York, I thought I needed to reclaim myself. Danny. I'd been shattered in ways I didn't see at first. I thought the only way to rebuild was to bury the pain—get over him by getting under someone new. For a while, it worked—or I thought it did. The dizzy high of being wanted never lasted. Each time I woke alone, staring at a stranger's ceiling or fumbling for clothes, emptiness returned heavier than before.

I didn't see how self-destructive it was until one night, I couldn't look at myself. Mascara smudged, hair a mess, I felt empty, trying to fill a bottomless void. I hated the pattern—the cycle of searching for love in all the wrong places. That night, I promised to stop. So I did. Cold turkey. I cut off the distractions—the men who saw me as a temporary escape. For a year, I focused on rebuilding what Danny broke. Celibacy wasn't a choice. It was survival. A reset for a life spinning out of control.

I glanced at the clock. Still early. My shift at the thrift store didn't start until one p.m., which meant plenty of time to shake off this energy. And I knew exactly how: the beach. The thought steadied me. Thirty minutes later, I was dressed and out the door—black leggings, teal sports bra, and a hoodie loose against the morning chill. I laced up my sneakers and headed for the car.

The drive was quick. It hit me when I stepped out—gravel crunching, the air smelling of salt and seaweed. The sky blushed pink and orange as the sun broke the horizon. Seagulls cried overhead, their calls mingling with the crash of waves. I walked to the beach and took in the shimmering ocean. The path cut clean through the sand, promising escape.

This was my sanctuary, the only place where the noise in my head quieted. I stretched at the path's start, shaking off tension. Salt-laced wind filled my lungs as I scrolled through my playlist. My thumb paused on the album *Tidal* by Fiona Apple—her blue eyes eerily familiar. It felt right this morning. The bassline of *Sleep to Dream* kicked in, drums pounding. I let the music guide me. My feet fell into rhythm, the world fading. Her voice was defiant, unvarnished, matching the fire simmering inside me. I picked up my pace, the cool wind brushing my face.

Danny's face surfaced. His smile, once comforting, now stung—a reminder of everything I'd tried to escape. He had promised love and freedom, but it was all a lie. I drove harder into the pavement, breaths ragged. Fiona's words hit like a punch. I wouldn't go back—not to Danny, not to my father's suffocating grip. Every man I'd trusted had tried to mold me. I was done. Then *Sullen Girl* began, and my steps faltered. The melody hit like a wave. Sadness felt too real—like the song was written from my life. I focused on the horizon, but the lyrics pulled me under.

Tears burned. I let myself feel it: loneliness, the lingering ache of Danny—my first heartbreak. He'd promised salvation after my father's strict rules, yet he controlled me too, loving me only on his terms. Broken promises felt like chains I hadn't noticed until it was too late. My father's control was different, but just as heavy.

He dictated everything—what I wore, who I saw, even music. He called it love, but it was a jail. Danny had been another. Memories crashed. I pounded the path harder, feet slamming like I could outrun it. Breath came in jagged bursts; my body burned, but I didn't stop. The ocean rolled beside me, vast and calm, its steady rhythm mocking my turmoil. Life moved forward, so why did I always feel left behind, dragging expectations and heartbreak behind me?

By the time *Shadowboxer* played, I was pushing my body to its limits, legs burning as I sprinted. Frustration churned—a storm I couldn't contain. My feet slammed the path, each step a release of the mess Kevin had stirred.

His face invaded—his smile, dangerous and tempting. Kevin saw me in a way no one else had. And last night...last night had been everything. The way he watched me in that wind tunnel, eyes unwavering, like he knew exactly what I needed. Not just the thrill, but the freedom of letting go.

The memory curled tight in my ribs—a mix of yearning and fear. Kevin didn't make me feel like another conquest. He made me feel like I mattered. More than my scars. And that scared me. If Kevin saw the chaos inside me, what would he think? He didn't know my past or the things I carried with me. Yet he looked at me like I was whole, not defined by what I'd been through. The scariest part—he made me feel like I didn't have to explain everything, and it wouldn't matter, like he could see through the cracks to something worth holding. And God, I wanted him to hold on—even as fear threatened to pull me under. I ran harder, breath ragged, body screaming—but I didn't stop.

Amid the turmoil, fear gave way to a deep, aching pull. Celibacy wasn't fun. I was irritable, and my vibrator felt like a cruel joke—a Band-Aid on a bullet wound. I needed release—real release. The kind that only came with connection, with touch. The kind I knew Kevin could give me. My body flushed as images of his lips, hands, and the heat in his stare flooded my mind. The way his voice dipped saying my name, the way he moved, like he was made to ravish me. I didn't just want him—I needed him. Desperately.

I hadn't even noticed the shift in my playlist until Fiona's voice pierced my thoughts—low and sultry—as *Criminal* played. The timing was too perfect, almost mocking, as if the universe was calling me out for the way my body was betraying my better judgment. Kevin had stirred something in me last night. Freedom. Desire. Hope.

I stopped, chest heaving, hands on my knees, salty breeze cooling my skin. The ocean stretched out, waves crashing in a rhythm meant to calm me. But it didn't. My mind was stuck on Kevin's text, his words echoed in my head: *Tonight wasn't enough—I want more of you, and I won't pretend otherwise.*

I straightened, staring at the endless expanse of water, his face vivid in my mind, his eyes saw something in me worth holding onto. The pull was too strong. The need, too consuming. "Screw it." My voice was lost to the wind. Pulling out my phone, I typed quickly, thumbs shaking slightly, but my resolve was solid.

Me: I know we just saw each other last night, but would you want to see me again? Tonight?

I hit send and started jogging, like I'd finally let myself exhale. Three miles and a shower later, my phone buzzed.

Kevin: What do you have in mind?

A slow smile spread across my face. Tonight was going to be different. Tonight, I was choosing to let go.

11

— • —

UNWRITTEN RULES

BETHANY

Humid summer air clung to my skin as I watched Kevin take in the axe-throwing venue. He stood near the entrance, eyes sweeping the room with equal parts disbelief and intrigue. The loud thwack of axes hitting targets echoed off the wooden walls, mingling with laughter and conversation. Kevin's brow arched, lips twitching like he was fighting a smile.

"This your idea of fun?" His tone was a blend of curiosity and skepticism.

I crossed my arms and leaned against the counter, smirking. His plain white T-shirt hugged a chest that looked carved, veins tracing the length of his forearms before vanishing beneath the sleeves. Without the leather jacket—thanks to the heat—I had an unobstructed view, and I wasn't complaining. He caught my stare; I glanced away, pretending I hadn't been openly checking him out.

"What?" I widened my eyes. "You thought I'd take you somewhere boring? A movie? Mini golf?" He turned fully toward me, amusement sparking in his eyes.

"Something like that. Didn't peg you for the hurl-sharp-objects-for-fun type. Guess you've got layers."

"Plenty of layers," I shot back, letting my eyes linger just long enough to make the point. "Stick around and you might see a few more." I grabbed his hand. "Come on—let me show you how it's done." I laced my fingers through his and led him to our lane. My heart jolted with the memory—arms around his waist, wind roaring, heat pressed between us. That ride was impossible to forget. And now, with his scent still lingering, the want returned full force.

Tying my hair into a messy bun, I picked up an axe and stepped into position. Tonight's outfit was built to leave an impression: high-waisted denim shorts, a white tank showing off the girls, red-and-black flannel at my waist, black Dr. Martens to complete the look. I felt his gaze on my curves, so I took my time before raising the axe, certain I had his full attention. "Pay attention, rookie." I tossed the words over my shoulder. With a practiced flick, the axe spun and thunked just off-center. I turned, arms raised in mock victory. "Not bad, huh?"

Kevin stepped closer, a smirk playing at his mouth. "Impressive." His voice dipped. "But can you teach? I'm not exactly...skilled with axes." The subtle pause sent a shiver down my spine. Handing him an axe, I brushed his fingers.

"All right—start with your grip." He held it awkwardly—fingers tense, stance wrong. I bit back a laugh. "Oh no. That's bad. Really bad. Here." Moving behind him, I adjusted his hold, my hands lingering a beat too long. "You're not trying to kill it, just hit it. Unless you've got aggression to work out." His breath hitched; he turned, our faces inches apart.

"Plenty of aggression." His voice was rough, challenging. "But I'm not sure this is the best outlet."

Pulse racing, our eyes locked. "Focus, Kevin." Sliding my hands to his shoulders, I guided his stance. "Just...let it fly." When he finally landed a bull's-eye, he flashed a grin so cocky it should've been illegal.

"How's that, coach?" I tilted my head, pretending to consider.

"Not bad. Let's make it interesting. Best of three—if I win, you buy drinks. If you win...I'm open to suggestions."

His smile darkened, hunger flickering in his eyes. "Oh, I've got a suggestion, but I'm not sure you're ready for it."

Challenge accepted. I admired the strength in his arms, how his jeans hugged his hips. His first two throws barely kissed the target, and on his final turn, when the axe finally stuck with a solid thud, I knew I'd let him win. He rested a hip against the table, studying me.

"Even though I won," he murmured, "I'll still buy you a drink." We headed to the bar. My body still buzzed with adrenaline and the thick tension that had been building all night. Kevin walked beside me, close enough that our arms brushed, each touch sparking a jolt that made my heart skitter. Inside, the low light played across his features, sculpting them, and I was captivated all over again. I stepped up to the bar, ordering a drink, and

Kevin followed suit, resting against the counter just enough for his arm to brush mine. His fingers brushed my knuckles—just enough to spark something deep in my chest.

"All right." His teasing tone sent a shiver down my spine. "I've got to know—where'd you learn to throw like that?" I smirked and took a lingering sip, letting his eyes trace every movement of my lips. Setting the glass down, I tilted my head at him, feigning innocence.

"Wouldn't you like to know?" Kevin's eyes locked on mine, lips quirking into a dangerous smile.

"Yeah, I would." His tone dipped darker, more intimate. "You've got a way of keeping me guessing."

"Well," I said, shrugging as I leaned just slightly closer, letting the heat of his presence wash over me, "let's just say I've had practice keeping people on their toes." His eyes dropped to my lips, lingering for a beat too long.

"You're full of surprises."

I nudged him lightly, breaking the tension just enough to keep it playful. "And how exactly are you planning to collect this reward of yours?" I asked, the question laced with challenge.

Kevin's laugh was low and rich—the kind that felt like velvet against my skin—and the sound made something deep inside me tighten. He moved in closer, his lips brushing my ear, and I burned with need.

"Finish that drink," he murmured, "and I'll show you." He knew exactly what he was doing—and loved every second of it. Never one to back down from a challenge, I met his gaze, picked up my drink, and downed it in one smooth motion—the burn of the alcohol no match for the fire coursing through my veins. His smile widened, the look in his eyes turning downright predatory, and before I could process what was happening, his hands were on mine. Without a word, he led me out of the bar, each step sending a fresh wave of anticipation coursing through me. The cool night air hit my skin like a shock, but Kevin's presence burned hotter than anything else. His stare tangled with mine, and in that moment, I knew—whatever came next, there was no going back.

Kevin parked along a quiet Koreatown street. The night carried the scent of late-night food. Narrow sidewalks ran alongside worn apartment buildings, their stucco facades chipped and fading. Neon signs in Korean script flickered above corner shops and bakeries. Swinging off the bike, I slipped my hand into Kevin's. He led me down the block, the soft scuff of our boots the only sound in the stillness. My pulse quickened with every step, anticipation bubbling in my chest. Where was he taking me, and what kind of prize did he think he'd earned for winning the game? More important, was I really ready for whatever this was?

We stopped in front of a laundromat, its fluorescent lights spilling onto the sidewalk and illuminating the cracked pavement. Above the entrance, a flickering sign in faded red letters read WASH & DRY 24/7, the "W" stubbornly half-dark. I folded my arms, staring through the bright windows in disbelief. Inside, a guy in a hoodie stood against a dryer, scrolling on his phone. A woman folded clothes while a child tugged at her sleeve. The hum of tumbling machines provided a monotonous rhythm. I turned to Kevin, one brow arched.

"A laundromat?" I asked, trying—and failing—to hide my grin. "Please tell me your prize isn't free laundry." His smirk widened, that confident glint in his eyes making me want to smack him—or maybe kiss him.

"Not quite." He held the door open like it was some grand gesture. "Do you trust me?" I hesitated, then stepped inside. The sterile scent of detergent slapped me in the face. A pair of kids argued over a vending machine while an older man flipped through a magazine on a plastic chair.

"If this is your idea of fun," I teased, "we may need to revisit your definition of the word."

"Patience," he said, nodding toward the back. We wound through rows of humming machines and stopped at a dryer beneath a neon sign that flashed CYCLE IN PROGRESS. "Okay, now I'm convinced this is some kind of weird laundry cult," I muttered. Kevin laughed, a rich, low sound that tightened something inside me.

"You'll see." He swung the dryer door open. Instead of a drum of clothes, a narrow staircase glowed with LED strips. Bass thumped from somewhere below. I gaped at him.

"You've got to be kidding me."

"Told you to trust me." He motioned for me to go first.

Heart hammering, I descended. The beat grew clearer, and suddenly I recognized the track—*Levels* by Avicii. My steps matched the rhythm. At the bottom, neon lights pulsed hot pink, acid green, and electric blue. Fog machines hissed; laser beams carved the haze. The music was loud enough to vibrate through my bones, each drop making the underground space feel alive. I stared, awestruck.

"This is insane," I shouted over the sound. Kevin leaned in, his breath brushing my ear.

"In a good way?" Laughter slipped free, tension melting from my shoulders.

"Yeah. In a good way."

"Come on." He tilted his head toward the bar. "Let's grab another drink."

We weaved through the crowd, the pulsing beat of the music vibrating through the floor. The bar was a neon-lit oasis.

Kevin stood casually against the counter and turned to me. "What are you having?"

I tilted my head, feeling a rush of boldness under the flashing lights. "Two shots of tequila," I said teasing. His brows shot up, and I caught the glint of surprise in his eyes.

"Tequila?" A grin tugged at his lips. He studied me for a moment, then chuckled. "I see you want to be free tonight."

Before I could respond, he turned to the bartender. "Four shots of tequila. Two each." He turned back to me, his movements smooth and confident. He handed me my shots and raised an eyebrow. "You need a lime or a chaser?" His tone was half-teasing, half-challenging. I shook my head, meeting his smile.

"Nope."

He laughed softly, shaking his head as he lifted his glass. "Alright, cheers to freedom."

"Cheers." I clinked my glass against his and tipped the shot back. The tequila burned as it slid down, spreading through me like fire. I set the empty glass on the bar and caught Kevin staring at me, his lips curled in that crooked, mischievous smile that made my stomach flip. "What?" I raised an eyebrow, keeping my tone light. He shook his head, the smile never leaving his face.

"Nothing." But the way his eyes lingered told a different story.

"Nothing?" I leaned in, pressing him.

"Nothing," he repeated, his grin widening as he grabbed his second shot. "Come on. Round two."

I rolled my eyes but laughed, grabbing my second glass. We raised them together and knocked them back. This time, the tequila went down smooth, the heat spreading faster through my chest. I felt lighter, like the night had blurred into something dreamlike. And then the familiar opening notes of *Sandstorm* by Darude cut through the room, the beat sending a ripple of excitement through the crowd.

I froze for a second before letting out an excited yell. "I love this song!" Grabbing Kevins hand I pulled him toward the dance floor. His laugh followed behind me as we plunged into the pulsing sea of bodies. The beat dropped, the lights strobed, and for a moment, nothing else existed but the music and the way we moved.

The beat throbbed around us, the bass pounding in my chest, and I let myself go. My body moved instinctively to the rhythm, swaying and spinning as if the beat had taken control. Kevin's hand lingered on mine; his grin was so infectious it felt like pure electricity. The DJ transitioned seamlessly into *Don't You Worry Child* by Swedish House Mafia, the lyrics soaring over the crowd like a quiet promise. The melody hit something deep within me, and I felt a rush of happiness so pure it made my heart ache.

I laughed, throwing my head back as the lights flashed in waves of blue and white, their glow making the room feel otherworldly. For once, there were no worries, no overthinking, just the pulse of the music, the tenderness in his eyes, and the joy of being alive. His eyes never left me, a mixture of awe as he watched me lose myself. His gaze was locked, entranced by every move. And I loved it. Loved feeling free. Loved feeling seen. For a little while, there was no past, no future—just me, Kevin, and the music wrapping around us like a cocoon, telling me it was okay to simply be.

As the music shifted into the sultry, hypnotic rhythm of *Lose Control* by Meduza, Kevin's hands slid to my hips. He moved behind me, his chest flush against my back, every inch of him moving in sync with mine. I stretched my arm back, my fingers curling around the nape of his neck, pulling him closer as we danced. Every move was hungry, his touch sending a delicious shiver through me.

The crowd around us blurred into the neon-lit haze, their movements a distant backdrop to the energy crackling in the air. Kevin's lips brushing the back of my neck—light, teasing, and just enough to make me dizzy. His breath lingered, igniting a need that spread like fire. A spark of boldness, of pure sexual confidence, surged within me as I tilted my head slightly, giving him more access. The sensation took over, making me feel powerful, and close to losing control. Unable to resist, I turned to face him, my eyes locking with his stormy gray ones. His pupils were blown wide, his desire clear, as if he were silently pleading for what came next. The intensity was undeniable, and I felt the world shift beneath us.

I didn't hesitate. I closed the gap, my lips capturing his in a kiss that was equal parts hunger and defiance. The kiss was electric—his lips soft, demanding, moving with an unrelenting rhythm. His hands grabbed my hips, anchoring me as the music pulsed, every beat amplifying the tension. My fingers tangled in his hair, pulling him closer as the heat built. It was consuming—the kind of kiss that left no room for thought, only feeling.

Our bodies never stopped moving, swaying to the hypnotic beat as we lost ourselves. I pressed against him in a slow grind, and I felt the unmistakable hardness of him through his jeans. A jolt shot through me, and I pushed into him harder, the friction intensifying the ache deep inside. Kevin groaned softly against my lips, his hands slipping lower. I felt invincible; his touch made the room, the crowd, even the music disappear. All that mattered was us—this moment, this connection, this fire that threatened to consume us both.

The music shifted seamlessly, the tempo slowing just enough to change the mood, but we didn't stop. We stayed close, our bodies moving together in perfect sync, lost in the rhythm and each other. Sometimes his lips found mine, soft and lingering, stealing kisses that left me breathless. Other times, we simply let the music take over, swaying in a way that felt effortless. At some point, Kevin came closer, his breath hot against my ear as he murmured, "I'm ready to collect on my reward."

I pulled back just enough to look at him, my brow furrowing slightly, thinking this—our closeness, the way we fit together—was the prize. His lips curled into a slow, knowing smile as he slid his arms around my waist, pulling me closer.

"Do you want to go to my place?" he asked, his voice low and full of promise. "I live down the street."

There was no hesitation, no second-guessing. I stopped moving, caught in the moment like it might swallow me whole.

In all seriousness, I simply said, "Yes." His smile was slow and knowing, and he didn't let go of my hand as we stepped into the night. Cold air nipped at my skin, sobering me just enough to snap everything into focus. I was tipsy, yes, but not lost—the tequila had simply stripped away the usual layers of doubt. Kevin's fingers laced with mine as we walked, the city's hum broken only by distant traffic and the rustle of trees overhead. Each step felt intentional, anticipation building with every heartbeat.

When we reached his motorcycle beneath a flickering streetlamp, Kevin stopped. Without a word, he framed my face in his hands—the roughness of his fingertips sending a shiver down my spine. He held me, eyes searching. Then he kissed me. Not hurried or wild like on the dance floor, but slow and sensual—a quiet confession. His tongue brushed mine in a measured rhythm that left me aching for more. My hands found his belt loops, tugging him closer until the cold brick of the building pressed against my back, heat radiating through my clothes.

When he finally pulled away, our breaths mingled in the chill. He slipped a hand into his pocket, drew out his keys, then lifted my hand to his lips, pressing a soft kiss to my knuckles, tender, almost sweet. Goosebumps rose across my skin. We crossed the courtyard in silence, tension thick enough to touch. At his door, Kevin unlocked it and held it open; one final charged glance before I stepped inside.

The living room was minimalist but inviting: a sleek gray couch, a single worn book on a simple coffee table, a guitar resting on its stand, and a vibrant fiddle-leaf fig adding the only splash of color. White cabinets in the open kitchen gleamed under soft lighting. Everything was precise—like him. Kevin's eyes followed me as I took it all in. The clink of keys dropping into a ceramic bowl broke the quiet; my pulse jumped at the sound.

"Your place is nice," I said, despite the butterflies.

"Thanks," he replied.

I turned away, feeling nervous energy gather beneath my skin. I tucked a strand behind my ear—an attempt to mask the nerves.

"Do you want some water?" Kevin asked, his tone casual but his eyes piercing.

"Sure," I answered softly, the word almost an exhale. He moved to the refrigerator, retrieved two bottles of water, and handed one to me. As our fingers met, a spark zipped up my arm. I flushed, silently willing myself to stay composed.

Kevin opened his bottle and took a sip, his movements slow and controlled. I watched his throat work as he swallowed, my mind racing while the silence stretched. Gathering my courage, I managed a playful smile.

"So," I began, my voice tinged with curiosity and tease, "you still haven't told me how you're going to collect your reward." His lips curled into a faint, wolfish smile as he finished swallowing. He capped the bottle with unhurried slowness, every movement measured and intentional, as if building suspense. His eyes darkened, taking on a predatory look. A shudder ran down my spine.

Without breaking eye contact, he walked toward me, closing the space with an easy confidence that made my breath hitch. Gently, he took the bottle from my hand and set it aside, his touch lingering just long enough to leave me breathless. Before I could process what was happening, his hands found my waist. In one smooth motion, he lifted me onto the counter; the cool surface beneath me was a stark contrast to the heat radiating from him.

A small gasp escaped as I steadied myself, palms pressing against the counter. Kevin stepped closer, his eyes locking onto mine with an intensity that sent a delicious thrill coursing through me. The room shrank, tension buzzing between us. He slid a hand to my waist—slow and intentional—and loosened the tie in my hair with a single pull. Strands cascaded over my shoulders; he sifted through them as if memorizing their texture.

"I love your hair," he murmured. "I love the way you look with it down."

Heat flooded my cheeks. Instinctively, I glanced away, but Kevin wasn't having it. His hand found my chin, guiding my face back.

"Do you know how fucking beautiful you are?" The words jolted straight to my core. "Watching you on the dance floor tonight," he continued, thumb stroking my jaw, "you were so goddamn sexy, Bethany. Do you know that?" He studied my face, already knowing the answer. His hand drifted from my chin, tracing the curve of my jaw until his fingertips brushed my lips.

"And these," he whispered, thumb grazing my lower lip, "they're so soft. I don't know how I'll stop kissing them."

Before I could speak, he stepped in, his body fitting between my legs. His closeness lit a fuse low in my belly. His lips found mine—soft, teasing—then deepened. His teeth caught my bottom lip in a playful nip that left me wanting more. Every sensation sharpened: his hands gripping my waist, his body flushed against mine, his mouth claiming me with unrelenting hunger. Fire consumed every thought until only the connection remained.

I looped my arms around his neck, but he caught my wrists, pinning them against the cupboard, as a soft moan slipped out. His lips trailed heated kisses down my neck; I squirmed, desperate for more. When his mouth reached the top of my breast, I gasped, anticipation coiling tight. Just as pleasure crested, Kevin lifted his head, storm-gray eyes calm yet intense.

"Now, time for my reward," he murmured, releasing my hands. His fingers slid to my waist, deftly unbuttoning my shorts, then paused. "You can tell me to stop. If you want me to, I will. Do you understand?"

"Yes," I whispered, barely getting the word out.

"Do you want me to continue?" he asked, voice thick with hunger.

"Yes," I breathed, the word trembling on my lips. His kisses were frantic and everywhere. Kevin's hands found my ass, fingers digging in, and I moaned into his mouth. He was aggressive, and I loved it. I nipped at his chin, trying to match his neediness, teeth scraping his neck. He growled, low and throaty, and with one swift motion, he lifted me, tugging off my shorts and panties. They caught on my boots, but he yanked them free.

I froze, pulling back to look at him. His pupils were blown—almost no gray left. Biting my bottom lip, I panted in anticipation. Kevin's fingers drifted from my ribs to the dip of my pelvis. He licked his lips, eyes locked on mine, silently asking. I nodded. He caught my chin and claimed my lips again. Our tongues tangled while his hand slid to my pussy.

"Oh God," I purred.

His fingers caressed my folds; my pussy pulsed at every rub. One thick finger slid inside, teasing slowly. I was so fucking wet that it urged him to add another. The feeling was too good—I clenched around him as he pumped. My hands flew to the cupboard as I squeezed my eyes shut and surrendered to the rush.

"Do you like this, Bethany?" he murmured, thumb circling my clit.

"Yes," I whimpered.

"Good. I'm ready to collect my prize." He withdrew, and my body ached at the loss. I watched him slip those fingers into his mouth, dragging them out as if savoring me. I exhaled shakily. Fuck, he was so fucking sexy.

"I know what you need, Bethany." His strong hands pulled me to the counter's edge. Before I could reply, he dropped to his knees and met me with the wet heat of his tongue. I moaned, voice cracking as sensation surged through me. My back arched; one hand smacked the cupboard for balance. Kevin's grip on my thighs. His tongue moved in slow, devastating strokes, and when he slid a finger inside, my hips bucked, a strangled groan tearing free.

"Fuck," I gasped.

I tried to pull away for breath, but he tightened his arms, dragging me closer. His fingers curled in time with his tongue, white-hot heat flooding my veins. My hands tangled in his hair, desperate for something to hold. He groaned against me—low, primal—vibrating through every nerve. Instinct took over; I rolled my hips into his mouth, chasing the friction.

"Kevin," I cried, voice cracking as his tongue flicked my most sensitive spot—relentless, knowing. He didn't stop. Lips and fingers worked together, driving me higher, pressure coiling low and tight.

Obscene sounds filled the room: my breathless cries, his groans, the slick rhythm of his mouth. Body taut, vision blurring, I was seconds from falling apart. He felt it—the way I clenched around his fingers, the way my thighs shook. He growled, holding me tighter. And then I shattered. Pleasure ripped through me in waves, my scream echoing off the kitchen walls. I convulsed, tugging his hair, drowning in the rush.

When reality returned, Kevin stood, wiping his mouth with the back of his hand. Lips glistening, eyes dark with pride and raw hunger, he watched me.

"What a way to break my celibacy," I whispered.

His head tilted, brows lifting. "What did you just say?" The rough tone made my thighs clench despite how wrecked I felt. Heat flooded my cheeks.

"I—uh—I didn't mean—"

"You said you've been celibate." He stepped closer, his grin wicked. "Is that true?"

"Yes," I admitted. "I mean, I was—until now." A softness passed through his eyes before he smirked and kissed me deeply. I was on his tongue, and fire flared all over again. Kevin pulled back slowly, crouching to slide my panties up my legs. His hands grazed my skin, each touch sending shivers down my spine. He glanced up, dark eyes smoldering, then dropped his eyes to my feet.

Without a word, he removed my boots with a quiet care that made my pulse stutter. His fingers lingered at my ankles for a heartbeat, heat shooting straight to my core. Standing, he took my hand and led me out of the kitchen toward his bedroom.

The lamplight lit the room as Kevin opened a dresser drawer and pulled out a black T-shirt. Turning back, his stare roved over my bare skin, each pass stealing the breath from my lungs.

"Take off your top and bra." His voice was low, commanding. I did what I was told. His eyes darkened; he looked torn, like he was holding himself back by sheer force of will. Then, hands trembling slightly, he drew the T-shirt over my head, the fabric soft against my flushed skin. He stepped back and pulled off his shirt. Broad chest. Sculpted abs. That deep V vanished into black boxer briefs, hugging every hard line. My mouth went dry, tracing each curve of muscle. He caught me staring; the corner of his mouth quirked.

"See something you like?"

I could only nod—brain short-circuited. He pulled back the covers and motioned me in. Sliding beneath the sheets, I buzzed with anticipation. He joined me, heat radiating off his body. Cupping my face, he kissed me—slower now, savoring. When he drew back, his eyes were soft but burning.

"I want you, Bethany," he rasped. "But not like this. Not tonight."

"Why not?"

His thumb brushed my bottom lip. "Because when I have you, I want you to remember it. We've both been drinking—you deserve better." I started to argue, but he silenced me with a tender kiss. Then he lay back, pulling me against him, arm draped around my waist, my head tucked under his chin. His fingers traced lazy patterns on my back. The ache still pulsed between my thighs, but his warmth lulled me. He reached over, flicked off the light, and darkness settled—nothing but the rhythm of our breaths and the promise of what's coming.

12

MIDNIGHT CONFESSIONS

BETHANY

I jolted awake, blinking at the sunlight and tangled sheets. This wasn't my bed. For a second, I thought maybe I'd forgotten to close my blackout curtains—but no, this wasn't even my room. My head throbbed.

"Ugh." I rubbed my temples, trying to piece it all together. As my eyes adjusted, the realization hit me like a freight train. This wasn't my room. Panic and clarity clashed. "Holy shit...Kevin." Last night flashed back—axe throwing, laughter, dancing, kissing. So much kissing.

A wicked smile tugged at my lips. He'd pulled me close, like I was the only thing that mattered. I laughed softly. But then, the memories deepened, and heat flooded my cheeks. We hadn't just kissed. My mind spun back to the kitchen—cool counter, his mouth on me, hungry in a way I'd never felt. And God, I'd wanted him to.

"Oh my God." I clutched the covers as the memory of his mouth on me resurfaced. He hadn't just kissed me. He devoured me, and I'd let him. I'd wanted him to.

I buried my face under the covers. Embarrassment clashed with exhilaration. I'd had partners before, but never felt so exposed—and that vulnerability thrilled me. The thought of Kevin's lips, his tongue, his fingers...My body tingled, a rush of butterflies swirling in my stomach. And yet, he had stopped. I accidentally said out loud that I was celibate, and despite the fire burning between us, he respected that boundary. Instead, he held me in his arms as I drifted to sleep. My heart ached at the tenderness of it all.

Still cocooned under the covers, I wasn't ready to face him. Dressed in nothing but his T-shirt and nerves, I cringed, desperate for a bathroom and a time machine.

"Why didn't I just go home?" I muttered. The door creaked. I froze, breath held, body tense. Footsteps padded softly into the room, followed by the sound of drawers opening and closing. I squeezed my eyes shut, hoping I could somehow will myself invisible. The mattress dipped as Kevin sat down beside me. The covers shifted, and then they were pulled back just enough to reveal my face. His gray eyes locked onto mine, humor dancing in them as his lips curved into a teasing smile.

"Good morning, sleepyhead." His voice was laced with mischief. "Did you sleep well?"

I nodded, unable to find my voice, hyper-aware of the mess I must look like.

"Yeah."

His grin turned wicked. "You were out cold. Like you were completely...spent for some reason."

Heat flared in my cheeks, and I rolled my eyes to deflect my embarrassment.

"Do you have work today?" he asked casually.

I shook my head. "No." My voice came out quieter than I intended.

"Oh, Bethany." He came closer. "Cat got your tongue?"

I sat up, clutching the covers around me as a barrier. "No, Kevin. I don't have work today." I tried to match his playful confidence. He chuckled, his hand grazing my leg, sending a rush of heat straight up my spine.

"Good. How about spending the day with me? Here?" I wasn't prepared—no clothes, no toothbrush, probably a disaster. But spending more time with him was tempting.

"I'd like that," I admitted softly, "but I don't have anything to wear."

Kevin reached beside him and held up a pair of his shorts. "These will do for now." He winked. "Though, for the record, I wouldn't mind if you just walked around in my T-shirt." I laughed, and he smiled, reaching out to brush a strand of hair from my face. "I went down to the corner store and picked up a toothbrush for you," he said. "There are some clothes and a towel in the bathroom if you want to shower. I'll make us breakfast while you freshen up."

My chest swelled at his thoughtfulness. "Thank you." My voice was laced with gratitude. "I must look like a mess." His expression softened, and he reached for my chin, tilting it up to meet his.

"You're wrong. You're fucking beautiful." He kissed my forehead. "I'll let you get to it." He headed for the door. "Bathroom's on the right. Sorry about the manly soap." As the door clicked shut behind him, I exhaled, my heart still fluttering. Kevin had a pull I couldn't ignore—the kind that might be my undoing.

Kevin was a liar. My mascara was smeared, my skin blotchy—every inch screamed hangover. With a groan, I splashed water on my face, determined to fix myself up. After handling the basics, I ripped open the toothbrush package like it was the answer to all my problems and brushed my teeth with more force than necessary. The mint hit instantly—one small victory this morning.

Turning on the shower, I let the water heat up until steam swirled around the room. When I stepped in, the heat melted everything—sleep, tension, even traces of last night. I skipped washing my hair—it was already styled, and stepping out like a drowned rat wasn't the vibe. Instead, I grabbed Kevin's soap, flipped the cap, and took a quick sniff. Cedarwood and Bergamot. Pure Kevin.

When I got out, I grabbed the clothes Kevin had left for me: a white T-shirt and a pair of gray sweatpants. No clean underwear meant I had to go commando—a choice I rolled the too-long sweatpants at the waist, trying not to overthink. Before leaving the bathroom, I gave myself a final once-over in the mirror. My hair hung loose around my shoulders, just like Kevin had said he liked it last night. Taking a deep breath, I picked up his clothes, dropped them in the hamper, and stepped out.

The air was rich with something savory and spiced. My stomach growled in response. Kevin was in the living room, casually setting plates on the coffee table. The omelet was perfectly golden, packed with spinach, tomatoes, and peppers.

"Glad you're out." Kevin smiled. "I just finished up. I hope you like omelets. It's pretty much all I had in, eggs and veggies. I try to eat clean." Kevin motioned for me to sit, guiding me to a spot on the floor across from him at the coffee table. "Sorry for the setup," he said with a shrug. "My place is too small for a dining table. But this works, right?" He disappeared into the kitchen for a moment and returned with a mug, handing it to me.

"I noticed you drink your coffee black." His voice was casual, like it wasn't the most thoughtful thing anyone had done for me in a long time. I stared at the dark liquid, overwhelmed by everything about this moment. Kevin—this gorgeous, sexy guy—had made me breakfast. He'd noticed little details about me. This wasn't anything I was used to in the dating world.

"You noticed." My voice dropped to a whisper. "Thank you."

As always, Kevin sensed my unease. "Eat," he said gently. "Tell me what you think." The first bite of the omelet was like heaven. The eggs were fluffy, the seasoning spot on, and the vegetables added just the right amount of texture and flavor. There was a hint of garlic and maybe a pinch of paprika that gave it a subtle kick. Without thinking, I let out a soft, involuntary moan of approval. Kevin stiffened, his fork hovering midair as he glanced at me from the corner of his eye. "Are you okay?" His voice was amused.

"Yes!" I laughed. "This is...amazing, Kevin. I just got carried away for a second." He gave a satisfied smile before taking a bite. I set my fork down and turned to face him, the words spilling out before I could think. "Can I ask you something?" My tone was more serious than I meant, and I saw the subtle shift in his expression.

Kevin pressed back against the couch, setting his plate aside. "Sure, go ahead."

I hesitated for a second, but curiosity won out. "Why are you single?"

He stiffened, his shoulders going rigid, and I immediately felt the tension rise. Undeterred, I pressed on, trying to lighten the mood.

"I mean, you seem like an amazing guy. And you're not bad on the eyes." I gave him a small smile. "I'm sure women hit on you all the time. So...why?"

Kevin let out a long, heavy breath, running a hand through his hair. His eyes dimmed.

"That's...a big question." He glanced at me, then away, as if weighing his words. "I'm single because, for a long time, I didn't want to date. Or maybe I couldn't. My circumstances didn't exactly make it easy." His voice turned vulnerable. I stayed quiet, letting him continue. "I told you my brother and I moved out here to start over, right?"

I nodded, careful not to interrupt. He drew in a breath, his jaw tightening slightly.

"My brother got sick when we were in high school. It wasn't just some short-term thing. He was hospitalized for a very long time. When our parents died..."

He paused, swallowing hard, his Adam's apple bobbing.

"When they died, it hit us both hard. We had our uncle and aunt, and they tried, they really did. But it was the bond between me and my brother—losing Mom and Dad together—that kept us close, it made us lean on each other." His tone grew quieter, heavier. "Eventually, he got better, and we decided to move here for a fresh start. But it wasn't easy. He has these...bouts sometimes. And when they happen, I have to step in. For a long time, that left no room for anyone else. No time for dating, no time for connection."

My chest ached, but he kept going, voice lifting just slightly.

"But over the last few years, things have changed. He's doing better now, really better. He even took off out of state for a while, living his life. No health scares, no emergencies. It's freed up a lot of my time." Kevin's eyes softened, and he smiled. "Funny enough, he's the reason I ended up at the bar the night we met. I was supposed to be meeting him there, but his flight got delayed."

I sat there, throat tight, guilt creeping in for prying.

"Oh." I managed a weak smile. "I understand." He stared down at his food, and I fidgeted with my hair, shifting awkwardly on the floor. What could I say that wouldn't feel shallow or misplaced? Before I could come up with anything, Kevin—ever attuned—smiled softly and changed the subject.

"Are you done with this?" He nodded toward the sliver of omelet on my plate. The question caught me off guard. Instincts kicked in.

"Do not touch my omelet." I snatched up the plate and popped the last bite into my mouth.

Kevin grinned, the light fully back in his eyes. "Check. She loves my omelets." He muttered it just loud enough for me to hear. I smirked, setting the plate back down with a dramatic flourish.

"Done." I sat back with a small, satisfied smile. Kevin grabbed the plates and turned back, grinning.

"Relax on the couch while I clean up."

"I can help."

"No, Bethany. You're my guest. I've got it." He waved me off.

Left alone, I picked up the worn book from the coffee table—The Alchemist by Paulo Coelho. Kevin was a thinker, drawn to stories with meaning. Smiling to myself, I set it down and let my eyes wander the room until they landed on the guitar in the corner. The Martin D-28 called to me, its golden finish catching the sun. I stepped closer, fingertips grazing the polished surface. It felt like it held a thousand stories. I brushed the strings, something familiar stirring—nostalgia, maybe, or quiet longing. I strummed once, and the pull deepened.

Kevin's voice rang out from the kitchen. "You play?" I glanced over my shoulder.

"Something like that. I know a few songs." He leaned casually against the archway, drying his hands with a towel.

"I was learning to play, too. Why don't you play something for me?"

Shaking my head, I stalled. "I don't think I'd be good. It's been too long."

Kevin grinned, easygoing as always. "Bethany, you'll never know until you try. Go ahead, I won't judge. My guitar playing is just as bad as my axe throwing." He winked and turned back to the sink.

The guitar felt natural in my hands as I carried it to the couch. I sat, my fingers hovering. The chords came awkward and stiff—until muscle memory kicked in. The familiar melody began to flow. I closed my eyes and began to sing *Landslide* by Fleetwood Mac. The water shut off. Kevin stood in the doorway, gray eyes locked on me, intense, like he didn't want to miss a moment. I couldn't stop now. Lost in the song, I smiled and sang louder, letting joy loosen something inside me. The chords flowed. I let the last one linger, like greeting an old friend.

When I turned to Kevin, his expression was unreadable, his eyes still fixed on me with a force that made my stomach flip. I cleared my throat, breaking the silence.

"Sorry about that. Kinda got carried away." I laughed nervously, trying to ease the tension. Kevin blinked, like pulling himself out of a trance.

When he spoke, his voice was tender. "I've only heard you sing twice, and I'm already convinced you were meant to do it, Bethany. Your voice...God, your voice is incredible. Everything about you is beautiful."

I blushed. He stepped closer.

"Play something else for me. Please." He looked at me like saying no wasn't an option. I was stunned. Singing for anyone—especially in a moment like this—wasn't something I was prepared for. That part of me—the performer—I'd let go long ago. But Kevin pulled things out of me like they'd never been buried.

"Can I take a rain check?" I forced a nervous laugh. "I'm suddenly feeling very self-conscious." Kevin's eyes darkened, a smirk tugging at his lips.

"Let's make a deal." His voice turned teasing. "You sing me one more song, and I'll do whatever you want. And I mean whatever." The ache from last night returned—his words electric, promising. My heart skipped. Kevin was challenging me again, and I knew how much I'd enjoy it.

"Hmm..." I mused, letting my voice dip into something lower, more seductive.

"Whatever I want?" His smile deepened. He stepped forward, voice nearly a growl.

"Whatever."

I motioned for him to sit on the couch, and he did, settling in like a man completely in control—or so he thought.

"Do you mind if I sing to a track instead? I think I have the perfect song for you," I said, letting just enough suggestion slip into my tone to make him raise an eyebrow.

"It would be my pleasure." His voice was smooth, laced with intrigue.

I set the guitar in its place and grabbed my phone from the counter. Boldness surged—fueled by his words, his eyes, his presence. Scrolling, I found what I wanted.

The first notes of *Alone with You* by Alina Baraz filled the room—low, hypnotic, pulsing. Turning to Kevin, I locked eyes and began to sing. My voice floated through the space, every word dripping with intent, drawing me closer with every step. His gray eyes tracked me, intense, memorizing every breath. Pressure mounted. At the chorus, I stepped between his knees and straddled his lap. A low groan slipped from him, I saw him off guard. I leaned closer, voice dipping sultry as I sang.

His hands slid to my hips, surprise fading into something primal. Still singing, I peeled his shirt from his shoulders. When he reached for mine, I caught his hands, wagging a playful no. His lips curled into a devilish smile, eyes burning with urgency. I let my lips brush his ear, purring about kissing—and then I kissed him. Soft, teasing, then deeper. When I tried to pull back, he wouldn't let me, hands tightening as he reclaimed the kiss with breath-stealing intensity.

"You're not playing fair, Bethany." His voice was rough with need. He nipped my earlobe; shivers raced down my spine. Catching my breath, I eased back just enough to continue the song, lips hovering inches from his. I traced his neck with my tongue, trailing kisses to his collarbone; his body went still beneath me. Between kisses, I murmured the lyrics, voice melting into the heat.

When I reached his chest, Kevin's hands closed around my wrists, tugging me up to face him. Gray eyes searched mine.

I smiled, voice a purr. "Didn't you say you wanted me to remember every second? I'm not drunk, Kevin. I'll remember." Something in him snapped. The fire from last night roared back—hotter. I surged forward, crashing my lips to his. He answered with equal fervor, like I already belonged to him. One hand squeezed my ass while the other roamed my thigh, leaving molten trails. Fingers hooked the hem of my oversized T-shirt, and with one swift motion, it was gone, leaving me bare. His eyes dropped to my breasts; lips parted like he needed a taste. A palm cupped one, thumb brushing my nipple—electric. Then came his mouth, tongue flicking the sensitive peak.

A gasp spilled into a moan as his other hand pinched my other nipple, the pleasure edging on pain.

I arched, hips grinding against him, chasing friction. His mouth moved between my breasts, worshipping each. Then his grip tightened, hands locking under my thighs as he lifted me. Legs wrapped around his waist, arms around his neck, our mouths met again, kissing like we were starving.

He carried us toward the bedroom, steps sure, breath ragged. Every inch fed the fire, stoking the ache until it burned wild. By the time he shoved the door open, my heart pounded; the world outside vanished. There was only him—his mouth, his touch, his need—and the way he lit me up from the inside out.

We reached his bed, and Kevin guided me to sit. The room felt charged, every breath between us heavy with anticipation. He moved to unbutton his jeans, but I reached out, stopping him. We locked eyes, the air thick with heat and tension. I took my time opening the button, my fingers brushing his skin. He stood perfectly still, hands loose at his sides, gray eyes burning and breath coming rough. I slid the denim down inch by inch; when the jeans finally pooled at his feet, I stilled.

Kevin wasn't wearing underwear. He stood there, powerful, unashamed—arousal thick and irresistible. His dick was long, heavy, pre-cum glistening at the tip. My cheeks flushed; eagerness thrummed through me. After everything he'd given me last night, I wanted to please him. I slid my palm over the head. Wetness coated my hand as I twisted gently.

"Fuck, Bethany," he rasped.

Stroking lazily, I looked up through hooded eyes.

"I'm not sure I can fit all of you in my mouth." I licked my lips.

"You won't know if you don't try." His teeth were gritted. With my free hand, I grabbed his base. I licked up and down his shaft like it was my favorite popsicle. He let out a guttural groan, trembling. My lips closed over the tip, sucking deep, taking him inch by inch until sweetness melted on my tongue. I worked him—wet, messy, relentless—because I fucking needed it.

Kevin watched, entranced, eyes darkening with every pass. His breaths came ragged; his filthy groans filled the room.

"Bethany," he murmured, voice cracked. I glanced up, licking him slow as sin, a wicked smile curving my lips. I wasn't stopping. Not when he trembled like that. "Bethany." He groaned again—raw, desperate—fists clenching.

I took him deeper, throat relaxing until my eyes watered. His hand shot to the back of my head, fingers curling in my hair, guiding me as his control slipped.

"If you don't stop..." He breathed hard. "I'm going to lose it."

Good. That was the point. I sucked harder, slid back with a slurp, then sank down again, showing him how much I wanted every inch. His guttural moan made me ache, soaked, starving to feel him inside me. I dragged my tongue along his length one last time, savoring every drop, then pulled off him, slow, dirty, hungry for more.

Leaning back, lips still slick, I caught his stare with a wicked glint. Kevin didn't hesitate. He kicked his jeans off, yanked down my sweats, leaving me bare, dripping, spread for him. His eyes roamed, hungry, and that sinful smirk from last night curved his mouth. He bent to grab his jeans, pulled a condom from the pocket, and tossed them aside.

"In your pocket?" My voice was thick with want.

"One should always be prepared, Bethany." He tore it open, rolled it on his dick, thick, glistening, ready to ruin me. Pushing me onto the bed, he crawled over me like a man who wouldn't stop until I forgot my own name. Hovering, eyes dark, lips parted, he brushed hair from my face and murmured, "I don't know where the fuck you came from...but I'm not letting you go."

Before I could answer, his mouth crashed into mine, weight pinning me to the mattress. I clawed his back, moaning as his hips settled between my thighs. His lips dragged to my neck, biting just enough to make me squirm. Then his fingers slid between my legs and found me—soaked and ready form him.

"Fuck," he breathed. "You're drenched."

I moaned shamelessly as two fingers pushed inside—slow at first, then faster, deeper, rougher.

"Kevin," I gasped, fisting his hair while he fucked me with his hand. His mouth closed over my nipple, tongue flicking before a light bite drew a cry. He sucked hard, switching breasts while his fingers pounded into me; then he added a third. I jerked, grinding down, riding his hand like it was the only thing keeping me together. "Fuck me," I begged, breath broken, hips frantic.

He withdrew and looked up, chest heaving. Without a word, he slid those fingers into his mouth, licking them clean as if savoring every drop. A shudder rolled through me.

"Please. Stop teasing." Smirking, he hitched my leg around his waist. His dick slid through my folds, the tip dragging over my clit—agonizingly slow. I trembled. He did it again. My hips bucked, chasing him. On the third pass, I reached down to guide him, but he slapped my hand away, shaking a finger just like I had earlier. That grin said everything—then he slammed into me.

One hard, deep thrust stole my breath. He pulled almost out, pushed back slow. Again. Again. A rhythm that stretched me open and filled me to the brink. When I tried to match his pace, he pinned me and fucked me even harder. I screamed, nails digging into his back as he took me—fierce, deep, relentless. I couldn't think—only feel: him in my throat, my belly, everywhere. Heart pounding, vision blurring, body locking tight. I looked down—his dick sliding slick and fast—and my world shattered. The orgasm rose like a tidal wave, then crashed: every muscle tight, stomach twisting, air gone. I screamed his name, legs clenching, body convulsing in wave after wave of brutal pleasure.

That's when Kevin lost it. He thrust deep, hips grinding through his release as he groaned my name, unrestrained. I felt every pulse as he came with me, body shaking, mouth at my neck. He didn't stop working us both through the aftershocks like he needed every last drop inside me. And God, I wanted it all. Holy fucking shit. It was the first time I'd ever come from just being fucked—nothing will ever compare.

13

DANGEROUS CURRENTS

BETHANY

I couldn't believe it. The orgasm was mind-blowing—from just being fucked? I wasn't inexperienced, but this was different. This was Kevin. Fireworks detonated inside me. My mind spun, body humming like it'd been jump-started—better than any vape, gummy, or high I'd chased. Every nerve was awake, flooding me with a rush so strong it left me weightless.

Kevin slipped the condom off, tossed it into the trash, then drew me toward the headboard. He wrapped his arms around me without a word, like he knew I needed something solid. My body melted against his; our breaths still tangled. Sticky, messy, completely spent—and it felt perfect. His touch shifted soft and slow, brushing hair from my shoulders. Fingers skimmed my skin, not to tease but to tell me I was safe. Seen.

He didn't rush—just touched me. Like he knew I needed quiet in the aftermath. A tender ache unfurled down my spine; time slowed; the world outside us faded. It clicked—this was where I belonged.

Finally, he spoke, voice calm. "How are you feeling?" He tried to sound confident, but I heard the nerves. I smiled, letting out a small, contented moan.

"Perfect," I purred.

His low, relieved laugh melted into the hush. "I'm glad to hear that." He kissed my forehead. His fingertips traced lazy patterns across my back. After a moment, he asked, "Hey, Bethany, can I ask you something?"

"Uh-huh." My voice stayed dreamy.

"Why are you still single?"

The question jolted me. I stiffened. Kevin's hand paused, then resumed long soothing strokes, silently promising I was safe. He'd been open with me earlier; I owed him the same truth. I sighed, clearing the fog.

"I was in a relationship that lasted four years...though only two of those years were in real life." Kevin stayed quiet, his nearness holding me in place. "I met him online while still living at home. He was charming—said all the right things. Promised me the world. Said he could jumpstart my singing career. And I believed him." My voice wavered. "So, when I got the chance, I left everything behind and moved to New York City to be with him. It felt like an adventure. Like I was chasing my dream. But it was all lies—just broken promises disguised as sweet words. I was young, and I thought it was love. I thought he loved me."

Kevin's hand paused, then kept moving. He didn't interrupt—just listened. And somehow, that made it easier to keep going.

"I gave him everything." My voice trembled. "Worked myself to exhaustion while he sold me pipe dreams. He convinced me to accept his idea of an 'open relationship.' " Bitterness crept into my voice. "He called it 'open,' but it was just an excuse to cheat on me whenever he wanted. And the worst part? I let him. I pretended I didn't care. Like it didn't rip me apart every time he left...or came home reeking of someone else." My voice cracked. I swallowed the lump in my throat.

"One night," I continued, "I came home from another terrible bar performance. Another gig he had lined up to make a few bucks, just enough to keep us going. He was supposed to pick me up that night, ride the train home with me like a real boyfriend would, like my manager should have done. But he didn't show. I took the train alone, got home around two a.m., and..." My breath caught. "And I found him...fucking some random girl on our living room couch." The memory slammed into me like a wave, the image seared into my brain. "I froze. Just stood there. I couldn't move, couldn't scream...couldn't even cry. And then I just...walked to our bedroom, shut the door, and stared at the wall. I didn't yell. I didn't throw him out. I just felt...empty. Like there was nothing left of me anymore."

Tears pricked my eyes, but I kept going.

"After that, I knew it was over. I stayed a few more days, pretending I could fix it. I knew I was done. I packed a bag and stayed with a friend." I shook my head. "Even after I was free of him, I still felt broken—like I had nothing left to give. I hated who I'd become."

I paused, voice shaking. "I needed to start fresh. That's why I moved here." I buried my face in Kevin's chest, cheeks burning. I'd just bared my soul—and waited for him to pull away. But he didn't. His hand moved in slow, sincere strokes, then slid to my chin. He tilted my face until our eyes met.

"There's nothing to be ashamed of, Bethany," he said softly. He sat up, pulling me with him. I bit my lip, fighting tears. "We all have a past," he said. "And yours doesn't make you any less incredible. You're still the most beautiful, amazing woman I've ever met."

His words shattered something in me. He pulled me close like he was stitching the broken parts back together. Maybe he was. For the rest of the day, we stayed tangled—talking, laughing, just being. Hours slipped by as we lay in bed, sharing stories and secrets. I couldn't remember the last time I felt this close to someone. Not since Danny. Not since those nights in my old bedroom, dreams close enough to touch. Spilling my heart into the dark, believing the world was mine. This was breathing again after holding it far too long.

14

— · —

THE COST OF SILENCE

BETHANY

This was love—the kind that sneaks up on you and swallows you whole. Being with Kevin felt like gravity had shifted, pulling me deeper with every touch. We were insatiable, lost in each other until time blurred. His touch, his voice, the way his eyes lingered on mine—he couldn't get enough of me, and I felt the same. It wasn't just lust. It was hunger—feral and consuming—like we were starving in ways words couldn't explain.

Even an hour apart, I felt the pull. An invisible thread tightening. The night air hung heavy as I parked my car and walked toward my apartment, keys clutched in one hand. In the other, my phone glowed while I typed a quick message to Kevin: I'll be ready in an hour. A smile tugged at my lips, anticipation building. He had this way of making even waiting feel electric—a slow burn that left me eager and restless. I could already hear his teasing voice, stretching the anticipation just to make my heart race. And damn, it worked every time.

I was lost in thought when something felt...off. Unease prickled. Was someone behind me? The question barely formed before it happened. The shove hit like a freight train, hard and sudden, knocking me off balance. My phone flew from my hand, clattering against the pavement with a crack. My keys slipped away as I stumbled forward. My knees slammed into the sidewalk, pain flaring up my legs.

"What the fuck?!" The words ripped out of me as I gasped, winded. Heart hammering, I scanned the street, and I was the only one on it. My knees throbbed. "What the hell just happened?" I muttered. My keys, phone, and purse were scattered. Groaning, I pushed to my hands and knees—every movement a jolt.

"Bethany? Is that you?"

Katie's voice cut through the silence. She rushed from the apartment gate, phone light illuminating her worried face. Dropping beside me, she grabbed my arms and eased me upright.

"What happened?" she asked, voice tight.

"Someone shoved me." I winced as I shifted.

"What?!" Her eyes widened, then narrowed with fury. She yanked a tiny can of pepper spray from her purse. "Who the hell did this?" Through the sting, a laugh slipped out. Katie's small frame and fierce glare looked ready to fight an army.

"I don't know," I admitted, shaking my head. "I didn't see anyone. One second I was texting Kevin, and the next...I was on the ground." Katie swept over the shadows.

"This is why I'm starting to hate this city."

I bit back a groan as I gathered my things. Using her phone's flashlight, we found my phone and purse, but the keys were gone. We searched the bushes and pavement cracks—nothing.

"Bethany, it's too dark," Katie said, resting a hand on my arm. "We're not going to find them now. Let's look in the morning. You need to ice those knees and sit down."

Reluctantly, I nodded. As she guided me toward the building, I glanced over my shoulder—the shove like an unanswered question. But beneath the ache, excitement flickered—scraped knees and lost keys wouldn't ruin my night. A quick check of my phone—just enough time to ice, shower, and get ready for whatever surprise he'd planned.

The unmistakable roar of Kevin's motorcycle echoed down the street, and my pulse skyrocketed. I grabbed my purse and practically flew out the door, too excited to care about the dull ache in my knees. By the time I reached the gate, I was full-on limping, but honestly, I couldn't have cared less. Swinging the gate open, I found him Kevin-ing again—dangerous, gorgeous, completely mine. One look, and my panties were wet. Knees be damned. He sat astride the bike like he owned the world, black leather jacket hugging broad shoulders, dark jeans a second skin, slate-blue shirt making his gray eyes blaze. Those eyes locked on me and, for a beat, I forgot how to breathe.

"Damn," I whispered, grinning. The moment he noticed my limp, he was off the bike, striding toward me, carefree confidence flipping to laser-focused concern.

"What happened?" His hand slid under my arm to steady me.

"I fell earlier," I admitted, embarrassed. I wasn't about to ruin the night by mentioning the shove. "It's fine—nothing serious." He stopped, eyes narrowing as he assessed the damage.

"You have a pretty bad limp. Are you sure you're okay? We can skip going out if you need to rest."

The mix of frustration and concern melted. I set a hand on his chest, feeling his heartbeat beneath my palm. "I'm fine." I met his eyes. "I've been waiting for this all day, Kevin. You're not getting out of this date that easy." His hands claimed my waist, lips crashing into mine—urgent, like he'd held it in for hours. Heat flared as his mouth devoured mine; my fingers tangled in his hair, matching his passion. A low growl rumbled in his chest. Each kiss came hotter, deeper, more demanding—overwhelming need with no room for restraint.

"God, you're dangerous," he murmured against my lips. Before I could reply, he scooped me up as if I weighed nothing, carrying me back to the bike. I gasped, laughing into his mouth as he set me down with surprising gentleness.

"I should fall more often if that's the welcome I get."

"I might start pushing you down if that's what it takes." He handed me my helmet. I laughed, slid on the helmet, and he swung a leg over the bike. The engine thundered to life. He finally stopped in front of a plain, unmarked building—the sort you'd pass a hundred times without noticing. No sign, no windows, nothing to hint at what lay inside. Removing my helmet, I shook out my hair and eyed the place with suspicion.

"What is this?" I narrowed my eyes. Hopping off the bike, he flashed that devilish grin that always meant trouble.

"You'll see. Just trust me." I slipped my hand into his.

"Trusting you has a dangerous track record," I muttered, though a smile tugged at my lips. He chuckled and led me to the door. The first room we stepped into was underwhelming, to say the least—bland gray walls, mismatched chairs, and a scratched-up counter that screamed waiting room. I frowned and glanced at him, but Kevin kept moving, completely unfazed. He walked straight to a door at the back, punched in a code like he'd done it a hundred times, and the lock beeped.

The door opened into a long, dimly lit hallway that immediately put me on high alert. Mechanical buzzing echoed down the hall. Lights flickered, casting uneven shadows.

"Kevin, where are you taking me?" He didn't answer—just shot me that same maddening grin over his shoulder, gave my hand a quick squeeze, and kept walking. We passed one door, then another, and a third. Each one was marked with a plain black number. At the fourth, he finally stopped.

When he turned to face me, something shifted. The playful spark in his eyes dimmed, replaced by something quieter, something that felt like it carried more weight than the moment should've held. He let out a slow breath.

"I wanted to bring you here the first time I heard you sing." The words hit harder than I was ready for, and for a second, I couldn't speak. The look on his face, the softness in his voice, it didn't feel like he meant just this room. It felt bigger.

Before I could figure out what to say, he turned, reached for the handle, and pushed the door open. Then he stepped aside, nodding me in.

"Go ahead," he said quietly, his eyes still locked on mine. With a deep breath, I stepped inside—and stopped cold. The room was dim, lit from the equipment inside. A massive console sat at the center, crowded with buttons, knobs, and sliders. Screens above flickered with shifting waveforms, like something out of a sci-fi film. Dark, angular panels lined the walls, swallowing the light and cloaking the space in a moody hush.

At the far end, a window revealed a smaller glass-walled room. Inside, thick foam lined the walls, and a single microphone hung suspended from a sleek metal arm. It gleamed under the low light, still, waiting. A music stand stood beside it, headphones resting from a polished hook like a ghost of my past, waiting to be summoned. It took a second for my brain to catch up, but then it hit me—this was a recording studio. A real one. Something inside me folded. A suffocating pressure settled over me, like I'd been dragged underwater. Emotion rushed in—happiness, fear, longing, anger, grief. My stomach twisted. My hands began to shake. I turned to Kevin, trying to make sense of what I was feeling, of what this was supposed to mean. He stood there, beaming, proud, like he'd just given me the world. But when he saw my face—really saw it—his smile crumbled.

"What is this, Kevin?" The words splintered with all I'd held in. His brows pulled together as he stepped forward, hands lifting in surrender.

"Bethany, wait—just let me explain."

"Explain what?" My voice shook, louder than I meant it to be. "Why would you bring me here? I told you—I don't want this. I told you I'm done with singing. Why can't you

THE DEVIL & THE DETAILS

just listen to me?" Kevin froze. His eyes searched mine like he was trying to rewrite the moment, trying to find the version of me that would understand what he meant. But I was unraveling, and I could feel it in every part of my body.

"I thought maybe this could be different," he said, his voice gentler now. "Not about pressure. Not about your dad. Not about anyone else's opinions. Just...you. Just your voice. I wanted to give you a space where it's about your happiness." His words chipped at my walls, but they didn't fix what was splintering inside me.

"You don't get it." I shook my head. "This place—it's not just a room for me, Kevin. It's failure. It's disappointment. It's heartbreak. I can't just walk in here and feel okay." He reached for my hand, and I let him, even though I shouldn't have. The moment he took my hand, a tremor rolled through me, and I hated how much I wanted to lean into it. He guided me gently to the chair in front of the console. I sat stiffly, hugging myself tightly, trying to keep myself from falling apart.

Kevin crouched beside me, his eyes never leaving my face. "I know you never got this far in your music before," he said softly. "And I wanted to give you that chance. Something new. Something just for you." But the words didn't reach me—not the way he wanted. I rubbed my thighs, trying to stop the tremor in my hands. The walls seemed to close in. Pressure built in my chest. I couldn't breathe.

"I need to get out of here." Panic spilled over.

"Bethany—" But I was already moving, bolting for the door. Heart pounding, I scanned the hall, eyes locked on the glowing EXIT sign. I staggered toward it, lungs screaming for air.

I gasped, bending over, I grabbed my knees. My heart still raced. My thoughts spiraled.

"Bethany!" His voice was close, laced with worry. He laid a hand on my back, rubbing slow circles. "Breathe," he murmured. "Just breathe with me, okay? In...and out."

I matched his rhythm.

"One," he counted, and I forced myself to follow. "Two...three...four..." By ten, my breathing had slowed, though my chest still ached. I straightened, pressing against the cold brick wall, the chill biting into my skin. Kevin stayed close, eyes searching mine.

"Bethany." His voice was low. "I didn't mean to upset you. I know you've had too many broken promises. I just wanted to give you an experience to remember. When you sing, there's so much joy and peace in your voice. I wanted to capture that—selfish, maybe, but I wanted it for myself." His confession caught me off guard. I stared, trying to process. His eyes softened. "You don't know how much your voice connects to me. It's like hearing it fills a missing puzzle piece. You're that missing piece."

Before I could answer, he kissed me—slow, deep. When he pulled back, he rested his forehead to mine.

"All I want to do is make you happy." Kevin wasn't Danny. He felt real, reliable, and right now he was mine. His arms tightened, pulling me close until our bodies aligned. A low thrum pulsed through me. I wanted him to know I wanted that for him, too. He deserved to feel it.

"I want to make you happy, Bethany." His voice slid down my spine. Heat coiled in my belly. "Let me..." His breath ghosted over my neck. "Please you." I cupped his jaw and kissed him back—my answer. His mouth took mine harder; need pulsed. He brushed the shell of my ear, trailing feather-light kisses along my neck until my nipples pebbled beneath my top. My eyes fluttered shut; my hands found his chest, hungry for more. His kisses turned urgent, pulling a soft moan from me. Breath hot at my ear, he murmured, "Sing for me, Bethany, and I'll do whatever you like."

My pulse pounded as his hand slid to my waistband, skimming my panties. The jolt had my pussy clenching—but reality intruded. I caught his wrist.

"Kevin, someone could catch us." He glanced at the dark alley, and smirked.

"Do you see anyone?" I looked—only shadows. "Didn't think so." His fingers returned; I let him. He slipped beneath the lace, unhurried, finding the place already slick for him. My breath hitched as he stroked through my folds, slick and practiced. When he circled my clit, the fuse lit. Each swirl pulled me apart molecule by molecule. Fingers curled deeper, like he'd memorized my body's language.

"Bethany," he rasped, gravel and heat, "sing for me."

A helpless moan escaped—his mouth caught it, kissing me hard. One hand braced my neck gently against the wall while his tongue matched the rhythm of his fingers. I clutched his shoulders, grinding down, chasing the high I'd been denied too long. "I'll do that thing with my tongue you like," he murmured, voice sliding hot down my neck, "I'll suck you dry." He nipped my earlobe; my whole body jolted.

He hooked his fingers, dragging over that deep spot—my leg wrapped around his waist. Wet sounds echoed in the alley, each thrust louder, and I didn't care. I wanted to get caught. His free hand gripped my hip, guiding my rhythm, forcing me to ride him fast and messy.

"Come on." His mouth brushed my ear. "Give it to me." My hips bucked; each drag of his knuckles lit me up. My moans turned frantic—his name, a plea.

"Kevin..."

"Sing for me, Bethany." His voice was ragged. "Let me hear it. Will you do that for me?"

Heat coiled—my back arched, body convulsing as release crashed through me. I let out a breathy, "Yes."

By the time we got back to the studio, the tight ball of nerves I'd felt earlier had nearly disappeared. What Kevin had done for me—what we'd shared—had melted much of my anxiety, leaving a strange calm in its place. Still, as we stepped into the quiet, humming space, a flicker of unease pulled at my thoughts.

Kevin didn't give me much time to dwell on it. He took my hand and guided me toward the recording booth, his confidence pulling me along like a tide. The glass door swung open, and we stepped inside. My eyes darted around the space, taking in the sleek microphone, the perfectly coiled headphones, and the small control panel brimming with buttons and switches. He moved around the booth like he belonged there, pointing out everything I needed to know.

"This button lets you talk to me," he said. "You'll hear yourself through these." He gestured toward the headphones, then picked them up. He adjusted the mic like it was second nature, lowering it to my height. His fingers brushed mine briefly, sending a faint warmth through me that left me feeling both exposed and oddly comforted. When he stepped back, he studied me. "You, okay?"

I couldn't speak. My throat tightened. I just nodded, swallowing the knot in my chest. "You don't need to have anything prepared," he said. "Just sing whatever comes to you. Whatever feels right." His words hung as he gently placed the headphones over my ears, fingers brushing before stepping back. He turned to leave, but I stopped him.

"Kevin?"

He paused, turning to face me, his expression unreadable but intense.

"You promise these vocals will be just for you?" I asked, my voice thin with vulnerability. "You won't play them for anyone else?"

Kevin's jaw tightened slightly as he walked back to me. "Bethany, this is for my ears only. I promise." He pressed a quick kiss to my lips. When he pulled back, his hand lingered briefly on my arm before he turned and left the booth, moving quickly, like he was afraid

I might change my mind. The door clicked shut behind him, and I was alone. The booth was silent, a cocoon bracing for what was about to hatch. I stared at the mic, my fingers brushing its sleek surface. This wasn't just for him; it was for me. Something I hadn't known I needed.

I took a deep breath, calming my anxiety, and let the first note rise in my throat. The booth swallowed the sound, amplifying it in a way that felt both intimate and exposing. Since this was for Kevin, I needed him to know how I felt when I was around him. I felt like a dangerous woman, and Ariana's song would reveal that to him. My voice came out soft at first, the words brushing against the stillness like a secret I wasn't sure I wanted to share.

As I sang, Kevin flooded my mind. I closed my eyes and gave in—his touch, his breath hot against my skin, his voice low and commanding. My body ached with the phantom weight of him pinning me to the wall, his hands tracing every inch like he had to memorize me. I wanted him. Desperately. The ache wasn't just emotional, it was physical, deep and unrelenting, spreading like a flame through my chest, my stomach, my thighs.

My voice grew bolder—every lyric a confession. My body remembered every mind-blowing orgasm. I gripped the headphones, trying to hold on, but I was slipping back into those memories—when his mouth claimed me. I let the lyrics carry me, each word pulling me deeper into the feelings I couldn't hide. The final note lingered, full of everything I couldn't say. I caught my breath, still burning. I opened my eyes and looked through the glass. Kevin stared, unmoving—his look unnerving, not intense but still, like he saw more than he should. A chill slid up my spine. For a moment, I felt exposed, stripped bare by the song I'd given him. But this was Kevin. I reminded myself there was nothing to fear.

I pressed the button, voice soft. "Was that good? Do you want me to go again?" That pulled him back. He moved quickly, pressing buttons and adjusting knobs.

His voice came through the speaker, even and measured. "I think we got it. Step out of the booth." I hung the headphones back on their hook, exhaling as I stepped out. The pressure eased, though something uneasy still clung to me.

"Do you want to hear the playback?" Kevin asked, his tone casual as he turned back to the soundboard. I shook my head. The emotions were still too close.

"No," I said quietly. "Not tonight." He nodded and turned back to the equipment, his hands moving swiftly to save the track. I watched him. He worked, jaw tight, fingers moving over the controls. Familiar. Yet something felt...off. I pushed the thought aside, brushing my hair as I prepared to leave. It felt like more than a song. I gave Kevin a piece of me tonight, and there's no way I was getting it back.

15

UNSPOKEN TRUTHS

KEVIN

I knew I'd probably pushed Bethany too far tonight, the realization sinking into my gut like a stone. But how could I help myself? She consumed my thoughts—her voice, a haunting melody I couldn't shake. When she sang, it felt like she reached into my soul and captured a part of me I hadn't known existed. I was desperate to hold on to that feeling—to her, to the magic she brought into my life.

The ride home from the studio unfurled in thick silence. Bethany sat behind me, arms wound tightly around my waist, clinging as though I were her lifeline. She held on tighter than usual, body pressed closer—a vulnerability I wasn't ready to face. That silent confession made my chest ache. I'd been selfish—so blinded by my own desire, I didn't realize how much I was asking of her.

As the motorcycle rumbled through the dark streets, my mind replayed the song she'd just performed—*Dangerous Woman* by Ariana Grande. Her voice sultry and unrestrained, every lyric echoing with want. I couldn't stop picturing her pressed to the mic, hips swaying, mouth parted. I wanted her. Needed her. I'd almost claimed her right there in the studio, imagined losing myself in the taste of her skin, the softness of her hair, the heat of her body.

Regret pressed against my chest like a bruise. I rubbed the hand resting on me, a weak attempt at comfort. I'd seen the sadness in her eyes as we left, the way her smile never quite reached them. What was I thinking? I'd reopened wounds she'd worked hard to close—and now her tears were on me. All I wanted was to make her happy after everything she'd survived—and I'd failed.

When we finally pulled up to my apartment, I killed the engine. My fingers clenched the handlebars, afraid of what I might see in her eyes. I eased off her helmet, and my heart shattered. Her bright blue eyes—usually alive—were bloodshot and brimming with unshed tears. Shit. I really had pushed her too far.

Sliding off the bike, I gathered her to her feet and into my arms. She melted against me, head tucked beneath my chin. I held her tight, wishing I could take her pain.

"I'm so sorry, Bethany." I threaded my fingers through her soft blonde hair. She pulled back to meet my stare.

"Kevin, there's nothing you should be sorry for." Her sincerity destroyed me. I cupped her cheek, thumb brushing her skin.

"Then why were you crying?" My voice stayed gentle but insistent. Her lip trembled before she trapped it between her teeth. I tilted her chin. She looked down, gathering courage.

"They aren't sad tears." She took a breath. "They're happy ones. I never thought...I'd sing in a studio. You made that happen. Thank you."

The admission hit like a tidal wave. She rose on her tiptoes and pressed the softest kiss to my lips—a fleeting brush that destroyed me. Without another word, she laced her fingers with mine and led us inside. Drained, we collapsed into bed. She whispered a thank you, voice so faint I barely caught it. Soon, her breathing slowed into a steady rhythm.

Guilt kept me awake. I traced idle circles on her, staring at the ceiling, replaying how one night at a bar became everything.

It wasn't supposed to happen. I wasn't even supposed to be there. Ian had picked the place—a dingy bar. A year had passed since I'd last seen him, and I'd been looking forward to catching up. I arrived early, ordered whiskey, and waited. An hour passed before my phone buzzed—flight delayed. Disappointment settled in my gut. I signaled for another drink, planning to finish it and leave. Then she walked in.

Bethany.

The deep-blue dress might've caught my eye, but it was the way she tugged the hem, like it revealed too much. She held her chin high, daring anyone to look closer, but I saw through it. Armor. She perched beside her friend, and I told myself to look away. My drink was nearly gone, and I debated heading out when her voice cut through the bar.

She sang *The First Cut Is the Deepest*, and the room fell silent beneath the raw ache in her voice. Each word landed like a slow punch, quieting the room until no one dared to breathe. Her voice wasn't flashy; it was vulnerable, trembling with a sadness deeper than the lyrics. Mid-verse, her eyes met mine, and it felt like she was singing only to me.

By the final note, I knew I had to leave. That voice—that woman—would undo me. Tossing cash on the bar, I walked outside, trying to break her hold. But her voice haunted me, tugging at something buried deep. I paused beside my bike. The hairs on my neck rose, like the universe dared me to turn. And I did.

She stood in the shadows near the doorway, vaping. A faint glow lit her face. The sight jarred me: a voice like hers, and she smoked? More than that, her squared shoulders didn't match the tremor in her hands. Her armor was cracking. I stepped forward, boots crunching gravel.

"That's unexpected," I said into the night.

She jumped, spun, then stumbled. Instinct took over; I caught her waist before she fell.

"I've got you," I promised, steadying her. Her body stiffened, then softened, a slight shiver coursing through her at my touch. Somehow, I got her talking. Her words were guarded, but beneath them, sadness cloaked in defiance, loneliness barely hidden. Her voice cracked. Tears fell. I didn't think—just held her and said it was okay. As she melted into me, something shifted: protect her. Keep her safe. It wasn't just concern; it was a fierce, relentless need to ensure no one hurt her again. Whatever haunted her wouldn't win. Not with me beside her.

I must've drifted off, because suddenly I was back in Colorado—and it hurt how real it felt. The sun hung low, casting gold streaks across the cracked asphalt of the high-school parking lot. I sat in my uncle's beat-up pickup, the cab still carrying its faint mix of pine and motor oil. Next to me was Allison McFarlin—Aly.

She was impossible to ignore, defined cheekbones that softened when she smiled, lips parted like she was about to say something. Her eyes—startling, glacier-blue—made you forget whatever you'd planned to say. Her honey-blonde hair caught the light like it glowed on its own. She was small, but the way she carried herself made her seem larger than life.

We were sixteen again, time suspended. Her hand rested lightly on my chest as we made out, lost inside the truck. Floral perfume drifted over worn leather; it felt too vivid to be a dream. Then a loud knock shattered everything. We jerked apart, breathless. My heart hammered as I turned—Ian stood outside the glass.

"Geez," I muttered, still scrambling for reality. Aly unlocked the door, fingers brushing my thigh. Ian climbed in beside her, popping our private bubble. She sat wedged between us, lips slightly swollen from the kiss, and the cab shrank as the dream lurched.

Fluorescent light flooded a police station. Tension thickened the air. My uncle and aunt clung to each other, fighting to hold it together. His jaw was locked to stop the tears; her muffled sobs rattled through her shoulders. Blurred voices: an officer's clipped questions, a phone buzzing somewhere unseen. My chest drew tight, but before I could piece anything together, the scene dissolved.

Now I hovered above a hospital room. I was strapped to a bed, thrashing, screaming nonsense. Gaunt and thrashing, I fought the bindings as green light pulsed with every shout. Shadowy figures stood motionless along the walls. Even my voice sounded foreign. I reached for myself, helpless to stop the nightmare.

I jolted awake, gasping. The dream clung. For a heartbeat, I swore someone watched from the hall, but the doorway was empty. Shaking it off, I pulled Bethany close and eventually drifted back to sleep.

A shrill ring cut through the early quiet. Half-blind, I fumbled for my phone.

"Yo, bro, you up?" The voice was unmistakable, though my brain lagged behind. Clearing my throat, I croaked, "Who is this?"

"Seriously? It's Ian. I'm in town—be there in an hour." The line went dead. I shot upright, heart thundering. Ian. Here. In an hour. Bethany lay beside me, golden hair fanned across the pillow like sun-rays. She had no idea the storm was heading our way. No damned way could they meet—not yet, maybe not ever. I kissed her forehead, heart pounding.

"Wake up, sleepyhead," I whispered, brushing her hair aside to kiss the curve of her neck. She stirred, a soft whimper slipping out before her blue eyes blinked open.

"Good morning," she murmured, voice husky. "What time is it?"

"Eight-thirty," I said. "And...don't kill me, but I just remembered I've got an appointment. I need to run you home early." She groaned and pulled the blanket over her head.

"Can't I just stay here?" I chuckled, peeled the covers back, and gave her a playful smack on the butt.

"Babe, I have zero food here. You'll starve and be bored. Don't you have laundry or something productive to do?"

She sat up with a dramatic pout, arms crossed. "Fine. Katie's off today—maybe we'll have a girls' day." She texted Katie while I watched, mesmerized. Even half-asleep in my T-shirt, which barely skimmed her thighs, she was a vision, stirring a possessive thrill low in my gut. She walked to the bathroom, bare feet thudding softly against the floor. I had to move fast to get her out before Ian showed up. Today was already off the rails.

When we pulled up to Bethany's building, she remembered she'd dropped her gate keys somewhere out front. Her brow furrowed, eyes sweeping the pavement.

"I think they're near the bushes." We started searching. After a few minutes, I spotted a glint of metal in a dense shrub, reached in, and fished out the keys.

"Found them." I held them up. Bethany exhaled in relief, but the image of her fall earlier twisted something in my chest. The thought of her delicate frame hitting the ground lit a simmering anger at the world for letting it happen.

She stepped close and slid her arms around my neck—everything else disappeared. I grabbed her waist, pulling her close. Her lips met mine, and my dick twitched—that's what she did to me. She kissed me softly, and as her tongue glided against mine, I hardened. A groan slipped out as I pressed against her, wishing I could freeze time. But I couldn't. I had to let her go. Forcing myself to break the kiss, I rested my forehead against hers.

"About last night...are you okay?" Looking at me and biting her lip. I brushed it free with my thumb. "Bethany, talk to me. What's on your mind?" Her sad eyes hit hard. She stepped back, resolve settling into her expression.

"Kevin, I know you meant well, setting up that studio session. But I need you to hear me. I don't want to be a singer—I left that behind for a reason. I'm still figuring things out, but I know singing isn't it. Karaoke is just for fun. Please, respect this boundary." Her words hit like a sledgehammer. My stomach churned. Good intentions, wrong result.

"Okay. I hear you. I won't bring it up again."

She nodded, her expression softer but still guarded, then turned and walked away. I watched her disappear inside as the morning chill sank into my bones. As the door closed, I realized how much I'd taken her—and her trust—for granted.

16

HALF TRUTHS & BURGERS

KEVIN

I opened the door, and there he was—my brother, Ian. Same dark hair, same gray eyes, but something about him looked softer now. He seemed healthy, fit—better than I'd seen him in a long time. A weight I didn't know I carried began to lift.

"Ian!" I pulled him into a bear hug, lifting him like we were kids again.

He laughed, patting my back in that awkward way that said he wasn't used to this much affection. "Alright, alright. You'll crush me before we even get inside."

I stepped back, giving him a once-over. "You look great, man." He shifted, shoulders hunching a little as a shy laugh slipped out.

"Thanks, bro. Life's been...better." I let it sit—whatever better meant.

"Take a load off. Water?" He hesitated, then smiled faintly.

"Actually, I'm starving. How about we grab food? My treat."

"If you're treating, I'm eating. What's the craving?" Seven minutes later, we slid into a booth at Cassell's Hamburgers, sizzling patties and warm buns mingled in the air. A waitress appeared, notepad ready, a playful spark in her eyes.

"Two for the price of one." Her eyes bounced between us, amused. "Lucky me. Ready to order?" I leaned back, smirking.

"Fried Chicken Sando, extra pickles." The double-dipped buttermilk chicken, spiced mayo, and tangy slaw were calling my name. Ian glanced up from the menu.

"Two-thirds-pound cheeseburger, hold the onions, extra pickles, side of fries...and an Old Fashioned."

"Perfect." She scooped up our menus. "Be right back, hon." With a wink and a bounce of red curls, she was gone.

I cleared my throat. "You sure about the drink? I mean...with your medication?" His jaw tightened before he forced a smile.

"It's fine, Kevin. Different meds now. The occasional drink won't kill me." I raised both hands.

"Had to ask. Booze and meds don't always mix." For a heartbeat, his glare was ice cold, then it thawed. He ran a hand through his hair and sighed.

"Stop being my overprotective big brother." I nodded, letting it drop. No point risking an argument.

"So...Indiana treating you well?" His shoulders eased. "Yeah. Really well, actually. Good community, joined a church, and..." He rubbed the back of his neck. "Met someone."

"Someone, huh? How long?"

"Haven't asked her out yet." His laugh was shaky.

"Timing, huh?" I prodded, but before he could reply, the waitress returned with our drinks. Ian raised his glass.

"Cheers." I clinked mine against his, returning the smile. He took a sip, then fixed me with that little-brother glint.

"So, big bro—seeing anyone?" I shifted against the leather booth.

"Dated a few women, nothing serious."

"Sorry to hear that," he said, a smirk betraying zero sympathy.

"Plenty of beautiful women here. Maybe we hit the town tonight? See what's out there." My gut clenched. I wanted an evening with Bethany, but dodging Ian wasn't an option. If I refused, he'd dig for answers I wasn't ready to give.

"Sure," I mumbled.

"Perfect!" He lit up. "I'm a killer wingman." Our food arrived. The conversation shifted to easier topics: road-trip disasters, summers with our aunt and uncle, two brothers laughing like the years and complications hadn't piled up.

When the check arrived, Ian grabbed it and headed to the register, giving me a moment alone. I stepped outside, leaned against the wall, and pulled out my phone.

Bethany: I already miss you. Can I see you later tonight?

I exhaled, rubbing the back of my neck. Through the window, Ian was still inside, chatting up the waitress. She laughed, clearly enjoying the flirtation. He didn't seem to mind. Turning back to my phone, I typed a reply: Raincheck? Got pulled into an emergency session—might run all night. I hated lying to her. She couldn't see Ian. Not yet. Maybe not ever. I hit send, shoved the phone into my pocket, and looked up just as Ian stepped outside.

"Ready to go?" He grinned like he didn't have a care in the world.

"Yeah," I said, matching his smile. "Let's do it."

We ended up at EightyTwo, a retro arcade bar in the heart of the Arts District. Neon lights bounced off polished concrete, buzzing and beeping filling the air. Ian's face lit up when he spotted the Street Fighter machine.

"You're going down, big bro." He dug quarters out of his pocket. For the next hour, we lost ourselves in the game. I let him win a few rounds, pretending to care. He drank just one beer, which eased the knot in my chest. He seemed in control tonight.

It was after midnight when we got home. Ian crashed on the couch since his flight wasn't until the afternoon. The next morning, we woke up around the same time. While he showered, I tossed him a change of clothes and started breakfast—my signature omelets. As I cracked eggs and diced peppers, my thoughts drifted to Bethany—her mouth on me, tongue dragging down my shaft, slow and dangerous. My grip tightened on the spatula. I shifted to shake the image. Focus. Ian was here. There'd be time for Bethany later. As I plated the omelets, a knock sounded at the front door. Frowning, I wiped my hands on a towel and checked the peephole. My heart dropped.

Bethany stood outside, coffee in hand, her smile bright enough to light the whole damn hallway.

"Shit," I muttered under my breath. The shower was still running. I cracked the door open and stepped out, closing it behind me.

"Hey." She kissed me softly and handed me the cup. "Surprise. I missed you—thought I'd swing by. Are you going to let me in?"

My heart kicked into overdrive. "Uh...babe, I can't." I shifted. "I'm heading back to the studio. Pulled an all-nighter, just came home to shower and change. Tight deadline—mix is due by noon." Her smile faded—disappointment flashed across her face. I hated seeing that look. So I kissed her, deep and lingering, pouring everything I had into it. She melted into me, a soft moan against my lips. When she pulled back, her voice was low.

"Okay. Tonight, then?" I brushed my thumb across her cheek. "Tonight. Thank you for the coffee." I watched her go, heart pounding. Tension eased—then snapped right back when the door opened.

Ian stood there, towel slung over his shoulder, brows raised. "Were you just talking to someone?"

I lifted the coffee. "Uber Eats. Needed caffeine." He stared at me for a moment too long. Not quite calling bullshit, but not buying it either. "Come on." I nudged him back inside. "Breakfast is ready."

We ate in silence, making small talk as we finished. When it was time for him to head out, I walked him to the door and clapped his shoulder.

"Safe travels, bro." He nodded and headed off to grab his bags and catch his flight. When the door clicked shut, all I felt was relief. Ian was gone. The close call was over. All I could think about was Bethany. Tonight, I'd make it up to her. Tonight, she'd be mine.

17

THE RHYTHM OF DESIRE

BETHANY

I sat in my car outside Kevin's building, gripping the wheel as mid-morning sun streamed through the windshield. Our earlier interaction replayed—the way he slipped out so quickly, shutting the door behind him. His excuse sounded believable, but that nagging voice still crept in, whispering doubts I'd worked hard to silence. I leaned back, closed my eyes, and took a deep breath.

"Kevin is not Danny, Bethany. You're healing. You're not that girl anymore." My voice steadied me—a reminder that the past didn't control me. Trust didn't come easily, but I was learning. I wouldn't let my doubts win. Starting the car, I headed back to my apartment in Santa Monica. Katie greeted me with her usual enthusiasm, pulling me into the living room to hang out.

Last night, we went out for dinner, something we hadn't done in far too long. Over drinks, Katie teased me about how much time I'd been spending at Kevin's.

"So," she smirked over the rim of her wineglass, "how's Mr. Dark and Delicious treating you? You seem so...Zen lately. Like, glowing goddess vibes." I blushed, smiling as I picked at my plate.

"He's amazing." A shy smile crept across my face. Katie leaned in closer, her grin turning wicked.

"Girl, it's the sex, isn't it? Come on, spill it. He's got you walking around like the stress-free queen of the universe." I rolled my eyes, laughing harder now, but my silence said it all. She wasn't wrong. Kevin and I had a connection—intensely passionate, the kind that consumed every part of me.

"You deserve this." Katie squeezed my hand. "For as long as I've known you, there's always been this undercurrent of pain, like you were carrying something heavy. But since you've been with Kevin, it's like that weight has lifted. Seeing you like this—it's refreshing. It's everything." Her words lingered as we lounged watching movies. Katie had always been the one to see me clearly, the one who could cut through the shadows of my doubts and remind me of the woman I was beneath it all.

That evening, I showered and slipped into one of Kevin's band T-shirts. Soft and thin, it barely skimmed below my butt, exposing the curve of my cheeks. I wandered to the record player, craving the nostalgia that only music gave me. I pulled out *Everybody Else Is Doing It, So Why Can't We?* by The Cranberries and carefully placed the needle on *Linger*. I grabbed my headphones and slipped them on.

The first notes crackled to life, and I closed my eyes. I got lost in the music, dancing around my room. When the chorus came, I tilted my head back and sang softly, the words spilling from my lips. I felt free. As I spun around, my eyes fluttered open, and I nearly jumped out of my skin. Kevin stood leaning in the doorway, arms crossed, a playful smirk lighting up his face.

"You scared me!" I pulled my headphones off, laughing despite myself. "How did you get in?"

"Katie," he said with a shrug, stepping inside. "What are you listening to?"

"The Cranberries," I said. He walked over to the record player, glancing down at the spinning vinyl. "'Nineties alternative. Not bad. You always surprise me, Bethany."

I smiled, watching as he crouched by my crate of records, flipping through them with interest.

"You know," he said casually, "I just realized I've never been in your room before. Why is that?" The question caught me off guard.

"I guess it's because we don't really have privacy here. Katie's always around, and it's just easier at your place...you know, for all the things we do." I gave him a small, teasing smile.

His gaze flicked up to mine, and the energy in the room shifted instantly. His eyes, darker now, held a heat that made my breath hitch. Suddenly, the space between us felt impossibly small. My mouth dried as the slow burn spread through me. The look in his eyes wasn't just desire—it was overpowering, and I could feel it sinking into my skin, awakening a hunger I couldn't ignore.

"Fair enough." He stood and closed the distance. He cupped my face, eyes never leaving mine. His lips met mine with a slow, smoldering kiss that made my knees weaken. It ignited something between us that felt combustible.

He pulled away, leaving my breath coming in short, uneven bursts. His lips curved into a devilish smile as he turned and walked to my door, the quiet click of the lock echoing in the room. I panted, not knowing what was coming next. His hand lingered on the doorknob for a moment before he spoke, his voice low and smooth.

"Think Katie would mind if we played music on your speakers?" The question felt loaded. He didn't look at me as he spoke, his focus on the room itself, as though setting the stage.

"No, it will be okay," I replied. Uncertainty coursed through me, mingling with a heady anticipation. What was he planning?

Kevin crossed the room with a confidence that made it impossible to look away. Kneeling by my record crate, his fingers moved through the collection, slow and methodical, like he was savoring the process. His eyes scanned the titles, and when he found what he was looking for, he plucked it from the stack with quiet satisfaction.

He removed the record from the player, sliding it off the turntable and slipping it back into its sleeve. He unplugged the headphone jack. Then, removing the vinyl with care, he slid it from its sleeve, flipped it to the B-side, and placed it on the turntable, setting the needle down.

The first notes filled the room—a sultry hum that seemed to thicken the air itself. *Glory Box* by Portishead.

The sound was dark, sensual, almost hypnotic. My pulse quickened as Kevin turned to me, his eyes shadowed with an intensity that made my body tighten. Without a word, he crossed the room, his presence commanding but calm. Sitting on my bed, he reached out and took my hand.

"Come here."

Kevin guided me onto his lap, positioning me so my back was flush against his chest. Heat radiated off him, surrounding me in something feral and possessive. He removed my shirt inch by inch, exposing my breasts to the room—and the mirror. He reached up and unfastened the clip from my hair, letting it tumble down in messy waves. The slide of it against my skin made me shiver. I met his eyes in the mirror—dark, full of fire, already claiming me. He let his knuckles drag along my jaw as he spoke, "Keep your eyes on the mirror. Don't close them. Not once."

The mirror reflected everything—my parted lips, the flushed rise and fall of my chest, the way his arms draped around me like I belonged there. Like I was already his to use. His hands slid from my shoulders down my arms, slow enough to make me ache. When he finally cupped my breast, I gasped. The pressure of his palm, the graze of his fingertips—none of it rushed. All of it intentional. He pinched my nipple, hard enough to make me jolt.

"You like that?" He watched me closely.

"Yes," I breathed, soft and desperate, a confession dragged from somewhere deep. His grin ghosted against my skin. He enjoyed watching me squirm. His fingers returned to the other nipple, rolling it slowly, tugging, teasing. He flicked it with purpose, then gave a harder pinch that had me biting my lip to keep from crying out. My nipples throbbed. I needed his mouth on them. I needed to grind against him. I needed to be filled.

I shifted in his lap, trying to relieve the pressure building between my legs. His hands clamped down on my hips, holding me still, his mouth grazing the shell of my ear.

"I said—be still." His voice was tight with control. I whimpered, clenching around nothing, my hands clutching his thighs for support. He kissed my neck, licking a line down to my shoulder while his fingers played with my nipples—pinch, pull, twist. Over and over. Just enough to keep me moaning but not enough to push me over.

"I know what you want, Bethany." His voice was thick with hunger, breath hot against my neck. "But I need you to watch what I do to you. I want you to see what you look like when you're desperate for me."

The sound I made landed between a moan and a sob. My whole body was vibrating, drenched with need. I couldn't stop watching the way he touched me—the flex of his hands, the confidence in every move. My nipples stood hard and flushed. My legs trembled. I needed to feel him inside me. I needed to fuck this ache away. "Please," I whispered, barely able to speak. The mirror showed the flush in my cheeks, the mess of my hair, the way I was panting for him as though I'd been starved.

Kevin scraped his teeth along my neck, and my whole body twitched. It wasn't only the pleasure—it was the control. The way he didn't rush. The way he held every second in the palm of his hand made me beg for more without saying a word. He let go of my breasts and slid his hands down, spreading my legs until they matched the width of his, holding me there, open, exposed, soaking wet. Then he reached into my panties like he already knew what he'd find.

"Already wet for me."

Then came the sound—crisp and merciless: the tear of lace. My breath caught as Kevin ripped them clean off, tossing them aside like they were made of paper. Now I was bare—and he hadn't even really touched me. He let the moment sit, my legs open, his body behind me, the cool air licking my skin while his heat wrapped around me like a spell. I felt completely exposed—and I loved it. The ache between my thighs pulsed harder. His finger drew a lazy, feather-light circle over my clit. I moaned into his neck, but he stopped. With his free hand, he caught my chin and turned my face to the mirror. His touch wasn't rough, but it left no room to disobey.

"No. Watch." His voice was velvet laced with heat.

The reflection was sinful: my bare body splayed across his lap, nipples hard, lips parted, legs spread wide while he sat behind me, fully clothed, perfectly in control. He looked like he owned me; in that moment, he did.

"Keep your eyes on me, Bethany." Then he moved. His thumb rubbed my clit slowly, not giving me what I needed, just enough to keep me aching for more. My hips twitched, but his arm around my waist locked me in place. And then—finally—his finger slid inside me. I gasped; his other hand curled around my breast, thumb grazing my nipple, then pinching harder than before, a sting that made my back arch.

"You like that?" His voice dripped with pride.

"Yes." Another confession soaked in want. His smile in the mirror was pure sin. His fingers tugged and twisted my nipples with purpose, using my body like an instrument he knew by heart. Each pinch was a lesson—teaching me to take it, teaching me to crave more. I was panting, legs shaking, soaked. I needed to feel him deeper. Needed to ride his hand until the ache inside me exploded. "Please."

He chuckled, teeth scraping my neck. "Want to cum, baby?"

"Yes...please."

"Then stay still." He added a second finger, and my body tried to move—tried to grind down, to fuck the rhythm he'd set—but his hand flattened on my thigh, holding me in place.

"No," he murmured. "You don't get to take it. I'll give it to you." Every thrust of his fingers slow, filthy, wet. The sound—obscene. He made me listen to it, watch it.

He flicked my clit with his thumb between strokes, just to feel the way I clenched around him. His eyes never left the mirror.

"Look how fucking pretty you are like this." His voice was lower now, as though it cost him to keep control. His fingers worked deeper, harder, owning my body, my breath, every broken sound spilling from me. "Gonna take what I give you?"

"Yes."

"You going to keep your eyes open when you fall apart for me?"

I nodded. Kevin's hand returned to my breast, squeezing and pinching as his fingers thrust with wet, aching precision. He bit down on my neck and groaned against my skin.

"Fucking hell, you're perfect like this. So ready. So mine. I want you to cum for me, Bethany," he growled. His fingers sped up, thumb circling my clit in messy, hungry arcs. My thighs trembled; my chest heaved. His grip at my waist kept me from floating away—until his hand slid to my throat, not choking, just there. His mouth crashed onto mine, tongue commanding, while his fingers kept moving.

I shattered. The orgasm tore through me with a cry caught in my throat, my body clenching and trembling against him, soaking his hand as he held me down and fucked me through every wave. He didn't stop—just kept his mouth on mine, drawing out every drop of pleasure until I was spent and boneless in his arms.

He finally slowed, his fingers sliding out of me with a wet, lingering drag. One last soft stroke—gentle between my legs, a promise he wasn't done. He kissed my jaw, then my neck, and whispered against my cheek.

"Now that," he said, smiling into my skin, "was fucking beautiful."

The room fell silent except for my ragged breathing and the soft crackle of the needle spinning on the now-silent record player. I dared to lift my eyes to the mirror. Kevin's eyes locked on mine—dark, blown wide, burning with a hunger that punched the air from my lungs. No smirk. No hesitation. Just pure, silent possession. My pulse stuttered. I turned, needing to taste him again. Our mouths collided—breath hot and open. I bit his lip, sucked his tongue, desperate to drag every filthy sound from him.

"I need you now," I whined.

Kevin yanked me upright and turned me so fast my head spun. He shoved me against the wall, lifting me, my legs locking around his waist, heat to heat. His mouth never left mine. Our tongues were frantic. I clawed at his clothes, ripping until only his briefs were

95

left. I didn't stop; I needed him naked, now. I slid my hand down. He was already hard. I pushed his briefs down and moaned—thick, flushed, perfect.

"Please," I breathed. That was all it took. Kevin slammed into me in one brutal thrust. I screamed, head hitting the wall, nails digging in as he drove deep. Again. Again. No rhythm, no tenderness—just him, fucking me like it was the only thing keeping him alive.

I held on, choking on moans, sweat slick between us. His hands grabbed my thighs, bruising tight, bouncing me on his dick as though he had to own every inch.

"Fuck, Bethany," he growled, voice ragged. "You feel so good—fuck—so tight."

I couldn't speak—only cry out as each thrust stole my breath. He didn't slow; he fucked me harder, faster—hips snapping like he had to carve himself into me.

"Say it," he panted. "Tell me who you belong to."

"You," I whimpered.

His mouth landed on my neck, sucking hard, leaving proof. "Louder."

"You, Kevin. I'm yours."

"Goddamn right you are." He was wild now—sweat dripping, muscles flexing, every thrust shaking the wall. My clit rubbed his pelvis with every bounce, pressure building until I was gasping, clawing, holding on for dear life.

"Don't stop," I cried.

"I'm not fucking stopping until you scream." His mouth crashed to mine, swallowing my cries as he pounded into me. My body burned. Every slam pushed me closer. He was everywhere—in my bones, my breath, my soul.

"Cum," he gritted. "Cum for me."

"I—fuck—I can't—"

"Yes, you can." He slammed harder. The wall trembled. One hand slid between us, rubbing my clit in tight, dirty circles.

I broke. The orgasm tore through me, my cry hoarse as my body clamped around him. Kevin didn't stop.

He breathed, still thrusting with punishing force. "That's it," he growled. "That's my girl."

"Kevin—"

He bit my shoulder, marking me. "I'm close—fuck—I'm right there."

"Do it. Cum inside me." That was it. He let go, hips jerking, dick pulsing deep as he groaned my name. His body tensed, then sagged against me. Slick and panting, we clung to each other—sweat and need melting into something dangerously close to more. When Kevin couldn't hold me anymore, we collapsed to the floor. I landed half on top of him, laughing breathlessly.

"Well, that was dramatic." A dazed giggle escaped. Kevin's booming laugh followed, rich and infectious, vibrating beneath me.

"You knocked the strength out of me." He brushed hair from my face with a matching grin.

"Why did that feel so damn good?" he panted. "You realize that was our first time without a condom?"

Kevin froze. "Fuck—I didn't mean to—"

"I'm on the pill," I said, cutting him off with a kiss. His eyes said it all—relief, hunger, and the promise that round two was already loading.

18

—·—

THE SHIFT IN THE AIR

BETHANY

As I rang up the last customer, my thoughts drifted to Kevin—especially last night, which had been something else. The memory of us made my skin flush. Kevin was like forbidden fruit—every glance, every word, stirring a craving I hadn't known I had. Each touch unraveled a tether I didn't know held me. With him, I felt unshackled, as if I had stepped out of the shadows of mere existence and into the vivid, unfiltered experience of truly living.

I finished closing and waved goodbye to my coworkers as they climbed into their cars. One by one, they pulled out of the lot, headlights cutting the darkness before disappearing down the street, leaving me completely alone. I leaned against my own car, letting the stillness settle over me while I tilted my head to the sky. The stars glimmered above, and there they were—the Big Dipper and the Little Dipper, perfectly in place. A pang of nostalgia hit as I traced their familiar shapes, memories of Mom flooding back. On clear nights, we'd race to find them; I could almost hear her laugh, feel her hand guiding mine. The thought warmed me, even as it ached—a bittersweet reminder of life before everything changed.

A faint rustling pulled me from the stars. It came from behind the car, just loud enough to make me freeze. Pulse quickening, I glanced around, but nothing moved in the shadows. Probably a stray cat, I told myself, even as my fingers tightened on the keys. I turned the key. The engine sputtered, struggled—then died. I tried again, pressing the pedal slightly. Nothing. "No, no, no." I slammed my palms against the steering wheel. "Perfect timing." Digging out my phone, I called AAA. Forty-five minutes until a driver could arrive. Great.

I slumped back, staring at the ceiling liner. My car wasn't flashy—just a 2010 gray Ford Fusion—but it had been with me since I moved here. I could afford an upgrade; selling Dad's business left me comfortable enough. Yet spending that kind of money felt wrong. Dad's voice echoed: "Money isn't evil, but the love of money is." The lesson stuck, even when I wanted to ignore it.

I scrolled to Kevin's name and tapped. He answered on the second ring. "You miss me already?" His voice was teasing.

I smiled despite everything. "Maybe." I inhaled. "But my car won't start. I'm stuck at work waiting for AAA." A frustrated sigh slipped out.

"What do you mean your car won't start?" His voice turned serious. "Why didn't you call me first?" I blinked at the sudden shift.

"Kevin, it's not a big deal. AAA is on the way. I'll be fine."

"You're sitting in a parking lot. Alone. At night," he snapped, as if I'd committed a crime. "That area isn't safe, Bethany."

"It's fine." I kept my tone light. "I've worked here for years. I know the neighborhood. I've taken care of myself so far without you, Kevin. I can do it now, even with you in my life."

His frustration bled through the line. "Taking care of yourself doesn't mean you have to do it alone. I could've been there, waiting, making sure you didn't have to deal with this. Why didn't you tell me you were leaving work?"

I exhaled slowly. "Because I didn't think my car would die. And I've never texted you when I leave work—why start now? AAA is on the way." A door slammed on his end.

"I'm coming to get you." His voice was final. "Give me fifteen minutes."

"Kevin, I said it's fine—"

"Stop arguing, Bethany." His voice cut in. "Stay put. Don't get out of the car. I'll be there soon." The line went dead. I stared at the phone, a mix of exasperation and something softer curling in my chest. Most people might call his behavior controlling, maybe suffocating. To me, it wasn't. It was endearing—utterly and completely. Kevin cared like I was the center of his world. His need to protect me—no matter how over-the-top—didn't feel stifling; it felt like devotion, the kind of love I'd dreamt of but never thought I'd find. As the minutes passed, the night seemed darker, the quiet a little too loud. But knowing Kevin was on his way settled something inside me. However intense he got, he always made me feel safe.

Kevin wasn't lying—fifteen minutes later, the low rumble of his motorcycle broke through the stillness. I spotted him as he pulled into the lot, his helmet catching the glow of the streetlights. He swung off the bike with effortless ease, his leather jacket clinging to his broad frame. He looked just like he had last night—coolly magnetic and infuriatingly irresistible. I stepped out of my car, crossing my arms as I scuffed my foot against the gravel. Sarcasm shielded me.

"Look at that—I managed to stay alive without you."

Kevin pulled off his helmet, running a hand through his dark hair as he walked toward me. His smirk was soft, tinged with guilt.

"I deserved that." Taking my hands in his, his voice dropped. "I'm sorry for overreacting. I just don't like you being out here alone. Anything could happen, and I'd never forgive myself if I thought I could've stopped it." His kiss blended apology with possession, leaving me spellbound.

Pulling back, he nodded toward my car.

"Why don't you pop the hood so I can take a look?" I slipped into the driver's seat and pulled the latch. When I joined him at the front, he was already inspecting the engine. "Turn on your flashlight and point it here." He motioned to the tangle of hoses. I held the light steadily, watching him work. A few moments later, he tugged out a torn hose and held it up. "Here's your problem. Your vacuum hose is ripped. When's the last time you had it serviced?" I looked away, suddenly interested in the gravel.

"It's been...a while." I bit my bottom lip.

Kevin wiped his hands on his jeans, stepped closer, and tilted my chin, brushing my lip free with his thumb.

"Did you know that's your tell?" His mouth found mine again—soft and slow—and all I could do was melt into him. He pulled back, grinning like he knew.

"Alright. We'll wait for AAA, get it towed to my place, and I'll fix it. In the meantime, I'll take you to work on the bike."

We climbed into my car to wait. The windows quickly fogged as we filled the silence with small talk—words lost. At some point, conversation gave way to silence—and then to something else entirely. The world outside faded until a loud knock on the window startled me. The AAA driver gave us a bemused look. Kevin rolled down the window and handled everything, arranging for the car to be towed to his house. When we got there, we waited for the truck to arrive. Kevin drove me home, knowing I had an early shift.

I only stayed at his place if I had the next day off or a closing shift, but tonight, as he walked me to my door, I felt the pull of wanting to stay. Kevin made me feel independent and cared for—and I wasn't sure which I needed more. As we reached the door, his voice was casual, but carried that familiar note of control.

"Are you hungry?"

Right on cue, my stomach growled loudly, and his lips curved into a knowing grin.

"I'll take that as a yes. Hand me your key. I'll grab Chinese. Go shower—by the time you're out, it'll be ready." I fished my keys out of my bag, unlocked the door, and handed them to him. Before I stepped in, his hand slid around my waist, pulling me close. His lips met mine in a kiss that was hard, greedy, and left me momentarily dazed.

"You're lucky I'm starving." I giggled and stepped inside, shutting the door behind me. With it locked, I sank into it and let out a breath.

I dropped my bag on the counter, rummaged through it, and pulled out my phone.

"Katie, are you home?" I called. Silence. Then I remembered—Tuesday. Her night class wouldn't end for hours. Shrugging, I headed to the bathroom and turned on the shower, letting the water warm while steam curled against the mirror. The hum of the water was comforting as I walked to my bedroom. I grabbed the charger from the nightstand, plugged in my phone, watched the screen light up, then set it down. Satisfied it was charging, I grabbed a fresh towel and returned to the bathroom.

Hot water rinsed off the day's tension. I loved the thrift store—every item told a story—but dust clung to me by closing. I sighed as the water poured over me, melting stress from my muscles. I lathered shampoo, savoring the lavender scent, then heard something just outside the bathroom. I froze.

"Kevin?" Nothing. I rinsed my hair, trying to shake the unease. Probably building noise. Reaching for conditioner, I tried to focus on the heat of the shower—then heard it again: the sound of what seemed to be a door closing in the apartment. My stomach knotted. "Kevin, are you back?" My voice rose, tinged with worry. No answer. I finished quickly, shut off the water, and wrapped the towel tight.

I stepped into the hallway.

"Kevin?" Nothing. Just the empty living room. I returned to the bedroom to dress, trying to calm myself. My phone sat on the nightstand, not on the charger. Frowning, I picked it up. The screen was locked, exactly as I'd left it—but I knew I'd plugged it in. A chill ran through me. I set it back on the charger and dressed quickly, heart thudding. As I pulled on my shirt, the front door opened.

"Bethany, I'm back." Light. Casual. "Got your favorites."

I wanted to believe him, but the unease wouldn't let go.

"Did you come back earlier for something?" I forced nonchalance. "I could've sworn I heard the door while I was in the shower." Kevin set the food on the counter, movements slow, cautious. He turned to me, face calm, though something flickered in his eyes.

"No." He shook his head. "You probably imagined it. The water must've made it sound like the door." I nodded, brushing it off—but the shadow in his eyes stayed with me. Something about it didn't sit right, no matter how I tried to explain it away.

19

FALLING QUIET

BETHANY

It was Friday, and my car still wasn't ready. Normally, that would have frustrated me, but not today—not when it meant Kevin was my personal chauffeur. I loved riding behind him, arms wrapped around his waist. The engine roared beneath us, my hair tangling. Pressed against him, everything else melted away. I was in love with this man, and spending every free moment with him felt like a dream I never wanted to leave.

Kevin promised he'd fix my car over the weekend, so I decided to stay at his place. It was our kind of night—cozy, private, full of indulgences. He brought dinner from Papa Cristo's, my favorite spot, and when I opened the bag, the aroma of grilled calamari and smoky shrimp kebabs filled the room. The calamari was tender, drizzled with lemon and olive oil, a hint of char lingering on my tongue. The shrimp was juicy, bursting with garlic and spice, and the flaky, honey-soaked baklava curled my lips into a smile. Kevin watched with a teasing grin, but I saw the softness in his eyes.

After dinner, we settled on the couch, Kevin insisting on an '80s cult-classic double-feature: Weird Science and Christine. The first had me doubled over with laughter—the idea of two nerds "accidentally" creating the perfect woman was so over-the-top it was endearing. Then came Christine, and I groaned when the haunted car began its rampage.

"Who thought a possessed car would be scary?" I asked, tossing popcorn at the screen.

Kevin chuckled, arm over my shoulders, fingers brushing my skin. Moments like that deepened my love for him—the way he never took life too seriously, how easily he pulled me into his world. By the credits, I was nestled against him, warm and content. The night ended as always: tangled in the sheets, his hands on my skin, his lips tracing soft, lingering kisses—gentle yet passionate, his love in every touch. I drifted off, certain I'd never felt so safe, so adored.

Saturday morning shattered the calm. Kevin's phone rang shrill and persistent. When it kept ringing, I nudged him.

"Kevin, your phone." He grumbled, rolled over, and reached blindly.

"Hello?" he answered, voice thick with sleep. A woman's voice—urgent, words indistinct—came through the speaker. Kevin sat up, muscles tense, gray eyes narrowing. "Yeah," he said, tone clipped. "Okay...I'll take care of it."

I placed a hand on his forearm. "Is everything alright?"

"Can I call you back? I can't talk right now." He ended the call and leaned in, lips barely brushing mine. The smile that followed never reached his eyes. "I need to take you home," he said, avoiding my eyes. His voice was calm, but something in it made my stomach tighten.

"Is something wrong?"

"No—just...a friend needs help. It's an emergency." The words sounded rehearsed, too careful.

I wanted to push, demand answers, but held back.

"What about my car?" Kevin blinked, as if only just remembering.

"Right. I'll work on it now. Grab a shower—by the time you're ready, it'll be done." I nodded, swallowing the lump in my throat, and headed to the bathroom. Under the hot water, questions swirled: Who was the woman? Why was Kevin acting so strange? Kevin wasn't Danny; he didn't owe me everything. Still, doubt crept in.

When I stepped outside, Kevin sat behind the wheel of my car, turning the ignition on and off. He handed me the keys with a tight smile.

"It'll get you home," he said. "But you should take it to a shop for a full tune-up. I know a guy who can look at it." I slid my arms around his neck, rising on my toes to kiss him. He tensed, easing back as though he didn't want me in his space, eyes darting up and down the street. It was subtle, but I caught it, and my stomach sank. I leaned in again; he turned slightly, and my lips landed on the corner of his mouth.

"I'll call you later." He stepped back. "Drive safe." His words were distant. I climbed in, clutching the steering wheel as I drove away. What happened? Did I do something wrong? Maybe I was reading too much into it.

Six days passed without a word. At first, I rationalized—Kevin was busy, always juggling a million things. But as my texts went unread and calls rolled to voicemail, worry hardened into something darker—like a pit opening in my chest. Sunday bled into Monday. Even at the thrift store, amid dusty donations and curious customers, my mind wandered to him. By the time I got home, I was drained—thoughts on repeat. I crawled into bed, hoping sleep would quiet the storm.

Tuesday morning greeted me with the same emptiness. Instinctively, I reached for my phone—blank screen. No text. No call. My stomach churned; I slammed the phone onto the nightstand. I needed to burn off the frustration before it consumed me. A quick shower, shampoo hastily rinsed, then leggings and a tank top. I needed to run full-throttle, rage-fueled. Keys in hand, hoodie on, I drove—knuckles white on the wheel. Each red light felt like an insult. At the lot, I paused, staring at the gray sky and ocean. No calm today.

Headphones in, I found the playlist crafted for moments like this—Screaming at the Waves—created back when Danny and I broke up. Too fitting now. I cranked the volume; *You Oughta Know* exploded in my chest. Without stretching, I sprinted—feet pounding the damp path. I wouldn't think about him or the whispering insecurities telling me I wasn't enough. Rage powered each stride. *Killing in the Name* blared, guitars driving me harder.

After what felt like miles, my body gave in. I staggered to a stop, bent for breath, hands on knees.

"Excuse me," a jogger snapped behind me.

I stepped aside, muttering "Sorry" as they passed. I straightened, brushed my hair back, and returned to the car. A pamphlet was tucked under the wiper. He Is Calling You Home sat above a simple church sketch, address, and service times beneath. I barked a laugh, crumpled it, and tossed it onto the back seat.

"Perfect," I muttered, slamming the door. Exhaustion swept over me—body and soul tired. The doubt still gnawed, relentless. Why wasn't I enough for a call?

Wednesday came with no mercy. Desperation had taken root, winding through me like an invasive vine. My shift at the store was a blur of halfhearted greetings and robotic movements; it was my day to cover the registers. As soon as I clocked in, I slipped my phone onto the shelf beneath the counter—close enough to check without anyone noticing. Every few minutes, I glanced down, my heart stuttering with fleeting hope that

I'd see his name. But the screen remained dark, unyielding. Each silent moment twisted the knife, the ache deepening inside me.

By lunch, the war in my head had peaked. I sat alone in the break room, picking at a sandwich I wasn't hungry for, telling myself over and over that I wouldn't call again, wouldn't text again. I couldn't keep humiliating myself, giving pieces of me to someone who seemed content to let them fall away. Still, I crumbled. My hand moved almost involuntarily, dialing his number once more.

"Hey, this is Kevin. Leave a message." I hung up before the beep...only to redial seconds later. Nothing changed. I lost count of how many times I hit call, the act felt as automatic as breathing.

When my shift finally ended, I dragged myself home, exhaustion pressing down like a weight. Seasoned meat and warm tortillas greeted me the second I walked in. Katie had made tacos, and seeing her in the kitchen made me feel grateful—and disconnected.

"Dinner's ready." She set a plate in front of me. She did most of the talking, her voice hummed while I pushed food around my plate. My thoughts—unanswered questions, aching doubts—drowned her out. "Are you even listening to me?"

I blinked. "I'm sorry, Katie." Guilt weighed on my voice. "I wasn't paying attention. I'm not feeling great. Can you handle the dishes? I think I'll head to bed." Concern flickered in her eyes, but she didn't press.

"No problem. Feel better, okay?"

I nodded, muttered thanks, and retreated to my room. A scalding shower failed to calm me. In bed, staring at the ceiling, questions spun: What did I do wrong? Why hadn't he called? Turning onto my side, I buried my face in a pillow that still smelled like him and drifted into uneasy sleep.

By Thursday night, I crossed a line I never thought I would. Hoping to get his attention, I slipped into a black lace negligee I'd bought months ago and never worn. Hands trembling, I snapped a photo and hit send before I could change my mind. I waited for any sign of a reply. None came. Each silent hour felt like a choice he was making, and that stung the most.

By Friday, I was completely drained—emotionally, mentally, and physically. I couldn't face another day of pretending everything was fine, so I called out of work. The hours dragged. By afternoon, I was still in bed. The soft fabric of my blue fuzzy fleece pajamas felt suffocating, a reminder of how little effort I'd put into the day. I hadn't even made it to the shower. Clutching my phone, I stared at the blank screen, willing it to light up with his name. It didn't. It never did.

Katie's voice pulled me from the spiral. "What's wrong, Bethany?"

I turned my head. She stood casually in the doorway, arms crossed, head tilted as if to say I already know. She looked effortlessly put together, as usual: a floral off-shoulder top, denim miniskirt, pristine white sneakers, and bold red lipstick. Her hair was down, slightly messy, but in a good way. Meanwhile, I was cocooned in pajamas and knew I looked awful.

"Still not feeling well?" I muttered, rolling over to avoid her. I felt ridiculous—pathetic, even.

"Really? Because it seems your sudden 'illness' has a lot to do with Kevin falling off the face of the earth." She stepped in, hands on hips. Heat rushed to my cheeks as I turned my back, hating how transparent I was, pining like a lovesick teenager.

"I'm fine."

Katie didn't buy it. She crossed the room, grabbed my shoulder, and rolled me onto my back with surprising strength. Her brown eyes locked onto mine.

"Bethany, what's really going on? I'm here. Talk to me." Pride battled desperation, but her hand stayed until the words spilled out...the emergency call, the six days of silence, unanswered messages, the photo, and the nothing that followed.

Katie furrowed her brows and sat on the bed, leaning back to weigh her words.

"Something's definitely going on with him," she said at last. "Kevin doesn't strike me as the type who would just ghost you. He said it was an emergency—maybe it truly was." Her logic offered hope, but the ache stayed.

"What if I did something wrong?"

"No, Bethany. This isn't about you. He'll call. Let him explain—and when he does, give him absolute hell for putting you through this, okay?" A small smile tugged at her lips—and mine. She leaned over and kissed my forehead. "You'll be okay. But seriously, don't let him off easy—he owes you an explanation." Her sneakers squeaked on the hardwood as she left. I stared at the doorway, clinging to her words like a lifeline.

20

SALT IN THE WOUND

BETHANY

Saturday was worse, like salt in a wound that wouldn't heal. I felt exposed. Every thought of Kevin was torture. How had it come to this? Confused. Angry. And in love. This was why I built walls too high to scale. Relationships were messy, unpredictable, and painful. I was proof of that.

I kicked off the covers, the tangled sheets a cruel reminder of another sleepless night. My chest felt tight, suffocating. I couldn't stay here another second. I grabbed my running clothes, yanked them on, and laced up my sneakers like I was suiting up for battle. Keys jangled in my hand as I headed out, desperate to escape. I wanted the ocean. I wanted waves crashing—steady and unchanging, unlike the chaos inside me. Somewhere along the way, my car turned toward Koreatown. Toward Kevin.

When I pulled up to his apartment, his bike was parked outside like nothing had happened—as if he hadn't been ignoring me for days, as if my heart wasn't in pieces. My stomach twisted, betrayal tightening with every breath. He wasn't going to get away with this. Not without an explanation. I climbed out of the car and headed toward his building, my footsteps heavy with purpose. The anger drowned out the part of me that whispered to turn around. To walk away before I got hurt even more. By the time I reached his door, my anger had morphed into something more fragile. My heart pounded so loudly I could hear it in my ears, and my hands shook as I raised one to knock. I hesitated, sucking in a breath. Then I knocked—hard. The door opened after a few seconds, and I stopped cold.

A woman stood there, tall, stunning, and completely at ease, like she had every right to be answering his door. Her straight brown hair fell past her shoulders, glossy and impossibly smooth, like she'd just stepped out of a shampoo commercial. Her hazel eyes met mine with a flicker of curiosity and nothing more. No guilt. No discomfort. No sign she felt out of place. And somehow, that made it worse. She wasn't scrambling or covering up. She looked comfortable. Confident. Like she belonged. She was wearing one of Kevin's white T-shirts, there was no mistaking it, and a pair of blue lounge shorts that barely peeked out beneath the fabric.

"Can I help you?" she asked.

I swallowed hard and forced myself to speak. "Is Kevin here?" She nodded, turning her head slightly toward the apartment without a second thought.

"Kevin!" she called, the word ringing out casually, as if she were letting him know the mail had arrived or his coffee was ready. I could see into the apartment. My heart sank when Kevin stepped out of his room. He was bare-chested, his hair tousled like he'd just rolled out of bed. He was buttoning his jeans as he walked, the undone waistband revealing a sliver of his lower abs. My heart broke. When his eyes met mine, his entire body froze. His gray eyes widened in shock, and for a moment, the apartment felt deathly still, like the air had been sucked out of the room.

"Bethany." My name slipped from his lips like a question, voice thick with disbelief. I couldn't respond. My body moved before my mind caught up, and I fled down the hallway. Tears blurred my vision, but I refused to stop. Not here. Not in front of him. Behind me, I could hear his footsteps pounding against the floor and his voice echoing after me, desperate and frantic. "Bethany! Bethany, wait!"

I didn't stop until I reached my car, and I fumbled with the door handle as panic surged. Just as I was about to open it, Kevin caught up to me, his hand slamming the door shut before I could climb inside.

"Bethany, please." His voice cracked as he tried to catch his breath. "Let me explain." I turned, chest heaving, body trembling with a toxic mix of anger and heartbreak. He was barefoot, his jeans barely clinging to his hips, and his eyes—those damn gray eyes—looked panicked and pleading.

"There's nothing to explain, Kevin," I spat, my voice breaking. "I've seen enough." His jaw tightened.

He stepped closer. "It's not what it looks like."

I laughed bitterly. "Not what it looks like?" I gestured toward the apartment. "Kevin, I can see what's going on." I glanced over his shoulder, and there she was—the woman from his apartment—standing in the doorway, watching us with an expression I couldn't quite place. Concern? Pity? I didn't care. The sight of her made my stomach churn. Kevin followed my gaze, jaw ticking when he saw her.

"Bethany," he said again, his voice softer this time, almost breaking.

"Let me go, Kevin." I fought the tears threatening to spill. "Just let me go." He didn't move, his hand still pressed against the car door, his eyes searching mine for something—anything—that could fix this. But eventually, he sighed and stepped back, his shoulders slumping in defeat. I climbed in, clutching the wheel like a lifeline.

Without meeting his eyes, I pulled away. Couldn't. My tears stayed buried until my feet hit the sand, waves crashing in front of me. I stared out at the ocean, its endless expanse mocking the chaos in my heart. And there, with the salty breeze tangling my hair and everything I'd been holding breaking loose, I cried until there was nothing left.

I didn't know how long I stared at the horizon. By the time I stood, salt air stung my lips, and my legs felt heavy, like the weight of it all had seeped in. I couldn't sink into the depression that once consumed me. I had already been there with Danny, drowning in heartache and hopelessness, and I swore to myself I would never let anyone put me through that again. Not even Kevin. No matter how searing the pain, how deep the cut—I refused to lose myself in it.

The sun was starting to dip lower in the sky as I made my way back to my car. I slid into the seat and scrolled until I found Katie's name. Without hesitation, I hit dial. She picked up on the second ring, her familiar, upbeat tone immediately lifting my spirits.

"It's time for singing and whiskey."

Katie let out a delighted laugh. "Yay! Time to get our karaoke on!" Her excitement was contagious. For the first time that day, I smiled. It wasn't much, but it was something. I'd drown my sorrows not in tears, but in laughter, songs, and a stiff drink. Tonight, I would sing one song for Kevin—a symbolic farewell—and then I'd drink away every last shred of sadness. Tomorrow would be a new day, and I was hell-bent on making sure it would be better than this one.

When I stepped through the door, Katie's voice rang out like a bright melody. "Hello!" Her smile lit up the room, bright enough to melt ice. The moment her eyes locked onto mine, that smile faltered, crumbled into concern. Her eyes flickered with worry as she rushed over, arms circling me in a tight hug. "Oh, hun, what happened?" Her voice broke against my hair. She pulled back just enough to examine me, her hands holding my arms. "Sit down."

I tried. I really did. I fought to keep it together, willing my voice past the lump in my throat. Every time I opened my mouth to speak, the tears broke free, spilling down my cheeks in silent defeat. Katie sat with me on the couch, rubbing small circles into my back, patient like the best friend she had always been. I sucked in a shaky breath and forced the words out, recounting everything—my confusion, the gut-wrenching moment when I saw the woman in his house, wearing his damn shirt.

"I just can't believe it," Katie finally said. "I never took Kevin for a fuckboy." She shook her head. "Bethany, I am so sorry. You don't deserve this." She reached for my hands, squeezing them between her own, her fingers gliding over mine in a slow, comforting motion. "What can I do?" Her voice dropped to a tone I rarely heard. "Should we go over to his house and take a bat to his bike?" That earned her a watery laugh. I wiped at my eyes, shaking my head.

"Absolutely not. We can't afford to go to jail."

"But it would be satisfying." Her lips twitched with the ghost of a smirk.

"It would," I admitted. "But honestly? You're already doing everything I need. Just being here for me."

She pulled me into another tight hug, squeezing like she could somehow press all my broken pieces back together. When we parted, I sniffled and smirked. "Actually, there is one thing you can do for me..." I tilted my head, letting the mischievous glint in my eyes speak for itself. Katie's grin stretched.

"Oh? Do tell." I leaned in.

"Let's go get fucked up." She burst out laughing, bright and loud. She hopped off the couch, hands on her hips.

"Now that, I can help with!" Without another word, she grabbed my hand and dragged me to my bedroom. "Okay." She flung open my closet. "We need to find you something hot."

I groaned, already knowing where this was headed. "Katie, I am not in the mood for a short, revealing dress. I just want to drink and forget about tonight—not attract more assholes." Katie huffed but relented. After an hour of back-and-forth, I settled on my ripped gray jeans, my favorite black cropped tank, and my belted leather jacket. The look was casual, edgy—something that felt like me. To top it off, I laced up my chunky black boots, standing tall, ready to drown this night in whiskey and music.

When we arrived at the bar, the energy was already buzzing. The place hummed with laughter and clinking glasses. The stage area was just beginning to fill up, and we managed to snag a spot up front.

"I got first round," Katie announced. "What's your poison?"

"Whiskey." I didn't hesitate. "It's that kind of night."

While she went to the bar, I made my way to the DJ booth. DJ Dewayne had been spinning records at this bar for years. He was an irreplaceable fixture in its heartbeat. He was tall—maybe 6'2"—with broad shoulders and a bald head that caught the light overhead. A little heavy, but it suited him. Something about him felt solid, like you'd be safe around him. His deep brown skin was smooth, his salt-and-pepper goatee adding a touch of wisdom and warmth. He looked like someone who gave good advice...and really good hugs. Maybe it was his voice, or the way he greeted everyone like an old friend, but somehow, the whole bar felt a little more like home when he was in it.

"Bethany, how you doin', suga'?" He drew me into a side hug, his Southern twang coated the words like honey.

"I'm good," I lied, forcing a small smile. His eyes crinkled like he didn't believe me.

"Missed you 'round here. You singin' tonight?"

"Yeah." I exhaled. "Where's the sign-up sheet?" He handed me a clipboard, and I quickly scribbled my name.

"Can't wait to hear you," he said. I nodded and headed to the restroom for a quick mirror check. I didn't need a mirror to know I was barely holding it together, but at least I looked ready to have a good time. As I stepped back into the crowd, a tense scene caught my attention. My stomach dropped. Katie stood rigid, her arms crossed tightly over her chest, her face red with fury. And in front of her—Kevin. Shit.

I froze, watching. Kevin talked fast, hands pleading. Katie looked ready to rip him apart. I saw her jab a finger into his chest.

"Shit, shit, shit," I muttered under my breath, picking up my pace. I grabbed Kevin's arm and spun him to face me. He looked weary, with dark circles under his eyes I hadn't noticed before. But it didn't matter. I didn't care.

"What are you doing here?" I spat, anger surging to the surface.

"Bethany, please. Let me explain."

I folded my arms. "Explain what, Kevin? How you ghosted me all week? How you shoved me out of your house on Saturday like I was some inconvenience? Or do you want to explain the woman in your house at seven a.m. wearing your damn shirt?"

His lips parted, but no words came. He searched my face, then ran a hand through his hair with a hard exhale.

I scoffed. "Exactly." I squared my shoulders. "Leave me alone. We don't have anything to talk about." I turned on my heel and walked back to Katie, grabbing my whiskey.

Kevin lingered, hands twitching. But after a long pause, he let out a slow breath and finally turned away, disappearing into the crowd.

Katie reached over and squeezed my hand. "I'm proud of you." I knocked back my shot and slammed the glass down. A sharp ugh slipped out as the burn hit my chest. Katie laughed.

"Another round?" We did. And another.

As we sat back, watching other people take the stage, the familiar voice of DJ Dewayne filled the room. "And now, comin' to the stage, one of my favorite voices in the house—y'all give it up for Bethany!" Applause erupted. The noise rattled through me. I took off my jacket, stood tall, and made my way to the mic. Dewayne leaned in, voice low. "What's your song tonight, suga?" I whispered my song in his ear.

I stepped on center stage and held the mic. I closed my eyes, breathing slowly as I waited for the music. This is for Kevin. Tonight, I'd put my heart on the line. I scanned the bar, searching for him. There he was—sitting exactly where he'd been the night we met. His gray eyes, once full of light, were now dull. He looked frozen, holding his breath. Then the music started.

21

— · —

THE SOUND OF LETTING GO

KEVIN

I stood there, rooted, watching Bethany's car disappear. My chest tightened like a vise—like she'd taken the only piece of me that mattered. How the hell did I let this happen? I raked a hand through my hair, pulse hammering. I thought I'd done everything right. I kept my past where it belonged, far away from Bethany. I locked up my family, my history, and my mistakes in a separate world. And for four months, I had her—everything I ever wanted, everything I never thought I deserved.

She was smart, funny, and real—so damn real. Vulnerable enough to make me want to protect her; fierce enough to crave her; loving enough to break me open. She was it. And with one phone call, one cruel twist of fate, I lost her. My throat burned as I swallowed the grief rising inside me. My hands curled into fists, nails digging into my palms. I felt unmoored—everything I'd built was crumbling beneath me.

A soft touch on my shoulder made me flinch.

"Kevin." Tara's voice was composed, unshaken, unfazed. "Come back inside." I barely registered her leading me through the doorway—my legs moved on instinct. Tara motioned for me to sit. I dropped onto the couch. She vanished into the kitchen; ceramic clinked, and moments later, she handed me a warm mug of coffee. I barely looked at it.

She settled on the floor across from me, legs folded beneath her, steam curling from the teacup in her grasp. She didn't rush me. Instead, she took a slow sip, waiting. Words wouldn't come. The door, Bethany's shock, her flight—it blurred. Her betrayed eyes burned into memory. My heart slammed against my ribs. Tara set her mug down gently.

"Are you going to tell me who that was?" Her tone was curious but measured.

I held the mug tighter, the heat unnoticed against my numb fingers.

"That was Bethany," I finally managed, voice barely above a whisper. Tara repeated the name.

"And who is Bethany to you?" I exhaled shakily. Pain curled around my heart like barbed wire.

"Bethany..." The word came out like a breath, a prayer. "Bethany is my girlfriend. I mean—was my girlfriend. I mean..." A hollow laugh died in my throat. My knuckles turned white around the mug.

Tara sighed—neither judgment nor comfort. "I see. Your girlfriend." Her eyes narrowed. "Does she know about your past?" I shook my head, throat tight. "Don't you think she should know?" Her question settled like a suffocating blanket. Regret, shame—the truth I swore I'd avoid: keeping secrets. Lying by omission. Now she was gone.

Silence stretched, thick and heavy. Tara sipped her tea while I stared ahead, lost in the wreckage of what I had destroyed. I barely noticed when she stood, the hush of her footsteps fading down the hall. It wasn't until she leaned down in front of me that I snapped back. She placed her hands on my forehead, touching light with quiet affection. Then, with a softness that spoke of understanding and care, she leaned in and pressed a motherly kiss to my forehead—a silent reassurance, a wordless comfort.

"Tell her", she whispered. Her words lingered before she pulled away. "I'm going to take a shower," she said, turning toward the hallway. "My Uber will be here in an hour to take me to the airport." She walked away, her steps measured, but just before reaching the bathroom door, she paused. Turning back to me, she looked at me, something flickering in her hazel eyes.

"She kind of looks like Aly." Without another word, she turned and disappeared into the bathroom, closing the door behind her.

I sat on the couch, staring at the space Bethany filled, the emptiness swallowing me whole. It closed in—heavy, unrelenting—the full weight of losing her impossible to ignore. It wasn't just the absence of her presence—it was the absence of us. I didn't know how to put myself back together.

As I walked Tara outside, her suitcase rattled over the uneven sidewalk. We stood side by side as we waited for her Uber. She shifted on her feet, her fingers drumming lightly against the handle of her bag. I could feel her hesitance like a tangible thing, pressing between us, making the silence heavier. Finally, she turned to me.

"I feel like I should stay," she said softly. "To make sure you're alright." Her voice was gentle but unwavering, laced with concern that had followed me for years. I looked up—and there it was. The same look she gave me back in high school—after Aly—when she stood by me at my worst. The kind of look that saw right through me.

I shook my head. "No, Tara."

She sighed, lips pressed together like she was considering her next move. With the same careful tenderness, she reached out and placed her hand on my arm.

"I can call Jason. He'll understand," she said. "I could book another flight for tomorrow. Or Monday."

"Tara, I'll be fine. I promise," I said, but my voice wavered at the end, betraying the lie even as I tried to sell it.

She tilted her head, skeptical. "When's the last time you called your therapist?"

I stilled, staring at the sidewalk cracks like they held the answer. "It's been a while," I admitted. She exhaled sharply, her expression tightening with something between frustration and concern. I knew she wanted to say more—how I always did this, pulled away when things got rough, never let people take care of me the way I took care of them.

Before she could, the chime of her phone sounded. Her Uber had arrived. The car drove up to the curb, its tires crunching lightly over the asphalt. Tara turned back to me, her face softening. She gave me a tight hug. I closed my eyes, letting myself sink into it—the comfort of her, the quiet understanding we had always shared. When she eased back, she placed a kiss on my cheek, her palm smoothing over my arm.

"If you need me, do not hesitate to call. Do you hear me, Kevin? Call me."

The Uber driver got out and took her suitcase, loading it into the trunk. Tara opened the back door, then turned to look at me one last time. Her eyes in the afternoon sun held something unsaid—concern, love, maybe frustration.

"Call your therapist," she said. And then she was gone, the car door shut behind her with a quiet finality. Frozen on the sidewalk, I watched as the Uber drove her away. Her words stayed, settling into my bones. I turned back to my apartment, head spinning. She wasn't wrong.

For hours, I sat in my living room, staring at my phone, my thoughts tangled in a relentless loop. I needed to fix this. I needed to get her back. Every call went straight to voicemail. On the next attempt, I discovered I'd been blocked. My stomach twisted. An ache settled in my chest. Bethany was gone—she hadn't even given me a chance to explain. Should I tell her the truth—the one I'd spent years burying? She ran without knowing—what would she do if she did?

I knew exactly how the morning must have looked: Tara, dressed in my T-shirt and lounge shorts, answering the door like she belonged; me, shirtless, buttoning my jeans, looking every bit of a man who'd just rolled out of bed. Bethany had no reason to doubt what she saw. She didn't. But she was wrong—just not in the way that mattered.

Tara is my mother's sister, my aunt, only twelve years older than me. When my parents died, she and Jason had been married a year. They were twenty-six, barely out of their honeymoon phase. They could have traveled, partied, and lived freely. Instead, they became parents overnight, taking me and Ian in because there was no one else. They never had children of their own—just us. I owe them everything.

Now, because of a misunderstanding, Bethany thought I'd slept with Tara. I could explain Tara's presence, but not why I ignored Bethany all week. How did I tell her I was drowning in my past—that every time I reached for her, I feared dragging her into waters too deep, too dark? I couldn't lie. But the truth was too damn hard. I had to find a middle ground.

I stepped into the shower, scalding water cascading over my head and back. The heat eased my muscles, the ache settling deep in my chest. Hands braced on tile, breath heavy, the realization hit like a gut punch: I was in love with Bethany. The thought burned hotter than the water, sinking deep. Frustration clawed beneath my skin. I slammed my hand against the wall—the dull pain lost in the storm inside me. Once it consumed me, the climb back was steep and unforgiving. I forced a deep breath, pushed it down. I needed to fix this. Moving on autopilot, I toweled off, dressed, and grabbed my keys. One thought burned: get Bethany back.

A block from her house, my pulse hammered—then I saw her: Bethany and Katie slipping into the back seat of a car. I acted. Without hesitation I followed, weaving through traffic as I trailed the Uber across town. When it pulled up to the bar where I first met Bethany, something in my gut twisted. Of all places, why here? I parked, gripping the handlebars, running through everything I wanted to say. Apologies. Explanations. Promises. Would any of them even matter?

Shoving the doubt aside, I climbed off the bike and stepped into the bar. The dim lighting, the hum of conversation, the clink of glasses, it was all background noise. My focus was singular. I scanned the room, searching for Bethany. But she wasn't there.

Instead, I spotted Katie near a table in the front, her expression unreadable as she nursed a drink. Determination pushed me forward, and my steps were quick. When I reached her, I tapped her shoulder.

She turned, and I immediately knew this wouldn't go smoothly. The usually lighthearted, bubbly Katie was gone. In her place was a woman radiating hostility, her expression hard with anger. Her lips curled in disgust.

"What the hell are you doing here?" I ignored the venom in her tone. I didn't have time for it.

"I'm looking for Bethany. Where is she?"

Katie straightened, crossing her arms over her chest, her stance unyielding. "That's none of your business anymore. You had your chance, and you ruined it. Where's your friend from this morning?" I exhaled. Of course, Bethany had told her. The misunderstanding had already cemented itself into something bigger, something I had no control over.

I tried again. "Katie, I promise you—it's not what it looked like. Please, just tell me where she is." Her expression darkened with disgust.

"Are you fucking serious right now?" she hissed. "You think you get to stand here and just ask about her like nothing happened? Like you didn't completely wreck her?"

I swallowed hard. "I just need to talk to her."

"No." She leaned in. "You don't get to talk to her. You don't get to smooth things over or make yourself feel better. You ghosted her for an entire week, Kevin. A week. And then this morning? You let her show up to that? Jesus Christ, do you even understand what you did?"

Guilt twisted like a knife, but I held my ground. "I know how it looked—"

"Shut up," she snapped, her jaw tightening. "You don't know anything. You didn't see her face when she came home, how fucking broken she looked. Do you know what she did when she got there? She sat on the couch and cried—deep, gut-wrenching sobs that wouldn't stop. I stayed beside her, consoling her for almost an hour, trying to get her to understand that she wasn't the problem. That's what you did to her." A sharp pang shot through my chest.

Katie wasn't finished. She stepped closer, stabbing her finger into my chest. "Bethany has been through enough, Kevin. She didn't deserve this. She doesn't deserve someone who clearly doesn't give a shit about her."

"That's not true," I shot back, my voice cracking slightly.

She laughed bitterly. "No? Then where the fuck have you been? Where were you while she was waiting by her phone like an idiot? While she was blaming herself for whatever the hell she thought she did wrong? Bethany gave a shit about you. She would've done anything for you. And you threw it in her face."

I clenched my jaw, keeping my voice calm. "I swear, Katie. It wasn't what it looked like. Where is she?"

Her eyes burned as she jabbed her finger into my chest, punctuating every syllable. "Again. THAT. IS. NONE. OF. YOUR. FUCKING. BUSINESS." And just when I thought this night couldn't get any worse, I felt a hand on my forearm. Bethany turned me to face her, eyes storming. My heart plummeted.

She was breathtaking even in her fury. But the tenderness I once knew, the softness I had memorized in every stolen glance, was gone. Her eyes, those eyes that used to light up when she looked at me, were now cold, guarded, filled with fury.

"What are you doing here?" she demanded. My pulse hammering, I just wanted to tell her how fucking sorry I was. But I had no right. I clung to the only thing I could offer—an explanation, even if I wasn't sure she would let me give it.

"Bethany, please. Let me explain." My voice was stripped to the bones of desperation. Her lips pressed into a tight line, arms folding across her chest in a stance so closed off it made my stomach twist. Ready for war.

"Explain what, Kevin?" she shot back, her glare scorching. "How you ghosted me all week? How you shoved me out of your house on Saturday like I was some inconvenience? Or do you want to explain the woman in your house at seven a.m.—wearing your damn shirt?" Her words sliced through me. My mouth opened, but everything tangled—excuses, justifications, the truth. I'd replayed this conversation a hundred times, imagined every way to make her understand. Yet face-to-face with her anger and pain, I realized just how badly I'd fucked this up.

This wasn't how I wanted it to go. Not here. Not in a crowded bar with half-drunk strangers looking on. I needed privacy to show her I wasn't who she thought—that I hadn't betrayed her; that I'd stayed away because I was drowning in a past too heavy to voice. But Bethany wasn't giving me that chance. Frustration coiled in my chest. I raked a hand through my hair. I was losing her.

She scoffed. "Exactly." She squared her shoulders, her expression hardening. "Leave me alone. We don't have anything to talk about." And just like that, she turned back to Katie—no second glance. She sank into her seat and knocked back a shot of whiskey, drowning whatever was left between us. I stood frozen, silently begging—pleading—for her to look at me, just once, long enough to see how much I hated myself. Still, she didn't. Defeat settled deep in my chest. With no other choice, I headed for the bar, claiming the same damn stool I'd sat on the night we first met.

"Bartender," I muttered. "Beer on tap." I wasn't leaving her here—not like this. Bethany had a plan—I saw it in every reckless toss of whiskey, the burn in her eyes. She meant to drink until she was numb—until she forgot what was eating her alive. I wouldn't let that happen.

I nursed a single beer, fingers clutched around the sweating glass as I took slow, measured sips. I didn't want to drink—or even be here—but I had to blend in, not be the guy alone, watching her self-destruct. It was karaoke night, and the bar was alive with the kind of energy that made it easy to get lost—except Bethany and I weren't. We stood in the middle of it, drowning in the void. She laughed at all the right moments, leaned in when she was supposed to, but I saw it. I could always see it: the act, the mask.

I heard her name. I snapped from my thoughts as Bethany slipped off her jacket and strode to the DJ, confidence drawing every man's attention. Dim lights traced her curves—ripped gray jeans clinging to her hips, black cropped tank baring just enough skin to make my jaw tighten. Too many eyes were on her. It pissed me off. That stomach—on display for every damn person—was the one I used to trace with my tongue, feeling her tremble as I unraveled her. I shifted in my seat, holding my beer tighter, my body reacting to memories I shouldn't indulge.

Bethany climbed the stage, stood center, eyes scanning like she was searching. For someone. Me. The music started. The first haunting notes of *No Light, No Light* by Florence + the Machine hummed through the speakers, drifting through the bar like a haunting whisper. Conversation dipped; a ripple of quiet told everyone something big was coming. The harp shimmered—gentle, heavy—and my chest clenched. I knew this song was for me.

Bethany's voice poured into the mic, smooth as honey. The lyrics were clear proof I was still in her mind—hit me square. She swayed, body melting into the music, every movement unhurried, hypnotic. Her hips rolled in rhythm, like the song pulsed beneath her skin. As she sang, her voice wove through the lyrics—rich and full—flowing through the melody with a pull that drew everything around her into its orbit.

She crossed the stage with easy rhythm, boots tapping the worn wood, arms drifting upward, fingertips tracing her waist. Head tilted back, she let the melody consume her, lips parting as she poured herself into every note. A gentle spin, denim shifting over the soft expanse of her stomach; stage lights cast shadows that made my pulse jump. With every bar, she surrendered more, breathing with the beat, nothing existing but the song in her lungs.

She looped the mic cord loosely around her fingers, pressed it to her heart as though to drive the words deeper. Her hand brushed along her hairline as she sang. Logic versus love—the war hammering inside me. Her voice ached with every syllable, thick with emotion like a storm. The drums hit, melody swelling—then she froze. And changed the words. It wasn't blue eyes. She sang gray eyes. My pulse stuttered.

Every note after that pulsed with everything she couldn't say, emotions left to rot beneath the surface. She wasn't just singing; she was confessing, releasing, laying herself bare. At the bridge, she snapped upright, arms outstretched in a crucifix, voice soaring—a vulnerable cry of how hard it was to admit the truth she buried beneath silence and pride. The note held—forever—until the ground beneath me shifted.

When the note finally broke, the room erupted: cheers, whistles, applause. She twirled, letting the music own her. For a heartbeat, she looked at me, eyes locking as she sang the line that said it all: she wasn't ready to talk. Not about this. Not with me. Her voice was defiant, but her eyes were anything but. I'd seen enough. She turned back to the crowd, her voice weaving through the air, no longer meant for me. I grabbed my jacket, slid into the sleeves, and didn't wait for the song to end. The door swung open, and I stepped into the night, her voice fading behind me. A sound that should've pulled me back, but only reminded me of what I'd already lost. There was no fixing this tonight.

I felt defeated.

22

WHEN THE MUSIC FADES

BETHANY

As I stepped off the stage, the room closed in—not overpowering, but in an unexpected rush of energy. People turned in their seats, some reaching out, some stopping me in my path, their voices blending into an overwhelming chorus of praise.

"That was incredible!"

"You have such a beautiful voice!"

"Damn, girl, where have you been hiding that talent?"

Hands clapped my back. Fingers brushed my arm, I smiled, nodding, murmuring, "Thank you," on repeat. I barely knew half the people, but for five minutes, I was caught in a current of strangers moved by my voice—by the emotion I'd spilled onstage. It felt surreal—like stepping into someone else's life. Yet beneath their praise, something deeper awakened. Realigning. Locking back into place. By the time I reached the last line, I felt it. Music had always been there, waiting for me. And tonight, I had finally let it back in. But Kevin...

I never thought he would show up. When I saw him trying to explain, I knew it was pointless—just wasted breath on words that wouldn't change a thing. Even after he walked away, I knew he hadn't really left. He was still there, somewhere, watching me. I hadn't even chosen a song to sing until that moment. When he turned his back, slipping into the crowd, I knew exactly what needed to be said. The lyrics weren't just words—they were everything I'd wanted to scream. Everything I'd held back for too long. So I let the music speak for me.

When my eyes found him from the stage, I felt it—that faint, aching hope that maybe this wasn't the end. That there was still something left to salvage. But I knew better. It was foolish to believe otherwise. Still, the question gnawed at me. How the hell had he known I'd be here? How? It wasn't a coincidence. Couldn't be. I finally reached my seat, still dazed.

"Oh my God, Bethany, that was amazing!" Katie threw her arms around my neck. I laughed, hugging her back.

"Yeah," I said. "It was." Katie slid back, her excitement dimming into something more cautious.

"Where did he-who-shall-not-be-named go?" Her voice dripped with disdain. I swallowed hard, gripping the edge of the table.

"I don't know." I shrugged. "Who cares?" Kevin was my past now. If I said it enough times, maybe I'd believe it. "Let's order another round."

By the time we stumbled through the door, it was well past one a.m. The bar had long since closed, but the heat from the night still clung to my skin. Alcohol buzzed in my veins, hazing everything, thoughts thick with more than just drunkenness. I was hot, flushed—not just from the drinks, but from something else entirely. A hunger. A longing. A craving that had nothing to do with food. I wasn't going to drunk-dial Kevin. I refused. But not even a day had passed, and I already ached for him.

My body betrayed me, rewinding to when I locked eyes with him—his shirt stretched across those shoulders, lips parting as he looked at me. I hated him. But the alcohol blurred that hate into something reckless. Dangerous. I was starving for him. Want twisted low, heat spreading like wildfire. I was going to miss the way his strong arms wrapped around me, holding me tight, possessive, like I was something precious and fragile in his grasp. The way he could lift me with ease, pinning me against the wall. His body pressed into mine. Breath was hot and uneven on my neck. And his hands—those hands knew every inch of me. Teasing. Coaxing. Claiming. Until I was trembling, gasping his name. I missed all of it. And it was killing me. No. Not tonight.

I muttered a rushed goodnight and stumbled to my bedroom. Tossing my phone onto the bed—far away from temptation—I flicked on the light and walked straight to my dresser. My fingers trembled slightly as I yanked open the top drawer, reaching inside. If I couldn't have him, I'd settle for the next best thing. B.O.B. never let me down. Battery Operated Boyfriend—always ready, never disappointing, and best of all, no complicated feelings attached. But when I pulled my hand out, it wasn't B.O.B. I was holding.

It was a Bible.

I blinked at it, my alcohol-soaked brain struggling to process what the hell I was looking at. That's...weird.

How the hell did that get in there? The thought flickered like a dying lightbulb—there, then gone. Didn't matter. I tossed the Bible on the dresser and plunged my hands back in, digging with drunken determination. Clothes. Socks. An old receipt. Everything but what I was looking for. I yanked the drawer open farther, shoving things aside, and frustration bubbled under my skin. Where the hell was it? It'd been a while, sure, but I knew I left it in there. It wasn't the kind of thing that just disappeared.

I sighed, slamming it shut as I kicked off my shoes. Next came my jeans, peeled off haphazardly as I nearly tripped over myself. My top, bra, and panties followed—fabric trailing behind me. My body still burned, alcohol amplifying every sensation, every lingering thought. Near the bed, I spotted one of Kevin's shirts—his scent clung to the fabric, faint but there. I hadn't washed it, and didn't care. I grabbed it, slipping it over my head. I stumbled to the light switch, the room spinning. My fingers fumbled over the wall for a second before I finally found it, plunging the room into darkness. I exhaled, steadied myself, and climbed into bed, nearly losing my balance.

The only glow came from my phone's screen as I reached for it. Tonight, my fingers would take his place. With a sigh, I opened my browser, letting the heat under my skin take control as I searched for female-friendly porn to feed the hunger clawing inside me. I fell asleep mid-stroke. The pleasure is just out of reach. Too drunk. Too tired. Desire faded into exhaustion before I could finish. A singsong voice yanked me out of the heavy fog of sleep.

"Honey, I need to head out to work. There's a glass of water on your bedside table with some aspirin," Katie said. I groaned, voice barely a whisper.

"Thanks." She kissed my forehead; her perfume lingered as her footsteps faded down the hall. The front door clicked shut, and silence settled once more. I sank into the sheets, sleep lulling me under.

When I woke up, the day was half gone. My phone glowed dimly beside me—battery nearly dead, last night's browser still open. I locked the screen without looking. A dull throb hammered behind my eyes as I forced myself upright. My stomach churned. The aspirin. I fumbled for the glass. The water was tepid, but I tossed the pills in and drained half of it. In the mirror, I looked like hell—rumpled shirt, tangled hair, blotchy skin, alcohol-soaked eyes. "Ugh," I muttered.

I stood, wobbling slightly as the dizziness passed. Near my dresser, the Bible caught my eye. A knot formed in my stomach. How the hell did that get there? I hadn't seen that Bible since returning from Indiana—since the day I buried my father. I could've sworn I'd shoved it into the back of my closet, buried beneath forgotten clothes. Yet there it was. A chill crawled over my skin. My fingers hovered, then grabbed the book and shoved it back into the closet where it belonged, slamming the door. Nothing against God—just the institution my father forced on me. That part of my life was over.

In the bathroom, I scrubbed my teeth, trying to erase the memory of last night. Steam curled around me as the shower roared to life. I stepped under the spray, let it pound my skin, but no heat burned the ache in my chest. I pressed my palms to the tile, memories crashed like waves. I knew what I saw: Kevin with her. Yet he came looking—that had to mean something. Danny never did that. Whenever I caught Danny cheating, there was no remorse, just a shrug: It is what it is. But Kevin's eyes—there had been desperation. Something real. Doubt twisted inside me. I was the one who ended it; I never gave him a chance to explain. Maybe that was for the best...wasn't it? Tears blurred my vision; shampoo stung my eyes, and I blinked hard. Reality's slap. I had to stop wallowing, quit second-guessing.

The rest of the shower passed in hushed silence. I stepped out, body heavy. I put on flannel pajama pants and Kevin's old hoodie—the one he gave me the night I forgot my jacket. I lifted the fabric to my nose, hoping for his scent, but caught only crisp fabric softener. Nausea churned. I pulled the hood up and collapsed onto the mattress. I didn't bother with my hair. I lay there, staring at the ceiling, listening to the nothingness of my own heartache. Maybe I drifted off, mind numbed by exhaustion, lost in nothingness. I wasn't asleep, but not fully awake either. I drifted in the in-between, where time blurred and feelings dulled enough to make it bearable.

Then I heard it—a knock. Faint at first, a whisper of sound against the hush. My eyes fluttered; my breath went shallow. Had I imagined it? The knock returned—louder. Again—harder, faster, more insistent. I blinked several times, my sluggish mind struggling to process the noise. It was coming from the front door.

I rubbed my face, wincing at the headache clinging to my skull. Who the hell was knocking like that? And why wouldn't they stop? Getting up felt like wading through fog. Each step pounded through my skull. I reached the door, ready to snap—but something in my gut warned me to pause. I looked through the peephole and sucked in a breath. Kevin.

A rush of anger, longing, fear—tangled together—shot through me. I clutched the knob, forcing myself to breathe. He stood, shoulders sagging, hands shoved deep in his pockets like he was trying to hold himself together. Hair a mess, jaw rough with stubble, clothes rumpled—maybe the same outfit as last night. He looked terrible, as if he hadn't slept, as if something inside him had snapped. I pressed my forehead to the door, willing my heartbeat to slow. He hadn't seen me. I could walk away. Pretend I wasn't home. Ignore the ache in my chest. But, as if he sensed me, he stopped knocking.

"Bethany."

My name came out hoarse, strained, as though it hurt him to say it. His voice seeped through the door, curling into places I wished were numb.

"I know you're in there. Please, just let me explain." That pull—aching, inevitable—dragged me. I squeezed my eyes shut. Through the peephole, I watched him drag his hands down his face. Restless. Anxious. "Please." His voice cracked—just enough to make my stomach flip. "If you let me say what I need to say, I'll leave you alone."

I should've walked away. But my fingers trembled as I slid the deadbolt. The metallic click echoed in the silence. Kevin's eyes snapped up—dull, defeated. And I hated that part of me still wanted to fix it. Wordlessly, I stepped aside. He slipped past me, his presence filling the apartment the way it always did. I shut the door, exhaling before facing him again. I motioned to the couch. He sank onto it, elbows on knees, hands clasped like he was bracing for impact. I stayed near the door, arms crossed—a barricade. The silence was unbearable. I fidgeted, unsure what to do with my hands.

"Um...do you want something to drink?" The words sounded awkward; I bit my bottom lip.

Kevin let out a short, humorless laugh, raking his fingers through his hair—his tell. He was nervous. Good. So was I.

"Kevin," I said, "I'm waiting." His throat bobbed. Something flickered before he straightened. Hands fidgeting, jaw tight, he drew a breath—and finally began.

23

THE WEIGHT OF CLOUDS

KEVIN

I couldn't believe she let me in. I'd knocked with nothing but hope and words I wasn't sure would matter. I hadn't thought she'd open the door—hadn't thought she'd let me step into her space, into this moment. But here we were. Bethany stood across the room like she couldn't bear to be near me. And fuck—she looked like a beautiful mess. She wore my blue hoodie, the one I gave her the night she forgot her jacket. It hung off her small frame, worn by distance and the walls she was rebuilding. The hood slipped back, revealing damp waves clinging to her neck.

I'd left her at that bar last night, walked away because I thought it was the right thing to do. But it wasn't. I didn't know if she got home safe, was alone, or—not. I cut off the thought before it could fester. Bethany wasn't reckless like that. She wasn't the type to erase me by falling into someone else's arms. But I'd still fucked up—gave her every reason to believe I touched another woman.

Bethany's eyes locked on mine—dark, guarded, rimmed with exhaustion that made my chest ache. She looked drained of whatever fight she had left for me. She bit her bottom lip—a habit I knew too well—and asked if I wanted something to drink. Her tone was casual—too light—but I saw through it. She was nervous. So was I. A bitter laugh slipped out before I could stop it. I wanted to pull her close, bury my face in her neck, and whisper a thousand apologies. I hadn't cheated, but it was still my fault she was hurting.

"Kevin." My name pulled me back. Bethany stood with her arms crossed, unreadable. "I'm waiting." Two words. Enough to crush me. I swallowed hard; my pulse thundered. Stick to the script. Say what you came to say. I drew a slow breath and met her stare.

"The woman you saw at my house yesterday morning wasn't who you thought. You're the only woman for me, Bethany."

She closed her eyes, body stiff, bracing for impact. She shivered—barely, but I saw it. I pressed on.

"The woman you saw...her name is Tara." I paused; Bethany didn't move, didn't blink. "She's my aunt." Her eyes snapped open, shock flashing like lightning. She said nothing—just stared, weighing whether to believe me. "She came down here for a family emergency," I added, my voice even though my throat felt hoarse. Her brow furrowed, lips parting, but she didn't speak. "I know she looks young because she is," I continued. "She's only twelve years older than me." Bethany's expression changed. Wheels turned in her eyes.

"When my parents died, she was barely twenty-six," I continued, my voice dipping lower. "Your age now." Saying it hit harder than I expected. I'd spent so much of my life carrying that loss—what it meant for Tara, for my brother, for me. But seeing Bethany at this age, with her own burdens, I realized how young Tara had been—how much had been thrown onto her shoulders before she'd even lived her own life. I looked away, sadness edging in. "She gave up everything to raise us, two teenage boys, a life that wasn't hers to fix. But she did it anyway."

Bethany hadn't spoken, but she didn't need to. The hardness in her eyes softened—she was listening, and that alone kept me from breaking.

"That's who called me last Saturday," I said, voice lower, as if admitting it made it real. "She called to tell me my brother is missing." My throat tightened. Bethany's eyes met mine, full of sadness, like she already knew what was coming. I drew a slow breath. "Again."

The word left the sting of regret and fear. Pressure clamped around my ribs, making it hard to breathe. I felt the couch dip. Bethany's warm hands found mine, her fingers curling around them. I held on to the feel of her skin while I worked to slow my breathing. I opened my eyes after a few beats.

"Tara got a call from Ian's fiancée," I said, voice wavering. "I didn't even know my brother had a fiancée." The words felt foreign. During Ian's visit, he insisted he hadn't even asked her out. And now he was engaged? I ran a hand through my hair, frustration rising. "He came into town for a surprise visit last month. That was the last time anyone saw him. He never flew back. I was the last one to see him."

Bethany finally spoke. "What did you mean by 'again'?"

I hesitated, choosing my words, walking the line between truth and burden. "I should've known something was wrong," I muttered. "He was acting...off." I pressed my fingers to my temples, replaying our last conversation for signs I missed. Bethany watched, no judgment—just quiet understanding. "This isn't his first time going missing," I whispered. "It's his fifth."

Bethany inhaled sharply, but didn't look away. "My brother has relapsed." I searched her face, needing her to grasp how hard this was. "That's why I didn't call this week," guilt in every word. "I spaced out—my brother..." My voice cracked as I clenched my jaw. "Ian's all I have left." Bethany's fingers tightened around mine, but I couldn't hold on. I slipped free and dragged my hands down my face, trying to wipe away the exhaustion clawing at my chest.

"I went to every place I thought he might be," I said, voice thick with frustration. "I'm sorry, Bethany. I never meant to hurt you—never meant to shut you out." My hands clenched. "I couldn't call. Not until I found him."

I pushed off the couch, tension coiling through every muscle. I paced to the window and stared out at the cloudy, gray sky.

"I usually find him. Last time, it took three days." My voice lowered. "But this time..." I faltered. "I have no idea where he could be." My fingers curled against the glass, absorbing the chill. Helplessness seeped in. "No idea."

Bethany moved. No hesitation, no permission asked. She simply came to me, arms holding me, her cheek resting on my shoulder. Silent comfort. She was crying—for me. That was all it took. I turned and cupped her face, crushing my lips to hers. She kissed me back, arms sliding around my neck like she could piece me back together with her touch.

24

— • —

FREEFALLING BETWEEN BREATHS

BETHANY

This afternoon was chaotic. Kevin bared his soul, every word soaked in pain, each confession cutting deeper than the last. I'd never seen him like that—so unguarded and unraveled. And Ian...his brother was missing. Missing. The word echoed in my mind, heavy and impossible to shake. And the relapse—God. Kevin never spoke about Ian—not in passing, not even when the past crept in uninvited. I never asked—I knew what it meant to bury things, to pretend some chapters didn't exist. I'd spent years doing the same. But today, the walls he built cracked open, spilling everything he held in. I felt it all, the guilt, helplessness, and the fear he carried in every movement.

I swallowed hard, moving slightly, careful not to wake him. Kevin let me see him at his lowest, trusted me with the darkness, and it scared me. After we finally broke apart, lips still tingling from the kiss, I guided us toward my bedroom. He didn't say anything—and he didn't need to. Exhaustion was etched into him: shadows clung beneath his eyes, subtle but telling, tension in his jaw, the way his shoulders sagged now that he was somewhere safe. He'd been running on adrenaline and guilt. "Take your clothes off."

He blinked, caught between exhaustion and reluctance. I lifted the hem of his shirt and drew it over his head. He didn't resist. Piece by piece, I stripped him to his boxer briefs—not for sex, but so he could rest. I pulled the covers back and guided him into bed, tucking the blanket around his body as he exhaled, sinking into the mattress like it was the first softness he'd felt in days. Maybe it was. I slid in beside him, listening as his breathing slowed. He was already asleep. Reaching for my phone, I typed a quick message to Katie.

Me: Kevin's here. I was wrong about everything. We'll talk in the morning.

I hit send, set the phone down, and padded to the bathroom. I climbed back into bed and closed my eyes, exhaustion finally hitting.

Kevin's lips brushed the back of my neck, waking me. His breath fanned over my skin, his stubble grazing me as he worked his way down, leaving a trail of heat that curled low in my stomach. I whimpered—my body recognizing him before my mind caught up.

Kevin never rushed. His kisses were slow, restrained, leaving no room for doubt. A sigh escaped from my lips as my body melted into his. His arm rested heavily around my waist, his fingers splayed across my stomach, holding me close, like he had no plans of letting go. His other hand moved higher, sliding beneath my shirt, claiming the curve of my breast. Kevin's palm was rough in all the ways that made my skin tighten and my pulse stumble. Pleasure bloomed in my chest—hot, immediate. I blinked, a slow inhale catching in my throat as I glanced down. His fingers were stroking me, teasing, sending tiny ripples of sensation curling through my body.

A soft moan slipped out before I could stop it. Kevin pulled me closer, pressing me flush against his chest. I felt his breath against my hair—slow and deep—before he buried his face in it, inhaling me like something he had been missing for a long time. I let my eyes close again, content to stay nestled against him until reality forced me to move.

"What time is it?" I mumbled sleepily. Kevin's lips grazed my ear.

"Early enough to do this." And then, without warning, he pinched my nipple. A loud gasp tore from my throat, my body jerking at the unexpected sting.

"Ouch!" I yelped, breathless. Kevin chuckled—low and rough—as he kissed below my jaw.

"Too much?" he asked, but there was nothing apologetic in his voice. Just amusement. Just knowing. And damn him—he always knew. I swatted at his hand, but he was already smoothing over the sting with teasing strokes. A moan escaped as heat surged in place of the sting, rippling pleasure through me. My body surrendering to the rhythm of his hands. Just as I relaxed into it, another jolt shot through me. I sucked in a breath, my body jerking as he pinched my nipple again, harder this time. A whimper escaped me, half protest, half something else entirely, as I reached to stop him. But he was faster. Before I could push him away, he caught my wrist and pinned it down against my chest.

"I don't think so," he growled. A shiver ran through me, fire licking up my spine as his words tangled with the ache between my thighs. He knew exactly what he was doing—how to pull me apart piece by piece. He nipped my ear, teeth scraping, another spasm shooting through me. This was his favorite tactic—slow, torturous, calculated to the inch. He pushed me higher with wicked precision, only to snatch it away with each pinch, every flick of his fingers. I whined, the frustration bubbling into something needy, desperate.

"Please," I purred, breathless, aching.

Kevin laughed. "Please, what?" His tone was smug and knowing. Damn him. His fingers dipped below my panty line; my skin burned. I parted my thighs, craving the way he undid me. His fingers slid through my wetness—teasing—until they found my clit. A slow, familiar pace, one he'd perfected, making me arch. And then—that pinch. A burst of pain collided with pleasure so intense it stole my breath. My body shuddered, a helpless gasp slipping past my lips as the sensation shot through me. I loved this. He played my body like a song he'd memorized, building me up, leaving me trembling, barely holding on.

"Kevin, please," I begged, my voice shaky with need. Reaching behind me, I found his lips, crushing into them with desperate hunger. I needed him. I needed this. My body ached for the release he was so cruelly keeping just out of reach. A low, wicked giggle vibrated against my mouth before his fingers returned to my clit, soft flicks sending sparks through me. And then—he thrust two fingers inside, deep and unrelenting. I gasped, my walls tightening around him, my back arching as a cry tore from my throat.

"You like that?" he whispered, dark and teasing.

"Yes," I panted, grinding against his hand for more friction.

"Or do you love it?" His fingers curled inside me, finding my G-spot with infuriating precision, and a fresh wave of ecstasy crashed through me. I rode his hand, grabbing his wrist, every stroke pulling me closer to my release.

"Yes," I panted, breathless. "I love this."

He drove deeper, fingers knuckle-deep, filling me in the most delicious way. Ragged breaths filled the space as our bodies moved in sync. It came—that warmth, that rush—flooding me like a crashing wave. I convulsed, overwhelmed, clutching his wrist as the waves overtook me.

25

A DEAL WORTH MAKING

KEVIN

We made love all morning, lost in each other. Bethany was my anchor, the only thing keeping me from drowning in the search for Ian. As much as I wanted to stay, reality didn't pause for me. I'd already neglected too much work, responsibilities, everything outside, and the desperate need to find my brother. The studio deadline was waiting; I couldn't let everything slip through my fingers.

Bethany was still asleep when I left, curled in the sheets, her hair a tangled halo. Part of me wanted to crawl back beside her and pretend the world didn't exist, but I grabbed my keys and left. The second I stepped inside, reality hit hard. I stripped down and took a long, hot shower. By the time I emerged, towel around my waist, my phone rang on the nightstand. Tara.

I hit the speaker. "Hey." I kept my voice even, like this wasn't already a burden.

"Hey, Kevin." Her tone brimmed with concern. "How are you doing?"

"Better. Took a while, but I got through to Bethany. We're okay." Saying it felt good.

"That's good to hear..." Tara hesitated. "Did you tell her about your past?" I stilled. There it was. I sat on the bed, rolling my shoulders.

"Bethany knows enough." I'd told her what mattered.

Silence stretched before Tara spoke again. "Kevin, I think it's important you don't just tell her 'enough.' You need to tell her all of it. You can't keep running. You need to talk about Aly."

My jaw clenched. I yanked the phone off speaker. "No need to bring her up," I snapped. "She's irrelevant. I don't ever want to hear her name again." I paced, caging my temper. "That will never happen again, Tara. Do you understand me? I will do everything in my power to keep Bethany safe." Silence. Damn it. I closed my eyes, dragging a hand down my face. "Look, Tara, I'm sorry."

"No need to apologize," she said evenly. "But you need to know where I stand. You can't keep burying your past. It'll catch up with you. One day, Bethany's going to need the whole truth."

Now wasn't the time.

Then her voice softened. "I hired someone to find Ian. I thought you should know."

"Tara, it's a waste of money."

"How is it a waste, Kevin?" she challenged. "He's our family."

"How many times are we going to let him take over our lives?" My voice dropped, heavy with exhaustion. "I'm tired, Tara. I'm tired of dropping everything for him. This time it almost cost me the most important thing in my life." My throat tightened. "I don't want to do this anymore. I can't." She stayed quiet, so I kept going, "I love my brother. My door's always open if he truly wants help. But letting him destroy every bit of happiness I have left? That has to stop. I spent my twenties worrying about him. I want to build something real with Bethany, and I can't do that if I'm constantly chasing him."

"I understand," Tara said at last. Beneath her words was sadness—like she'd known this was coming. The silence was heavy but final. I cleared my throat.

"I've got to go. Studio's waiting."

"Okay," she said softly. "If you need anything, call me. I mean it."

"I know." She hung up. I stared at my phone, waiting for relief. It didn't come. I closed my eyes. The memory swallowed me. Aly. She had always been beautiful—blue eyes so striking they could pull me in and make me forget everything else. But that day they weren't bright; they were wide, frantic, blown so big the color barely showed, darting around the room as if searching for a way out. She was hyperventilating. And when she looked at me—really looked at me—her face twisted into something I never wanted to see: terror. Her hair—God, her hair. Jagged, uneven cuts replaced what were once soft waves. Strands stuck out at odd angles, the choppy ends barely grazing the tops of her ears, a brutal echo of how it used to frame her face. It was never supposed to be like that.

She shook so hard it looked as if her body might give out. Her fingers twitched, unsure whether to fight or flee. Each breath jerked her shoulders, tremors running through her without end. I took a step forward, reaching for her, desperate to make her understand, to make her stop.

"Get away from me!" she screamed. Her voice cracked; she fought like her life depended on it—arms flailing, legs kicking, nails scraping across my skin and drawing blood, though I barely felt it.

"Aly, stop." I kept my voice calm, but she only screamed louder.

"Get away! Get away!" Tears streaked her cheeks, sobs gutting the air. I reached for her again and—pain. A blinding crack against my face, the heel of her foot slamming into me before I even saw it coming. The room spun. My vision tunneled. Blackness.

My eyes snapped open, chest rising and falling with uneven breaths. Sunlight streaked the walls, but the nightmare clung to me, stitched into each inhale. The past crept in, sinking its teeth into me. I exhaled, rolling my shoulders, forcing it back. That was then. This was now. I stood and shook it off before it took hold. Bethany was where I wanted to be, where I could breathe, but I had work to do. I'd already lost too much time, and as much as I wanted to turn back—to fall into her and let her pull me out of my own head—I couldn't. The studio would have to be enough.

My hoodie was draped over the chair, and my sneakers were where I'd kicked them off. I grabbed them, pulling them on, barely aware of the motion. I had to move, focus on anything but the spiral. I'd be working through the night, maybe longer. In the studio, I could drown it out. In there, the only thing I had to face was the music.

It was well after one a.m. when I finally finished mixing the project. The studio felt different at night. During the day—even with a closed session—distractions crept in. At night, it was just me, the hum, and the music. No noise. Just control. I clicked the mouse and brought up Bethany's track. I pressed play, and her voice filled the room. *Dangerous Woman*. Her rendition was sexy—sultry, confident. She didn't just sing; she owned it. I leaned back, eyes shut, picturing her in the booth—lips parting around each note, body swaying, lost in the music. She was so damn beautiful. I thought about this morning—how she looked at me, bare and open. She'd sealed her fate with me. Bethany would always be mine. The depth of it hit like a punch to the gut: I fucking loved this woman. Not the kind that faded—but the kind that rewrote everything. I would do anything for her, fight for her, die for her if it ever came to that.

Tara's words haunted me. I should've told Bethany about Aly—but I couldn't. I wasn't just falling for Bethany—I was already gone. She deserved better. I listened again. Bethany had the kind of voice that made the world stop. Her sound didn't just echo—it marked you. Changed you. I'd spent years in the industry working with top talent, and I knew when someone had it. Bethany had it. She was it. So why wouldn't she chase this? Why wouldn't she just go for it? I'd do anything to support her, to make sure she had every opportunity. I had connections—producers, label execs, A&R reps always hunting for the next breakout artist. And then it hit me—like the idea had been waiting all along.

I just had to master the track and get it to the right people. I wasn't her ex feeding her empty promises. I'd make it happen. I could phone in a few favors and place her demo in the hands of someone who'd hear what I heard—someone who would understand that Bethany wasn't an artist you simply listened to; you felt her. My mind was made up. Reaching for the controls, I pressed stop. No more waiting. Fingers flying, I fine-tuned every note, breath, and pause to perfection. I wasn't just going to shop this demo; I was going to get her a deal. She deserved everything. I wouldn't stop until she had it.

26

SIX MONTHS TO THE BOLDEST CHOICE

BETHANY

It had been two months since Kevin and I broke up, for less than a day. Looking back, I'm glad. It was a turning point, a necessary fracture. After we came back together, we were stronger, more honest, and more real. Kevin let me in—not just the easy parts but the ones that haunted him: his brother, Ian—missing. An addict. Heartbreaking.

I can't imagine carrying that. The constant worry, the helplessness of not knowing where someone you love is, whether they're safe, whether they even want to be found. Ian is still missing, and even though Kevin tries to keep moving forward but I can see how much it gnaws at him. Sometimes we're in bed, his arms around me, but his mind is elsewhere. Other times it hits mid-movie, over dinner, or while we walk hand in hand. His jaw tenses, fingers still against mine, eyes darkening like he's staring at something only he can see. He's thinking about Ian.

I never push. I give what I can—a touch, a kiss, a hug. A silent promise. But behind closed doors, when it all threatens to pull him under, I offer him something that no words can fix. He presses me into the mattress, heavy with desperation. His hands roam, searching for solace, control, escape. His lips find mine—rough, urgent—as if afraid I'll disappear if he doesn't hold on tight. But I'm not going anywhere. I give him my body the way he gives me his truth. Completely. My fingers dig in, promising I'm here—that no matter how lost he feels, he can find his way back. When he finally lets go—takes without guilt—I meet him there, molding to him, drowning in him like he drowns in me. In those moments, the pain fades. The world vanishes. As he buries himself in me, whispering my name like it's what tethers him, I know—this is how I love him best. I'm getting really good at that.

Kevin's been there in ways I never expected. Even when I pretend I'm fine or avoid what I'm not ready to face, he sees right through me. He never pushes—never demands. He just stays. I can't avoid this anymore. My father's house—my childhood home—still hasn't been sold. I left it untouched, like the memories I won't unpack. Every time I think about it, my chest tightens. I told myself it was logistics, that I was busy, that I'd get to it eventually. But Kevin saw through it.

When I finally admitted it—told him about the house and how I'd avoided it—he didn't judge. He pulled me into his lap, nuzzled into my hair, lips brushing my neck and sending a rush through me. "I think it's time to confront your past," he murmured, voice soft. His kisses trailed my skin, coaxing me into letting go. My head tilted as his lips brushed my jaw. "You realize," he continued, "the only reason you haven't sold it is because you're not ready to let go."

I stilled, breath catching. His hands traced circles on my thighs. I closed my eyes, letting the truth settle deep. Kevin doesn't let me hide. He caught my lip, guiding my face to his. His stormy gray eyes held nothing but patience.

"I know," I whispered. "I can't put it off any longer. He's been gone six months...and he can't hurt me anymore." His arms tightened, pulling me close. I buried my face in his shoulder. "I'll call the realtor tomorrow morning," I muttered against his skin. He didn't speak. Just held me. It's time to move on.

Katie and I wandered through the aisles of Victoria's Secret, the scent of vanilla in the air as we sifted through lace and silk. I was on a mission—six months with Kevin deserved something special. Six months together, and I wanted to surprise him with something he wouldn't forget. Katie rummaged through racks with a playful grin.

"And maybe I'll find something for myself," she mused, holding up a sheer red babydoll lingerie piece against her frame. She smirked at me. "You know, just in case I ever meet someone actually worth taking my clothes off for."

I laughed, shaking my head as she wiggled her eyebrows. That was Katie—shamelessly confident, effortlessly flirtatious, and completely unbothered by the idea of settling down. I glanced at her, wondering again why she was still single. She was stunning, petite, with striking features that could pass for Lucy Hale's long-lost twin. Men noticed—drawn to her wit and easy laugh. But no matter how many flirtations sparked, she never let them catch fire.

I smiled as she tossed a lacy black number into her bag. She deserved someone who made her feel the way Kevin made me feel. Someone who looked at her like she was the only one in the room.

"I wish you'd let someone in," I murmured, mostly to myself. She turned, catching my expression, and her smirk faltered just slightly before she waved me off with a laugh.

"Trust me, B, I'm good. But you? You better find something that'll blow Kevin's damn mind."

I rolled my eyes and flipped through fabric. I was already picturing the look on Kevin's face. I needed bold—something that didn't whisper confidence but roared it. A piece that told Kevin exactly what I wanted. I wanted him to look at me—and lose control. As we wandered through the store, my eyes caught on something just beyond a mannequin—a flash of fabric so bold it practically dared me to wear it. I stepped closer, and the second I saw it, I knew. Stunning. Daring. Absolutely sinful.

Katie stepped beside me, eyes widening as she took it in.

"You gotta be fucking kidding me," she blurted out. I stood still, heart pounding, imagining Kevin's face when he saw me in it. "Bethany, this is...wow." She let out a low whistle.

"This is bold. Even for me." I ran my fingers over the fabric, anticipation curling through me. Could I pull this off? Yes. A slow smile tugged at my lips as I grabbed the hanger. "I think I'm gonna do it," I said, more to myself. Katie blinked, still processing, but I wasn't second-guessing. This was what I wanted—what I needed Kevin to see me in.

We stood in line. Just as I was about to comment on the ridiculous upcharge on lace, my phone rang—the vibration buzzing against my palm. I glanced down, and the second I saw the name flashing, my stomach soured. Cheyenne. I groaned under my breath, resisting the urge to ignore it. I knew the number by heart—Cheyenne Campbell had been a pain in my ass since we were fourteen. Unfortunately, she was also the only real estate agent in Willow Creek, which meant I had no choice but to deal with her. With a deep inhale, I pressed accept, forcing as much politeness into my voice as I could muster.

"Hi, Cheyenne. What's up?"

"Guess what?!" she shrieked, voice shrill enough that I had to pull the phone away from my ear. "We got a cash offer at asking price! One-eighty! Can you believe that?!" She was so over-the-top giddy, I almost forgot I couldn't stand her. Almost. I pressed my lips together, ignoring the way my fingers clenched around the phone.

"That's great." My tone was neutral, careful. "Any contingencies?"

Katie mouthed, "What's going on?" I covered the receiver.

"Cash offer on the house." Her face lit up. "Oh my God, that's amazing!" Cheyenne was still rambling, barely pausing for breath as she rattled off the details.

"Nothing major! Just a twenty-one-day closing period. They want all personal belongings removed before then, the house in broom-clean condition at closing, and they're taking it as-is. No inspections, no repairs." I should've been relieved, ecstatic even. But the idea of stepping into that house—sorting through the remains of a past I'd spent years outrunning—had me second-guessing. I'd have to fly back to Willow Creek in two weeks. Take time off, clean the house, and go through it one last time. No avoiding it now.

"Send me the offer," I said finally, sealing my fate. "As long as everything checks out, I'll accept."

A high-pitched squeal blasted through the phone. Jesus Christ. "AHHH! Bethany, this is huge! I'll send it over right now!"

"Great," I muttered, rolling my eyes as I ended the call. Cheyenne being unprofessional? No shock.

Katie nudged me. "Congrats!"

"Don't congratulate me yet," I said, slipping my phone into my purse. "I'm gonna need your help."

She raised a brow. "With what?"

"Ever been to Indiana?" Her face went blank. "Uh, no. But sounds like I will."

I smirked. "You sure will." Before she could argue, the cashier waved us forward.

"Next customer!" We paid and left, heading straight home. There was no turning back now. When we got back, Katie wasted no time pulling out two wine glasses and pouring generous amounts. She lifted her glass, smirking at the Victoria's Secret bag on the counter.

"If you're really wearing that tonight," she said, wiggling her brows, "you're gonna need all the liquid courage you can get." She handed me the glass, giggling as I took it. I laughed, lifting it in a silent toast before taking a long, slow sip. Between laughing over old stories, talking about my trip to Willow Creek, and polishing off the bottle, time flew.

When it was finally time to get ready, I took a quick shower, letting the hot water work some of my nerves out. When I stepped out, Katie was already in my bathroom, setting everything up. She pulled a chair to the mirror and motioned for me to sit.

"Alright," she said, tying her hair up in a messy bun. "Tonight, we're going for bombshell." I rolled my eyes but didn't argue. Katie was a magician with makeup and hair—able to turn me into whoever I needed to be. And tonight, I needed to be confident, sexy, in control. She ran her fingers through my damp hair. "We're doing something different."

Normally, I wore my hair straight, but tonight, Katie curled it, letting the loose waves tumble down my back before pinning it up in a classic pin-up style. I hadn't realized how long my hair had gotten—mid-back. In Katie's hands, it was perfect. Next was makeup. She lined my eyes in one clean sweep, brushing on mascara until my lashes looked impossibly long. She handed me the mirror, and I hardly recognized myself. My blue eyes looked electric, standing out like never before. And then came the final touch—ruby red lipstick.

When she stepped back to admire her work, she let out a low whistle. "Damn," she breathed. "You look fucking delicious." I turned to the mirror, and my breath caught. Holy shit. I looked...powerful. The kind of woman who walked in and owned the room. Who knew exactly what she wanted—and how to get it. This was exactly how I wanted Kevin to see me. Katie grinned, satisfied. "Now, go get dressed. It's time to make that man putty in your hands." She tugged me up and swatted my ass. I laughed, shaking my head as I headed to my room. It took longer to get ready, but I didn't care. I missed this—laughing with her, feeling like myself again. A girls' trip—even to Willow Creek—suddenly didn't seem so bad.

I found my long tan Calvin Klein trench coat, pulling it out of the closet before slipping into the lingerie I had picked out earlier. My heart pounded as I fastened the belt, nerves and excitement swirling while I made sure nothing underneath showed. My phone buzzed, Uber was outside. I grabbed my purse and headed for the door. Katie leaned against the counter, smiling as she watched me.

"Good luck," she teased. I tied the belt—one breath, one bold choice—then stepped into the night.

27

— • —

A TASTE OF PLEASURE

KEVIN

Bethany texted out of nowhere—she was on her way. We hadn't made plans, but I wasn't complaining. Truth was, I'd gotten used to spending nights with her—so used to it, my place felt too damn empty without her. A knock at the door pulled me from my thoughts. I didn't waste a second. The second I opened the door, the sight of her knocked the breath out of me. Fuck.

Bethany stood in my doorway like a fucking dream—straight out of a vintage pin-up. Curled hair, sultry makeup, deep-red lips made for sin. And that trench coat—tan, cinched tight, hiding whatever she wore beneath...if anything. My dick stiffened instantly—a reaction I couldn't control. She arched a brow, lips curving into a smirk.

"Are you gonna let me in, or are you planning to let me freeze out here?" Her voice was sultry and playful. I stepped aside, watching her stride past—heels clicking, confidence radiating. I shut the door and locked it—I wasn't letting her leave anytime soon. I turned to face her, drinking her in.

"You look beautiful."

Bethany pouted like I'd insulted her. "Beautiful?" she echoed, tilting her head. Did I say something wrong? "Stunning," I corrected quickly, watching her expression for any sign of approval. She sighed dramatically, pouting even more.

"Stunning?" she repeated, like the word offended her. Shit. I had no idea what I was doing wrong. "Uh—what am I supposed to say?"

I stepped forward, but she backed away, keeping space just to make me crazy. Her face unreadable, eyes locked on mine, dark and teasing. My pulse pounded. Whatever game this was, I was already fucking losing.

"Tonight," she said, her voice dipping lower, softer, "I don't want you to call me beautiful. I don't want you to call me stunning." She reached for the belt, toying with the knot until my breathing turned shallow. "I want you to call me..." She tugged the belt loose and held her coat open, holding it wide so I could take in every inch of what she had on. My body constricted. Jesus. My mouth watered as the coat dropped to her feet. "...sexy as hell."

A devilish smile curved her lips as she spun slowly, letting me drink her in. My breath caught. My body—a loaded spring, ready to snap. She wore a pastel-blue lace bodysuit that looked fucking painted on—sheer in all the right places, just enough to drive me out of my mind. My eyes locked on her tits—full, perfect, straining against that lace like they wanted to be in my mouth. Fuck. My jaw clenched. I was already hard, already imagining them in my hands—heavy, soft, mine. How she'd react when I sucked them, tongued them, bit down just enough to make her squirm. I wanted to rip that lace open with my teeth and bury my face between them until she was grabbing my hair and begging me not to stop.

That bodysuit was fucking evil—white stitching barely covering her, like someone designed it just to fuck with me. The straps ran over her shoulders and down her sides, framing every curve like a damn invitation. Her waist dipped just right, her stomach smooth and soft-looking, and all I could think was how good it would feel under my hands, my mouth, my tongue. She was made to be touched. Licked. Marked. And I was two seconds from tearing that shit off her and giving her everything I'd been holding back.

She turned with grace, dragging it out like she knew she was turning me on. Sweat formed on my skin as my eyes raked down her back, thin straps tracing her spine, dipping to the satin bow at the small of it. But below that? Fuck. Her ass was a goddamn masterpiece—full, round, perfectly framed by lace barely clinging to her hips. The thong—if I could even call it that—was nothing more than a teasing scrap of fabric, sitting high on her waist before disappearing between her cheeks, leaving nothing but bare skin and temptation. My fingers twitched to grab her, cup those perfect curves, sink my teeth into soft flesh, and mark her.

Jesus. I wanted to kiss every inch, run my tongue along the smooth curve of her ass, eat her—hear the way she'd gasp when I took my time devouring her. The way she stood there—knowing exactly where my mind had gone—made it worse. Made me harder. Hungrier. She wasn't just showing off—she was fucking torturing me. My eyes swept lower, and fuck, it just got worse—better. Deadlier. Soft blue garters clipped to lace stockings that clung to her legs like a damn invitation. I hissed, my dick aching as I imagined her spread out beneath me, those garters digging into her skin while I held her open. The contrast of lace against the filthy things I wanted to do had me rock-hard.

Those heels—ivory straps encircling her ankles, elevating her legs—longer, leaner, dangerous. I wanted them on her writhing beneath me, thighs over my shoulders, my face buried between them. My mouth filled with her sweet and soaked. I pictured her bucking, my tongue dragging, thighs gripped tight enough to bruise. The thought made my head spin, teeth grinding until they ached. I wanted to see her like that—heels digging into my back, garters straining, stockings hugging her legs while I ruined her, making her scream my name. She turned, head tilted like she was saying, Well? Turning me into a fucking animal—and loving it.

Bethany was playing a dangerous game—one she couldn't win. She thought she was in control, calling the shots. But in that sheer, teasing outfit, there was no way I was letting her dictate how this would go. I stepped toward her with a predator's grace, eyes locked on hers. We stood on a fault line, both waiting for the shift that would split everything open. She held my gaze, but I saw it—the flicker of anticipation. She wanted the game, but she'd already lost.

I took her chin, tilting her face up until she had to meet my eyes. My voice was rough, thick with hunger.

"You look fucking sexy as hell," I said, my thumb brushing the corner of her mouth. "Just looking at you has my dick hard." Her lips parted with a sharp inhale—but she didn't look away. Brave. Foolish. Perfect.

I pressed against her, making damn sure she felt what she was doing to me. The second my mouth crashed into hers, she melted—soft and yielding, her body molding to mine like she belonged there, like she'd been waiting for me to take what was already mine. The kiss was slow, deep—I wanted her to feel every ounce of restraint I barely held on to.

When I pulled back, her cheeks were flushed, and her breathing was uneven. Yeah. I'd already won.

"Come here," I said, taking her hand. "Let me get a good look at you." I led her to the coffee table, lowering myself onto it, eyes locked on her. My fingers trailed lazily over her left thigh. I took my time, watching her breath hitch as I moved lower, past her knee, all the way to her ankle. I lifted her foot and guided it onto the table beside me. The position left her exposed. Exactly how I wanted her.

A shaky breath escaped her; I felt it more than I heard it. I traced the back of her calf, kneading gently before sliding up her inner thigh. I made slow, teasing circles there, saying nothing—just watching her react: the way her muscles tensed beneath my touch, waiting for something more. Bethany shivered. I smirked.

"So," I said, letting my fingers nudge the strap of her garter before snapping it lightly against her skin. She gasped, jolting. "What's the occasion for this little outfit choice?" Her eyes darted away, a sheepish flicker crossing her face. When she spoke, her voice was barely above a whisper.

"It's our six-month anniversary."

I skimmed my fingers along her thong, tracing the lace, my touch barely there.

"I didn't get you anything," I murmured, voice low and rough. My fingertips pressed just enough to make her squirm. I looked up—eyes dark, full of promise. "We're gonna have to do something about that." I wanted to rip the lace off and claim every inch of her, but I made myself take my time. I wanted her writhing, needing me as badly as I needed her. With just my fingertip, I stroked her over the fabric, feeling her already soaked for me. My dick twitched at the realization.

"I see you like this." My voice held a note of amusement as I met her gorgeous face. Her breath was shaky—eyes closed—but she shook her head, feigning innocence. I smirked. "Good." I hooked a finger into the crotch of her thong and dragged it aside, exposing her silky, bare pussy. The second I touched her, I swallowed a groan. She was dripping. Hot. I traced her folds, slow and teasing, then circled her clit just enough to make her gasp. She trembled, the pulse under my fingertip throbbing. I slid a finger inside. No friction, no resistance, just pure, soaked need. I cursed low and added another, stretching her just a bit; her breath tumbled into a moan. The sound ruined me—soft, hungry, mixed with the obscene smack of my fingers.

She cried out, rocked onto my hand, and fuck—the way she purred had my dick throbbing. If she kept making those noises—kept dripping down my fingers—I wasn't going to last. And when I finally got inside her? There wasn't a chance in hell I'd be gentle.

146

I curled my fingers, and she seized my wrist, body tensing, a broken sound escaping her lips. Nails dug into my skin, but I didn't let up. I wanted that needy little plea. And there it was, trembling past her mouth, her body already about to break. I leaned in, voice rough.

"You think you can walk in here dressed like that and just fuck me?" I tsked, shaking my head. "I don't think so, Bethany."

To prove it, I withdrew my fingers. She gasped, jerking forward, chasing what I'd taken. A frustrated whimper spilled out—and fuck, I felt it in my bones. I was torturing both of us, but she needed to learn—needed to feel how badly I wanted to fuck her. My dick was a ticking time bomb—straining, aching to be buried inside her. But not yet. Not until she broke.

I listened as she tried to steady her breathing. When it came, that soft exhale of surrender, I held her stare, dark and unrelenting, and growled, "By the time I'm done with you, that sweet pussy is going to be so sore, you'll remember this night every time you sit down."

Lifting her heel from the table, I set it gently on the floor. My mind was already ahead, planning exactly how I wanted her. I stood, took her hips, and backed her up, turning her around in one smooth motion. With both hands, I steadied her and reached for the bodysuit, fingers hooking into the thin band of her thong. Slowly, I peeled it down, savoring the way it dragged along her skin—how she stood completely still, barely breathing, waiting. The second the lace slipped past her thighs and pooled at her feet, I dropped to my knees behind her. And fuck. Look at her.

That perfect, creamy ass, framed by the blue garters still hugging her thighs, had my throat tightening, my restraint hanging by a thread. I ached to squeeze her, brand every inch of her—but then an idea hit me.

I smiled as I spoke. "I haven't eaten tonight." My voice was rough, teasing, full of intent. "Get on the couch. Keep your back to me. On your knees." I felt her hesitation—saw the way she stiffened before obeying, stepping forward and placing her hands on the back of the sofa. She dropped to her knees, arching her back. The position was perfect—damn near filthy—and she knew it.

A sweet pain hit my dick—I had to undo my jeans, yank the zipper for relief. The ache was unbearable, the desire to be inside her all-consuming. But first? First, I had to taste her. I spread her knees to the width of my shoulders—no space. Nothing in my way. And then I moved in, inhaling deep. She smelled like pure fucking perfection—warm, sweet, completely drenched for me. I couldn't wait. Couldn't please. I shifted, now sitting on the floor, looking up at her. With one swift motion, my tongue flicked out, fast and hungry, lapping up every drop of her wetness like I'd been starving for it.

Bethany let out a guttural cry—needy, breathless—sending a pulse of want through me. Fuck. This woman was going to be my undoing. My dick swelled, but all I could think about was what was right in front of me. I positioned my head between her legs. And there she was—her glistening cunt spread open just inches from my face, slick and dripping with need. My mouth watered. My fingers tightened on her thighs as I took in the sight—flushed, swollen, waiting.

She started to speak. "What are you..." But didn't finish. I grabbed her thighs and yanked her down onto my face, burying myself in her. Bethany gasped, a broken sound ripping free as her hands flew to my hair. I didn't ease into it. Didn't tease. My tongue slid through her slick folds in fast strokes, dragging over every swollen inch before circling her clit.

The second I had her in my mouth, I groaned against her, keeping her exactly where I wanted. I scraped my teeth over her, just enough to make her quiver, to make her body jolt. I sucked, my lips closing around her, tongue flicking fast and relentless. She cried out, thighs shaking, pushing closer—like she didn't know whether to escape or sink deeper. I needed this. Needed to fuck her with my mouth.

She was intoxicating—pulsing, dripping onto my tongue like the sweetest sin. I lapped her up greedily, drinking in every drop, tongue working her in fast, frantic strokes.

She shook, her moans breathless, broken. I felt her unraveling—her body climbing higher. And I wasn't stopping. Not until she came apart, screaming my name, sopping my tongue the way I needed her to. I felt it—the way her body tightened, every muscle coiling, her breath coming in sharp, panicked gasps. She was teetering on the edge, and I was about to send her flying. One last flick, then a gentle bite to her clit—just enough to push her over. Bethany exploded. Her scream merged with my moans —unrestrained harmony echoing through the room like a lover's song. Her body convulsed, thighs trembling against my face as she came, drenching my mouth, my chin. I didn't stop. I couldn't stop. I swallowed her down, guzzling every drop, letting her release coat my face as I held her firmly in place.

She started to collapse, her body limp. I held her tighter, keeping her balanced as she rode out every last pulse of pleasure. She was light in my arms, delicate, but I could handle her—I wanted to handle her. And when the last tremors faded, when her moans softened into shaky exhales, I finally loosened my hold. She sank onto her knees, her hands grabbing the back of the couch like she needed it to keep from falling. I eased out from beneath her, wiping my mouth with the back of my hand, tasting her lingering on my lips.

My smile was slow, taunting, as I spoke. "That was an amazing appetizer. I think I'm ready for dinner." Bethany's head turned slightly, her voice still thick, dazed.

"Appetizer?" I pushed myself up, standing behind her, my palm molding to the thick curve of her ass, squeezing, testing the give. Tight and sculpted, built from miles of running, from strength and discipline—every inch of her made to be held, fucked, ruined. My fingers flexed, kneading the muscle, and fuck, if I thought I couldn't get any harder, I was dead wrong.

The garter belt hugged her waist, straps stretched across her tight, perfect ass and pulling against her hips, framing the kind of body men lost their minds over. My dick pulsed hard, aching with the need to bury myself so deep inside her she'd feel me for days. The way the lace hugged her only made it worse, made it better—too pretty to rip off, too tempting not to.

I dragged my hands down, tracing the thin straps that disappeared along the back of her thigh-high stockings. My fingers twitched as I skimmed over them, feeling the tension, the way her skin radiated heat even through the fabric. Bethany tossed her head back, her breath ragged, her eyes locking onto mine. Waiting. Daring. I drank her in one last time before a wicked grin curled my lips. She had no idea what was coming next.

"Yes, Bethany. You heard me right. Appetizer." I slapped her ass hard—the crack echoing in the room. Bethany yelped, her body jerking forward slightly. I chuckled, dark and low, stepping out of my jeans and briefs, standing at attention. Pulling my shirt off, I began to stroke myself.

"I meant thoroughly fucked. And I still haven't done that yet." I placed my hand on the small of her back and pressed down, guiding her forward until her upper body lowered, arching her just how I wanted. The sight before me was enough to steal the breath from my lungs—her body, flushed and supple, her curves displayed like something made to be worshiped.

My fingers trailed down, brushing over her swollen, soaked pussy, and I groaned as I gathered her juices, stroking it along the length of my dick. She was already trembling. She was sensitive from what I'd done to her before, but the way her body reacted told me she was ready for more. Ready for me. Positioning myself behind her, I stroked myself at the base and guided the tip to her entrance, caressing the heat of her. The second I pushed forward, the sensation hit me like a lightning strike.

"Fuck," I muttered under my breath, my fingers flexing against her waist as I fought for control. I needed to focus. Think of something else. Baseball. The capital of North Dakota...Boise? No, that wasn't right. It didn't matter. Nothing mattered but this—her. I pushed slowly, feeling her body stretch to take all of me, milking me so tight it was like she was trying to pull me in and never let go. A gasp tore from her lips, her nails digging into the couch, her back arching as she fought to adjust.

She was clinging around me like a fucking dream—hot, slick, and squeezing down so hard it sent a violent shudder through me. Bethany let out a choked moan, hips rolling back, wanting more, her body begging even if her lips hadn't formed the words yet. My fingers digging deep, holding her still, making sure she felt everything—the stretch, there wasn't a single part of her untouched by me. Mine.

"Kevin..." My name fell from her lips in a breathy, trembling sound, and fuck, I felt it everywhere. I bottomed out, burying myself so deep she had no choice but to take it. No space. No room for anything else but this. A growl rumbled from my chest as my forehead fell to her back. She was mine. In this moment, on this couch, she belonged to me.

I started slowing, dragging each thrust out, letting her feel it all—the depth, the way I filled her, the delicious torment of pulling back just enough before slamming back in. Her body shook, caught between the aching spread and the overwhelming pleasure, torn between bracing for more and falling apart completely. She was molding to me, surrendering, and fuck if that didn't make me want to push her even further.

I bent down, chest tight to her back, my breath hot against her ear as I thrust deeper, slamming into that spot that had her gasping for air.

"You feel that?" My voice was rough, thick with control I was barely hanging onto. "How fucking tight you are? How perfect you feel around me?"

Her breath hitched, fingers twisting into the couch as she tried to hold herself together. My hand slid from her waist to her stomach, pressing down just enough to make sure she felt me inside her, to remind her I wasn't going anywhere. A dark chuckle rumbled from my throat as she clenched around me, her body betraying just how much she loved this.

"You like that, don't you?"

Bethany whimpered, her head tipping forward, her body pushing back, taking me deeper, offering herself up like she couldn't take another second without more.

"Yes," she screamed. I gritted my teeth, every muscle in my body wound so damn tight it was a miracle I hadn't cum. My instincts demanded I take her, fuck her the way we both needed—but not yet. Not until I had her exactly where I wanted her. Not until she was undone beneath me, pleading for it.

I slowed, drawing it out, letting her feel every inch of me. I spoke, my voice laced with promise.

"Do you trust me?" Bethany let out a soft murmur. "Yes."

"Do you want to cum hard? Like you've never come before?" I punctuated my words with a slow, deep roll of my hips. She gasped, her hands fisting against the couch.

"Yes," she yelled. I reached down, caressing the curve of her ass, savoring the feel of her bare skin beneath my palm. She pushed back against me, moving in time with my rhythm, letting herself sink deeper into bliss. I dragged my thumb along the rim of her ass, coaxing a reaction. I pushed in. Her body tightened, my lips brushed the shell of her ear.

"I promise you'll like it," I said. "You'll cum so hard, Bethany. I want to hear you scream my name." I nipped at her ear before pressing soft, open-mouthed kisses along every exposed inch of her back, feeling the tension in her body dissolve with each touch. The moment she relaxed, I moved again.

My thumb stayed right where it was, giving her time to adjust to the sensation, and when I felt her body fully surrender to me. I slowed my thrusts, dragging out each stroke as I leaned down, my lips brushing against the small of her back. Her skin was hot beneath my mouth, her body already shaking from how deep I was inside her. I traced my tongue along the dip of her spine, taking my time, tasting her, before pressing an open-mouthed kiss just above the curve of her ass.

Bethany let out a desperate, breathless sob, her voice quivering with want as she begged, "Please, Kevin...don't stop. I need this. I need you." I lifted my thumb to my lips, sucking it, wetting it thoroughly before pulling it free. But that wasn't enough. I wanted to make sure she felt it, that she was drenched, that there was nothing between us but heat and need.

I licked the center of her back again, this time with enough pressure, enough spit, to let it pool before it began its slow descent, trailing down the crease of her ass. I watched, mesmerized, as it slid lower, teasing, marking her, making my dick throb inside her.

Her body shuddered, her fingers clinging to the couch like she needed to hold on to something—anything to keep from completely losing herself.

"Oh God," she exhaled, her voice shaky, the words falling from her lips in a breathless plea. That was my cue. I picked up my pace, slamming into her, making sure every movement sent her reeling, had her too caught up in the pleasure to notice what I was about to do next—until she did.

The second my thumb pressed inside her, she gasped. Her body was rigid before melting all at once, the needy sounds slipping from her lips. My other hand tightened around her hip, holding her in place as I eased my thumb inside, slow, working her open as I continued to drive into her.

"Just take it. Let me have you." A ragged moan tore from her lips, her body shuddering in response. "That's my good girl," I groaned, feeling her get even wetter around me. So perfect. So fucking mine. My other hand slid beneath her, finding her breast, freeing it from the lace that barely held it. I rolled her nipple between my fingers, tugging her up so that her back angled closer to me.

"Kevin," she gasped, her voice thick with pleasure. Her moans had turned louder, needier. Plunging deep, could feel the way her body tightened, barely holding on, so close to coming undone. Her walls clenched around me, gripping me like a fucking vice, hot and soaked, pulling me in, demanding more.

Every drag, every stroke, sent a jolt of pure pleasure straight up my spine, making it damn near impossible to hold on. She was squeezing me, milking me, her body begging for release, and fuck if I wasn't right there with her, teetering between control and complete fucking ruin.

"I want you to cum with me, Bethany," I growled, my pace becoming faster, unstoppable.

She was falling apart. Sweat dripped from my forehead, landing between the crack of her ass, mixing with the heat of her skin. Our bodies were slick with sweat, the heat between us intoxicating, her body taking everything I gave, every deep, punishing thrust. "Cum with me, Bethany," I pleaded, my voice rough, worn out.

Bethany's breathing turned frantic, each exhale breaking apart as her body stiffened. Her hips bucked, her back arching as she gasped, voice shaky.

"Oh—my—God," she choked out, her words splintering between moans. "It feels...I can't...I'm about to—" Her body seized up, muscles tightening like she was trying to hold on, trying to fight it, but it was useless. I knew I had her, knew she was near. And then I felt it—the tremor, the first crack in her control.

She was pulsing around me, and that was all it took. I slammed into her one final time, sinking so deep I swore I could feel her heartbeat around me. A guttural groan ripped from my chest as the last thread of my control snapped, pleasure detonating through me in a violent, consuming wave. Her scream and mine merged into one, a perfect, unrestrained harmony, echoing through the room like a lover's song—beautifully unbound and all-consuming. The moment she shattered, I followed.

My fingers dug into her hips as I pulsed inside her, filling her, claiming her. My mind went blank, lost in the way she squeezed me, taking every last drop. My vision blurred, pleasure so intense it bordered on being unbearable, leaving me breathless, spent, completely hers. I slowly slid out, wincing at the loss. My hands lingered on her waist, reluctant to break the connection. Bethany stayed where she was, breathing deep and slow, arms draped over the couch. She looked beautifully ruined—flushed skin, relaxed limbs, forehead resting on the cool wall.

Heading toward my bedroom, though part of me didn't want to leave her even for a second. At the dresser, I grabbed a pair of boxer briefs and a T-shirt before making my way to the bathroom. The light flicked on, and there I was—hair a mess, skin dewy, lips swollen from devouring her. I smirked. The look of satisfaction was undeniable. Turning the faucet on, I let the water warm before soaking a washcloth and wringing it out just enough. The distance from her made me restless. I shut off the water and headed back, towel in hand.

Bethany hadn't moved—still lost in whatever world she'd drifted into, unaware of my return. Her eyes were shut, breathing even, head bowed.

"Bethany, you okay?"

She hummed softly. "Hmm? Uh...yeah. That was..." She pushed off the couch, legs wobbling as she stood. Her voice was still thick, dreamy. "Amazing." Her lashes fluttered open, locking onto mine. That look—soft, vulnerable, unguarded—tightened my chest. I smiled at her.

"Yeah, it was," I said, stepping closer. "Come here. Let me clean you up."

She let me—no protest. Just trust. I knelt in front of her, towel in hand, and gently wiped her clean. When the cloth met her skin, she shivered, breath catching—something dark and possessive tightening inside me. I stood up, letting my hands glide over her arms before gently turning her around so her back was to me. I traced the elegant curve of her spine. "We need to get you out of this."

She exhaled, already relaxed beneath my touch. When I reached the first clasp of her bodysuit, I unhooked it with ease, the fabric loosening slightly under my fingers.

"If you stay in this," I said, fingers trailing to the second hook, undoing it, "we'll never rest." Bethany let out a small laugh, breathy and sweet, and fuck if that didn't make my heart ache.

I slid the straps from her shoulders, watching as the delicate fabric slipped down her body, falling to her feet. As if drawn by an invisible force, she slowly turned to face me, her eyes meeting mine. She didn't move to cover herself, didn't shy away. She stood—bare, beautiful, trusting—like she knew she was completely mine. I bent down, removing her thigh highs and heels. I reached for the T-shirt, sliding it over her head, letting the fabric fall over her small frame. It swallowed her in my scent, and seeing her in my shirt—taken care of—settled something deep in me.

I stood, wiping myself clean before stepping into my boxer briefs, my body still thrumming with the aftershocks of her. And as I looked at her again, standing there in my clothes, still flushed from what we'd just done, I knew—I'd never seen anything more perfect in my life.

I guided her onto the couch with me, settling back as she curled into my side, her body fitting perfectly against mine. Wrapping my arms around her, I held her close, breathing in the soft scent of her skin. She nestled her face into my chest, her fingers lightly tracing over my side as if she needed to keep touching me.

"Are you cold?" I murmured, reaching for the throw blanket she bought me a couple of weeks ago.

"Not really," she answered dreamily, her voice soft, barely there. Still, I covered us both, tucking the blanket around her before running my hand down her thigh, caressing her gently.

"Did I hurt you?"

Bethany shook her head, just slightly.

"No," she whispered.

Relief crept in. I kissed her—soft, slow, lingering. I love this woman. Having her in my life is a true blessing. I'm lucky I found her. I kissed her forehead, my lips resting there.

"Thank you for the anniversary present."

Bethany let out a soft laugh, her fingers grazing over my skin. "I should be thanking you."

I chuckled. "The pleasure was all mine."

She shifted slightly, and I noticed the pins in her hair starting to loosen. As she reached up to remove them, I caught her hand.

"I got it."

Carefully, I worked the pins free, letting her hair tumble down in soft waves around her face. My fingers sifted through it, pushing the long strands back, watching the way her lashes fluttered as she began to drift.

"I love the way you did your hair," I said, brushing my knuckles against her cheek. "Who did it?"

"Katie," she mumbled, her voice thick with sleep. "Worked her magic."

"Remind me to thank her. And send a tip."

Bethany smiled, her eyes barely open. "Before I forget to tell you..." she yawned, nuzzling closer. "I got a cash offer on my father's house. At asking price." I felt her words settle.

"Congratulations," I said, tightening my hold on her, placing a kiss to the top of her head. "Contingencies?"

"Yeah," she said, her voice growing softer. "But for the most part, it's simple. The only thing is, I'll have to go down in two weeks to clean the house out. Twenty-one-day closing."

My mind immediately started working. Could I take time off? I wasn't sure—I had three major projects due, and the money from them wasn't something I could afford to pass up. I was still calculating when Bethany tugged my hand, pulling me back.

"Sorry," I said. "What were you saying?" She let out a small breath of laughter.

"I knew you were in your head..." She paused, kissing my chest before continuing, "I was saying, I know you probably want to come down and help, but if you don't mind, I want Katie to come with me."

I arched a brow. "Katie?" Bethany nodded and kissed the middle of my chest.

"Since you and I got together, we haven't spent as much time with each other. She's in her final year of school, and since her winter break coincides with the cleanup schedule, I'm turning it into a girls' trip."

I let her words settle before nodding. "That's perfectly fine with me, Bethany. I'd love to go, but I'm swamped at work. You two have a good time." She hummed, sinking deeper into my hold. I dragged my fingers gently down her spine, feeling the way she relaxed further, her breathing evening out.

"Get some rest," I murmured. "We'll lie here a bit before heading to bed." Less than five minutes later, she was asleep in my arms, her body tucked against mine, completely at peace. I held her closer, listening to her breathe, her warmth settling into me like she belonged. And she did. This—her, us, everything—was exactly where it was always meant to be.

28

WINTER'S BITE

BETHANY

Two weeks passed in a blink, the countdown slipping away faster than expected. Katie and I had no trouble getting time off—she worked part-time anyway, and I had vacation saved up. With everything booked, we were set for a sleepover-style getaway—just us, movies, and overdue best friend time. I didn't argue. It had been a while since we'd spent real time together, and this trip was about more than clearing out my dad's house.

On the morning of our flight, we left before the sun had even thought about rising. The airport was busy but manageable, and after a smooth flight, we finally touched down in Fort Wayne.

The second we stepped outside, an icy gust slammed into us. Katie was not prepared for the weather.

"Oh, hell no! I want to go back to Santa Monica," she groaned, hugging herself.

I couldn't help but laugh at the sheer misery on her face. I warned her—multiple times—to dress in layers, but of course, she didn't listen. Instead, she had shown up in what she thought was a winter outfit: a thin, long-sleeved brown shirt, black yoga pants, and a scarf that did little to shield her from the biting cold. Her *coat* was a lightweight California jacket, better suited for a breezy beach evening than a brutal Midwestern winter. Californians had no real clue what winter actually meant for the rest of the country.

At least she had somewhat heeded my warning about footwear. Her feet were tucked into dark brown Uggs instead of her usual flip-flops—a small victory on my part. But judging by how she shivered like a leaf in a storm, that small win wasn't helping much. Meanwhile, I was bundled like a pro—cozy and layered, exactly how a Midwest winter demands. I was perfectly fine. Comfortable, even. Katie dashed to the rental car fumbling with her duffle bag as she dove into the passenger seat. I strolled over while she glared at me through the windshield, eyes full of betrayal.

As soon as I climbed in, she barked, "Turn on the car. Heat. Now!" I burst out laughing, my breath fogging the air as I caved. The second the engine roared to life, I cranked up the heat, watching as she huddled closer to the vents like her life depended on it. "This is abuse." Katie shivered. I chuckled and shifted into drive.

"Next time, just listen to me."

"Never," she shot back, voice muffled by her scarf. Shaking my head, I pulled out of the lot, the warmth finally spreading through the car as we set off toward the hotel. Since this was our first girls' trip, I wanted to go all out. No corners cut, no budget motels with stiff sheets and flickering lights—I wanted something that felt like an experience. So, when we pulled up to The Bradley Hotel, I couldn't help but feel a little smug.

I'd never stayed there before. Not because I didn't let myself, but because I couldn't. There was never a moment in my life when dropping this kind of money on a hotel was even an option. As a thrift store employee, I barely made enough to cover my bills, let alone splurge on something like this. Every paycheck was stretched thin—rent, groceries, gas. Luxury wasn't in the budget. But now I finally had a chance to experience something different. Plush robes, room service, and a bathroom big enough to spin around in—things I had only ever seen in movies. For once, I wasn't just looking—I was here. Check-in was smooth. The front desk staff were polished and professional, greeting us like we belonged. No sideways glances, no forced politeness like they sensed I usually stayed where the carpets were stained and the water was iffy. This? This was different.

I let Katie walk into the room first, already knowing what was waiting on the other side of that door. Katie stepped inside and gasped.

"Holy shit!" she shrieked, spun, dropped her bag, and launched into a full-body hug. I laughed, stumbling back.

"Calm down! You're squeezing the life out of me!" She finally let go, grinning like a kid on Christmas. While she ran around touching everything, I took my time soaking it in.

Deep blue and green tones gave the room a cozy, boutique feel, like something out of a design magazine. Two massive beds sat side by side, dressed in crisp white linens with textured gray throws folded at the foot. The headboards were floral and intricate, giving the space a touch of elegance. Each detail felt deliberate. A sleek desk sat beneath a modern lamp, paired with a mustard-yellow chair for a pop of color. But the bathroom? That was what sealed the deal.

I stepped inside, boots clicking against deep-blue tile. It looked like a spa—soaking tub, marble counters, gold finishes. The vanity stretched across one wall, dark blue with gold accents, double sinks, and neatly rolled towels stacked beside them. But the wallpaper got me—zebra print. Bold, unexpected. Just enough personality without going overboard.

This was the kind of hotel I used to see in movies, the kind I never thought I'd actually stay in. But here I was, standing in the middle of it, and for once, I wasn't thinking about the price tag or if I deserved it. I just let myself enjoy it.

"Okay, this is officially the best decision you've ever made," Katie said, flopping onto one of the beds. I grinned, setting my bag down.

"Yeah," I said, looking around one last time. It really was.

I kicked off my boots and sprawled onto the other bed with a satisfied groan. The mattress swallowed me whole. I stretched, arms above my head, sinking into bliss.

"Oh my God," I sighed, rolling onto my stomach, my fingers curling into the plush comforter. "This bed feels amazing. I wish I could ship it straight to my bedroom."

Katie sighed. "I know. Can't we just stay here forever?" She turned onto her side, facing me, her expression half-dreamy, half-serious. I rolled to my side and propped my head on my hand.

"I wish, but we both know that's not happening. We can't afford to live like this," I said, nose scrunched in mock disappointment. "And I'm not blowing my savings pretending we can." I pouted, and Katie mirrored me. We burst into laughter at the same time. I took a breath and cleared my throat. "I was thinking..." I said. "We can start clearing my father's house tomorrow. Today, let's just stay here and rest. Jet lag's real—I already feel like a zombie." I slid my arms under the pillow. "The hotel has a restaurant and a rooftop bar. We can eat here, keep it easy. Though I'm not about to freeze my ass off drinking on a rooftop in this weather. What do you think?"

Katie sat up, shrugged off her jacket, and gave me that unreadable look she always wore when something serious was coming. "It sounds like a good idea," she said. After a beat, she asked, "Are you okay with being here again?"

I exhaled slowly, staring at the ceiling before meeting her eyes. "First, thank you for being here. There's no one else I'd rather have—not even Kevin." She nodded. "You already know how I feel about this place. About him." I swallowed hard. "I've talked to Kevin about a lot of it, but you...you've seen it."

I drew a deep breath and forced out the truth that sat like a rock in my chest.

"This week is going to be hard. Harder than the funeral. That house was my prison. It's where I learned silence, shrinking, survival on his terms." My throat burned, but I kept going. "Going back to that town...everyone there still calls me 'Bethy,' still sees the pastor's quiet daughter. And now I have to sort his things—pieces of my past that used to mean everything."

I sighed.

"I know I'll cry. I know there'll be moments when I want to walk out. But I need this. I need to let go—to move forward." I managed a small smile. "I'm ready." Katie squeezed my hand. That was enough.

We spent the day drifting between naps and room-service bliss—grilled sandwiches, truffle fries, chocolate mousse—lounging in fluffy robes like queens.

We eventually showered and headed to Arbor Restaurant. Candlelight danced across navy banquettes and coral chairs, dark floral wallpaper broken by gold-framed mirrors and bold abstract art. Something rich and buttery scented the air.

"This is definitely date-night vibes," Katie whispered. "Maybe one day I can eat somewhere like this with an actual adult male."

I smirked, eyeing the intimate tables and imagining Kevin's hand brushing mine. A sigh slipped out. I grabbed Katie's hand with mock gallantry as the hostess approached.

"I can't give you what you need, but I'll try to be a good substitute. My lady."

"You're ridiculous." She giggled. Menus, cosmos, and laughter followed. "So," Katie began, "have you talked to Kevin? Must be withdrawals not being attached at the hip."

I rolled my eyes. "We can manage, thank you."

She moved closer. "You never told me what you did for your anniversary. Did he love it?" Heat rushed through me.

I pressed my thighs together under the table. "I am not talking about that here," I hissed.

"Oh, so he definitely loved it." She sipped smugly. Then, softer: "Come on, you're the only one of us having sex. Let me live through you." She flagged the waiter. "Another round?"

I stared. "I haven't even finished my first."

"Well, hurry up and catch up."

I groaned and tossed back the last of my drink. "Fine." I gave her just enough to satisfy her curiosity—nothing scandalous enough to scorch the linen. Cocktails flowed, laughter rose, and by dessert, Katie was swirling the final sip of her Cosmo.

"Where can I find my Kevin? This guy gives you your first orgasm, makes you his top priority, thoroughly—" brow waggle "—fucks you." She burst into giggles.

I tossed my napkin. "Shut up."

Her expression softened, turning serious. She reached across the table, took my hand, and squeezed. "And he loves you."

I knew Kevin loved me; I felt it in my bones.

I squeezed her hand back. "One day you'll find your guy. You're too amazing not to. And when it happens, we're double-dating."

"Yeah, right. I only attract losers and idiots." She snorted. I shook my head but let it drop. We rose—stomachs full, heads light from cosmos—and curled beneath the blankets to watch 13 Going on 30, one of our favorites. The last thing I remembered was Katie's soft laughter, the TV's glow, and the comfort of knowing I was loved.

I woke restless, my body tense, before my mind caught up. A sinking feeling settled in my gut. Today is the day. Willow Creek loomed like a storm cloud—heavy and inescapable. I stared at the ceiling, wishing I could slow, rewind, or freeze time—but it marched on, and the hardest day since my father's funeral had arrived, ready or not.

I rolled over and checked my phone: five a.m. Too early to be up, too late to sleep in. Lying there felt suffocating, so I slipped from the covers, careful not to wake Katie, and changed in the bathroom. It was too cold outside for a run, so I headed to the hotel gym. It was empty. Good. I needed the silence. After a stretch beside the treadmill, I slipped on my headphones, cued my Fleetwood Mac playlist, and tapped The Chain. As the first notes hit, I eased into a jog, my feet finding the driving beat. Movement helped, but memories clawed up—my father, and our last conversation.

Three years had passed since that call. I'd just started at the thrift store when the phone rang. Busy helping a customer, I barely noticed until my coworker James called out, "Bethany, phone for you." No one ever called me at work. Unease crawled up my spine as I took the receiver.

"Um...hello?"

A voice I hadn't heard in years—deep and commanding—answered.

"Bethy, this is your father." Cold fear crashed in, knocking the breath from my lungs. My stomach twisted in on itself. Time collapsed, pulling me into childhood shadows. I was no longer a grown woman in a thrift store—I was a little girl again, small and powerless.

I could feel his presence towering over me, his shadow stretching across the floor. My father's voice filled every room—not with comfort, but with authority that demanded obedience. His sermons were loud and unrelenting, hammering the pulpit like a stone. I remembered my tiny hands clutching the hem of my Sunday dress, fingers twisting fabric while he roared about sin and redemption, veins bulging, face flushed with conviction. I sat perfectly still in the front pew—too afraid to move, too afraid to breathe wrong. His words weren't to inspire—they were to control.

Now, after years of freedom, his voice was in my ear again, dragging me back. My knuckles whitened around the phone. I couldn't move. Couldn't breathe. His voice tightened like a noose, squeezing the air, wrapping me in chains I thought I'd broken.

"Are you there?" His voice was harsh, demanding. I swallowed hard as the old fear rose—thick, suffocating, pulling me under. For a fleeting second, my voice wavered, small and uncertain. Then something shifted inside me—like a door bursting open. No. Not anymore. I wasn't that scared little girl who cowered beneath his booming voice, who bent under the weight of his control.

I'd clawed my way out—built something real, something mine, where my choices were mine. I'd spent years silencing myself to survive. But I wasn't small anymore. I gritted my teeth, forcing my voice to stay strong.

"How did you find me?"

"We need to talk," he said, ignoring the question.

"I can't talk right now. I'll call you back."

"I need to talk to you right now. Do you hear me?" His anger sliced through the line like a blade.

"You're calling me at work," I said, steel in my voice. "I'll call you back on my break. Do not call me here again." I hung up before he could speak, hands trembling. I shut my eyes, taking deep, even breaths. He's not here. He's not here.

The rest of my shift crawled by, the call looping until the thrift store walls closed in. When my break finally came, I bolted outside. I dialed *67 before his office number, blocking my ID. He'd found me once; I wasn't making it easier.

162

He answered on the first ring.

"Father," I said, voice distant.

"Bethany, how dare you disrespect me like that?" he thundered. "I did not raise you to be rude and ungrateful! The Bible commands you to honor your father and mother, but instead, you disgrace me with your defiance. Do you think you are above God's law? Do you think you can just turn your back on your own flesh and blood without consequences?"

I clutched the wheel. "How did you find me?"

"I did not raise you to be defiant," he snapped. "You have lost your way, Bethany. You need to come home, repent, and beg the Lord's mercy for your rebellion. This world has poisoned you, filled your head with nonsense, but I will not stand by and watch my own daughter stray from righteousness. You will come home, and you will do as you are told. Do you hear me, Bethany Martin?"

My name sounded like a verdict. He didn't see me—never had. I pinched my nose as anger simmered. He kept going—demanding, condemning—each word a hammer strike. Come home. Repent. Obey. Submit.

Something snapped. "Stop talking!" I exploded, voice shaking with everything I'd held back.

Silence followed—I'd stunned him.

"You don't control me anymore." My voice cut like a blade. "You don't tell me where I belong or who I should be. Those days are over. I will never come back to you, your church, or Willow Creek. That chapter is closed. Do not call me again. Do not call my work. If you can't respect my choices, we have nothing left to say." He didn't argue. He simply hung up. That was the last time we spoke.

The Chain by Fleetwood Mac thundered in my ears. I cranked the treadmill and ran—harder, faster—until my legs burned and my mind went quiet. An hour later, I staggered off, drenched in sweat but still heavy-hearted. Upstairs, Katie paused mid-stretch.

"How was the gym?" she asked, voice light, eyes knowing.

"Good," I muttered, hand raised before she could pry. "Shower time—we need to leave in an hour and a half." I disappeared into the bathroom, letting hot water pound down, hoping it would wash away what refused to leave.

29

NO PLACE LIKE HOME

BETHANY

The drive to Willow Creek was quiet. I felt bad—Katie had come all this way, and I barely had the energy to hold a conversation. But she understood. She always did. She scrolled her phone, fingers absent-minded, giving me space without making a show of it. As we pulled off the highway exit, I cleared my throat, breaking the stillness.

"I'm sorry I'm so temperamental this morning. Between the hangover and coming here, I didn't get any sleep."

Katie set her phone in her lap. "I totally get it. You needed to mentally prepare, so I thought I'd give you space. Don't worry about it." Of course, she understood—Katie never bailed when things got hard.

"Thank you." I turned my focus back to the road. As we crested the last hill before town, I lifted a hand in a mock-grand gesture. "Welcome to Willow Creek."

Katie's head swiveled, taking it in. "Wow." She peered out the window. "No wonder you left this place." The two-lane highway stretched endlessly, disappearing into the horizon like a path to nowhere. The town itself sat in a quiet valley, thick trees hemming it in as though hiding it from the rest of the world.

Willow Creek was the kind of town time forgot. Katie rolled down her window, and the crisp scent of burning wood filled the car, curling into my lungs like a ghost of childhood. We turned onto Main Street—if you could call it that. The town's heartbeat was a short stretch of brick-front buildings: a diner, a gas station, a post office, and the thrift store where people traded more gossip than goods.

The streets were lined with houses that had seen better days, their peeling paint whispering of years gone by. Most were old Victorians or farmhouse styles, porches sagging where rocking chairs once creaked through quiet conversations. Some yards were pristine, flags hanging still. Others looked abandoned—rusted pickups on cinder blocks, relics of another time. Fences were mostly for show. No one locked their doors unless they had a reason to. And then there was the church.

My father's church—the tallest in town, with its white steeple piercing the sky. An unshakable monument to everything I'd tried to leave behind. On Sundays, its lot would be full of people in their best clothing, shaking hands, offering smiles that never quite reach their eyes.

"That's where I spent most of my youth." Bitterness clung to every word. Katie glared at the building, lips pressed into a tight line. Her indignation made me smile. I loved how protective she was.

I turned down a desolate road, the town shrinking in the rear-view mirror as the landscape stretched open. The last row of houses gave way to sprawling fields, golden and endless, patched with grazing cattle and the skeletons of barns leaning precariously against the wind. Finally, we arrived. I pulled up to the last house on the block and shifted into park. Neither of us moved at first.

Stepping out, I let my eyes settle on the house. It looked taller than I remembered, a two-story shell that had been full with the comings and goings of churchgoers but now stood quiet and emptied out. The wraparound porch sagged under neglect. Faded yellow paint peeled back to weathered wood; the white trim had dulled to gray, curling at the corners. The roof held, but time had left its mark. Soot streaked the chimney, and the porch railing bowed where too many hands had leaned. A tattered wreath still hung on the front door—from some forgotten Christmas. The yard wasn't wild or tended—just tired. Brown grass tangled with weeds pushed through the brick walkway. Two old planters flanked the steps, their flowers long dead and gray. The whole place felt suspended, waiting for someone to breathe life into it. I was glad it wouldn't be me.

Every instinct screamed to turn around, get in the car, and catch a flight to LA—leave this behind like a bad dream. The temptation was so strong that my feet felt cemented.

"Come on." Katie squeezed my hand. "You got this. You're not alone. We'll do it together." I nodded and stepped forward. The front stairs creaked beneath my feet, just as I remembered. I swung the old screen door open; Katie caught it, holding it in place as if afraid it might slam and trap me outside forever.

My fingers trembled as I fished out the key. It felt heavier than it should, cool metal biting into my palm. I slid it into the lock—first the familiar resistance, then the subtle give. My hand hovered over the doorknob. I wasn't ready.

"I can do this. I can do this. I can do this." The mantra slipped out in a whisper, more plea than affirmation. With one last breath, I turned the knob. The door swung open, and I stepped inside. I kept my eyes shut. The air was thick with stillness, scented with aged wood. Exhaling, I forced my eyes open. It was like stepping into a time machine.

Everything was as I'd left it five years ago. The furniture, muted colors, and eerie stillness made the place feel untouched, as if I'd never left. My father didn't believe in comfort. Everything here had to serve a purpose—or it didn't belong. No extras. No softness. Just structure. The room was as lifeless as the memories trapped inside. I swallowed hard and stepped in. A stiff brown couch faced a matching loveseat, both untouched, like museum pieces. A red-and-white quilt draped over the back, its colors faded with age. I remembered sitting there as a child, feet dangling, listening to my father read scripture. That couch had never offered comfort.

In front of it sat a brownish-orange coffee table piled with religious books, their spines creased, pages ink-marked. The Bible lay on top, its cracked leather cover worn from years of his hands pressing it open. It had always been present, more than love ever was.

The loveseat beside it bore the same permanent grooves from Bible-study nights. I still heard the hum of prayer, the rustle of pages, the silence when he spoke. The walls were eggshell white—blank, cold. No family photos. No framed memories. Just a tarnished cross, shadow haloed in dust. Across from it hung The Last Supper, glass smudged, the solemn faces locked in devotion. I used to wonder if any of them felt trapped, too.

A lump formed in my throat. The house hadn't changed—but I had. The bang of the screen door snapped me back to reality. Katie stepped inside, boots scuffing the floor, eyes sweeping the room with disgust and disbelief.

"This is where you grew up?" she asked, nose scrunching at the lifeless space. Before I could answer, she hip-checked me, hard enough to send me stumbling.

"What the hell, Katie?" I caught myself on the ugly brown couch. She giggled.

"Had to snap you out of it. You looked like you'd seen a ghost."

I exhaled, rolling my shoulders. She wasn't wrong; memories had swallowed me whole.

"Thanks. I needed that." The fog lifted—just a little. Katie wandered, poking at the furniture. Then she stopped, hands on hips.

"Where's the TV?"

"You won't find one. My father didn't believe in them."

"Wait. Ever?"

"Ever," I confirmed. "I used to go to friends' houses just to watch Saturday morning cartoons. This place was all scripture, all the time." Her shudder made me smile—proof I wasn't trapped here, just passing through. In a corner sat a neat stack of boxes. Cheyenne had arranged their delivery—efficient as ever, already organizing the donations.

"How do you want to start this?" Katie shrugged off her sweater and draped it over the loveseat. I unzipped my jacket and tossed it onto the couch.

"The house isn't that big—living room, kitchen, two bathrooms, two bedrooms, and my father's office. The big stuff gets picked up Thursday night, so we'll stage everything in here for now."

The walls still felt like they were closing in, the past pressing at my back.

"As much as I'd love to give you the grand tour, I need to ease into it. Let's start simple—the living room and kitchen. The kitchen should take a couple of hours if we work together. Before we leave, we'll walk the rest of the house and make a game plan. Sound good?"

"Sounds great." Katie clapped. "Anything in here you actually want to keep?"

"Absolutely not."

She grinned. "Good. Then let's get to work." We cleared the living room, stripping away a past I had no intention of keeping. Having Katie here made everything easier; somehow, she could turn even the most unbearable situations into something almost fun. She kept me laughing, her jokes easing the tension that had lived in my chest since I walked in. At one point, we started reminiscing, letting the past distract us in a way that felt safe. I nearly doubled over when she mentioned convincing me to get my nose pierced.

"You were so dramatic." She grinned, shoving a box toward the door. "I swear you almost cried before the needle even touched your skin!"

"I did not!" I feigned offense, though we both knew she was right.

"You clutched my arm like I was walking you into surgery."

I groaned. "Okay, fine. But at least I didn't almost pee myself in a nightclub."

Katie froze. "You wouldn't."

"Oh, but I would." I leaned against the counter, smirking. "Remember? The women's line snaked around the building, so you bolted into the men's room and peed in a urinal."

167

"Bethany!"

I dodged the dish towel she hurled at me, cackling.

"Don't you dare tell anyone that story! Seriously, I had no choice—and the way those guys looked at me!"

"Some looked horrified—some looked a little turned on." We broke out into breathless laughter. For a moment, the house didn't weigh me down; it was just us—two best friends, laughing like always.

"Hello?" The single word sent an icy shock through me. Cheyenne stepped into the kitchen, polished heels clicking on worn linoleum. My laughter died. The moment soured. "Oh, Bethy, there you are! I was knocking. Did you hear me?" Her voice was polite, but her eyes told another story. She stood like she owned the room, emerald-green pantsuit tailored to perfection, a satin-purple blouse making her eyes pop. Glossy black hair framed high cheekbones and a sculpted nose. Minimal makeup, pink lips, silver hoops, that dainty heart-shaped locket—every detail intentional. To anyone else, she was poised, polite, perfect. But I knew better.

I rolled my eyes, biting back words. Cheyenne was a polished veneer hiding something insidious. She was the snake that slithered close, pretending to be your friend, only to strike when you least expected it. Before I left, I discovered she'd been the one who exposed my YouTube channel to my father. She knew exactly what it would cost me: his disappointment, judgment, and punishment. Meanwhile, she'd lived a double life—partying, attending community college, breaking rules beneath the illusion of perfection. Her father had been my father's right hand for as long as I could remember; by all accounts, we should have been close. She'd never seen me as a friend. Maybe she hated me. Now, forced to work with Willow Creek's only realtor, I had no choice but to deal with her. My body tensed on instinct.

"Apparently not." Katie's tone sharpened. "Do you usually just walk into someone's home without an invitation?"

Cheyenne smiled. "In Willow Creek, we don't wait to be let into friends' homes. Everyone is family. This house was like a second home to me, especially for the last five years." Her eyes flicked to me, a silent reminder that I'd been gone. Katie folded her arms as Cheyenne stepped forward and extended a manicured hand. "I'm Cheyenne Campbell. And you are?"

Katie shook it firmly. "Katie—Bethany's roommate. Best friend."

I sighed. "I go by Bethany now, Cheyenne. What's up?"

She leaned against the counter. "Just checking on you—seeing if you need a hand." I raised an eyebrow.

"Sure looks like you came to help."

"Oh, honey, I wouldn't be physically helping—more like managing your time. Just like old times. You always had trouble finishing school projects."

Katie inhaled, but I cut in. "People evolve, Cheyenne. They change. They move out of town; they don't all stay stuck." Something flickered across her face. She recovered fast, eyes narrowing.

"Is that a nose ring?"

I barely moved. She smiled, triumphant. "Boy, if your father could only see that," she mused, shaking her head. "He would've had a fit."

Katie stepped closer. "Well, he's not. And Bethany's a grown woman who can do whatever she wants with her body."

Cheyenne's eyes slid between us. Fingertips traced idle circles in the dust before she lifted her hand to let the light catch a delicate ring.

"Oh—did I tell you? I'm engaged." Katie and I glanced down at the dainty band.

Katie tilted her head. "Oh, is that what that is? An engagement ring?" I nudged Katie's foot.

"Who's the lucky guy?" I kept my voice bland.

"No one you know. He moved here after you...ran away." She said it lightly, watching for the sting. "He's on a business trip, but maybe next time you're in town..." She paused. "Are you seeing anyone these days?"

God, she was insufferable. I needed her out of here before she drained whatever patience I had left.

Ignoring her question entirely, I said, "I'd love to catch up, but Katie and I need to finish packing. Thanks for coordinating the movers." I turned to the cupboard; Katie resumed sorting her box. Cheyenne hovered like she was waiting for an opening.

"You know, Bethany," she said lightly, "funny how life works. Some of us leave, thinking we're moving on to bigger and better things, only to end up right back where we started."

I didn't react. Not at first. I took my time, placing the dish I was holding into a box before turning to her, feigning a look of realization.

"You're absolutely right, Cheyenne. Some of us do end up right back where we started. Others just never leave." Her smile faltered. Something flickered behind her eyes—annoyance? Embarrassment?

I turned back to the cupboard and pulled out a stack of plates, pretending to be too focused to notice her. A few seconds later, the sound of the front door opening and closing signaled her exit. I relaxed, rolling my shoulders to shake off the tension.

"What a fucking bitch," Katie said.

I laughed. "Yes, she is." We laughed hard before getting back to work.

We packed the kitchen an hour later, right on schedule. Church volunteers arrived promptly to collect the boxes—a mix of familiar faces and new ones. Some of the high-school kids were almost unrecognizable, teenagers now instead of the children I once saw tearing around the church courtyard. It made me feel impossibly old, like I'd skipped whole chapters of life here. Once they'd gone, I led Katie through the rest of the house. With each cleared room, a cool detachment settled over me. The living room and kitchen were done, their memories folded into boxes and carried away. Only a few rooms remained: the bathroom and my father's office.

We peeked into the bathroom—nothing remarkable, just outdated fixtures and the same dull beige tile I remembered from my childhood. At my father's office, I paused, hand hovering on the knob. The door was closed. My fingers twitched, but I couldn't bring myself to open it. Not yet. Wordlessly, I started up the stairs. The second floor felt muffled. The upstairs bathroom looked nearly identical to the one below. I showed Katie the linen closet, releasing the faint scent of faded detergent and old fabric.

We reached my father's bedroom.

Stepping inside, I expected grief, nostalgia—anything—but felt nothing. Even when I still lived here, he barely used this room. Most nights, I'd find him asleep on the couch or locked in his office. He kept a narrow cot in the corner of his office, as if he'd stopped using the bedroom altogether once my mother left. Everything looked frozen in time. The bed was made, an ugly plaid blanket—green, black, and red—pulled drum-tight. A wooden dresser stood against the far wall, bare except for a single Bible, its pages faintly curled, a set of prayer beads, and a pair of initialed cufflinks aligned with military precision, as if still waiting for him. A trace of his cologne still hung in the air —even seven months after his death—and my stomach twisted. I backed toward the hall.

"This won't take long to pack." I shut the door. "There's barely anything in there."

We stopped outside the next room. My room.

"This was my room." I imagined it exactly as I had left it. My father never liked change; he preferred things to stay just as they were. There was a way everything had to be done—a certain order he expected, from how my bed was made to how my dresser was arranged. Even how long I could keep my door closed wasn't up to me. And yet, it had been my room. He wouldn't have touched it. He wouldn't have let anyone else touch it—not because it meant anything to him, but because in his mind, I was always supposed to come back.

The moment I opened the door, the air caught in my lungs. Everything was destroyed. My blankets were flung across the room as if they'd been ripped from the bed in anger. Clothes that had once sat neatly in my dresser now lay twisted in heaps across the floor. The dresser itself was overturned—one leg snapped clean off, drawers yanked out and tossed aside. My mattress—my entire bed—had been flipped, half hanging off the frame. Books, childhood trinkets, Bible-study notebooks—torn apart, like he needed to erase my existence.

My knees buckled, throat burning. I had known my father was cruel; I'd lived under his strict, suffocating control for years. But this—this was entirely different. This wasn't control. This was rage. His rage. My stomach twisted. My hands trembled. He hated me for leaving, for defying him, and this ruin was proof. Even in death, he needed me to see how deeply I'd disappointed him.

"Holy hell." Katie stood behind me. I stepped inside, eyes sweeping what was left of my old life, but the pressure in my chest turned unbearable.

"I can't—" My voice broke. I blinked back the sting in my eyes. Abruptly, I grabbed Katie's wrist and ushered her out before she could say anything. "I'll deal with this on the last day." I forced the words out. "I can't right now."

Tears blurred my vision as I rushed downstairs, barely focusing while I grabbed my purse and keys. I needed to get out of this house. Katie didn't argue; she simply followed, silent and understanding. I shut the door behind me, fingers numb, chest hollow.

We drove back to the hotel in silence.

30

— • —

LINING UP THE PIECES

KEVIN

It had been two days since I last saw my girl, and I fucking missed her, not in a casual, wish-you-were-here way, but in a restless, something's-off-in-the-universe kind of way. Bethany was my air. Without her, everything felt heavier—harder to breathe. I knew she was strong—probably one of the strongest people I'd ever met—but even the toughest minds had breaking points. She was back home, digging through a past she'd spent years escaping. I knew how that kind of shit could drag you under. I avoided my past. Buried it. Moved forward, because looking back only dragged me down. But Bethany? She wasn't just looking back—she was ripping open old wounds, standing in the wreckage, sorting through pieces of herself she thought she'd left behind. And I wasn't there. That gutted me.

Katie was with her, and I knew she'd help—but there's nothing like a lover to pull you out of your own head. To remind you you're not alone when the walls close in. I should've been there, not across the country, letting her do it alone. Maybe I failed her by staying behind, convincing myself she'd be fine when I should've fucking known better.

I grabbed my phone and checked the time. Six p.m. in Indiana. Still nothing from her. That wasn't good. We always talked—even just a text or voice note. Something. Silence from her wasn't normal, and the longer it stretched, the more the anxiety built. I dragged a hand down my face, exhaled, and typed a message.

Me: Hey beautiful. Just thinking about you. Are you okay?

I stared at the screen. Nothing.

My jaw clenched as I hovered over the call button. I needed to hear her voice. Just to know where her mind was. I wouldn't push—I just needed to make sure she wasn't

172

sinking into a place she couldn't pull herself out of. I had my phone halfway out when something moved in the corner of my eye. Collin Conners. Even with sunglasses on, I could tell he was smirking. I shook my head, already knowing how this was going to go. "Well, well, look who it is."

He strode up like he owned the place. I pushed up from my seat, meeting him halfway as he grabbed my hand, pulling me in for a quick, rough hug—a couple of hard slaps to the back like we were trying to outdo each other. "Damn, man." Collin stepped back. "What's it been, a year? Looks like you've been skipping the gym."

I scoffed. "You fucking wish." He jabbed at my stomach—not that I felt it.

"You sure? Looking a little soft, bro."

I rolled my eyes. "Says the guy who skips leg day. You forget they make weights for the lower half of your body, too?"

Collin laughed and dropped into the seat across from me. This was our routine. Other guys dapped up—we sized each other up like assholes comparing dick size. It was tradition.

I settled back in my chair, watching as he leaned back, stretching out like he had all the time in the world. He was always like that—laid-back as hell, moving through life like nothing ever really phased him. It wasn't arrogance, just confidence that made people pay attention without him trying. The guy was a solid 6'4", broad shoulders, built like someone who actually used his gym membership instead of just paying for it. I wasn't short, but next to him, I almost felt it. Women lost their shit over him. I did fine in that department, but Collin? He walked into a room, and the girls within ten feet forgot what they were talking about.

Today, he had on a light linen shirt, sleeves pushed up just enough to show off strong forearms, paired with worn-in jeans that made it look like he hadn't tried at all. And he probably hadn't. That was Collin—he didn't need to. I caught the women at the next table eyeing him, whispering, probably debating whether they should say something. They didn't even know what color his damn eyes were yet. Collin pulled off his sunglasses like he hadn't just shattered the room's focus. The women at the next table let out a moan—one of them actually fucking whimpered.

I groaned, shaking my head. "Can you stop with the smug shit for five minutes?" Collin smirked, feigning innocence.

"What smug shit?"

With an eye roll, I muttered, "I knew I should've met you at your office."

He laughed, stretching out like the most relaxed motherfucker in the world. He knew. We all did. And he loved every second of it.

Our waitress practically tripped over herself getting to the table, eyes locked on Collin as if he were the sun. She barely spared me a glance—hell, I could've been a chair. But Collin had her at his beck and call. It was almost disgusting. Almost. She tucked a strand of hair behind her ear and smiled.

"Can I get you guys started with anything?"

"Two beers," Collin said, voice smooth as silk, "and two burgers—medium—with fries." She nodded so fast I thought her neck might snap.

"Coming right up."

I shook my head. "Don't you ever get tired of that?"

"Tired of what?" he asked

"Never mind." The waitress returned with our beers. I took a slow sip. "So, what the hell have you been up to?"

"London. Six months. Label sent me to scout talent—I hated it. Gray, cold. Pretty sure I caught seasonal depression. Just got back last week."

"London, huh? Anyone worth signing?"

"Nah. Just wannabes chasing trends. One more sad boy with a guitar trying to be Ed Sheeran and I'll lose it."

I laughed. "So, you bailed?"

"Pretty much." He shrugged. "Told the label they were wasting my time—threatened to quit." He said it casually, but I knew he'd do it. Collin never backed something he didn't believe in. He took a sip and looked at me. "You've never asked for a favor. Then I get a random text to listen to this song."

I shrugged. "What'd you think?"

He swirled his beer, dragging it out to piss me off. "Who is she to you?"

"A friend."

"Bullshit." He crossed his arms.

I groaned. "Fine—she's my girlfriend."

Collin choked, then grinned. "Holy shit! Kevin Sinclair has a girlfriend." He stretched the word like it was foreign. I tossed a fry. He dodged it with annoying ease.

"Yeah. A drop-dead-gorgeous girlfriend with more talent in her pinky than you'll ever have. Cocksucker."

He laughed and slapped the table, earning a few looks. "Thought you were destined to be a loner." His laughter faded. "Happy for you, man."

I nodded back, but I wasn't letting him off the hook. "So?" Being the dramatic asshole he was, he took a long swig of beer, then picked it back up and finished it. I clenched my jaw, resisting the urge to smack it out of his hand.

Finally, he set the glass down and looked me dead in the eye. "She definitely has something."

A rush of pride surged through me. I knew it. Collin continued, "It was so good, I sent it to one of the execs." My brows lifted slightly. That wasn't nothing. "He listened," he went on, more serious now. "And he was intrigued. He wants me to meet her. Hear her sing live. If she sounds the way she does on that demo..." He paused, watching me. "I wouldn't be shocked if he tried to sign her."

I stared at him, heart pounding. Tried to stay calm, but inside I was lit the fuck up—every nerve sparking hope. Bethany deserved this. After everything she'd clawed her way out of, this could change everything. Collin leaned back, waiting.

He knew I was holding it in. "Cool," I said, drumming my fingers like I wasn't.

He smirked. "You're so full of shit." I ignored him. "When can I meet her?"

"She's out of town until Friday. She usually sings at a karaoke bar. That work?"

He considered it for a second before nodding. "That works. I'll get a real sense of how the audience responds to her. Let me know when, and I'll be there."

"Will do."

We finished our food, trading the same easy banter as always. It was a needed break from everything weighing on me. Collin checked his phone and groaned. "Shit—industry party."

I smirked. "Poor you."

"You have no idea." He slid on his sunglasses. "See you."

I exhaled, running a hand down my face as he left. This was real. Bethany had a shot—and I'd make damn sure she took it.

31

— • —

PLAYBACK DENIED

BETHANY

As Katie and I worked through the rooms, the heaviness began to ease. The silence wasn't heavy, just comfortable, as if she knew I needed this

Last night's drive back to the hotel was quiet. I wasn't in the mood to talk, and Katie didn't push. When we reached the room, she gave me space, letting me vanish into the bathroom without question. I ran the water until steam curled against the mirror, then slipped into the tub, sinking beneath the surface. My body ached, but it wasn't just exhaustion—it was the emotional toll, the way my mind had been unraveling since stepping back into that house.

While I soaked, Katie went downstairs to grab dinner. She didn't ask—probably knowing I wouldn't have had an answer. The truth was, I didn't even have the energy to call Kevin. His concerned messages waited, but I ignored them. Answering meant reliving everything—putting words to emotions I needed buried. Deep. So deep that not even I could dig them up again. By the time I dragged myself out of the tub, Katie still wasn't back. I slipped beneath the hotel comforter—its cocoon muffling the world outside—and I meant to wait for her, but the moment my head hit the pillow, sleep pulled me under and granted me the first real peace I'd felt in what seemed like forever.

This morning felt lighter. Maybe it was the sleep, or maybe today was a reset—but I could breathe again. I finally texted Kevin, promising to call later, telling him yesterday had been rough, but I felt better now. It was only half a lie. Gratitude swelled as I looked at Katie, my constant. I picked up breakfast to thank her and gave her the biggest hug.

"You are the best." I meant it. She squeezed tighter.

"You don't have to say that." Her voice was light, but I heard the emotion beneath it.

176

We split the tasks: Katie tackled the bathroom and hallway while I faced what remained of my father's bedroom. The air felt stale, untouched, with shadows of his life lingering in every corner. I had almost finished when an odd sensation crept up my spine—an inexplicable urge to look under the bed. It wasn't rational—just a feeling, like something waited in the shadows. I crouched and stretched my arm beneath the frame until my fingers brushed something hard.

A blue vintage travel case. Rectangular, rounded corners scuffed, dust puffing up as I dragged it out, making me sneeze. My pulse quickened. I'd never seen this suitcase. The dust suggested he hadn't touched it in years—maybe since the day he shoved it under there. My hand paused on the latches as an uneasy thought slithered in: Pandora's box. Did I really want to open it? My father had been guarded in ways I'd only begun to understand. If I opened this, would I peel back layers I wasn't ready to face? I lifted my hands away just as Katie entered. "What's that?" She dropped beside me.

"I don't know. It was under the bed. I've never seen it before." My voice wavered.

"Have you opened it yet?"

"No." My fingers curled into my palms. "Maybe I shouldn't."

Katie's expression softened. "You should. He was too private. What's inside might answer some questions."

"I don't know if I can handle more surprises. My room was enough."

She laid a reassuring hand on my arm. "It'll be okay. You're not alone. I'm right here." I nodded and exhaled slowly. With shaky hands, I popped the latches. They clicked open, echoing in the still room. Inside, the first thing I saw was a photograph. Dust slipped off as I lifted it. My parents on their wedding day. I'd never seen a picture of it. They stood at my father's church altar. My mother was breathtaking—long blonde hair cascading over her shoulders, a delicate tiara and veil, a timeless lace gown pooling at her feet. Her smile lit her eyes. She looked happy. Beside her stood my father, rigid in a tux, bow tie perfect, boutonniere matching hers. His expression was a stark contrast—serious, almost emotionless. A tightness bloomed in my chest as I passed the photo to Katie.

"Wow...you look so much like her," she whispered, comparing us.

"Talk about the '90s—that dress is something else." A somber laugh escaped me. I set the picture on the floor and reached back into the suitcase. More photographs. In everyone, my mother smiled, my father remained unreadable. Then I found a picture of

Mom pregnant. A blue-and-white floral dress stretched over her belly, hands cradling the bump. Her smile was still there, but dimmer, restrained.

"Wow. I've never seen her pregnant." I sifted through more: Mom holding me as a baby, her smile fading year after year. I didn't notice my grip tightening until Katie's voice pulled me back. "He was sucking the life out of her," I said softly. The realization settled bitter and unforgiving, just like he'd tried to do to me.

I exhaled and reached again—this time touching paper, not photos. A handful of envelopes, edges yellowed. My breath caught: everyone addressed to me.

"What the hell?" I thumbed through them, hands shaking. Each return address was the same—my mother's. Postmarks spanned a decade. Ten years of letters I'd never seen. A vacant feeling opened inside me. She wrote? The same woman who signed away her rights? None of it made sense. If she truly wanted to be part of my life, why had no one given these to me? Frustration bubbled. I clenched the stack like pressure could squeeze out answers. I couldn't do this—not now.

I tossed the letters back into the case, followed by the photos, and slammed the lid. The latch clicked shut as though sealing everything inside could keep it from unraveling me.

"I'll deal with it another day. Let's get out of here." I stood, holding the suitcase handle with one hand. With the other, I clasped Katie's, and pulled her to her feet. The simple contact steadied me— reassured me that I wasn't alone. She nodded, understanding this storm inside me needed to be left untouched.

"We'll order room service and watch a movie." I forced lightness into my tone. "What should we watch?" At the same time, we answered, "The Devil Wears Prada." Laughter bubbled between us, easing the tightness in my chest. As we walked out, the discovery still pressed at the back of my mind—but for now, I refused to let it pull me under.

Back at the hotel, I collapsed onto the bed, staring at the ceiling. I hadn't let go of my phone, clenched so long it left a faint imprint on my skin. I'd spent the last hour debating whether to call Kevin. The suitcase sat by the door, untouched, gnawing at me. I didn't know when I'd face it. I unlocked my phone: three missed calls, three unread messages from Kevin.

Kevin: I know today was a lot. Call me when you can.

Kevin: Thinking about you.

Kevin: Bethany?

That last one hit different. It wasn't really a question, but in my head, I heard his calm, patient voice waiting on the other side of the silence. I finally typed.

Me: Sorry, I missed your calls. It's been a long day.

His reply came almost instantly.

Kevin: Figured. How are you?

How was I? Exhausted body, messy mind, emotions I couldn't begin to sort. Dust clung to memories—my mother's face, smiling, then not. Those letters. Ten years of words hidden from me.

Me: Tired, but okay.

Kevin didn't push.

Kevin: I wish I could be there.

A small smile touched my lips.

Me: Me too. I'll call you tomorrow.

Kevin: Okay.

I let the phone drop onto the mattress. Across the room, Katie flipped through the channels, the background noise reminding me I wasn't alone. Tomorrow I'd tackle my bedroom, then my father's office, maybe even open those letters. But not tonight. Tonight, I just needed to breathe.

The next morning, I wasn't sure which would be harder—Dad's office or my bedroom. One thing was clear: I had to face my room alone if I ever hoped to let go of what this place had buried inside me. I walked Katie to the office door. It had been five years since I'd stood here—five years since leaving a letter on his desk saying I was gone and not to look for me. I had expected never to return. Taking a slow breath, I turned the handle and pushed the door open. Memories swallowed me.

I pictured Dad bent over this desk, pen scratching sermons in precise handwriting, Bible pages rustling, his deep voice murmuring scripture. The room had held the scent of ink, old paper, and cologne. But that wasn't what I saw now. The mahogany desk was shoved into a corner, as if it no longer mattered. In the middle of the room sat a cot: a thin mattress, a single pillow, a neatly folded blanket. My stomach twisted. Even stranger—a television and DVD player. I froze, breath catching. "This is...weird."

"What do you mean?" Katie stepped beside me.

"My father had never owned a television. Called them a distraction. And this isn't how he kept his office." It no longer felt like his space. In the years I was gone, things had changed, and he had become someone I didn't recognize. Dust clung to my fingers as I touched the desk. This room was no longer about sermons and scripture. I swallowed hard. "Pack everything up," I said, nodding toward the closet. "His sermons should be in the file cabinet." Katie didn't ask; I didn't give her the chance. Without another word, I turned and headed upstairs.

In my childhood bedroom, I stood amidst the wreckage of what was once mine. The walls, the floor—everything felt smaller than I remembered, yet the memories pressed in on me, unrelenting. My eyes swept over the destruction, my mind trying to make sense of it, grasp the fury my father must have felt to tear through this room like a storm.

I crouched down, my breath shallow as my fingers brushed over a piece of torn fabric. A dress—purple plaid, its hem frayed, ripped apart viciously. I had worn this dress when I taught Bible study at the Children's Church. A good girl's dress. A dress that made him proud. Now, shredded. Destroyed.

I let out a slow, trembling breath and whispered, "Father, I'm sorry I had to leave." I hated the words the second they left my lips. I wasn't sorry—not for choosing myself.

I shoved the dress into the trash bag with more force than necessary, my hands shaking. Another ruined piece of clothing. And another. Each one a testament to his rage. Each one a reminder that I had never truly belonged here—only existed in the space he allowed.

"You never let me be myself," I muttered. I grabbed another ripped shirt, clenched it, and tossed it into the pile. "I had to do what I was told." Even saying it felt bitter. I shut my eyes, but the memories flooded in, his voice deep, commanding, sharp as a whip.

"Bethy, children are to be seen and not heard."

I could hear it as if he were standing behind me, as if his presence was still woven into the very bones of this room.

A harsh laugh escaped. "Seen and not heard," I muttered, vision blurring as I grabbed another torn blouse. "It was moments like that," I whispered, "that made me leave. That made her leave."

My mother. I sucked in a breath. She had stood here once, voice soft but full of the same warnings. "Just do what he says, Bethy. Just don't argue." As if obedience were a shield. As if silence could keep me safe. And for years, I had tried. Tried to be the daughter he wanted. Tried to be the good girl, the obedient girl, the one who spoke when spoken to, who smiled in front of the congregation, who bowed her head in silent submission. It had never been enough.

Now I sifted through the wreckage of a life never truly mine. I tossed another torn dress into the bag, my breath coming in quick, shallow bursts.

"Using religion to control us." My voice was barely above a whisper, but the truth of it burned like acid. Trash bags piled up, each filled with pieces of my childhood that had been picked apart and destroyed. There was nothing left to salvage. Nothing left that I wanted to keep. As I worked, something strange happened. The anger clawing at my insides, the resentment that had burned so fiercely, began to shift. Not fade—not completely—but change. Instead of rage, there was understanding. A brutal, gut-wrenching understanding. He never knew how to love me—at least not the way I needed.

I straightened. "You don't control me anymore." The words were stronger than I expected. And in my mind, I saw him. Standing in the doorway like he always did, arms crossed, stern face. The same way he used to look at me when I dared to speak out of turn. When I dared to want more than what he was willing to give. But this time, he didn't interrupt me. I wasn't a child, or afraid.

"I know you meant well," I said. "But your control did more harm than good." His expression never changed. Cold. Unforgiving. "You could've prepared me for the world instead of caging me in your own A tremble ran through me." I forced the words out. "You could've just let me live."

A tremble ran through me. My voice dropped, but the anger remained.

"You could've let me go to college. Have real friends—not girls like Cheyenne, who only knew how to pretend." Another hollow laugh. "You could've let me laugh in my own damn house." The ghost in the doorway didn't move. Didn't speak. Turning away from the image of him, from the past that had lived inside these walls for far too long. My chest heaved, my heart pounded, but what once chained me to this place no longer felt unbreakable. That's when I realized—I wasn't his prisoner anymore.

I grabbed the Precious Moments figurines from the shelf—little porcelain versions of the daughter he had wanted me to be. Soft. Silent. Fragile. One by one, I dropped them into the church's donation box.

"I had to learn on my own," I whispered, the confession barely escaping past the lump in my throat. "You failed me." The words landed like a punch. The painful truth I had never let myself say out loud before.

Tears blurred my vision, hot and relentless. They weren't just for what I had lost, but for what I had never been given in the first place. A father who saw me. A father who let me exist beyond the constraints of his faith. A father who loved me as I was, not as he wanted me to be. I wiped my face, inhaling deeply. I sensed it instantly. The storm in me went still. Not in defeat. Not in surrender. In peace.

I met his cold stare. He never changed. But I had.

"But I forgive you." The words weren't for him—they were for me. No more tears. No more regrets. He disappeared. I packed in silence, moving at my own pace. It took time—sorting, folding, discarding. No more outbursts or sadness. Just the simple task of boxing my past, one piece at a time.

As I pushed the mattress back onto the bed frame, something caught my eye—a sliver of black and white tucked between the wooden beams of the box spring. Reaching down, my fingers curled around the worn spine. A composition notebook. I held it, breath caught in my throat. I forgot this existed. I sat on the bed, flipping through the pages, my fingers tracing the words I had written so long ago. Lyrics. Songs. Dreams I had once dared to have.

"Bethany, can you come down here for a second?" Katie's voice cut through my thoughts. Closing the notebook, I stood, making my way downstairs to my father's office.

Katie stood by the TV, turning as I entered, excitement in her eyes. "I was wrapping up in here and was about to pack the DVD player, but something told me to check if there was anything inside." Her lips curved—part disbelief, part curiosity. "You are not going to believe what was in there." She pressed play.

The screen flickered, static gave way to an image, blurry at first, then sharpening. A little girl stood on a stage, hands neatly folded, small and poised under the glow of soft church lighting. She wore pale blue with white lace, curls falling over her shoulders. Then she began to sing:

"He's got the whole world in His hands." Her voice filled the room, clear and sweet, untouched by doubt.

Katie fast-forwarded. The same girl—older now, different dress, same posture—waiting for approval.

"He's got you and me, sister, in His hands." A tightness coiled in my chest.

Another skip. The girl was taller, a teenager. Her voice polished, bearing practiced—like she knew the congregation's eyes were always on her.

"He's got all of us here in His hands. He's got all of us here in His hands." A violent shudder tore through me. The office walls closed in. That melody—my father's favorite—echoed. Coaching. Correcting. Controlling.

Without thinking, I surged forward and slammed the eject button. The tray slid out with a quiet click, revealing the disc that had survived all these years. It wouldn't survive another second. I yanked it free and snapped it in half. The crack echoed through the office. Katie recoiled.

"What the hell?" My breath quickened, pulse hammering. I stared at the broken pieces trembling in my hands.

"If there are any more DVDs like that, break them. I don't ever want to hear that fucking song again."

I turned and walked out, my body humming with a mess of emotions I couldn't unravel. I was so fucking tired of this shit. That child on the screen—sweet voice, practiced smile—was a stranger.

Bethy was gone. I wasn't her anymore.

32

SOME THINGS LINGER

BETHANY

Nothing compares to the crisp bite of California air after a long flight. At LAX, Katie stretched her arms wide, inhaling like she could drink it in.

"Home sweet home!" she beamed. The city buzzed—horns blaring, voices overlapping, airport chaos around us. Our suitcases thumped as we weaved through the crowd toward the rideshare pickup. I adjusted the strap of my bag, stealing a glance.

"Thank you for putting up with my emotional, moody behavior. I know I was a lot to deal with. Katie, I owe you big time." She didn't immediately respond, which made me uneasy.

"Yeah, you were difficult to deal with. I regret going."

I stopped mid-step. Had I really been that unbearable? Katie kept walking, unaware I'd stopped. A pang of guilt shot through me. Maybe I had been too much, too emotional, too reactive. Maybe I should've done it alone. She turned to look for me and frowned when she saw me standing there, my fingers curled tightly around the handle of my suitcase like it was the only thing keeping me upright.

"Earth to Bethany!" Katie waved in front of my face. I blinked, trying to gather myself.

"I..." My voice faltered as I struggled to find the right words.

And then she burst out laughing. "I was just joking!" She sprinted back to me, throwing her arms around my shoulders in a tight squeeze. Relief flooding my body.

"You gotta lighten up," she teased, pulling back with a playful shake of her head. With a wicked smirk, she added, "You've been wound up all week. Give me your phone—let's call Kevin, see if he can help you relax." She waggled her eyebrows suggestively. "Pretty sure he wouldn't mind putting in the extra effort."

I groaned, shoving her lightly as she giggled. "Oh my God, Katie."

"What?" she asked, feigning innocence. "You know I'm right."

I rolled my eyes, but a small laugh escaped me. Sitting in the back of the Uber, I pulled out my phone, my fingers moving instinctively as I typed out a message to Kevin, on my way home. Just sending it gave me a sense of peace. I couldn't wait to feel his arms around me, hear him say everything would be okay. He was my refuge; the one place I could always find comfort. I hadn't realized how much I needed to hear his voice until that night at the hotel, after I'd spent the entire day packing up my childhood bedroom. I had collapsed onto the bed, exhaustion sinking into my bones, but my mind wouldn't rest. Every box held a memory. Every drawer felt like erasing a piece of myself. The finality left my chest tight, my hands clutching the phone like a lifeline. And Kevin, with that smooth, reassuring tone, knew exactly what to say.

"You're not losing anything, baby. You're making space for something better."

His words were the breath I desperately needed. He let me spill every emotion, never rushing me, never making me feel like I was too much. Instead, he soothed the ache with soft encouragement, helping me make the pain manageable. By the time we hung up, I felt lighter—maybe this wasn't an ending but a beginning. I leaned back into the seat, closing my eyes. My heart swelled just thinking about him.

Before Kevin, my life had been...predictable. Safe. A carefully curated existence built on routine and caution. I had been fine with it, content even. But with him, fine wasn't enough anymore. Kevin made me feel alive. He pushed me outside my comfort zone—to live, not just exist. He always knew what to say, what I needed before I even realized it. And when it was hard—when I hesitated, when my fear of change reared its ugly head—he never let me retreat.

"I've got you," he'd say, his voice dripping with certainty. And I believed him. With Kevin, I felt complete.

Just as I felt myself drifting into that hazy space between consciousness and sleep, Katie's voice sliced through the quiet. "Bethany...you know how you keep saying you owe me?" Her tone was light, but I could hear the setup coming. I cracked an eye open; my head was still tipped back against the seat.

"Yeah?" She hesitated for a beat before pressing on.

"You can make it up to me tonight."

Both eyes snapped open as I sat up straighter.

"How?" My voice carried suspicion. I knew Katie, and this would derail my plans. Before I could even start forming an excuse, she grabbed my hand, her face set with determination.

"Before you say no, hear me out."

I let out a slow breath, already bracing myself. "Go on."

She straightened her posture like she was about to present a life-altering case to a jury.

"I want to go out tonight—"

"Absolutely not."

"Bethany, please," she whined, drawing out the word like a child begging for candy. "You owe me. Once you and Kevin reunite, you'll disappear into your little love cocoon, and I'll be left alone. I want one last night to have fun. I want tequila. I want to sing. I want bad decisions and no regrets!" She pouted, pressing her hands together like she was praying to the gods of persuasion.

I groaned, already torn. I did owe her. She had stuck by me through my mess of emotions, through my overthinking and self-doubt. All I wanted was Kevin. His apartment, his couch...or that damn coffee table. My entire body heated at the thought of that damn coffee table.

"Fine," I said, the word dragged out like it hurt. She squealed and yanked me into a chokehold hug, her arm locking around my neck like she was wrestling me into submission. "Let go, I can't breathe, Katie," I laughed, trying to pry her off.

She released me and said, "Tonight's gonna be epic." I sighed. I'd regret this. I couldn't believe my eyes when we pulled up to the apartment. My stomach flipped, pulse racing like I'd just stepped off a rollercoaster.

"Holy hell," Katie muttered. Because there he was. Kevin leaned against his motorcycle like he belonged in a magazine—jeans and a white T-shirt. He looked effortlessly sexy, like he hadn't thought once about those muscles flexing beneath the fabric. My breath caught in my throat at the way his arms—those sculpted, powerful arms—curved around the flowers in his hands. Roses and sunflowers, with a single welcome home balloon.

The second my feet hit the pavement, I was running. The moment I reached him, I launched myself into his arms. His solid body radiated heat through the thin barrier of my clothes. I locked my thighs around his waist; hands tangled in his hair as I crushed my mouth to his. Kevin exhaled hard against my lips, fingers tightening around my hips. I felt his resistance before he gave in. His kiss turned possessive, his tongue sweeping into my mouth like he was determined to take every single part of me for himself. The taste of him was intoxicating and never enough.

I moaned into his mouth, pressing my body harder against his, chasing the feel of him. Every inch of him was solid muscle. I felt it everywhere—his arms holding me like I weighed nothing, his chest pressed to mine, his hands sliding lower, cupping my ass, heat pooling low in my belly. I giggled against his lips, my body burning with hunger, and I didn't even try to hide.

"Woah, Bethany," Kevin breathed. His grip flexed, like he was trying to stay composed, but I felt the tension ripple through him. Everything in me begged for the man holding me.

"Excuse me, can I get some help here?!" Katie's voice shattered the moment.

Kevin sighed, kissed me one last time, then reluctantly set me down. My legs went weak, my breath uneven, fingers still clinging to his shirt like I couldn't let go.

"Sorry about that," I muttered, glancing at Katie. She rolled her eyes so hard I was shocked they didn't get stuck. Kevin chuckled, completely unbothered.

"Here, let's trade." He handed me a bouquet of roses and extended the sunflowers toward Katie.

"Sunflowers are your favorite, right?" Her irritation melted as her fingers brushed the petals, a small smile tugging at her lips.

"Yeah...they are." Kevin gave me a slow, knowing smile. Damn him.

"It feels so good to be home." I stepped into our apartment, inhaling the scent of vanilla candles and fresh linen. It felt safe—mine. No more hotels, no more packing, no more holding my breath through memories I wasn't ready to face. Just home.

"I bet in more ways than one," Katie muttered under her breath, just loud enough for Kevin and me to hear. I whipped around and glared. She smiled, eyes wide with faux innocence. "Give those here." She plucked the roses from my hands before I could protest. "I'll arrange them and put them on the kitchen table."

I rolled my eyes, but the amusement tugging at the corner of my lips betrayed me. Classic Katie. I shook my head and turned toward my bedroom, Kevin close behind.

"Hey, you two..." Her teasing lilt made me turn, already bracing myself.

"Yes, Katie?"

She emerged from the kitchen, a glass vase in her hands, too smug. "Just a reminder—our walls are thin. Very thin. Whatever you're planning…" She lifted a brow at Kevin.

Kevin smirked and stuffed his hands into his pockets. "Uh-huh?"

"And," she went on, ignoring my mortified expression, "don't forget we're going out tonight…so please don't wear her out before I get my night out, Kevin. I would never forgive you."

I gasped. "Really?" My face burned as I hissed through clenched teeth.

Katie grinned, her eyes twinkling with mischief as she spun on her heel and disappeared back into the kitchen, her laughter echoing. I groaned, rubbing my hand down my face.

Kevin chuckled. "She's got a point."

I whirled around, jabbing a finger at his chest. "Not. A. Word."

He grinned and stepped closer until his breath tickled my skin. "Whatever you say, baby."

Kevin's hands were on me the moment we entered the bedroom. His hold was possessive—his touch setting every nerve ending on fire. He kicked the door shut behind us, the soft click of it closing sealing us into our own private world.

"Since we only have a few hours, let's not waste time," he murmured against my ear. His teeth scraped my earlobe, sending a shiver down my spine. I melted against him, every inch of my body craving the way he made me feel—how easily he could strip away every thought but him. I had just spent hours on an airplane. I felt gross and sticky. I needed a shower.

Kevin groaned, grinding my hips, pulling me flush against him.

"I like it when you're dirty," he growled, his lips skimming the curve of my neck. "Let me help you out of these clothes." I let out a breathy laugh and shuffled away from him, placing my palms against his chest and pushing back.

"Kevin, just let me take a quick shower."

He took a step forward. I took a step back. His eyes darkened with amusement as he watched me.

"Bethany…" he drawled.

Raising a hand, I shook my head. "I'm serious. Give me fifteen minutes."

"That's fifteen minutes we could spend reconnecting," he said, licking his lips slowly.

My thighs pressed together at the promise in his eyes. I was torn between the need for cleanliness and the need for him.

"Ten minutes," I bargained, tossing my bag onto the bed. My movements faltered. My bed was unmade. That might not have meant anything, except...I knew I had made it before leaving for the airport. I always did. A habit, something small that made returning home feel less chaotic. But now, the sheets were slightly rumpled, the comforter folded back just enough to suggest someone had sat there. Or laid there. A strange chill swept up my spine. Kevin smiled and kicked off his shoes.

"Clock's ticking, Bethany. Shower quick." His voice was all dark, silky heat, sending a swarm of butterflies loose in my stomach. I giggled and bolted to the bathroom, dodging his hands.

My shower was quick—just long enough to scrub away the grime of travel, to reset, to breathe. I brushed my teeth, wrapped myself in a towel, and walked back into the bedroom, my skin damp, tingling with anticipation. I froze. Kevin sat on my bed, fingers skimming my Bible before placing it gently on the nightstand. I frowned. Why was that out?

"Why do you have that?" I asked, shutting the door.

He looked up. "It was under your pillow. I lay down and felt something bumpy. Didn't know you still read it." My brows furrowed. Unease prickled at the back of my mind. I didn't put it under my pillow. I put it in my closet before I left...The thought barely settled before Kevin tugged at my towel. His lips curled into a devilish grin.

"What do you have under here?" His voice dipped, thick with want. "Are you clean enough for me now?" Heat coiled in my belly, sinking lower. He pulled me onto his lap, my knees bracketing his hips, arms locking around me. He inhaled deeply at my neck. "You smell heavenly," he murmured, his nose trailing up the curve of my throat.

My breath hitched. I trembled as his tongue traced down my neck in lazy, teasing strokes.

"And you taste..." His mouth found that sensitive spot behind my ear, teasing waves of need. I trembled, a moan slipping free.

"Kevin..." His lips drifted down my collarbone to my nipple. His tongue slid over me, sparking under my skin, as I dripped with need.

"Oh—" I gasped, arching as pleasure rippled through me.

"You like that?" he purred, dark and satisfied.

"Yes," I breathed, my fingers dug into his shoulders.

He lifted me, laid me back, eyes burning into mine. "Let's see what else you like," he murmured. Then his lips were on me again, unraveling me kiss by kiss.

33

— • —

KARAOKE NIGHTS

KEVIN

The last few hours were fucking bliss.

Being with Bethany—tasting her, pleasing her—was what we needed. I felt it in how she clung to me, how her breath hitched when I whispered against her skin, how her body melted into mine like she was made for me. Leaving her was the last thing I wanted to do. If it were up to me, I'd have stayed tangled with her all night, listening to her sleep, breathing her in like she was the only thing keeping me sane. But fucking Katie.

She had to keep her damn promise to go to karaoke on a Friday night. I should have known. Bethany was loyal like that—always following through, even when she didn't want to. It pissed me off—having to let her go when all I wanted was to keep her with me—but this was an opportunity. A perfect setup. Collin wanted to hear her live, and tonight was the perfect way to make that happen. I called him on the way home, still high from being with her.

"Well, shit. You sound like a man who just got laid."

"Shut the fuck up," I muttered.

He laughed. "What's up?"

"Bethany's going to be at a karaoke bar tonight. Thought you might want to come."

I heard the curiosity in his silence. "What time?"

"Nine. Don't be late."

Collin let out a low whistle, but for once, he didn't have a smart-ass remark lined up. "Perfect. I'll see you there."

I gave him the name of the bar, adding, "And keep it low-key. None of that Hollywood bullshit."

191

He scoffed. "Please. I know how to blend in."

"Sure, you do." I drove the rest of the way alone with my thoughts, mind spinning on how the night would play out. Bethany had no fucking idea what was coming. Neither did Collin.

The second I walked in, my eyes found her—like they always did. She stood near the stage, waiting to write her name, eyes lit with anticipation. Fingers tapped the table, lips curving with the music. Her dress—damn. Black with red hearts, hugging every curve. The lace hem brushed the tops of her thighs, testing my patience. That white T-shirt underneath gave off a laid-back vibe. My pulse jumped. I clamped a hand on my neck to stop myself from crossing the room and tasting that dangerous smile. Her wild curls short-circuited my thoughts, and those black boots said she didn't care about fitting in. She never did. Delicate. Defiant. Soft lips. Dangerous curves. Every time I looked at her, it hit me low. Fierce. Undeniable.

All I thought about was getting her alone. When Bethany reached the table, I cut off whatever plan she had to sit. My hand caught her waist, yanking her in, and before she could speak, I kissed her hard. She met me fierce, chest to chest, soft curves pressing into mine. Her fingers grabbed my shirt like instinct, like she couldn't wait another second. Heat tore through me. I slid one hand down, pulling her tighter so she felt exactly how much I'd missed her.

"I see you missed me," I murmured.

Bethany's nails raked down my chest, brushing my dick. Her lips curled into a smirk as she whispered, "I see you missed me more." Fuck. I growled low, giving her ass a hard slap, just to remind her who she was teasing. She bit her lip, smirking like she wanted to push me further.

"Can you not?" Katie's voice cut through, exaggerated and annoyed. "Jesus, you two saw each other a few hours ago—you act like it's been weeks."

Bethany rolled her eyes and peeled off me slowly, making me feel every inch of the distance. She dropped into her seat beside Katie. I went to sit next to her, Katie grinned.

"Lover boy," she sang, "grab the first round? Tequila? You know how Bethany gets with it."

Bethany glared. "Katie."

She shrugged. "I'm just saying."

I smirked. "Yeah, all right."

Before I left, I leaned down, catching Bethany's lips for a slow, intense kiss, making sure she felt every ounce of restraint I was holding.

"Ugh, disgusting," Katie groaned. I laughed and headed for the bar.

I ordered their shots and a beer for myself, glancing back toward the table once. Bethany watched me, lip caught between her teeth, eyes heavy with want. A voice cut in.

"Make it two beers." I turned, already knowing who it was. Collin tried to blend in, but even his laid-back look belonged on a movie set. Gray crewneck, sleeves pushed up—trying to look relaxed but still put together. Khaki pants—casual, but too damn fitted to be something he just threw on. His beanie—slouched just enough to seem natural. But I knew better. Everything about Collin was intentional, even when he pretended it wasn't. He stood out—even in a crowded bar. Even the bartender moved faster. Women whispered, sneaking glances, already trying to place him. Collin leaned on the bar, casual. Comfortable.

"This is your low-key?" I said. "You gotta be fucking kidding me."

Collin chuckled. "What? I can't help that I look this good dressing down." His grin deepened, cocky as ever. The bartender handed us our beers and the shots. "What's our cover?" Collin asked.

"Simple," I said, grabbing my drink. "You're back in town. I invited you out. Easy."

He took a swig from his beer, nodding. "That's doable."

I sipped and slapped his back. "Let's go." Drinks in hand, we headed back to Bethany and Katie.

34

UNEXPECTED COMPANY

BETHANY

"Oh my..." I murmured, eyes shifting from Kevin to the man beside him. "Who's his friend?" Katie barely looked up from her phone.

"Who?"

I gestured toward them as they made their way through the crowd. Kevin was easy to spot—but the guy next to him? Taller, muscular. A build that filled out a shirt exactly right. As they stepped closer, dim lighting carved shadows over his chiseled jaw. He looked like a taller Liam Hemsworth.

Katie finally glanced up, started to speak, then stopped. Just...stopped. Her head tilted slightly, her mouth opening again, but no words came out.

I stared at her, then smirked. "I never thought I'd see the day."

Before she could snap out of it, Kevin and his friend reached our table. He handed me my shot before pulling out his chair and sitting beside me.

"Bethany, Katie—this is my friend Collin," he said. "He called while I was changing at home. Just flew in from out of town and wanted to grab a beer. Since I was already heading here, I invited him. Hope you don't mind." He placed a light kiss to my cheek before moving away just as quickly. A kiss on the cheek? Kevin was being modest.

Collin placed Katie's shot on the table in front of her before pulling a chair from the empty table behind us. He set it down across from us and took a seat, completely at ease.

He turned to me, extending his hand. "Bethany, nice to meet you." His voice was deep, smooth, with just enough rasp to catch attention. I shook his hand. It was surprisingly smooth. He wasn't a man who did physical labor. Collin turned to Katie next, offering his hand. She didn't move. Didn't blink. I kicked her under the table, snapping her out of it. Katie jolted, her face flushing a deep shade of red as she grabbed his hand in a rushed shake.

"Hi," she squeaked.

She let go quickly, twisting her mouth to the side—her nervous tell. She snatched up her phone, scrolling like she hadn't just glitched. I knew that mouth twist. It gave her away. Collin leaned back in his chair, and I caught the faintest trace of amusement in his expression. I set my glass down and glanced at Kevin.

"I don't mind," I said with a grin. "The more, the merrier." Kevin's lips curved slightly, a hint of amusement flashing in his eyes before he turned his attention back to his drink.

"I've heard so much about you," Collin said, his tone friendly but teasing.

"Really?" I arched a brow, giving Kevin a playful look. "Like what?"

Collin, catching on, leaned forward slightly, a knowing smirk playing at his lips. "Like how you captured this loner's heart." Kevin nearly choked on his beer. He coughed, set the bottle down, and eyes narrowed as he wiped his mouth.

"Oh really?" I teased, enjoying this little revelation.

Kevin shot Collin a look. "Oh no, I see what's happening here." He pointed at us. "Don't even start."

Collin held his hands up in mock innocence. "What? Is it not true? As long as I've known you, you've never been with anyone." I turned to Kevin, blinking. He gave a small shake of his head, mouth twitching like he was trying not to smile. A flicker of embarrassment crossed his face before he masked it with a slow sip of his drink. I reached under the table, lacing my fingers through his.

"Maybe he captured mine," I replied, smiling softly at him.

He didn't speak, but the look he gave me said everything. I turned my attention to Katie. She stayed glued to her phone, scrolling in long, exaggerated strokes like she was totally absorbed in whatever she saw. Her classic move—listening while pretending not to. I smiled and nudged her elbow. "Come on, we're doing the shot."

She blinked, finally looking up like she had just remembered she was at the table. "Oh, right." Clearing her throat, she set her phone down and reached for her glass. I gave her a pointed look.

"Uh-uh. You better look me in the eyes and cheers me, bitch. You don't want to risk seven years of bad sex."

Katie blushed instantly. Coolly, she said, "Not something I'm willing to risk." Her eyes flicked to Collin. Interesting.

Locking eyes with me, she clinked her shot glass against mine, dead serious. We tossed them back. The tequila burned, but I didn't flinch as I set the glass down.

Collin smirked. "Not a tequila girl?"

"I can hold my own," I shot back.

Kevin chuckled, reaching for his beer. "She can, but I wouldn't put her against Katie in a drinking contest." Katie grinned, still pink but herself again.

Collin raised a brow, intrigued. "That confident?"

Katie said matter-of-factly, "I have a talent."

"She's being modest," I added. "It's more like a superpower. Girl's got an iron liver."

Collin let out a low, impressed chuckle, sipping his drink. "Noted." He set his glass down and glanced at me. "What do you two do?"

"Katie and I work at a thrift store," I said.

Katie lifted a hand, adding, "Part-time. I'm studying Cyber Security."

Collin's eyebrows lifted slightly. "That's a shift from retail."

Katie shrugged. "Gotta pay the bills somehow."

He nodded. "Completely understand." His stare lingered. Was he interested in her, too? Hmm. Katie wouldn't ask what she really wanted to know, so I took the lead. I leaned into Kevin as he sipped his beer.

"Do you live in L.A.?"

"I do."

"So why haven't we met until now?"

"I was in London for the past six months for work."

"London?" I repeated. "Sounds fun."

"Nothing about London was fun. I hate it there. Too cold, too gray."

"You sound like someone I know." I flicked a glance at Katie. She didn't look up, but her scrolling slowed.

"What kind of work takes you to London?" I smirked.

Collin paused before answering. "I work in the industry."

My brow furrowed. "Which industry?"

Kevin answered before he could.

"We work in the same field."

"Music?" I asked, raising a brow, watching Collin carefully. There was something about Collin I couldn't pin down. I tucked my questions away for later. Beside me, Katie kept sneaking glances at him, like she couldn't help herself. By round two, she was back to her quick-witted, confident self. Collin seemed to enjoy her banter, eyes flickering with amusement whenever she shot back something clever. Even Kevin relaxed, draping an arm along the back of my chair.

DJ DeWayne's voice cut through the music. "Alright, folks, we've got a treat for you tonight. Coming up next is one of my favorite singers—I managed to convince her to do a few songs for us. Give it up for Bethany!"

My stomach flipped—excitement and nerves tangling.

Katie's head snapped toward me, brow arching. "A few songs?" she repeated. I smoothed my hands down my dress and stood.

"Yes," I confirmed. Kevin's lips curved, gray eyes glinting with curiosity.

"What are you singing tonight?"

Coming closer, My breath brushed his skin, my voice a sultry whisper. "I was feeling a little nostalgic. Figured a little country wouldn't hurt." Kevin's brows lifted, expression softening. But before he could respond, I added, "The first song is for you." I walked away, turning toward the stage with a sway of my hips. Glancing back, I caught his stare. A devilish smile spread across my face. His eyes burned as I stepped onto the stage, fingers curling around the mic, and the lights softened as the first notes played.

35

CENTER STAGE

KEVIN

This girl would be the death of me. I knew it the moment her sweet ass swayed toward the stage, fully aware of the chaos she stirred in me. I tightened my grasp around my drink.

Collin chuckled. "Showtime." I gave him a nod, a silent acknowledgment that whatever Bethany had planned would be good—hell, I knew that much—but I hoped it would be enough to blow Collin's damn socks off.

Across the table, Katie narrowed her eyes, suspicion flashing across her face. She wanted to know what the hell was going on. She wouldn't have to wait long. Bethany adjusted the mic stand, fingers trailing the metal as she flashed that teasing smile, just for me.

"This first song," she said, "is dedicated to a special someone in the audience." Her eyes locked onto mine—and damn, my dick hardened. That look of hers was lethal. Then the beat kicked in.

Katie gasped as excitement sliced through the music. "Oh my God," she shouted over the first few beats. "I can't believe she picked this one!"

She turned to me, eyes wide, already caught in it.

Katie threw her arms up. "Woooo!"

Collin and I exchanged a look, both lost. The track was fast, upbeat—nothing like the raw, soul-stirring melodies I was used to hearing from Bethany. This was playful, almost...poppy? Something out of the late '90s, maybe?

Katie scoffed. "You don't know the song?" She rolled her eyes. "Oh, you are in for a treat." She turned back to the stage, completely absorbed. I swallowed hard, eyes on Bethany.

The bar erupted the moment she started singing, the energy shifting like a live wire had been dropped into the room. Women shot to their feet, swaying their hips to the beat, their excitement contagious. Laughter and cheers filled the space, a ripple of nostalgia washing over the crowd. I glanced around, confused as hell. Katie spun toward me, eyes wide with disbelief.

"Really, Kevin? Genie in a Bottle by Christina Aguilera?"

Ah. That's why the place had gone wild. '90s girl pop. It all made sense now. Bethany moved across the stage—confident, intoxicating.

Like a predator locking on, she sauntered toward me, eyes gleaming. She stopped inches away, leaned in, and sang, "Lickin'..." Her voice was smooth as silk. Right on cue, she rolled her hips, moving like sin itself. Jesus. The crowd lost it, the screams and whistles deafening.

She was so fucking hot. Her voice was flawless—but it was her presence, the way she owned the moment, that made it impossible to look away. Every move—a tease, a challenge. Then she straddled me. Instinct took over. My hands found her waist, heat flooding through me. As if she were reading my goddamn mind, she smirked and sang.

Just like that, she hopped off, wagging her finger at me. The bar roared. I was already laughing. She had me—exactly how she wanted me. Her timing was impeccable. Beside me, Collin shifted in his seat, getting a better view of the stage.

He clamped my shoulder and muttered with a chuckle, "Man, you are so fucked. She's got you eating out of the palm of her hand."

To drive it home, he threw two fingers in his mouth and let out a loud whistle. I raked a hand through my hair, pulse still pounding. He wasn't wrong. Bethany was magnetic. Up on the stage, she moved like she belonged there, seduction in every note, glance, and shift of her body. As the chorus kicked in, every woman in the bar—including Katie—joined in, their voices merging into one massive sing-along.

Bethany worked the stage, moving left and right, commanding attention like a seasoned pro. And this was just karaoke—it didn't feel like it. It felt like a concert. She transformed—became a vixen, body rolling like a snake as the music pulsed. By the final chorus, the entire bar had given in. Women, men—hell, even the guys who'd been nursing their beers in the back—were on their feet, dancing, singing along. Some swayed, others let loose—caught in her electric presence.

As the song hit its final note, Bethany struck a pose—one hand on her hip, the other grabbing the mic, her lips curled into the biggest, most satisfied smile. The room exploded in cheers. Everyone stood, clapping, shouting, caught in her spell. Bethany took a gracious bow, soaking it in before strolling to the DJ. She whispered in his ear. He nodded and stepped back. Returning to the center of the stage, she waited while the cheers faded into an expectant hush. She brushed the mic stand and scanned the crowd, a flicker of vulnerability crossing her face.

"This next song...you probably won't know it." She smiled slightly. "But the first time I heard it, something about the words—about her voice—hit home. I don't usually sing country, but as you can see, tonight I'm trying something new. So, will you indulge me for a little while?"

A voice from the back hollered, "Hell yeah!" Laughter rippled through the crowd, followed by more shouts of agreement. The energy shifted. People leaned in. So did I. Bethany glanced at the DJ, and with a simple nod, set everything in motion.

"The next song I'm going to sing is by an artist named Reyna Roberts," she announced. "It's called 'One Way Street.'" She gripped the mic as the first chord rang out.

The guitar rolled in—low, steady, heavy in your chest. Conversation died instantly; everyone felt it. And then she sang. Her voice changed—deeper, richer, carrying a hint of twang that hadn't been there before. It wasn't an act; it was real and unrestrained. Bethany stood rooted, eyes closed, as the first verse poured out. We were transfixed. The bridge lifted the tempo, drawing us further in. When she hit the chorus—her voice soaring on that first drawn-out "I..."—the bar erupted. Bethany was lost in the music. She was what I saw that first night: unfiltered, unstoppable. My siren.

Each note pulsed with power, shifting from vulnerability to strength. The instruments dropped out, leaving just drums and her voice—a single heartbeat beneath pure emotion. The crowd clapped along, caught in the rhythm as she finally pulled the mic from the stand and started to move, body flowing with the beat. By the last note the applause was deafening. Chest heaving, she opened her eyes to absorb it all. She had us. Had me. Exactly where she wanted.

Silence fell, everyone waiting. Like a headliner closing a concert, Bethany turned and smirked at the DJ.

"Now, this next song," she said, pausing to tease the room's eagerness, "was a special request from our fabulous DJ." The crowd cheered in good-natured fun.

On the other mic, the DJ's voice crackled through the speakers. "I mean, it is my birthday, so I figured—why not?"

Bethany grinned. "Well, happy birthday! Y'all ready to get down and dirty?"

"Fuck yeah!" Collin shouted. I turned, eyes wide at my usually composed friend, but he wasn't the only one caught up in the energy.

Katie jumped in next. "What you got for us?" Bethany's eyes flicked her way.

"Since my good friend Katie asked, I won't spoil the surprise. Birthday boy, play that song for me."

The DJ pointed at her. "I got you!"

The first notes hit—a slow, sultry guitar riff, thick with bluesy swagger. The kind of tempo that crawled up your spine—felt before it was recognized. Each note stretched deep and unhurried, curling into the air like smoke. Then the bass hummed low and slow, setting the stage for something darker, something with heat. Drums crept in next—subtle at first, a teasing pulse that built into a hypnotic groove.

Bethany swayed, like she was alone in her bedroom—just her, the song, and the night. The intro stretched, pulling us deeper. She stilled. A hush fell as her voice—soft as a whisper, smooth as silk—carried the first word.

"Mississippi..." Gentle, almost airy, yet soaked in a depth I hadn't heard from her before. I was transfixed, as she eased into the verse. The groove picked up; Bethany prowled forward—movements bolder, vocals raspier. She belted, "Black Velvet." Holy shit. My girl had arrived.

She threw herself into the music, her voice sending a ripple through the crowd. Her boots tapped in time, presence commanding, magnetic. The chorus hit like a perfect storm—strength and finesse, control and abandon. I glanced around. The crowd was with her: heads nodding, hands clapping, feet stomping. Pride surged in my chest. Bethany slipped into a honeyed tone, luring them in before unleashing the chorus again. The push and pull of vulnerability and force—mesmerizing. Katie shot up, clapping to the beat, and others followed—a swell of bodies, tables thumping, the room pulsed.

During the solo, Bethany shredded an invisible guitar, flashing a wicked grin—like she'd hidden this side all along. By the final verse, the entire bar was locked into the moment she created. She crooned the final line, soft as a whisper. The note lingered—tender and haunting. A beat of silence—then the bar erupted. Bethany didn't bask—she commanded.

As the final instrumental faded, she lifted the mic. "Don't forget to wish your DJ a happy birthday. And make sure you leave a tip!" She stepped off the stage. I jumped to my feet, clapping, heart pounding. She found me. Before I could speak, I caught her in my arms. She crashed her lips to mine—hot, heavy, stealing my breath. I loved this woman.

36

— · —

ALIGNMENT

BETHANY

That set was an exhilarating rush that left me breathless. Perched on Kevin's lap, arm draped around his neck, my pulse still pounded, skin warm from the lights and the thrill of it all. Another listener approached, glowing with excitement as they gushed over my voice. I barely processed the words, but the sentiment? That I felt. It swelled, deep and intoxicating; something I hadn't let myself feel in years, since New York. The love—the need to perform—had always been there, buried under doubt and time. But tonight, it roared back to life.

Kevin's breath skimmed my ear. "I can't wait to take you home and give you my own private performance." Heat curled in my stomach; my fingers twitched against the back of his neck.

I was about to respond when Katie's voice sliced through. "Will you two give it a rest? Some of us are trying to enjoy karaoke."

"Are they always like this?" Collin asked.

Katie seemed to forget he was there—she stilled, then slid into an easy stance.

"Absolutely." Her voice softened, almost careful. Her eyes stayed on him, as if she had more to say but held it back. I groaned, sliding off Kevin's lap into my own seat just as the next performer started. The room buzzed with energy. We laughed, sang—pure joy through music and good company.

After a while, Collin checked his phone. "Kevin, gotta head out. Early morning. Be at the gym by eight."

Kevin shook his head, but Collin was already rising. "No excuses." He turned to me, professional now. "Pleasure meeting you, Bethany. You're incredibly talented." Collin extended his hand. As I reached out, something pressed into my palm. "I'd love to work with you. Give me a call on Monday." Before the words could settle, he nodded at Katie. "Katie."

"Collin." Her voice was clipped. The heat between them stayed, even after he walked away.

Katie watched him disappear into the crowd. "What'd he give you?"

I turned the small card over between my fingers:

Collin Conners, A&R Representative – Shadowplay Records

Discovering the Sound of Tomorrow

I could feel Kevin's eyes burning into me. I handed Katie the card, my mind racing. Confused, I turned to Kevin. His gray eyes met mine, and there it was—guilt. The realization hit like a slap. I shot to my feet, chair scraping across the floor.

"Bethany, let me explain—"

I wasn't waiting. I needed to get out of here. I shoved through the bar. Seconds later, his hand caught my wrist, spinning me back. Kevin's eyes searched mine, desperate.

"Bethany—"

I ripped free. "What did you do?"

His expression tightened. "Please, let me explain." His tone was urgent—he knew he was already losing me. I sighed, shaking my head before motioning us down the building, away from the entrance and lingering bar patrons. I needed to pull myself together before I lost it in front of everyone.

We walked in silence, my mind racing, stomach flipping. I turned to him, folding my arms across my chest, bracing myself.

"Answer me this—was he even your friend? Or was this just some ploy to hear me sing for him?"

Kevin's eyes dropped to his shoes.

"Wow." I exhaled sharply. "I can't believe you," I muttered, shaking my head. He lifted his eyes to meet mine.

"Collin and I are friends. That part's true." I let out a skeptical hum, waiting for more.

Kevin rubbed his neck. "You're right. I wanted him to hear you—live." Live. The word dropped like a stone in my stomach. That meant...

My eyes narrowed. "That wasn't the first time he heard me, was it?"

He dragged a hand through his hair. "No."

My heart pounded. "When was the first time, Kevin?"

"Earlier this week."

The confession hit hard. I wasn't done pulling the truth out of him. "How?" I demanded. He looked away.

His voice was so low I almost missed it. "Because I sent him your song." The words sank in—*my song*. Meant only for him. The one he coaxed me into recording, promising it was just for him. Anger and hurt rose like bile.

He stepped forward, hands outstretched like he could hold me together. "Bethany, you're talented. You should share your voice with the world. I know you said you didn't want a career in music, but I think it's because you're jaded. The one person who promised to help you used you. I figured if I used that track as a demo, did the legwork, found the right person, you'd change your mind." He smiled, like he expected me to understand—like it was some romantic gesture. "And I was right. Collin was blown away tonight!"

My voice was quiet, but the fury was unmistakable. "I don't know what I'm more pissed about," I said. "That you took an intimate, private song—a song I sang for you—and shared it." My voice rose, shaking. "You said it was just for your ears. You lied."

I stepped back. The hurt cut deeper than I wanted to admit.

"Or maybe it's that you can't respect the decision I made for my life." My throat tightened. "You think you're helping me? All I see is you trying to control me—deciding what's best." I forced the words out. "Like my father. Like Danny." I shook my head. "You're all the same."

Kevin's expression cracked, his body tensing like my words knocked the air out of him. I swallowed against the lump in my throat, blinking past the sting in my eyes. Over his shoulder, Katie stood at the entrance, concern barely hidden. Kevin opened his mouth. I raised my hand.

"Just stop," I whispered, squeezing my eyes shut. I took a slow breath, counted to ten, pushed down the storm clawing its way up. When I spoke again, my voice was calmer, but the decision was already made. "I think I'm ready to go home."

Relief washed over Kevin's face. "Okay, we can talk later at my place."

"No." I shook my head. "I mean my home. By myself." His face fell. I couldn't tell who looked more hurt—him or me. His lips parted—like he wanted to fix it, rewind time. But there was nothing left to say. "I need time to think," I said. "And I'd rather be alone tonight." I stepped around him toward Katie. She didn't speak—just gave me a small, understanding nod. "I'm ready to go."

She glanced between us and pulled out her phone. "Okay, calling an Uber...we're in luck—two minutes."

"Good." I pulled out my vape and took a long drag. The inhale gave me a sliver of control as I unraveled. As I exhaled, watching the smoke curl, Kevin's eyes stayed on me. But I didn't look—I didn't trust myself to.

37

— • —

COURSE CORRECTION

BETHANY

I slept like a baby—and that should've been a good thing. But it wasn't. Because I was drained—mentally, emotionally, completely spent. And not just from last night. From everything. Seven months ago, things were simpler—maybe boring, but they were mine. My world had been small, but I built it—solid, controlled. My father was alive. I was single, and it never felt like a bad thing, because I didn't have to confront anything. No old memories. No ghosts waiting to be acknowledged. It wasn't exciting, but it was mine. My choices. And then my father died. Just like that, everything tipped out of my hands. My carefully built world shattered, spinning wildly. I scrambled to hold onto something, anything.

At the breakfast table, I stared blankly at my plate. Across from me, Katie talked, but I barely heard a word. My mind was too loud with thoughts I couldn't quiet.

"Are you even listening to me?" Her voice cut through the haze. I blinked, looked up.

"I-I-no. I wasn't. I'm sorry. What were you saying again?" My voice came out flat and distant. Katie huffed, setting her glass down a little too hard.

"All right." She crossed her legs, foot bouncing. "I can't do this anymore. We're not going to have a normal conversation until we deal with the Kevin of it all." I didn't respond. Her brow lifted as she stood. "I'm waiting." She scoffed, scraping her plate into the trash. She was pissed. Her movements were snappy, holding tight on the dish like it had personally offended her. When she turned off the water, she faced me fully. "Bethany, can I be honest with you?" I froze. I nodded anyway.

"Of course." She sat down. "You can be really self-absorbed."

The words hit hard. My back stiffened. Heat rose to my face. "That's not—" I stopped. Because deep down? She was right. Katie didn't let up.

"As long as I've known you, you've been so caught up in your own world—your problems, your emotions. You don't let people in. When you do, it's on your terms. It's always the Bethany Show. You never think about how your silence affects the people who love you."

I clenched my hands in my lap. I wanted to shut down—but not this time.

"Are we even friends, Bethany?" That one hit differently. I opened my mouth. "Yes."

Katie sighed. "Sometimes it doesn't feel that way. I love you, and I've tried so hard to be there for you. To hold you up when you didn't even know you were falling. Because you're not just my best friend—you're like a sister to me. But sometimes you act like you don't know me at all." She wasn't wrong. She'd been my anchor. And what had I done? Had I ever truly been there for her?

"I..." My voice cracked. "I'm sorry. You're right. I've been so caught up in my own mess that I haven't been a good friend to you." My eyes burned. "You've been patient—even when I didn't deserve it or when I shut you out. And I-I don't know why you've stuck around, but Katie...thank you."

Her expression softened. "I appreciate that," she said. "But we're not done."

"What else is there to say?"

She sat back. "Your religious upbringing made you think you always had the right answer. That your way of seeing the world was the only way. You don't even realize how much it still affects you. You don't see things from other people's perspectives." I opened my mouth, but she cut me off. "That's why you can't see Kevin wasn't trying to control you—he was trying to help you."

"Katie—"

"Just listen. If you could see yourself when you sing, you would get it. This is why I always push us to go to karaoke. Have you ever seen me pick up a mic? Not once. You know why? Because I can't sing to save my life. It was never about me. It was for you. Because I know what singing does to you—how it makes you feel."

I froze. I thought about Kevin—how he looked at me when I sang. Not like he was managing me. Like he saw me.

"I get it," she said. "Danny burned you. Bad. And you haven't been able to move past that. But Kevin isn't Danny. He's not trying to take advantage of you. He doesn't get anything from this except seeing you happy. He loves you. And you're about to throw all of that away because you're too scared to let yourself want this."

Her words landed like bricks. Katie pushed back, rinsed my plate like nothing had happened.

"Do us both a favor." She turned off the water. "Go to him. Figure this out. Because honestly? I cannot handle another one of your emotional downward spirals." She dried her hands and finally glanced at me. "And one of us should be having mind-blowing sex. It's clearly not going to be me anytime soon."

I laughed before I could stop it. She smirked and pulled me into a hug.

"Get out of your head. Go talk to your boyfriend." She shoved me toward the hallway. She was right. I needed to face it—face him. I got dressed, grabbed my keys, and headed to Kevin's.

38

A KNOCK AT THE DOOR

BETHANY

My stomach was in knots. I'd been outside Kevin's apartment for five minutes, staring at his door. Just knock. Get it over with. I exhaled, trying to calm the anxious pulse in my throat. But my hand wouldn't move. I didn't know what I was going to say. I'd rehearsed a dozen versions of this conversation, but now everything felt scrambled. He was home—his bike was outside. Why was this so hard? A breath caught in my lungs. I held it for a second, then forced my hand to move. My knuckles hit the door hard, each knock fueled by my need to fix us.

I shifted on my feet. Nothing. Maybe he really wasn't here. Maybe I was wrong about his bike. Or worse—maybe he saw me standing out here and didn't want anything to do with me. Heartbeat pounding fast. My stomach turned as I pivoted to leave.

The door flew open. I flinched, stepping back on instinct, breath catching as my eyes met his. He stood in the doorway with a duffle bag slung over his shoulder. No words—just a stunned stare, like he wasn't sure I was real.

"Bethany." His voice cracked on my name.

He looked awful. His bright gray eyes were clouded and bloodshot. The skin beneath them was bruised with exhaustion, a stark contrast against the rest of his face. His hair was a mess, sticking up in uneven spikes like he'd run his hands through it too many times.

A rough shadow darkened his jaw, making him look even more worn down. His black T-shirt was wrinkled, clinging to his frame like he'd been living in it. The way he stood felt off—like he didn't know whether to move or just wait. I wasn't the only one struggling to hold it together.

"I didn't hear you knock." His fingers curled slightly around the strap of his bag. "I was just on my way out." He sounded flustered. That wasn't like him.

"Oh." My voice was small. Searching his face for the right words, but everything felt tangled. "Can we talk for a second?" He paused, just for a second. His jaw twitched like he was biting back whatever response came first, and then he finally nodded.

"Yeah...sure." His voice was low, rough—like it hurt to speak.

I stepped inside, my heart hammering against my ribs. The door shut behind me with a quiet click. Kevin still didn't put the bag down. Swallowing hard, willing myself to focus.

"I know your intentions were good last night," I started, turning toward him. "But I wish you would've just told me the truth." His jaw ticked, but he didn't say anything. "You made me feel like...like I didn't have a say. I just—if you had told me your friend was there to hear me sing..." I trailed off. The space between us felt unbearable.

Kevin's fingers flexed on the strap, his stance stiff and guarded. I didn't come to make him shut down. Or hurt him. My hand lifted, my fingers brushing against the rough line of his jaw before I could stop myself. His breath caught, but he didn't pull away. His eyes flickered shut, breath slowing—like he was willing himself to stay in this moment.

"I'm sorry," I said. "For comparing you to my father. And to Danny." His lips parted, another breath slipping out. Seeing him—tired, worn, vulnerable—made me let my guard down. I wanted to give him something to hold onto, something real. Because no matter how messy things got—how much we fought, or how hard this felt—he would always know one thing. "I love you," I whispered.

Kevin's eyes snapped open. His face tightened, betraying a crack he hadn't meant to show. His fingers tightened around the strap, his throat bobbing like he was choking back words he couldn't let out. His voice was rough, thick with emotion.

"I love you, too." And then he kissed me. But not like usual. This wasn't the kind of kiss that burned, stole my breath, left me dizzy and clinging to him. There was no fire, no urgency pulling me under. Instead, his lips met mine—soft, slow, hesitant. It was careful, like he was handling something fragile, unsure if he should be kissing me at all. It wasn't bad. It was just...different. Almost innocent. Kevin pulled away first, forehead resting against mine. "Come with me."

"What?"

He lifted his duffle bag slightly. "I needed to clear my head. A friend has a cabin in the San Gabriel Mountains." His fingers tightened on the strap. "Do you have work tomorrow?" I shook my head. A slow smile crept onto his lips, but his eyes—his eyes didn't match it.

"Perfect." I laughed softly, wrapping my arms around his neck, my body pressing into his. "I don't have any clothes."

He lifted the bag slightly. "You can wear some of mine. Just a couple of days, Beth-any." The way he said my name stuck—like it was unfamiliar. He kissed my cheek, his hand sliding against my waist, fingers pressing in just a little too firmly before he pulled back. I ignored the flicker in my stomach and nodded.

"Okay."

Kevin sighed, brushing my wrist before adjusting his grip on the keys, knuckles whitening.

"Can we take your car?" he asked, voice raspier now. "My bike broke down this morning. I was going to get an Uber, but now I don't have to."

"Of course." Hand in hand, we walked to my car, his hold tight, like he wasn't letting go.

The afternoon sun hung low in the sky, casting long streaks of gold across the road as we drove deeper into the wilderness. I offered to drive. Kevin's eyelids looked heavy, and his posture was slumped. He could use the rest. He didn't argue—just handed me the keys and settled in, letting the hum of the car lull him. As the miles stretched on, I reached for my purse, fishing for my phone.

"What do you need?" Kevin's voice cut through the stillness, his hand suddenly on mine before I could grab it.

"I need to text Katie," I said, glancing at him before turning back to the road. "I don't want her to worry. She'll be expecting me to come home at some point this weekend."

"I'll do it for you. You should keep your focus on driving."

He put my purse onto his lap, pulled out my phone, and started typing. My chest warmed at the gesture. Taking care of things seemed second nature to him. Kevin rested—deep breaths, body still. I wondered if he was asleep or just lost in thought. Maybe he was replaying it all, just like I was—the tension, the cracks, the times we nearly fell apart. Now, sitting here with him, everything inside me finally began to feel normal. I felt like myself again. Getting away together, even just for the weekend, seemed like exactly what we needed. A break from everything outside of us. Just him and me.

Gravel crunched under the tires as I pulled up to the cabin. My foot eased off the gas, and I sat back, taking it in. It sat tucked among the trees—a true hideaway. Rugged and weathered, but still standing. Dark logs blended into the woods, like they'd always been part of it. Moss spread across the steep roof, while a narrow chimney reached from the top. The small windows, fogged over, gave nothing away. To the left, a covered porch extended out, held up by thick beams. Firewood leaned neatly against the wall. It looked untouched, like it had been waiting for us.

I stepped out of the car and stretched, letting the crisp air fill my lungs—pine and damp earth clinging to each breath. A breeze moved through the trees, brushing me enough to raise goosebumps. It wasn't the cold. It was something else—fleeting, buried. A feeling that threaded through my ribs, like a warning I wasn't meant to catch. I turned toward Kevin, but he was already at the trunk, pulling the duffle out. I told myself I was just tired.

39

HEAVY AIR

BETHANY

The air inside was abrasive, like the cabin had been holding its breath. Old wood, faint sweetness, a slight musty smell—but I didn't mind. Just dust, time, maybe a little neglect. Nothing a few open windows wouldn't fix.

"Ugh." I fanned my hand. "We need to get some air in here." I turned to Kevin, expecting him to agree, but he lingered in the doorway, watching me. His expression was indecipherable—neither distant nor tense, just...different. I'd never seen that look before. A flicker of something passed through his eyes, but before I could place it, it was gone. I smiled, letting it go. My eyes swept across the room as I took a few steps deeper inside. "Can the windows open?" I glanced over my shoulder at him.

The cabin had a rustic charm—simple, worn, lived-in. Not bare bones, but far from luxurious. The kitchen ran along the left side, its wood-paneled cabinets dulled by time, surfaces nicked and uneven. Open shelves sagged slightly under mismatched plates and dust-coated teacups. A gingham curtain hung beneath the sink.

I ran my fingers across the counter—gritty with old crumbs, sticky where spills had been left to dry. The stove stood along the far wall, iron doors streaked with soot, the metal darkened from years of use. A dented kettle rested on top. I didn't mean to reach for it, but when my hand passed over, a trace of heat brushed my skin. The counters told stories of rushed meals—scarred cutting boards, sticky oil bottles, and spice jars shoved into corners. A few dishes sat in the sink, food dried and crusted along the rim of a cast-iron skillet.

Turning back toward Kevin, I expected him to be moving around, settling in—but he was still by the door, watching me. He didn't answer, the pause stretching just enough to feel weighted.

"You okay?" I tilted my head. That seemed to snap him out of whatever trance he'd been in. He stepped into the cabin, shutting the door behind him.

The living room was small but inviting. An old sofa sat near the fireplace, draped with a faded hand-stitched quilt. A scuffed wooden coffee table stood in front of it, a stack of old magazines in one corner. At the center, a Bible lay open, its pages slightly curled, like someone had stopped mid-read and never returned. The sight of it made my stomach twist—a book left open felt oddly intimate.

The hearth was already set, logs stacked neatly inside. Near the window, a small table with two chairs stood ready. Along the far wall, a narrow bookcase leaned slightly, its shelves packed with worn paperbacks and dusty DVD cases. A metal stand beside it held a tiny television with a DVD player tucked beneath. A loud thud snapped me out of my thoughts. I turned to see Kevin had dropped his duffel bag by the door.

"This your friend's cabin?" I smiled. "When was the last time someone was here?"

Kevin gave a tight smile. "Yeah. My friend Bob comes here on weekends." There was something distant in his eyes. "Take a look around." His tone was easy, but the way the words came out felt a little off. I told myself not to read anything into it. I was so happy to be here with him, away from everything else. A weekend just for us. A weekend to think. I walked to the bedroom. There was a queen-sized bed with a red quilt, and an oak dresser stood beside it. A single window let in just enough light, and the greenish curtains swayed slightly. I locked eyes on the bed. I pictured Kevin above me, hands on my hips, breath hot against my skin. The thought sent a rush of heat through me, my pulse quickening, my body already aching for his touch. I could almost feel the weight of him, the way his mouth would claim mine, the way we'd lose ourselves in each other, tangled in the sheets until neither of us could tell where one ended and the other began. Desire burned through me, deep and insistent, settling low in my belly. This weekend wouldn't just be good—it'd be unforgettable.

I stepped out, fingers grazing the doorframe as I headed to the next room. The bathroom smelled of damp wood and old soap. Planked walls, warped and darkened with age, enclosed a clawfoot tub beneath a rusted pipe rack cluttered with half-used bottles. The sink slumped against a crooked vanity, mirror cloudy and speckled. Overhead, a single bulb flickered, casting a tired yellow sheen. The high-tanked toilet looked like it hadn't been used in ages.

I let out a breath, tipping my head. Not ideal, but livable for a few days. At the end of the hall, one last door sat alone, set apart from the others. Something about it felt eerie—maybe because it sat at the end of a dark hallway, swallowed in shadow. I reached for the knob, expecting it to turn easily, but it didn't budge. I tried again, jiggling it, but it wouldn't give.

Behind me, Kevin's voice said, "That door won't open." I turned, surprised by how close he was. He stood behind me—I hadn't heard him follow.

"Bob has the key." He reached out and took my hand in his. "Come," he murmured. "Let me make you something to eat." As he lifted my hand from the knob, a shiver ran through me while he led me back to the living room.

Kevin stepped into the kitchen, pulling out bread and peanut butter. He opened the small fridge, retrieving a half-used jar of grape jelly. "I hope you like PB&J. Food supplies are limited. There's a stream nearby. I'll go fishing tomorrow." I stretched out on the couch, kicking off my boots.

"Peanut butter sounds great." I peeked over the back of the couch. "Anything's good when I'm with you." He stiffened, as if I'd caught him off guard.

I frowned. "You okay?"

His shoulders eased—as though I'd pulled him back from somewhere—and when he turned, his smile was easy again. "Mmm-hmm." He set two steaming mugs on the coffee table, the soft clink of porcelain filling the quiet. The fire crackled, throwing a glow across the room. We sat side by side, eating our sandwiches in silence. Something felt off. Kevin was quieter than usual, his easy charm replaced by something heavier. He watched me while I ate, gray eyes unreadable, posture rigid. His stare lingered after I rose to gather our plates. In the kitchen, I turned on the faucet, sinking my hands into soapy water. Kevin stayed put, eyes fixed on the flames like they held answers.

I glanced over my shoulder at him, trying to shake the unease creeping up my spine.

"Your friend Bob must've left in a hurry," I said, scrubbing at a stubborn stain. Kevin didn't move—didn't even look my way.

"How do you figure that?" His voice stayed detached, like he was somewhere else entirely. I frowned, rinsing the soap from my hands.

"I mean, leaving dirty dishes? That's practically an invitation for rodents."

He said nothing; only the fire popped and filled the space. After a moment, he murmured, "That must be it." The flatness of his tone unsettled me. I wiped my hands, watching him carefully. Kevin was acting strange. I'd said harsh things last night, but he had set me up, well-intentioned or not. This was still my life, my choice. I sighed, pushing the thought away. None of this was unfixable. We just needed clearer boundaries, and I would make sure we had them. For now, I knew exactly how to lift whatever hung between us.

I loosened my ponytail, letting my hair cascade as I teased out the waves. Kevin loved my hair down. Straightening, I let my hips sway as I walked toward him, bare feet silent on the floor.

"Kevin." I purred. His head turned, expression impassive. "What's wrong?" My voice softened. He watched me—gray eyes darkening—but stayed guarded.

"I'm fine."

I gave a slow, knowing smile. "This won't do." Straddling him, I settled onto his lap. He stiffened. His hands stayed at his sides. I threaded my fingers through his hair, massaging his scalp, moving closer until my lips hovered over his.

"Baby, I know something's wrong. Tell me so I can fix it." I kissed him, coaxing him to meet me there. At first, he resisted—body rigid, lips barely parting. I deepened the kiss, tongue tracing the seam of his mouth, teasing, tempting. Something in him snapped.

He groaned—a guttural, needy sound. His hands on my waist tightened. The restraint he always carried crumbled. His mouth opened for mine, tongue tangling, hungry and desperate. I rolled my hips, feeling him respond as tense muscles slowly gave way. His hands slid up my back, fingers digging in, pulling me closer. His breath turned ragged, moans going feral.

My palms roamed his chest, feeling heat through his shirt, heart pounding beneath my hand. I tugged the fabric upward, nails scraping skin as I bared him. He sucked a breath, head falling back against the couch, throat exposed. I traced the hard planes of his chest with lips and tongue, savoring the new, broken sounds spilling from him.

I sat up to peel off my shirt, left in nothing but a white lace bra. I reached for the strap—Kevin's hands caught mine. Confused, I looked at him. His pupils were blown wide, gray irises nearly vanished. His breaths were ragged, barely controlled. Then, in an instant, his body changed. The hardness pressing against me moments ago was gone. He blinked rapidly, jaw locking, every muscle tense. Lifting me gently, he shifted me off his lap.

"Sorry," he rasped. "We can't do this tonight."

"I don't understand."

Kevin stood, tugged his shirt on. "I'm just too tired." Too tired? Kevin never turned me down. He handed me my top, and though he said nothing, the message was clear. Reluctantly, I slipped it over my head. He offered his hand; I hesitated before taking it. He dropped it the second I stood. "We have the next two days for that," he said. "I need rest. I'm exhausted." Maybe I was overthinking. He did look dead on his feet.

"Okay," I muttered.

Kevin pressed a quick kiss to my forehead, then led me to the bedroom. He retrieved one of his shirts and a pair of shorts for me. Turning his back, he waited while I changed; then he switched off the light and pulled on loose pants. We climbed into bed. He gave me a brief kiss.

"Good night." He rolled onto his side, back toward me. He didn't usually turn his back. I stared into the dark, my heart sinking. This didn't feel right. Maybe our problems were bigger than I thought. I closed my eyes, willing myself to sleep, but the ache in my chest clung like a nameless dread.

40

MARKED PAGES

BETHANY

I woke expecting Kevin beside me—his arm across my waist, our legs tangled like always. Instead, the bed felt empty. Too empty. The sheets were cool, his pillow untouched. Frowning, I sat up and rubbed the sleep from my eyes.

"Kevin?" My voice rasped. I strained to hear footsteps—any proof he was here. Nothing. Just silence. Unease rippled through me, but I shook it off. Maybe he was outside grabbing firewood or checking something out. I was overthinking. Again.

The bathroom mirror reflected a tired, messy version of myself—tangled hair, chapped lips, and sleep still clinging to my face. I splashed cold water on my face needing to wake up. In the kitchen I reached for a cup on the shelf when something caught my eye—a folded piece of paper, sitting alone on the counter. I picked it up and opened it.

Bethany,

Went to catch our lunch. Didn't want to wake you. Be back soon.

I pressed my lips together and hung my head. Seriously? He left without waking me? I sighed. I didn't love fishing, but I didn't hate it. And the idea of us spending time together, just the two of us...no tension, no overthinking...that had sounded really nice. But he'd just...gone. I grabbed the water and took a large gulp. It caught in my throat. I coughed, sputtering as I slammed the glass down. Jesus. I was annoyed—but not enough to choke over it. Maybe a shower would help.

As I turned toward the bedroom, a brief thought appeared. He invited me here...but did he want me here? Or had he done it because saying no would've sounded rude? That quiet doubt gnawed at me as I pulled open his dresser drawers. A T-shirt. Boxer briefs. Sweatpants. My hand paused. His clothes were unpacked—folded neatly in the drawer.

I didn't notice last night. Had he done all this this morning? I brushed the fabric, then shook my head. Don't spiral. Grabbing a towel and washcloth, I headed back to the bathroom. No steam. I tested the water—it was ice cold. I groaned.

"Of course."

Bracing myself, I stepped in. The water shocked my skin, making me gasp as I scrubbed quickly, muscles clenching against the cold. When I stepped out, goosebumps covered my arms. I dried off, dressed, and ran my fingers through damp hair. This morning was turning into a disaster. I told myself not to let it ruin the day. Kevin was probably just in his head. Maybe he thought I needed more rest than him.

Making my way into the living room and went to the couch to grab my phone. It wasn't there. I checked the cushions, the coffee table, and the stand beside it. Nothing. I searched the kitchen. The bedroom. Even the bathroom again. Still nothing. Confusion hit me. Perfect. One more thing to top off this morning. Where the hell was it? Maybe Kevin accidentally grabbed it. The realization hit like a weight: I was alone in a cabin, no Kevin, no phone. Pushing off the couch I walked to the front door. Opening it, I hugged my arms against the morning chill. The clearing was quiet—nothing but trees. No stream. No movement. Just the wind rustling branches.

I waited a beat, then stepped inside, shutting the door. Dropping onto the couch I rubbed my face. The phone had to be here. It couldn't have just vanished. I yanked off the cushions, ran my hands along the seams. Nothing. Slumping back, arms crossed. What now? No phone. No clock. No idea how long he'd been gone. I let my head fall back and stared at the ceiling.

Out of the corner of my eye, I saw it again—the Bible, open on the coffee table. A frown pulled at my face. An open Bible wasn't just left that way. Curiosity stirred in my chest. What had they been reading? I picked it up, fingers brushing the worn leather. I grew up with a Bible like this—practically lived with it in my lap. Now it felt...foreign. Pages flipped beneath my hands, my eyes landing on the highlighted passage. The hair on my neck stood up.

"Don't take the path of the wicked; don't follow those who do evil. Stay away from that path; don't even go near it. Turn around and go another way. The wicked cannot sleep until they have done something evil."

The words stared like a warning carved in stone. A shiver slithered down my spine. My breath shallowed. I'd heard this verse so many times before so often it was practically burned into my memory. My father's voice, deep and unwavering, came rushing back, thick with conviction.

"Bethany, the wicked cannot sleep until they have done something evil."

I could hear how he'd say it—slow, methodical, like the words held a truth he needed me to believe. My fingers curled around the book. It was nothing. Just a coincidence. Bibles always had highlighted verses. But the way it sat open, perfectly in my line of sight, it felt intentional. I snapped the Bible shut and tossed it on the table. The thud echoed too loud. The room felt smaller, the air heavier. I sighed, shaking off the unease in my veins. I was being ridiculous. It was just a book. Just words. A needed distraction.

Pushing to my feet, I walked to the bookcase, fingers trailing the spines. Nothing caught my interest. Air hissed between my teeth as my hand dropped, eyes scanning lower. On the bottom shelf, a stack of DVDs sat in a messy pile. Perfect. Kneeling, I rifled through the cases until I found one that seemed decent—a children's movie. Something light. Easy. I picked it up and turned on the TV. As the screen flickered on, I turned to the DVD player and pressed eject. The tray slid out, and I paused. A disc was already inside—blank. No title. No markings. A plain, silver surface stared back at me.

A strange feeling crept up my spine. I considered swapping it out for the DVD in my hand. That would be the normal thing to do. My fingers hovered, but something felt...off. I slid the disc back in and pressed play. The screen flickered on—grainy, unfocused. A crackling hum filled the silence. Pressing my lips together, I raised the volume. The static thickened, stretching into an uneasy stillness. The screen adjusted. A melody drifted through the speakers.

Dread crept up my spine, twisting my stomach. I knew that song. A slow dread settled over me. My body stiffened. A chill raced through me as the screen flickered again. Then, there she was. A teenage girl stood on a small stage, holding a microphone. Dim lighting cast long, eerie shadows behind her. Music played softly in the background—faint piano notes drifting through the silence. I stepped back. My legs wobbled, but I couldn't look away. Her voice floated, high and sweet, woven with innocence and worship.

"He's got the whole world in His hands..."

My breath hitched. Blood turned to ice. Her posture. The tilt of her head. The way she closed her eyes—I knew all of it. My heartbeat roared, drowning out everything else. The camera zoomed in. I staggered as my heel caught on the rug. The image sharpened. I stopped breathing. The girl on screen—the one singing with so much faith and trust—was me.

41

SHATTERED ILLUSIONS

BETHANY

The second the image of my teenage self disappeared from the screen, I lunged forward and shut off the television. My hands trembled so violently that I nearly stumbled against the TV stand. How did the DVD get here? None of this made sense. The cabin felt stifling, the walls closing in. Every nerve screamed—get out. Now. I turned, scanning for my purse and keys—then stopped.

Kevin was just...there. Silent. Watching. A breath lodged in my throat. My muscles went rigid. How long had he been there? Where the hell did he come from? It wasn't the front door. I would've seen him. I was practically standing in front of it. The stillness rang louder than words. My pulse pounded, hard and frantic. Instinct screamed at me to run, but I couldn't move—not yet. Not until I understood what I was seeing. This wasn't Kevin. Not my Kevin.

His eyes—gray but wrong—were eerily dilated like last night. His hair, normally tousled, was slicked back, pristine, a style he never wore. And the way he stood...his posture was rigid, calculated. Everything felt wrong. A shudder rolled through me as I forced the words out.

"Where did you come from?"

He didn't answer. His face remained blank, eerily still. Then, so suddenly, it made my skin crawl—he changed. His lips curved into a smile. It wasn't Kevin's smile. It didn't reach his eyes.

"Kevin?" I whispered.

A long exhale slipped past his lips, like he had been holding it in all this time. His hands folded, fingers intertwining. He stepped forward. I stepped back. He said nothing. The floor creaked as he took another step. My stomach churned. Every nerve vibrated with warning.

"How long have you been standing there?" I demanded, my voice shook, despite my attempt to keep it sturdy.

His jaw ticked. His eyes bore into me. Still—no response. He took another step. I took another back. This was wrong.

"Kevin, answer me," I said, trying to sound strong. "Or I'm leaving." Turning slightly, I measured the distance to the keys on the table. The door was right there, but not close enough. I wasn't going to make it. Kevin's look followed mine, his eyes looking at the keys. He knew what I was thinking. Swallowing hard, I forced my voice steady. "I'm sure you have an explanation for this." My fists clenched. Think, Bethany. Think. "Let's have a seat at the table and talk." Getting those keys was all that mattered. His expression didn't change. He stood there, measuring my words.

"Okay..." I let my guard down. "Bethy."

I froze. A jolt shot through my spine. My breath stalled. No one outside Willow Creek called me that. No one. I had never shared that name with Kevin. Katie hadn't even known it existed until the day Cheyenne said it in Willow Creek. Oh my God.

A dizzying realization crashed over me. Pressure crushed my ribs. Every breath was a struggle. He knew. Kevin knew something about me that I had never told him. Fear slithered in—cold, smothering. My instincts screamed: run. Fight or flight. The alarm in my head wasn't ringing—it howled. I lunged. My fingers brushed the keys when Kevin moved. Fast. Too fast. I bolted, shoving the door open so hard it rattled on its hinges. My pulse thundered, drowning out everything. He was behind me. Close.

I flew onto the porch, hope bursting—I was going to make it. Out of nowhere, there was a blinding pain. A white-hot explosion at the back of my head. The world blurred. The last thing I saw before darkness swallowed me was Kevin, lips curled in an insidious smile as he murmured, "Don't worry, Bethy, I'll take care of you."

42

WAKING TO DARKNESS

BETHANY

I woke to pain—searing and relentless, radiating from the back of my head and pulsing down my spine like an electric current. My skull throbbed, pressure building behind my eyes, each heartbeat a fresh wave of agony. A shallow breath slipped out as I reached up with shaky fingers. The moment they brushed the tender spot, an involuntary cry tore from my throat. My scalp felt torn like something had ripped through it.

When I pulled my hand back, my fingertips were slick and warm. Blood. The metallic scent filled my nose, nauseating, mixing with mildew and rot. Darkness pressed in from all sides. I blinked, straining to see—but the blackness was absolute. Panic tightened around my chest. Breaths came too fast, too shallow. Forcing myself to move, muscles aching like I'd been thrown downstairs. Cold seeped through my clothes, biting my skin. I curled my fingers, dragging them across the ground, rough, uneven concrete. Grit clung to my skin. My other hand swept forward, searching, trying to remember where I was.

Pushing up slowly, a dizzying wave crashed over me as I lifted my head. The room swayed. My stomach turned. Teeth clenched, I panting as I fought the pull of unconsciousness. My legs trembled, every movement stiff. Ahead of me, there was a sliver of light. It bled through a small gap near the floor. I staggered toward it, bare feet scraping the concrete—each step spiking pain through my skull. The light led me to the door. Fingers skimmed the wood—rough and damp beneath my touch—until they found the knob, cold and unmoving. I yanked with everything I had. It didn't move.

My ear pressed to the door, straining to hear anything. Footsteps. Wind. The faintest sign of life. Nothing. A tremor ran through me. Panic burned in my chest, rising fast. I didn't think—I moved. I hurled myself at the door, the impact sending a brutal shockwave through my shoulder, but I didn't care.

"Ugh," I groaned. "KEVIN!" My voice cracked, hoarse, frantic. I pounded with my fists, slammed into the wood again and again. The pain barely registered, drowned by the desperation clawing through me. "Somebody! Please!"

My throat burned, but I kept screaming, kept kicking, kept clawing until my nails felt like they were tearing away. The silence swallowed everything—not just absence, but a force, thick and unmoving, curling around me like a noose. The air thinned. Each breath was harder to catch than the last. My chest heaved, pulse pounding in my ears.

"Kevin," I whispered this time, my voice breaking. "Please."

I twisted the knob harder. My hand slipped. I jiggled it again, shaking the door like wanting it badly enough might make it open. But it didn't. The metal stayed stiff, like it was never meant to budge. I stared at it, breath catching, and tried again—this time with both hands, yanking until the wood creaked. Nothing. A dull panic started to hum beneath my skin. Quiet at first.

I pressed my head against the door, my fingers still holding the knob. Maybe it was stuck. Maybe I was doing it wrong. But the longer I stood there, the more I felt it—not just resistance. Refusal. The thought came slowly, like water seeping through a crack: I'm not getting out. Not right now. Maybe not at all. And then it settled, cold and final, in the pit of my stomach. No one was coming.

A choked sob wrenched from my throat, my knees buckling beneath me. I slid down against the door, my body shaking so hard my teeth chattered. I held the knob, clinging like it could save me, like holding tight enough might make it turn. It would open. I gasped in short, uneven breaths, my head falling back against the wood. The finality of it sank into my bones. My vision blurred with fresh tears. There was nowhere for them to go. Nothing to soak them up but stale, rotting air.

With my forehead pressed to my knees, curling in like being smaller might make this disappear. The dark didn't care. It seeped into my skin, whispering its cold promise. I wasn't getting out. Rocking slightly, my body trembled, my sobs quieting into shallow, broken gasps. Exhaustion swallowed me, dragging me into restless sleep.

I woke to the sound of footsteps on the stairs—each one heavier, the boards groaning beneath the strain. My body locked up, muscles tensing like pulled wire. Shooting upright, panic surged through me as I shoved myself backward with legs wobbling beneath me, weak and shaking, but I forced them to move. Had to move. Stumbling across the room, I felt my way through the dark until I reached the opposite wall. I pressed myself against it, the cold seeping into my skin, locking me in place. My heart pounded, each frantic beat crashing against my ribs.

The footsteps kept coming, closing the distance with keys jingling. I flinched. The lock turned with a loud click. The door creaked open, light spilling into the room, and there he was. Kevin. He stood in the doorway, calm as ever. Like nothing was wrong. Like I wasn't trapped in this room, shaking, my throat sore from screaming. He reached for the switch outside the door, flicking it on. The brightness stabbed through my skull. I squeezed my eyes shut, then forced them to adjust. When I looked at him again, his gray eyes were normal. Unbothered.

"I didn't want it to be like this," he said smoothly, stepping inside. "But you left me no choice." He carried a plate and a glass of water. My stomach twisted at the sight, at the terrifying normalcy of it. Kevin stepped forward, expression blank. "You took a pretty nasty fall outside," he continued, as if this were some casual conversation. "You're lucky I was there to bring you back in." He paused, tilting his head slightly. "You never know what kind of creature could've gotten to you."

The way he said it—so easy—made my skin crawl. It wasn't a warning. It was a threat. If I could melt into the wall, I would.

"Kevin, please." My throat burned, but I forced the words out. "Let me go. I swear, I won't tell anyone."

There was a sudden shift in him. Subtle at first—a flicker in his eyes, a slight tightening of his mouth. His shoulders squared, stance growing rigid as the illusion of warmth faded. His jaw tensed, the muscle ticking as his expression hardened—every trace of concern dissolving. Piece by piece, the softness disappeared until only the man who had locked me in here remained—the one I had every reason to fear. Without a word, he stepped to the side and placed the plate and cup on a small, dust-covered shelf. He turned and walked toward me. My instincts screamed at me to run, to do something. But there was nowhere to go. No escape.

Kevin stood so close that I felt his breath on my face. My jaw clenched as I willed myself not to flinch when he reached out. His fingers brushed against my hair, tucking it behind my ear with carefulness that made my stomach turn. I shuddered. The gesture should've been comforting, but from him, it wasn't. A mockery of tenderness from a man I didn't recognize. His hand trailed lower, fingers grazing my jaw before settling under my chin. I jerked away. His grip tightened, yanking me back. My skin stung beneath his nails, enough to make my eyes water.

"Now, Bethany," he murmured. "Now is not the time to be defiant."

I whimpered, sucking in my breath.

"Be a good girl," he continued, tilting my chin up until I had no choice but to meet his gaze. "Eat the sandwich. Drink the water." His face inched closer, so close his lips nearly brushed mine. "If you haven't eaten by the time I come back..." His voice dropped to a whisper, each syllable careful. "Bethy, you will regret it." His fingers dug in one last time, pain searing through my chin as I let out a choked cry. Kevin pressed a kiss on my forehead, then released me. He turned, smooth and effortless, like this was just a casual exchange. Without another glance, he strode to the door. The lock clicked behind him. And I was alone.

A dim light bulb hung from the ceiling. For the first time since waking up in the dark, I could see where I was. Empty wooden shelves lined the walls, their planks warped and covered in dust. No jars. No sacks of potatoes or canned goods. Nothing but the bare structure of what this place used to be. A root cellar.

I took a slow step forward, brushing my foot against something rough. A stained mattress lay on the concrete, sunken in places, the fabric darkened with patches I didn't want to think about. The stuffing bunched in uneven clumps, like it had been tossed there without care. Turning, my fingers trailed along the shelf, the wood dry and splintered beneath my touch. The longer I looked, the clearer it became. The door upstairs—the one Kevin said was locked, the one he claimed his friend Bob had the only key to—had led here. Kevin had lied. It was as simple as that. And now, this place wasn't just a root cellar. It was my prison.

I stared at the plate and cup sitting on the shelf. Fists clenched, nails digging into my palms. Eating or drinking was the last thing I wanted, but refusing came with it's own risks. Kevin's moods shifted—unstable, impossible to predict. If I pushed too hard, or tested his patience too soon, what would he do? My stomach flipped at the thought. I forced myself to move, stepping toward the shelf. My fingers shook as I picked up the sandwich and the cup of water. The plastic felt light. A reminder, Kevin made sure I had nothing breakable. Nothing to use against him.

I lowered myself onto the mattress, the smell of mildew and something worse seeping into my skin. The fabric sagged, stuffing pressing into my hip. I took a bite of the sandwich, my jaw working through the thick, dry peanut butter. Barely any jelly. It clung to the roof of my mouth, forcing me to take a gulp of water to wash it down. I needed a plan. I needed a way out.

Gripping the cup, my mind sorting through what little I knew. I was in a root cellar. Kevin had lied. That much was simple. But nothing else was. I forced down the last bite, throat tight. The plate and cup clattered as I set them back on the shelf. I wouldn't give him a reason to touch me again. I had to find something. A weapon. Anything.

Frustration burned in my throat as I crawled to the next, sweeping every inch. Breath quickened, heart hammering while my hands moved across bare wood. Nothing. Pushing up onto my knees, I reached into the shadows of the third shelf, movements sharp and frantic. I needed something—needed it now. Fingers skimmed the rough surface, desperate for a catch, a clue.

"Fuck!" The word ripped out of me. I stood too fast.

A white-hot wave crashed through my skull, a dull, pounding throb radiating from the back of my head. My fingers found the swollen knot. My legs wobbled, the room blurring until I had to squeeze my eyes shut. I stilled, straining to listen. No footsteps. No creaking from the stairs. He hadn't heard me. I let out a slow, careful breath and turned back to the shelf. Still two more.

I stretched for the fourth, rising onto the balls of my feet, fingertips barely grazing the back of it. My arms ached, body weak from too many hours crumpled on the floor. My vision blurred for a second, and I grabbed the planks as the world tilted. Blinked. It was the hit to the head. That had to be it. Squeezing my eyes shut, I breathed through dizziness, forcing my thoughts to focus.

I was looking for something. A weapon. I clung to the word like a lifeline, reaching back into the shelf—

The room lurched.

I staggered, hands slipping. My body swayed, a sudden weightlessness pulling me off balance. I caught myself before my knees buckled completely. Something was wrong. Grabbing hold of the shelf, fingers digging into the wood. It felt too far away, arms too heavy. My breaths slowed, thick, uneven. Limbs sluggish. Blinking hard, I tried to gather my thoughts, but they weren't coming together the way they should. Weapon. I needed a weapon.

I forced my hand forward again, but the moment I moved, my legs buckled, body folding in on itself. I had to sit down, just for a second. Dragging myself to the mattress, I collapsed onto it, limbs boneless. The ceiling swayed, my vision dimming, closing in.

"Lie down, Bethany," I murmured, my voice slurred, distant.

I sank lower into the mattress, body molding into the lumps and sagging fabric. My eyelids fluttered, too heavy to hold open. A yawn stretched through me, slow and deep, as a soothing heaviness crept through each limb. My fingers curled weakly. Muscles lax. I floated in hazy comfort. This felt nice. The bed was perfect. Everything was. A small smile tugged at my lips as I rolled onto my side. Whatever I'd worried about didn't matter. Nothing mattered. One last sigh—and I let go, floating into darkness.

43

— • —

MY SWEET BETHY

KEVIN

I had to think on my feet. She wasn't supposed to come. The plan was to take her last night. Alone. But she came to me instead—walked right up to the door. It was a sign. Last night had nearly broken me—the way she moved, breathed—she tightened around me like a vice. My flesh screamed; hands twitched, breath quickened, mind battling the need to claim what was mine. But I knew it wasn't right. Not yet. I had to wait. Do this properly. And this morning? I almost lost her. I'd been careless—leaving the DVD out was bad enough, but calling her Bethy changed everything. I saw it the instant understanding flashed—her breath caught, hands stiffened, body coiled like a trapped animal. She was afraid. She shouldn't be.

Her focus shifted to the table, then snapped to the keys. She moved too fast—lunging, fingers closing around them, twisting toward the door. I had no choice. I was outside before I realized I'd moved; the firewood was stacked like it had been waiting. My hand found a solid piece, bark biting into my palm. When I swung, the impact rang through my arm—a thick, splintering crack.

She gasped, stumbled, the crumpled; golden hair spilling like a wilted flower. The keys slipped from her hand. A slow exhale left my chest, heartbeat settling. Now Bethy was mine. I stepped over the body and shut the door; no one had seen, no one had heard. In the root cellar, she would be safe—made whole again. Beside the bed, I knelt and pulled the duffel from underneath, unzipping it.

Her Bible came first. I traced the worn cover, pages untouched for too long. Next, I lifted the dress, white and blue, with delicate floral stitching. Modest, feminine, pure. I smoothed it across the quilt.

"This blue will bring out your eyes, Bethy."

The hairbrush followed, bristles ready to glide through golden strands. Then a satin ribbon, cool and perfect between my fingers. Everything was ready. I walked down the stairs as the air grew cooler. The second key turned smoothly, the lock clicking open. I crept forward, letting my eyes adjust to the dimness.

My Sleeping Beauty. My Bethy.

Bethy lay still, lashes resting on pale cheeks, lips parted. She looked peaceful like this. Quiet. So...right. This was how I wanted her—innocent, clean, pure. I stepped forward, crouching beside her, then I slid my hands beneath her, lifting her into my arms. No stir. No resistance. Perfect. Time to cleanse her. Wash the world away.

44

SUNDAY CLOTHES

BETHANY

I woke in a fog, thoughts thick and slow to surface. The world tilted as I sat up, a dull throb pulsing from skull to spine. Every joint ached like I'd been dropped and left to splinter on this lumpy mattress—too thin, bunched, reeking of mildew. As my eyes adjusted to the dim light, something heavier weighed on me—a green wool blanket draped across my legs. It hadn't been there before. Breath caught in my throat. It had to be him. I must have been unconscious, drugged. Sludge crawled through my bloodstream, head throbbing, pressure thick behind my eyes.

My stomach flipped. I kicked the blanket off hard, my heel snagging it and sending it tumbling to the floor. That's when I saw it. I wasn't in the clothes I'd put on earlier. I was wearing it. A white-and-blue floral dress—fitted sleeves, modest hem— still haunting the corners of my mind. My throat clenched. I'd worn this every month growing up, on dedication days at my father's church. A dress meant for obedience, for purity, for everything I'd spent years trying to forget.

"No...no, no, no."

I clawed at the neckline, yanking at the seams. My braid whipped around my face, sticking to the sweat blooming across my brow. Shoving it back—I froze. My hair had been braided. A single, tight braid, finished with a satin ribbon. Blue. I tore the ribbon free and flung it like venom. A scream ripped from my throat, untamed and animalistic. It bounced off the stone walls and slammed back into me. I clutched the braid with shaking hands and yanked it apart, yanking at the strands as if they were shackles.

"I'm not her—I'm not her—I'm not Bethy anymore!" The words spilled out, half-choked. I wasn't that girl, the one who bowed her head on command, who sang songs

233

she didn't understand, who belonged to someone else. I yanked my arm halfway free, desperate to shed the skin he'd forced on me, when a sound stopped me cold. Click. A key slid into the lock. Heart pounding, breath lodged, I shoved my arm back through the sleeve and stumbled to the corner, pressing into the cold stone, willing myself to disappear.

The door burst open. Kevin stepped inside as if it were a Sunday morning service. He wore a blue plaid button-up, collar stiff, tucked into freshly pressed khakis. Hair slicked back, jaw clean-shaven. Calm. Precise. Proud. A black backpack hung from one shoulder; with his other hand, he dragged a scratched rust-orange chair. The legs screeched across the concrete, carving through the silence. My stomach knotted. He set the chair, turned it with careful intention, and sat, blocking the only exit—his posture almost peaceful. That made it worse.

"Now, Bethy," he began, voice rough with a twisted kind of delight. He folded his hands, calm, practiced—the way my father used to before every sermon. Or punishment. Kevin tilted his head. "Why so much noise?" A half-smile tugged at his lips—amusement cloaked in charm, sharp as a knife.

"I just want to go home." That smile stretched wide, slow, and poisonous.

"You are home, Bethy," he said, dragging my name out like a lullaby turned into a threat.

"I'm not," I snapped. The smirk vanished. He was on his feet in a blink, seizing my arms with bruising force; the room tilted as he shook me hard.

"What did you do to your hair?" he barked. "What did you do?" His fingers tightened; fire shot up my arms.

"This is unacceptable," he snarled. "It took me over an hour to get that braid right." He yanked me forward, dragging me across the floor until I stood in front of the filthy mattress. My heart slammed; my breath came in shallow bursts as I fought to pull away.

"What are you doing? Let go!" He bent in close, breath hot and sour against my cheek.

"When I enter this room," he thundered, "you are to stand here. Do you understand me?"

Caged, helpless, I forced out a whisper. "Yes."

"Answer me, Bethy!" he roared, spit striking my skin.

I winced and tried again, louder, "Yes."

He stared for a beat—chest heaving—then, as if a switch flipped, turned away and strolled back to the chair with eerie calm.

"Good," he said smoothly. "Now, fix your hair. Put the ribbon back." Panic drove my hands. I scooped the ribbon from the floor, fingers trembling as I re-braided, scalp throbbing from the pulling. The satin knot felt like ice against my neck.

Kevin's expression softened; unbelievably, he smiled. "There she is. My girl. You look so beautiful, Bethy." I stood rigid. "Manners," he prompted, singsong and smug. "What do you say when someone pays you a compliment?"

"Th-thank you." The words felt like poison.

"Very good." Something fractured inside me. He wasn't just delusional; he was becoming someone I thought I'd buried.

The cadence of his commands—the tone—was my father's voice wearing Kevin's skin. It didn't make sense. He'd reached into my most broken place and built a world from it.

"Today is a special day," he said. "The day you recommit yourself to our Father. We must purge all the evil from you." Acid churned in my stomach.

He unzipped the black backpack at his feet. When he pulled out the object, my heart stopped. My pink vibrator. Mine. I gasped. He held it like a trophy. "Been missing for months," he said lightly. "You've been unclean. Doing unclean things." He tossed it behind him; it hit the concrete with a dull thud.

Shame and rage collided in my chest, stealing my breath. He reached in again and drew out my Bible. I'd hidden it deep in my closet. The floor dropped away, and I staggered back, nausea rising. I tried to bury that book with the girl I used to be. The fact that he held it felt like a violation beyond words. My blood ran cold.

"Before we start today's Bible lesson," he said, voice smooth and cold, "I want you to sing."

I froze. His eyes narrowed.

"Sing," he said, jaw tight. "He's Got the Whole World in His Hands."

Swallowing hard, my voice wavered; body locked. I began to sing. When I finished, Kevin clapped once, slicing through the air like a blade.

"That was beautiful, Bethy. Absolutely beautiful," he said, voice dripping with twisted admiration. "So glorious...whenever I come into this room, I want you to stand right there and sing it. Do you understand?" His tone shifted. It wasn't just a question—it was a challenge. A test. Like he wanted resistance. Like he hoped I'd push back so he could punish me. But I didn't. I couldn't. The command reached into that buried place

235

shaped by pews, sermons, and fear disguised as faith. That instinct—that old, automatic obedience—snapped into place like it had never left.

My hands folded neatly in front of me, and my voice came out quietly. Empty. "Yes."

Kevin studied me, eyes narrowed like he was weighing my soul, deciding if I'd passed some invisible test. There was a flicker of something in his expression—hesitation, maybe. Or calculation. He cleared his throat and opened the Bible with careful hands, flipping through the pages until he found what he was looking for. In a deep, calculated voice, he began to read the scripture.

I held my breath, trying not to react to the familiar cadence of verses I hadn't heard in years. Each word hit like a stone in my gut. He wasn't reading to me. He was preaching at me. And I was the congregation. When he finished, he shut the Bible with a quiet thud and stood, brushing invisible lint from his pants.

"I want you to think about those words," he said, picking up the backpack and dragging the chair back to its place outside the door.

He didn't wait for a response. He just walked out and closed the door behind him. The lock clicked into place. I gasped, ragged and exhausted, like I'd been holding it for hours. Alone. I was finally—The door burst open again.

I jumped. Kevin stepped back inside with a jarring shift in energy. The pious calm was gone. He was different now. Hard. Cold. In his hands, he carried a cup of water and another dry, miserable peanut butter sandwich. He thrust them toward me like they were a punishment.

"Eat," he snapped. "Food better be gone before I come back."

I shouted, "I have to use the restroom!"

He didn't even look at me. His voice came flat, emotionless. "Use the bucket." The door slammed. The lock clicked again. Alone, with the sandwich, the cup, and humiliation pressing into my chest.

45

THE BREAKING ROOM

BETHANY

We played his game. Hours, days—maybe weeks. This place reeked of earth and mold. Time blurred until nothing felt real, not even when I was drugged and drifting in and out of myself. It's like waking inside a nightmare over and over, only to realize I'd never actually woken up.

When I was barely lucid, he'd stomp in like an unhinged preacher on a mission. And I already knew the routine; he'd trained me like an animal. I stood at the bottom of the mattress, hands clasped like I was waiting for communion. I could barely hold myself upright, but I did. There was no choice. Then I'd sing He's Got the Whole World in His Hands.

The sound of my own voice made me want to crawl out of my skin. Every word scraped at my throat, dry and cracked, but it calmed him. That stupid song was the only thing that pulled him from the rage spiral he whipped up before entering. Then—like flipping a switch—he'd smile, clap as if I were a little girl performing at Vacation Bible School, and launch straight into scripture, spouting verses with a twisted passion.

At first, I thought his questions were tests—checking if I'd listened, ready to punish me for failing. Then I realized it wasn't about the verses; it was about control. It reminded me of my dad's Bible-study nights—long lectures where only his interpretation mattered and I was expected to nod along. Kevin didn't want honesty. He wanted worship—wanted me to need his guidance. And I played along—nodding, engaging, smiling through the ache in my soul. The violence paused, drugs came less often, and sometimes he didn't forget I was down here. Inside, I screamed.

My body deteriorated—cracked lips, dry skin, a stomach twisted by hunger. The chill in the cellar was a living thing, burrowing into my joints until movement hurt. And when I had to relieve myself because what else can do you do in a cage? My shame burned hotter each time he grabbed it in disgust.

"You're disgusting." Kevin held the bucket at arm's length. "Filthy little thing." I wanted to scream, *Then let me go*, but I couldn't risk provoking him when he was already barely hanging on.

Worse than hunger and cold was the silence that followed. No one came, no one called out for me. Katie was the only one who might notice—but maybe Kevin had already lied to her; he was good at that. Making me disappear without anyone asking. One day, he came in with a darker light in his eyes. He said I needed to confess my sins, not to him but to God, as if he were a prophet sent to cleanse me.

"I want you to start with when you left your father's house," he said, calm as though he wasn't about to peel my soul open.

I dropped to my knees so fast my head spun, hands outstretched in a plea. My palms scraped the concrete, but I didn't care. Tears came first.

"Please," I whispered. "Please, Kevin. Don't make me do this." My voice cracked—small, pitiful. He didn't flinch. He stared with disgust, like I was no longer human. "If you won't confess," he said, voice so cold it burned, "then no food, no water, no medicine." Medicine—that's what he called the drugs, as though they were a gift.

Something hardened inside me. Pride was a luxury I couldn't afford. So I confessed. I opened my mouth and let the poison pour: the men, the moments that meant nothing—or too much. I called them sins, even though I didn't believe it, but I said the words he needed to hear: Jezebel, whore, a girl who had strayed.

He didn't respond right away—just paced, staring, his hands clenching and unclenching like he was holding himself back.

"How many?" he asked, his voice sharp as a knife against my skin. "Did you like it? Did you feel powerful when you sinned?" There was something sick in his eyes, a toxic mix of fury, disgust, and obsession. Kevin wasn't asking because he wanted the truth; he was asking because he wanted to punish me with it, and it worked. With every answer, I felt stripped. Not just naked, exposed in a way that made my insides burn. I was scraped open with every nerve on fire, and all I could do was hold myself together as his hatred fed on my shame. I had never felt so small.

Who the hell was he to judge me? This man—this sick, twisted hypocrite—who had taken everything from me? Who moaned my name while holding my hips, who couldn't get enough of me when I was on my knees with his dick in my mouth, now had the audacity to call me filthy? A whore? Like I had defiled him? He didn't seem to mind my *sins* when he was inside me. Didn't recoil when he came back for more, over and over again, like he was starving for it—for me. When he'd whispered, "You're fucking beautiful." As he traced circles on my skin, like I was precious. And now I was unclean?

He hurled those words like stones, trying to bury me beneath them. And I let them land, one by one, because I knew if I didn't, he'd starve me, punish me, drug me into numbness. But something inside me started to move, fracturing not from fear, but from rage. Every time Kevin made me speak those words—every time he made me shrink—I felt it grow: a deep, burning hatred for him. For the lies he told, for the part that once loved him. And then came the final blow.

"There's one more confession, Bethy."

My old name on his lips made my stomach churn. I looked at him, empty-eyed.

"I don't know what you mean." My voice barely rose above a whisper. His eyes changed—darkening, narrowing—as if something inside him had snapped and he no longer cared to hold it together. His chest heaved; his jaw clenched so tight the muscle by his temple twitched. He lunged and grabbed my wrist, his grip iron-clad, painful. I gasped.

"You've been singing the devil's music!" he growled. "The devil's music, Bethany!"

"What?" My voice trembled. "No—Kevin, that's not—"

But he wasn't listening. He didn't want an explanation; he wanted a target. Spit flew with every word.

"You were chosen, Bethany. God gave you that voice—an angel's voice. And what did you do with it? You didn't glorify Him. You didn't sing to lift up the Lord. No, you sang those filthy songs, those seductive lyrics—like a damn siren, luring men with your body, your smile, your little moans tucked into every verse. That voice was supposed to be a blessing, and you used it to lead them into sin. You turned it into a weapon of lust!"

His grip tightened, and I winced, trying to pull away, but he was too far gone, consumed by this storm of twisted righteousness.

"You think I didn't see it? How they looked at you? How you enjoyed it?" His eyes blazed. "You stood on that stage and soaked up the attention like it fed you. You wanted them to want you. You wanted to be their fantasy, not their salvation."

I tried to step back, to speak—anything—but the second my lips parted, his hand flew out.

Wham.

The slap cracked through the air like a gunshot. My head twisted sideways; I stumbled, the sting blooming hot and deep across my cheek. Everything went still—even him. In that silence, I heard my own breath: ragged, shallow, trembling. I looked up and saw his face change. His eyes widened; rage drained away, replaced by horror, like he didn't recognize what he'd done. Or maybe he did and couldn't believe he'd finally crossed that invisible line.

"I-I didn't mean to." His voice barely rose above a whisper.

He turned and fled, bolting out of the room like a frightened child, the door slamming behind him. The lock clicked. And just like that, I was alone again, shaking, burning, seething. I stood, body trembling, the sting of his hand still echoing on my cheek. I hugged myself and tried to breathe. He didn't come back.

Still hurting—empty, cold, terrified. He was gone. For once, Kevin was gone long enough, and he hadn't drugged me. I started searching. My body was weak, yet I moved. I flipped the bucket over, careful not to think about what I'd just dumped out. The smell was unbearable, sour, but I didn't care. I climbed, wobbling, balancing against the shelf with trembling fingers.

I searched again. Nothing on the second shelf. Waiting, I held my breath as the wood beneath me groaned—loud and traitorous in the silence. My legs shook, arms quivering as I strained upward—but I didn't stop. I was terrified it would give way—that the shelf would crack and he'd rush back in before I could climb down. Still, I had to check higher. Had to believe something was there.

I pushed myself one level higher; the old shelf groaned louder, screaming beneath my weight. My fingers moved blindly, scraping dust and splinters, groping through the crevice between two warped boards. Then something cool brushed my skin. Metal.

My heart skipped. I reached deeper, curled my fingers around it, and pulled it out slowly—afraid it would vanish. A meat thermometer—long, slender, the tip dull, the red gauge clouded with grime.

A choked sound escaped my throat—part gasp, part sob. The sight of it shattered me. My knees buckled. I sagged against the shelf, clutching the thermometer like a lifeline. Tears slipped down my cheeks before I realized I was crying—silent, stunned tears of joy. Not because I found a weapon. Because I found hope, it wasn't much, never meant for this, yet it would do. It could pierce.

Jumping down; my knees buckled on impact. Scurrying to the mattress, I ripped a hole near the top and shoved the thermometer inside, hands shaking. This was my chance. I would wait. I'd sharpen it on the wall if I had to. I'd listen for silence—for a break in his rhythm. And when the time came...

I'd stab my way out.

46

— · —

GUILT

KEVIN

I clutched the sink until my knuckles turned white, porcelain biting into my palms like it wanted to punish me, too. The stranger in the mirror was wild-eyed, flushed with fury and regret, hair sticking up like I'd come through a storm. Maybe I had. Maybe I was the storm. I couldn't believe I hit her. The moment kept replaying—her face jerking to the side, the brutal crack of skin against skin, the silence that followed. Her eyes...God, her eyes. Not fear. Not even pain. It was disappointment. Like something inside her had snapped loose and fallen away. Like I'd proven everything she'd been afraid of was true.

That wasn't what I wanted. Didn't mean for it to go that far. I just wanted her to see. To understand. She was lying to herself, drowning in sin. She needed someone to pull her out and hold her accountable. I wasn't trying to hurt her—I was trying to save her. I just needed her to be honest with herself. With God. But she fought me. So defiant, stubborn. Every word was laced with pride, like she didn't want redemption. And that pride—it's what set me off. I could feel it boiling under my skin, rising fast. Too fast. I told myself I was pushing her to the truth, to break down the wall between her and grace. But I lost control.

I saw the look in her eyes when my hand made contact—that flicker of something breaking. And then—me, backing away like a coward, running from the mess I'd made. I didn't want her to see that part of me. That violent part. The part I buried so deep I thought it was gone. But it wasn't. It came roaring back to the surface, and now she knew. She saw it, just like Aly.

My stomach twisted, a cold knot settling in my gut. Aly. Her name hit my throat like ash—dry, suffocating, impossible to swallow. She was the first. The one I couldn't get out

242

of my head. The one I thought I could protect, mold, and keep. She slipped through my fingers like smoke, no matter how tight I held on. She let the world have her—poison her, twist her up until she couldn't even see what was good for her. Until she looked at me like I was the problem. Like I wasn't the one trying to save her.

And now Bethany...

Bethany was starting to look just like her. The same defiance. The same fire in her eyes. Like she wanted to burn the whole world down—even if it meant taking herself with it, I could see it, clear as day—her standing on the brink of something dangerous. And teetering. Just like Aly. Just like before. But I wouldn't lose her. I couldn't.

I straightened, staring at the man in the mirror like he might vanish if I blinked. My hands trembled as I wiped at my face, breath still shaky, still thick with guilt. I'd start over. Rebuild what I broke. Re-earn her trust. I'd bring her back from that place because Bethany wasn't going to end up like Aly. Not if I had anything to do with it.

Aly. God, Aly. She wasn't just beautiful. She was perfect. Her hair was sunlight poured into silk—a golden halo that made everything else look dull. I used to watch it catch the wind like it was dancing just for me. I used to watch it for hours when she didn't know. And her smile...her smile did something to me. Made the noise quiet. Like everything ugly and broken inside me went still. A part of me that was hollow and aching finally felt full, like the world made sense. Whole. She filled in all my cracks.

She was meant to be mine. I needed her. I had her. I loved her. I made a plan. I laid everything out. Every detail. Where we'd go, how far we'd drive, what she'd need once we got there. It was going to be a fresh start. Just the two of us. She didn't need to understand. She just needed to trust me.

I told her I needed to talk. It was important. And she didn't second-guess—she came. She slid into the seat like she'd done it a hundred times. She looked at me with those soft eyes—the kind that made me believe she understood, even if she didn't have the words for it yet. There was trust in them. Love, even. Aly was mine. She knew I'd take care of everything. And I would. I was giving us a new beginning—clean, untouched by the world that kept trying to pull her away from me. Once we got far enough away, once it was just us, she'd see it too. She'd see I was right.

I took her to the place that mattered. The one that always felt like ours. Secluded. No one would find us there. That part was important. She changed—so fast I barely saw it happen. One moment, Aly was looking at me like I was the only solid thing in the world...and the next, she recoiled. Her voice panicked; she wanted to go home. That this wasn't what she thought it would be. She looked at me like I was someone else, like I'd done something wrong. She started pulling away, her hands trembling, calling me crazy. Accusing me. Like everything I'd done for us had suddenly become something to fear. But she didn't mean it. Aly was overwhelmed. Confused. She didn't understand—yet. So I did what I had to do.

I tried to help her shed the version of herself that was still clinging to the lies. I brought the scissors. I'd seen it in my head so many times—how peaceful it would be. How grateful she'd be after. Just a little trim. Enough to start fresh. But she screamed. Fought like I was hurting her. It was just hair. And when it was over, she was...radiant. Like a sculpture, stripped down to truth. Nothing false left behind. Just her. The way she was always meant to be. Then they came.

I still don't know how they found us. I was careful. No one knew where we were. They tore through like animals, ripping her from me, holding me down. Treated me like a monster. I know what happened, what she meant to say, what we could've had. They ruined her. They took her. They won't take Bethy. Not this time. No one can stop what's begun.

47

THE LAST PERFORMANCE

BETHANY

I'd been here too long. Throat raw—each swallow like sandpaper. No food, no water. Just me and the silence—cruel, pressing closer with every second he stayed away. Had he abandoned me? Left me to rot in this forgotten hole until my body gave out? The thought slithered in—cold, sharp, coiling around my chest as I hunched on the floor, meat thermometer clutched in a tight fist. My one weapon, my only hope. I didn't know if it could pierce muscle, let alone save me. But it was something, and something was better than nothing.

I dragged the metal tip across the concrete in small, controlled strokes, wearing it down without raising an echo. The sound was faint, a soft scrape barely louder than my breath. Grinding my teeth, I stayed quiet. I couldn't afford noise. Not now. Not with him possibly listening. This wasn't defiance—it was survival. Each scrape a whispered rebellion—a secret act of preparation. He thought I was weak, wilting, forgotten. Good. Let him underestimate me.

My stomach cramped, twisting from hunger. My limbs felt like wet sand, heavy and uncooperative. Staying awake was a fight, but I couldn't give in. Not now—freedom was crawling beneath my skin, whispering that I was close. It had to be two days. Maybe more. Time warped here. But the stillness—the absence of his footsteps, Kevin's voice—gave me time to think, to plan, to remember who I was before him. I paused, holding my breath, straining for the creak of a floorboard, the click of the lock, any change that meant he was coming. Nothing. The silence mocked me. Heat surged through my veins, furious and bright. He thought he could starve me. Erase me. He was wrong.

I pressed the thermometer harder to the floor and scraped again. At last, I lay on the mattress like a corpse—still, cold, empty. Arms splayed, fingers slightly curled. Not posed, but close enough to look like I'd given up. My face turned toward the wall, toward the bruise blooming in purple-yellows exactly where he left it.

The thermometer lay beneath my lower back, hidden in the mattress. Reaching it would only be possible if he was close—really close—and I was banking everything on him being the kind of monster who needed to witness his destruction. My body ached, but I let it go limp, slack as rope. Starving, dehydrated, shaking beneath the surface, I kept my breaths shallow, like I'd already started to slip away.

I heard it—a faint creak above me, floorboards groaning. I froze, every muscle tightening beneath the illusion of death. My heartbeat thundered so loud I swore it echoed off the concrete walls. Another creak. Then silence. Then—click. The lock. The door opened with that familiar, haunting squeal, followed by a whisper of air as he stepped inside. And then—click. He locked it behind him. We were sealed in together. His steps were slow, almost casual, as if he were entering a room filled with peace, not rot and dread. Something scraped on the shelf; he was setting something down—food? Water? Guilt in a glass.

"Bethy..." His voice trembled like a man delivering a eulogy. "First, I want to say I'm sorry." I didn't move.

"I didn't mean—" His words faltered. Silence swelled, thick and suffocating. Then his tone hardened. "Why aren't you standing in your spot?" A threat disguised as a question. Still, I let the dead calm answer for me.

"Bethy?" Panic bled into his voice. A step. A stumble. A thud as his back hit the door—like he'd lost his footing. His breath. Silence. Then a whisper so fragile it barely crossed the room.

"No..." A beat—then louder, frantic. "No. No, no, no." His breath ragged and broken. I heard the way it caught in his throat, as if he couldn't swallow what he was seeing. "Not my Bethy." His voice quivered. "Not like this. She was fine. She was fine. I brought food. I brought her food." He said it like that proved something. "She was just tired. She knew I'd come back. It was only two days—two days isn't too long. Not enough time to...No. She wouldn't do this. She wouldn't leave me like this." His voice pitched higher, climbing toward hysteria. "She was going to get better. She was going to see. I saw it in her eyes. She was softening. Bethy was changing. She just needed more time—just more time."

He began pacing—short, frantic steps, rustling his clothes; the thud of boots on concrete.

"Maybe she's asleep," he whispered, clinging to hope. "Yes. Just asleep. She's weak. That's all. She's resting." He stopped.

I felt his stare slither over my still frame. He was panting now. "She's not dead...Bethy's not." Pleading. "She can't be." Another step forward, then another. "I shouldn't have stayed away. I should've come back sooner—I thought space would help. I thought she'd miss me. I was trying to help her."

A beat of silence, then a whispered lie he forced into truth. "Bethy's just sleeping." He said it like a prayer, a desperate delusion. And then he moved. Closer. The mattress dipped under his weight. I nearly gasped—his body radiated heat beside me. Kevin's hand brushed the hair from my face, slow and trembling. He lingered over the bruise, his breath catching. "I did this to her..." The words were thick with tears. "I broke her."

His fingers traced my cheek, shaking. I wanted to scream, to claw at his face, but I stayed locked in the performance. I needed him nearer. I whimpered—just loud enough. His reaction was instant.

"Thank you, Lord," he gasped, relief crashing over us. Kevin pulled me against him as though rescuing me from something other than himself. "Thank you, God," he sobbed into my shoulder, tears hot on my skin. I fought the bile rising in my throat. "I'll never hurt you again. You have my undying devotion."

Now.

I slid my hand beneath the mattress, feeling for the cool metal. Found it. Wrapped my fingers around it. And struck. The thermometer tore into his neck with a wet crunch. He reeled back, gasping, hands flying to his throat as blood gushed between his fingers—thick, dark, arterial. It pulsed in jagged spurts, splattering hot and metallic across my face. His eyes went wide with shock, then confusion, and finally rage.

"You..." Blood coughed onto his shirt. "You bitch!"

He lunged before I could move. His hands found my throat in an instant, slamming me back into the mattress. The air ripped from my lungs. My legs kicked, but he was on top of me, all muscle and fury and blind wrath. His eyes were wild, foam forming at the corners of his mouth.

"I'm going to kill you!" Spit flew.

I grabbed the thermometer—still slick with his blood—and stabbed. Over and over. Into flesh. Into bone. Into whatever I could reach. Each thrust met a sickening resistance, followed by tearing meat and splashes of blood. I was dying. I could feel it—slow and certain. Lungs burned, begging for oxygen that wouldn't come. Parts of me went numb—arms heavy, fingers slack around the blood-slick handle. Thoughts blurred into static, white noise buzzing as the world pulled away. The pressure on my throat was absolute—his rage wrapped around my neck like iron, squeezing and squeezing. Vision sparkled with stars. My chest convulsed—desperate to breathe, but no air came. My legs kicked weakly, then stilled. I had stopped fighting. This was it. I was—

And then, his grip adjusted. Just barely. A tremor. A flicker of weakness. It faltered. His fingers loosened—not from mercy, but because something gave out, like a puppet with cut strings. Then his full weight crashed down on top of me—a collapsing mass of heat and blood. Dead weight. Unmoving. His breath, once hot and snarling, was gone. Still. Utterly, completely still.

Hot blood pooled between us, sticky and endless. His head lolled against mine in a grotesque mockery of tenderness. I lay beneath him, chest heaving, throat burning, soaked in the blood of the man who tried to destroy me. And I waited to see if I had lived. My limbs trembled as I shifted beneath him, the stench of sweat, metal, and death curling into my nose. Every movement was like wading through molasses—slow, dizzy, desperate. I pressed my palms to his chest and pushed. Nothing. My arms buckled.

I tried again, gritting my teeth, summoning strength I didn't know I had. This time, his body rolled just enough for me to slip out from underneath him. I scooted back on shaking legs, gasping, clawing at my throat as I dragged myself away. My fingers touched bruised skin—tender, swollen. His violence still echoed. I could breathe. Oh God, I could breathe. The first full breath hit my lungs like fire and ice. I choked, coughing, weeping, clutching my chest like I didn't trust it was real. Each breath was a miracle, a reminder: I was still here. I was alive.

I looked down at Kevin's body sprawled beside me. His blue jeans were soaked. His white shirt clung to his chest, already blooming dark crimson. Once, I loved him. Once, he'd been everything. That love had led me here, his blood on my hands and clothes, seeping into my skin like a curse. My heart barely beat. I could feel it slowing, the weight of what I had done pressing down until I could barely breathe.

Kneeling beside him, I reached out and touched his face. His eyes were closed, as if he were only asleep. I leaned in, pressing my lips to his cold mouth—a final goodbye to the man I loved and lost. My voice was barely a whisper.

"Why did you make me do this, Kevin? Why?"

I swallowed the scream clawing at my throat and forced my blurred vision to focus. Numb fingers searched his pockets. Left side. Nothing. Right side. Nothing. Panic scratched at my ribs. I rolled his heavy body, fumbling, desperate. Where is it? Where's the key?

A hollow ache sank beyond bone, buried in my core. A guttural sound ripped loose as I pounded his chest. "Where did you put the key?" The demand ricocheted off concrete, the only living thing in this tomb. I was trapped in the prison he made, and no one knew. No one would come.

I crawled to the wall, knees to chest, and rocked in silence. A broken lullaby slipped out—the same one he forced me to sing, the one that always reminded me of just how alone I was.

"He's got the whole world...in His hands...

He's got the whole world...in His hands...

He's got the whole world...in His hands...

He's got you and me, sister...in His hands..."

48

THE KEY & THE CAGE

BETHANY

I don't know how long I was out. Time didn't exist here; it dissolved into concrete, silence, and the dread beneath my skin. When I opened my eyes, my lashes fluttered against the crust of dried tears and blood. Everything ached—my ribs, my wrists, my soul. I blinked, once, twice, and the blur focused into a picture I didn't want to see.

Kevin.

His body lay twisted on the floor, lifeless and wrong. My brain short-circuited, then rebooted, forcing me to relive it in high definition—the fight, his breath, hands on my throat, my scream, the final thrust. The moment I stopped being prey.

Then another feeling crashed in—grief tangled with horror. Not for him, but for what he stole—the version of me I'd never get back, every moment he manipulated love into fear and touched me like he owned it, I hated him, yet surviving him felt like a different kind of death.

My chest seized, and I gasped for air that wouldn't come. My body froze, and a scream clawed up from where I'd buried everything. I wailed—loud, guttural, inhuman. I didn't want this. I didn't ask for this. Why me? I didn't know how I was going to get out of this hell, but I knew I had to try. My eyes squeezed shut as I curled in on myself, trying to disappear into the floor.

"God...please...help me."

I remembered the door. He'd locked it. He'd never locked the door before. What was he planning? Panic surged. I had two choices—sit here and rot beside his corpse, or find that damn key and get the fuck out of this place. I chose the latter. My legs shook as I pushed myself up, the cold concrete biting into my palms as I used the wall for balance. Don't look at him. Don't look at what you've done. I kept my stare in the shadows, scanning with feral focus. What did I hear when he came in?

Close your eyes, Bethany. Listen. He walked in. The door closed. Click. He locked it. That meant the key was still here. My eyes snapped open. The shelf. The food. The water. I staggered toward it, my legs barely cooperating, as if my body had forgotten how to move under its own will. I reached the shelf, hands shaking as I searched every inch.

Nothing.

"No, no, no!" I slammed my fist down. The cup of water tipped, splashing across the wood. The plate clattered, and I collapsed, sobbing into my palms. This was it. I would die here, buried beneath his secrets in a room no one knew existed. No one was coming. No one even knew where to look. I couldn't stop crying—harsh, guttural sobs that scraped my throat. When they finally slowed, the silence pressed in, thick and punishing. I curled into the corner, shaking, my face soaked, aching in places I didn't know could hurt. I opened my eyes and stared at the water, the clear liquid glistening like salvation. I knew he had been drugging me. I knew. What did it matter now? If I drank and it was laced, maybe I'd slip away without pain. Maybe I wouldn't feel the hunger anymore. Maybe I wouldn't feel anything at all. I was just so...tired. Tired in my bones. Tired in my blood. Tired in my soul.

I grabbed the cup and took a long gulp. The cold hit my tongue like rain after drought. It was heaven. It was mercy. It flowed down my throat as if it loved me. For a second, I closed my eyes and imagined being anywhere else—a beach, a porch, a safe bed, a world where Kevin never existed. I waited. Nothing came. No haze, no dizziness, no floaty silence. It's just water. Clean. Pure. Untouched. It felt so good, this time it broke me. He hadn't laced it. For once, he hadn't tried to control me, and that sliver of mercy felt like the cruelest part of all.

The sandwich sat in front of me, and my stomach growled. Fingers trembling, I peeled the bread apart. Tiny specks of white dotted the peanut butter, camouflaged like they belonged there. That's how he did it. The sick bastard used my hunger against me. A scream tore out as the plate was smacked off the shelf. The sandwich flew one way, the plate the other, cracking in two when it hit the ground. I stood seething, chest heaving, watching the pieces scatter like my sanity. Rage wouldn't save me. Not here. Eyes closed, I tried to breathe the way Katie taught me in yoga, back when the world made sense, when I could still trust people, trust myself. Think, Bethany. Think.

When I opened my eyes, something caught the light—a tiny glint near the edge of the shelf where the plate had been. My heart stopped. I reached out, terrified it wasn't real—just desperation conjured into metal. My fingers touched metal. The key. A sob tore free.

I held it like it was sacred, like it had a heartbeat, whispering over and over, "Thank you. Thank you. Thank you." Hope pulsed in my palm. My hand shook as I lifted the key, fingers slick with sweat. It felt too good—like the universe would snatch it away. I braced for disappointment, half-expecting the key to jam. Then—click.

The sound was the most beautiful thing I'd ever heard. The door creaked open, a rush of air sweeping in—crisp, real. It filled my lungs like life itself. My knees buckled. I crumpled, whispering, "I'm free..."

Louder now, broken and raw, "I'm free!"

Tears streamed as I lifted my face to the ceiling.

"Thank you!" To God, the sky, the universe, whoever had heard me. I wiped my eyes, pushed myself upright. My legs were weak, but they moved. That was enough. I staggered forward, up the stairs that had once felt like a path to hell, now leading me toward salvation.

Freedom.

I wanted out. I wanted to run until my legs gave out and the trees blurred behind me. I reached the kitchen, the dull light stabbing my eyes like it had never been off. It felt foreign. Wrong. Far too bright for a place that had held so much darkness. My eyes burned as they adjusted to the sudden change while I scanned the room. My car keys were there, sitting on the table, as if nothing had happened. I lunged for them, snatching them up with a shaky hand and clutching them as if they might vanish. My heart thudded against my ribs. Don't let this be a repeat. Don't let this be a trap.

I turned, heart racing, eyes darting around the room. I half-expected Kevin to rise from the shadows like a nightmare refusing to die, to grab me and drag me back down into that pit. But there was nothing. The cabin was still. I opened the front door and stepped outside. It was pitch-black out there, except for the pale strip of light glowing behind me from the cabin. I saw it—my car—and every part of me surged forward. My feet slapped the dirt, my breath ragged. I ran because my life depended on it.

I flung the door open and threw myself inside. No purse. No shoes. No charger. Just the keys. Just escape. I jammed the key into the ignition and turned it. The engine was dead. I turned it again, harder. Still dead.

"No, no, no!" I slammed my fists against the steering wheel. The horn offered a weak, pathetic beep. "You bastard...you knew I'd try to run."

My heart hammered as I looked around the car. I needed options—a new plan. If I couldn't drive, I had to call someone. I needed my phone. It wouldn't be in the cabin, not where he'd kept me. But Kevin was obsessive, controlling; he wouldn't let it be far. My eyes fell on the glove compartment. Too obvious—yet he always liked keeping control close. I hesitated, pulse pounding, afraid to hope. My fingers inched toward the latch. I opened it slowly, breath held, expecting emptiness—another cruel dead end. But nestled among forgotten papers and useless junk was my phone. I gasped. I couldn't move. I just stared, unable to believe it was real.

Grabbing it, I clutched it to my chest like it was a newborn. As I pressed the power button, I whispered a shaky prayer. "Please...please..." The screen lit. I choked on a gasp and dialed 911...no signal. "Shit!" I hissed, staring at the zero bars taunting me from the corner of the screen. I slid out of the car and started walking, bare feet hitting gravel with every shaky step. I didn't care about the cold or what waited in the dark. Let it come. I'd fight that too.

Holding the phone in front of me like a torch, I kept my eyes glued to the top of the screen, praying for a signal. Just one bar—please, just one. Then, it appeared. A single bar. The phone rang. Katie.

I answered with trembling fingers. "Hello?" My voice cracked.

"Geez." Katie laughed. "Look who finally decides to answer my calls."

Tears welled. "Katie..." My throat tightened. "Please. Please listen to me."

"Bethany? Are you okay?"

"Call the police. I'm in the woods. He held me captive, and I—" my breath hitched "—I killed him. Kevin. I killed Kevin."

"Bethany, slow down. What are you talking about?"

Beep. Beep. Beep. Three percent. "Oh God—Katie, I don't have time. You need to listen. Kevin—he locked me in the root cellar. I didn't think I was ever getting out."

"Where are you?"

"I killed him," I cried. "He was going to kill me, Katie—I had to fight back. You have to call the police!"

"You're joking, right?"

"I'm serious! The phone's dying. Call the police. I'm in the woods. You have my location—please find me!" The screen dimmed. "No, no, no—wait." The phone died, its light vanishing into black. "No..." I stared at it. "No, no, no..."

I turned and ran—stumbling, falling, scrambling back toward the cabin. I had to find my charger. I needed to be found. Inside, I tore through drawers, cabinets, and the floor by the bed. Nothing. No charger. No hope.

"God, please let her find me."

I looked down: my dress was soaked in his blood. I couldn't wear this, couldn't stay in this skin. I rushed to the hallway and locked the root-cellar door, slamming it shut like I was sealing away a monster. Stripping in the bathroom—the stench of sweat, fear, and blood choking me—I turned on the shower. Ice-cold water hit my skin, but I didn't care. I scrubbed like I could erase everything he touched. My skin burned; my knuckles bled; still, I kept going.

With no clothes of my own, I grabbed one of his T-shirts and a pair of sweatpants. They smelled like him. I wanted to burn them, but I had nothing else. Angry. Broken. How could I feel everything and nothing? The exhaustion hit me. The trauma caught up to me. My body was giving up even though my mind wanted to keep running. There was nothing more I could do. I crawled into the bed—the one I shared with him once. My body gave out before my mind did.

I don't know how long I'd been asleep. I heard a loud and urgent voice.

"She's in here!"

My eyes fluttered open, heavy with sleep and confusion. A man was in the doorway. I didn't recognize him. "Who are you?" I rasped. He stepped closer.

"Don't worry. You're safe now." Then he lifted me into his arms, and the world slipped away.

49

— · —

VITALS

BETHANY

I was warm, not the jolting kind, but a gentle heat that melted into my skin and soothed everything it touched. My body felt suspended—weightless yet heavy, held by something soft and slow-moving. No urgency, no pain. Just stillness—like slipping into a bath that hushes the world and lulls you into surrender. I couldn't move, couldn't open my eyes—but I could feel.

The world came to me in pieces—drifting voices, echoes through fog. Muffled. Warped. Strangers. But then, one clear note in the confusion: Katie. Her voice cut through, the only sound that reached the place I'd been buried in. She wasn't crying, but I heard the crack in her voice, the way she said my name like it was held together with paperclips and prayers. I wanted to answer her. I wanted to wake up. But I couldn't. My body didn't belong to me anymore. I was bone-tired. Soul-tired. All I could do was float—drift—sink deeper into darkness.

Light pressed against my eyelids—hot, harsh. I flinched, blinking slowly. The ceiling swam into view—white, sterile, too bright. The hum of fluorescent lights filled the silence. My chest felt heavy, my limbs unresponsive, my throat scorched and dry. I couldn't move. But I felt it—my hand, hot and slightly damp. Someone was holding it. I turned my head just enough to see, my neck protesting, sore and foreign. Katie. She was slumped in the chair, head on the mattress, fingers laced with mine like she feared I'd slip away. Her hair was a tangled mess, and her face—God, her face—looked like she hadn't slept in days.

"Katie," I rasped.

She jerked awake. Her head snapped up, eyes wide. "Bethany?" Breathless. "Oh my God." I tried to smile, but the skin cracked before it could form, pain blazing across my lips.

"Hey," I whispered.

Tears filled her eyes. "You're awake." The words spilled out in a flood she'd held back too long. "Oh my God. Oh my God, you're awake." She threw her arms around my neck, her body clinging to mine like she needed proof I was real. The pain lanced through me.

"My neck," I gasped.

She jerked back at once, eyes darting to the bruises blooming across my throat like ugly fingerprints. "I'm sorry," she whispered. "I forgot. I just...I was scared I'd never get to hug you again."

My mouth opened, but only a thin, broken breath came. Kevin's hands were everywhere—bruising memories into my wrists, my mind. The pressure. The darkness. The cold. I was back in that cellar with rot and silence. My chest tightened until I couldn't breathe. Not then. Not now. Not here.

I shook uncontrollably, my body trying to reject the memory etched too deep. Katie saw it. I wasn't ready for heartbreak. But there it was. She moved toward me slowly, as though I were shattered glass, and folded her arms around me, careful, trembling. I sank into her touch like I was falling through it.

"It's okay," she whispered, her voice barely a thread. "Bethany...it's over. He can't hurt you anymore. You're safe now. I swear you're safe." Safety didn't exist in my world anymore. Not really. Not after being locked away. Not after being told who I was, what I was, until I nearly believed it. My ribs shook with silent sobs, the scream I'd buried burning in my chest. I buried my face in her shoulder and let it go.

It was brutal and hoarse—a sound torn from someplace primal. The sobs came hard and fast, years of pain crammed into one broken girl.

"I killed him," I cried. "Kevin—I killed him!" The words slammed into the room, confession and curse in one. My body convulsed under their weight—because it wasn't just the act; it was everything it meant. I loved him. I needed him. And he'd turned me into something unrecognizable so I could survive.

Katie didn't pull away or hush me. She just held on, one hand grabbing my back, the other buried in my hair.

"I know." Her voice was thick with tears. "I know, Bethany. I'm here." She let the storm break and pass. No one rushed it; there's no timeline for this kind of pain. I don't know how long I cried for. When the storm finally faded, it left me numb. My throat was hoarse. My limbs felt carved from stone. Only silence remained—a quiet so deep I wondered if it would ever end. Katie drew back and wiped her eyes, blotchy, red. Her voice steadied as she said, "I'm gonna get the doctor, okay? They need to check you out."

I didn't answer. I just nodded. The exam felt endless. Every light, every touch, every question from the doctor pulled me further from the numbness I clung to. I could barely keep my eyes open, yet I registered the words he spoke—concussion, severe dehydration, pneumonia, shock. Each diagnosis sounded like it belonged to someone else, a stranger. Not me. But I nodded anyway; what else could I do? My body survived what my mind hadn't processed. When the doctor finally left, the room fell silent again—sterile silence, closed in, cold and confining like cellar walls.

The door creaked open. Katie walked in first, her presence a beam of light through fog. Two people followed—detectives, judging by their stiff posture and the cautious way they entered, as if afraid of shattering me further. The woman stepped forward. Tall, elegant, dark-skinned, probably late forties, hair pulled into a neat bun. Her gray pantsuit matched her strength, but her face was soft, her eyes full of empathy.

"Hi, Bethany." Her voice was soothing. "I'm Detective Matthews, and this is my partner, Detective Crosby." Crosby, older and stocky with a balding crown, stood a step behind her, scribbling in a worn notebook. "We're here to talk about what happened at the cabin. Do you feel up to talking?" I hesitated—not because I didn't want to, but because my throat still felt stitched shut. I glanced at Katie.

"Yes," I whispered.

Matthews nodded gently. "Good." She looked at Katie. "Do you mind giving us a moment?"

"No." Panic broke into my voice. "I'd like her to stay." I reached for Katie. She crossed the room, sat beside me, and squeezed my fingers: I'm here. I've got you.

"That's perfectly fine," Matthews replied, settling into the chair by my bed. "Can you tell me how you ended up at the cabin?" Crosby clicked his pen, ready.

I drew a shaky breath. "I went to Kevin's house. We'd argued the night before, and I wanted to talk. He was leaving when I got there, heading to the cabin. I caught him just in time."

Matthews and Crosby exchanged a look.

"After we talked, he invited me—said it'd be good to get away, to reconnect. I thought he wanted to fix things." My voice wavered, but I pushed on. "It sounded like a good idea. I didn't think..." The sentence withered; they already knew. They let me tell it—every flash of memory, every dark corner of truth. I didn't cry—just a dull ache behind my eyes. When I finished, Crosby looked up from his notebook.

"So you have no idea how that DVD came into his possession?"

I blinked, confused. "No," I said slowly. "All I know is...there was one like that in my father's office. Back in Indiana." Another glance passed between them. Crosby gave a small nod, and Matthews turned back to me, her expression sharpened. Katie's grip tightened.

"Bethany," Matthews began gently, as if searching for a way to land a blow without bruising, "we need to tell you something." I looked at Katie, but her face was unreadable. My pulse skittered. Something was wrong.

"The thing is—"

The door slammed open.

"Bethany!"

The voice ripped through me like a bullet. My body tensed before I could process it. No. No. No. No. Kevin. He stormed in, frantic, wild-eyed, voice cracking with disbelief and desperation.

"Bethany, you're alive! They wouldn't let me in—"

50

HALF THE TRUTH

BETHANY

I clung to Katie's fingers digging in as I curled into the top corner of the hospital bed. My body shook. I couldn't breathe. Panic swallowed my mind. Terror clamped my chest. No. No. No. Kevin. It couldn't be. I'd watched him die—I'd killed him. I remembered the meat thermometer piercing his flesh, the stillness, the silence, the blood. Yet he was here, alive—like a corpse.

I screamed—guttural—sure he'd come to finish it, to drag me back, lock the door, punish me for escaping. Detective Matthews shot out of her chair; Crosby stepped in front of him, both shouting, "You cannot be in here!" Their voices tangled in chaos.

Kevin didn't stop. "Please, let me explain." His voice cracked. "Bethany, please!"

Katie spun around, fury exploding from her. "Get him the hell out of here!" she screamed. "I told you this was a bad idea!"

"Please, no!" I clutched her tighter. "Please, not again!"

Kevin's voice rose. "No—Bethany, it's me! Kevin!" My head sank underwater, pulse thundering. I buried my face in Katie's shoulder, shaking, sobbing, choking on air that wouldn't come.

"You're scaring her!" Katie's voice cracked as she pulled me close, shielding me. Suddenly, the yelling stopped. The room went still, every sound swallowed whole. Had I gone deaf? I peeked over Katie's shoulder. Kevin stood motionless, arms limp at his sides, face pale, lips parted as though the wind had been knocked out of him. His eyes weren't angry—they looked lost. Wounded.

"I'm sorry." The words barely slipped past his lips. Then he turned. He didn't fight. Crosby followed close behind, ushering him out the door. The room was quiet except for my ragged panting and the frantic beeping of the heart monitor. I stared at the door, bracing for it to swing open again. The walls closed in. My thoughts spun. Nothing made sense. I looked at Katie, then at Detective Matthews.

"How? I don't understand. He was dead. I killed him." My voice cracked. I lifted my hands, sure they were still stained. I could feel the blood. Smell it.

"Bethany," Detective Matthews said gently. She took one of my hands while Katie held the other. "I'll tell you what we know, but I need you to calm down."

I couldn't speak. When my heartbeat finally slowed, the detective continued, "I'm going to give you all the information we have so far." I met her eyes, bracing.

"You didn't kill your boyfriend, Kevin," she said. "It was his brother who held you captive—Ian."

The words didn't land. Ian? Kevin's brother? That meant Kevin had a twin—an identical twin. No. He would have told me. Wouldn't he? Thoughts crashed. I blinked, trying to catch my bearings, but the floor had vanished. Detective Matthews must have seen the confusion on my face; her voice stayed calm, weighted with caution.

"It appears Ian kept an extensive journal," she said. "We found it in a drawer with his personal items—entries going back ten, maybe twelve years. It started after he saw a YouTube video of you singing Ocean Eyes." My chest caved inward. "That's when the obsession began." She paused, but I was frozen, made of stone.

"Go on." My voice came out dry and weightless.

"He downloaded your videos," she continued. "He studied every comment. He documented every time you replied to his messages. When your channel disappeared, his fascination turned darker."

A pit bloomed in my stomach. "I invited the devil into my life."

"No." Katie's voice sharpened. "Bethany, no. This isn't your fault."

I didn't argue; I was too tired. Matthews continued, "Ian figured out where you lived from one of your old videos. He went looking for you, but by then you'd already run away." My heart clenched. "He met your father instead. For reasons we don't yet understand, your father took him in—let him stay, even mentored him. Ian said living in your childhood home was the only way he could feel close to you."

I squeezed Katie's hand until I couldn't tell whose pulse I felt.

"He convinced your father to reach out to you, even hired a private investigator. When you refused to come home, he waited. Last year, he asked your father again to contact you, but your father refused." Matthews drew a breath. "Bethany...we can't say this with absolute certainty yet, but we believe Ian killed your father to bring you back to Willow Creek."

My jaw dropped. "No..." I shook my head, but the word felt meaningless, powerless against what I already knew. The truth had been coiled in my stomach all along; I just hadn't wanted to look at it. Now it screamed. My vision blurred. My ears rang. The room tilted. I held Katie's hand like it was the only thing tethering me to the bed. Not him. Not my father.

My chest clenched, breath hitching in ragged bursts. Something cracked open inside me—a scream, a sob, a truth too big to hold.

"He killed my father." The words tumbled out brittle. My throat tightened, and then I broke—no control, no grace—just sobs that doubled me over, wringing everything out of me. I shook my head, tears falling as bile rose in my throat. "It's my fault." I gasped. "All of this...is because of me."

Matthews stayed silent. It said enough. Once the realization settled into my bones, she continued, "After you returned, Ian stalked you. He shoved you outside your apartment, stole your keys, and made a copy. He was going in and out of your home without you knowing."

The words hit like a bomb. Images flashed—things slightly moved, that eerie sense of being watched. The week I went back to my father's house, my bed in my apartment looked slept in. Him. I looked up at Detective Matthews. Lips numb, mouth dry, I pushed the words out. "Did Kevin have anything to do with this?"

She paused a breath, long enough for doubt to crawl across my skin, then frowned. "No. He had no idea what his brother was doing."

Nothing felt right. My chest caved in. If Kevin truly didn't know, then why hadn't he told me Ian was his twin? Why let me fall in love with half the truth? My head swam. What was real anymore? I loved him—God, I loved him: the way he held me, listened, made me feel like I could breathe again. But now I couldn't tell if any of it was real or built on a version of him that wasn't the whole truth. Did I believe him? Did I believe myself? My brain warned me to run, to end this before it swallowed me again. Still, my broken, reckless heart reached for him in the dark. And that terrified me most of all.

51

SHATTERPOINT

KEVIN

It had been two weeks since my life shattered into pieces I couldn't pick up. Two weeks since Bethany had looked at me like I was a monster. Two weeks since I confirmed my brother's body, cold, still, and unrecognizable beneath everything I thought I knew about him. And the truth? I couldn't breathe without guilt clawing my throat.

Bethany was gone. The woman I loved—really, truly loved—could barely look at me without flinching. And Ian...Ian was dead. My twin. My brother. The other half of my history, of every childhood memory, is gone. And it was my fault. I should've told her. I should've told Bethany everything. About Ian. About us. About the shadows that followed him.

She knew the version of me that wanted a future, not the one who spent half his life putting out fires my brother lit behind closed doors. She didn't know the secrets I kept—warnings I tucked away and called "complicated history." I should've told her about the anger Ian carried—how it could flicker into something colder. I should've told her he could twist the truth to fit whatever story he needed to believe.

But I didn't. I wanted to believe he was different, that the sermons and second chances meant something. Maybe this time, he was actually healed. He found God. He said the right things. He looked me in the eye and made me believe. And I let that belief silence the part of me that knew better. I saw the cracks. I chose to ignore them. And Bethany...Bethany paid the price for my denial.

My stomach turned at the thought of him watching her, scaring her, hurting her. And the worst part? He found God through her father, manipulated his way into that man's home—into his trust—just to get closer to Bethany. I felt sick, poisoned by everything

I hadn't said or done. My fist slammed into the door. The pain came fast, but barely registered against the wreckage in my chest. I didn't care. I wanted to hurt. I deserved to hurt.

"Kevin, what the hell?" Tara's voice cracked as she rushed in. She was on me in seconds, grabbing my hand, inspecting the damage. "What did you do? Let me see. Jason, can you bring me ice?"

"I'm fine." I pulled away. "Just a bit angry."

Tara gave me that look, the one that said, you've never fooled me. "A bit angry?" she echoed. Uncle Jason stepped in, eyes going straight to the hole in the door. He didn't even ask—just passed the towel-wrapped ice to Tara like this was routine. He nodded once and left us, the way he always did when things got too heavy. Tara sat beside me, silent, the ice forgotten in her lap. They had both flown in to handle Ian's affairs because I couldn't. I hadn't even been able to sign the papers. When Tara's flight was delayed, it fell on me to confirm the body.

I closed my eyes. I still saw him—not Ian, but the shell—mouth slack, skin pale, like he'd never lived at all. That image sank into my bones. The worst moment of my life. He looked so still, so quiet, like a trick of the light. I waited for him to move, to sit up, to open his eyes and roll them at me the way he always did when I got too serious. But he didn't. There was no heartbeat beneath his skin. No breath. Just absence.

My twin. My brother. The last thread of my family—gone. I staggered back, then forward, like my body couldn't decide whether to fight or fall. I felt like a kid again, watching him through ICU glass at nine years old, begging God not to take him after he fell off that damn roof trying to prove he could fly. Back then, I prayed, I bargained—I thought losing him would break me. And now I was here, older, supposedly wiser, standing over his body with nothing but emptiness in return.

Part of me hated him. But, God, a bigger part missed him. We were born minutes apart. We shared everything—Christmas mornings, hand-me-downs, secrets no one else knew. He remembered Mom's hugs, Dad's laugh—even after time dulled the memory. He was the only person on this earth who knew what it meant to be me. And I couldn't save him.

I thought if I loved him enough, gave him space and trust, he'd become the man I believed he could be. I watched him pretend. I wanted it to be real. And now he was dead. I didn't know what broke me more—losing him, or still wanting him back. A sob cracked through. I pressed my knuckles to my lips, but it didn't help. I crumbled. There, in that sterile room, I came apart. Because no matter what he did, no matter how dark it got, he was my brother—my only family—and I still loved him.

Then the rest of it hit me, hard and painful: Bethany. The woman I'd fallen for. The woman I saw a future with. The woman I should have protected. She had trusted me—loved me—and Ian, my brother, twisted that trust into a nightmare she may never wake from. I hadn't seen it coming. I stood frozen between two griefs—one for the brother I couldn't save, one for the woman I might've lost. I didn't know which ache hurt worse.

Tara took my hands in hers, folding them gently between her palms as if trying to hold me together. Her eyes found mine—sadness, heartbreak, helplessness. Beneath it, something steadier: family.

Her voice was soft but direct. "Tell me what you're feeling."

The words clawed at my throat, but none felt like enough. My mouth opened, and all I could do was let them fall. "Lost. Confused. Angry. Sad. Guilty. Hurt..." I paused. "And heartbroken." I didn't look at her when I said it. I stared past her, into the wreckage of the last two weeks. Tara let the weight of my words settle before responding.

"As you should." Her voice softened. "This entire situation is...unthinkable. I'm still trying to process it all. I can't believe this has happened again." Her voice cracked, just slightly. "And I'm so sorry this has uprooted your life the way it has. I loved your brother, Kevin. We all did. But we did everything we could to help him. He had all of us fooled." She tightened her grip on my hands. "This wasn't your fault."

I yanked my hands back and stood, like her words burned me. "How can you say that? This is all my fault! Weren't you the one who warned me? You told me to talk to Bethany—to tell her about Ian, about my past. I didn't listen. I chose not to." I raked a hand through my hair, pacing, voice cracking under everything I hadn't said. "I could've protected her. I could've told her the truth—just one conversation. But I kept quiet because I didn't want to scare her away, because I thought I was protecting her. And now she's the one who's broken because of it."

Tara stood slowly. "Kevin, I told you to be honest with Bethany. Not because I thought Ian would do this again. I had no idea. None of us did. I just wanted you to stop hiding behind your brother's shadow—to stop living like you owed him your silence. I wanted you to have something of your own. Something real."

She crossed the room and faced me, her expression softening. "You finally started choosing yourself. You fell in love. You found someone who sees you, and I wanted you to have the support you deserve, not secrets."

I shook my head. "It's too late now." I scrubbed my face, worn down by sleepless nights and unanswered calls. "I've called her every day. Left message after message. Nothing. Not a single word back."

Tara tilted her head, studying me. "Do you love her?"

"Yes." The answer escaped before I could think.

She nodded once, as if she already knew. "Then go to her."

I looked away, unsure I deserved to. "Tara—"

"I know it's complicated," she said. "Hell, it's more than complicated. But if she's worth it—and I think you know she is—fight for her. Before Ian, what you had with Bethany was real. Don't let the past take that too. It won't be easy, and it may never be the same...but if there's even the smallest chance you can heal from this—together—you owe it to yourself to try."

She stepped closer and kissed my cheek. Her hand rested on my arm. Tears shimmered in her eyes, but her voice didn't waver. "You deserve to be happy, Kevin. Fight for her." Then she walked out, leaving me with the ache in my chest, her words echoing, and the one question I couldn't shake: How do you fix something you shattered with silence?

52

OMISSION

BETHANY

I spent five days in the hospital, tethered to beeping machines and IVs that bruised my arms. I didn't sleep—not really. Even dimmed, the fluorescent lights flickered. Nurses and doctors came in relentless waves. They came and went with gloved hands and sympathetic eyes, poking and prodding, as if any number could measure what I'd been through.

The detectives returned on the third day. Their voices were quieter, gentler, as if they'd finally started to understand. They said the DA ruled Ian's death a justifiable homicide—no charges, no court dates—just a box checked in their system, a tidy legal label for something that nearly destroyed me. They'd uncovered more about Ian—his past, his mind—but I didn't want to hear it. Knowing more wouldn't help; it wouldn't undo what he did—or how it felt when I realized it wasn't Kevin I killed. My silence was my boundary.

A psychologist visited next, sitting in the corner, clipboard resting on her lap. Her voice was calm, rehearsed. She told me I had PTSD—of course I did. She wanted me to see her regularly, said it would help me process everything. But all I wanted was to forget, to rewind to when life was uneventful and predictable, when the worst part of my week was folding secondhand jeans.

Kevin didn't come. Not once. For that, I was relieved. I couldn't see him. Not yet—maybe not ever. Katie was the only constant, squeezing in visits between classes and the life that hadn't imploded. She brought snacks I didn't eat, books I didn't read, and sat with me in silence. Discharge felt empty—bittersweet. I was cracked open, held together by sheer will and memory. Stepping into my apartment, I felt like an impostor in my own life.

My room still smelled like him—woodsy. But was it Kevin...or Ian? My stomach turned at the uncertainty. I stripped the bed like I was peeling off skin, shoved everything into the wash, hoping it would rinse away the confusion. I cleaned obsessively, as though scrubbing hard enough could make the room forget, too. Then he called. Kevin's name lit up my screen, and my heart clenched. I stared until it stopped ringing. A text came. Then another. I read the previews but didn't open them. I couldn't block him. I wanted to. Almost did. My finger hovered...then backed out. It felt less final, less like betrayal.

Days bled together like watercolors in the rain. A week slipped by unnoticed. I quit the thrift store with one call, no explanation. My manager was kind, confused, but didn't press. I had money from selling my father's business and the house. Rent was covered. Food didn't matter. I barely left my bed. I couldn't close my bedroom door. The thought of it shut—trapping me inside—made my skin prickle with dread. I kept it cracked. Just in case. The bathroom door, too. I couldn't take a full shower unless air moved freely, as if a closed door could suddenly mean I'd never come out again.

This afternoon, Katie dragged me out of my room like a child and parked me on the couch beside her. She put on cartoons—bright, safe, silly. She knew exactly what she was doing. Cartoons didn't require me to laugh or feel; they were noise, harmless, never pretending to be anything but pure, uncomplicated distraction. And right now, that was all I could handle. A sudden knock at the front door cut through the TV's chatter, snapping our attention from the screen.

"I'll get it," Katie said, already rising before I could move a muscle—not that I planned to. All I felt capable of was crawling back into my room and shutting the world out—again.

She peered through the peephole. She let out a breath, heavy and irritated. Turning just enough, I caught her jaw clenched, brows tight, angry, protective.

"Who is it?" I asked, though part of me already knew. The knocking came again, insistent but not aggressive. Katie didn't answer me.

She raised her voice. "Go away."

Then I heard him. "Katie, I need to talk to her." His voice. Kevin's voice.

My whole body tensed. I sat up too fast, breath caught in my throat. I wasn't ready—not emotionally, not physically, not in any way that mattered. My palms were slicked with sweat; my heart pounded in my ears. I gripped the couch like it was the only thing holding me together.

"She doesn't want to talk to you. Go away, Kevin!" Katie snapped.

Silence followed. Then, softly—brokenly, "Please, Katie. I know you're trying to protect her, but that's her choice to make...not yours." His voice cracked, twisting something deep inside me—pain, familiarity, longing...betrayal—all coiling against my ribs. I didn't want to hear him, and yet...I did.

"Please. Just ask her," Kevin continued, "Ask her if she'll let me explain. We don't have to be alone. We can sit in the living room. You can stay. I just—" His words faded, strength dissolving mid-sentence. Katie turned to me, expression hard yet unsure. Her eyes asked the question she refused to say aloud: Do you want me to let him in? I stood slowly, unsure whether my legs would carry me or collapse. Stepping into the hallway, I grabbed the doorframe as though it could ground me, then nodded once. Katie's shoulders tensed, her voice was steel laced with fire.

"I'm going to open the door, but if you come near her or try anything, I swear to God—I will fucking kill you."

"Yes." His breath sounded like it had been held for days, desperation softened by hope. Katie unlocked the top lock slowly.

"You come in; you go to the couch. Nowhere else. You don't move unless I say so." The bottom lock clicked. The door opened. And there he was. Kevin stepped inside, but I barely looked at him. My focus fixed on my own hand, clenched around the doorframe, knuckles pale. It was the only thing keeping me from shaking. He was here. And I was still deciding what to feel.

I couldn't look at him. I heard his footsteps against the carpet—familiar but no longer comforting. Just haunting. Then came the soft, reluctant creak of the couch as he sat. Katie locked the door and stepped between us, like she could still shield me from what he'd said or what I might feel. Pulse hammering, I stared at the wall, counting imperfections, pretending my knees weren't shaking.

"Bethany," Kevin said softly. "Can you please look at me?"

I shook my head, biting the inside of my cheek to stop the tears already threatening to fall. My hands clenched into fists at my sides.

"Please," he whispered again, almost pleading. Still, I didn't move. If I looked at him—even for a second—everything I'd held together would splinter.

Katie's voice sliced through the room like broken glass. "She said no. You wanted to explain? Then explain."

Kevin muttered, "Where do I start?"

"How about at the beginning?" Katie shot back, sarcasm lacing every word.

A short, weighty pause. Then Kevin spoke. "I'm so sorry this happened to you. I didn't know Ian would do this...again."

That word—again—landed like a slap, a truth that escaped before he could cage it.

"Again?" I turned to look at him for the first time.

He looked up slowly, and I saw him—not the man I loved, but a shell. Hair longer. Unkempt. A shadowed beard. Circles under sleepless eyes. A hoodie and sweatpants like someone who had stopped caring about anything, maybe even himself. We stared, but the warmth I once felt—that little pull—was gone. Only a cold ache bloomed.

He nodded. "Let me explain. I told you I had a brother, but I never told you he was my twin. At first, I didn't know why I kept it from you, but I do now. I think a part of me wanted to pretend the past didn't exist—or that it couldn't reach us. But it was always there. I see that now. I should've told you everything."

His shoulders dropped.

"Ian was sick for a long time. He didn't show real signs until junior year of high school. I was dating this girl, Aly. Ian didn't have many friends, so he spent a lot of time with us. He was quiet, shy...he kept to the background. Then one day, he pretended to be me."

Kevin looked down, eyes fixed on the space between his shoes.

"He convinced Aly to meet him. Took my truck. She thought she was meeting me. He drove her to a spot we used to hang out and tried to convince her to run away with him. I don't know exactly what happened, but I think she figured out it wasn't me. She panicked, tried to leave. He wouldn't let her. He...he cut her hair." He glanced at me, eyes clouded with guilt. His voice cracked. "It was blonde. Like yours."

My breath caught.

"She'd been gone too long, and it was getting late. Her parents started calling me, thinking I was with her. But I hadn't seen her—I was home all afternoon. They told me they'd seen her get into my truck. That's when I knew something was wrong. Ian—and my truck—were gone." His voice stayed controlled, but I could feel him slipping into the memory, each detail pulling him back. "I told Aunt Tara. We went looking. We found them at the hangout spot. Ian was...out of control. We had to call the police. I held him down while Tara got Aly out." Kevin stared into the distance, lost in the past.

"When the police came, they had to tase him to stop. He was admitted to the hospital. That's when they finally diagnosed him."

I wanted to look away, but couldn't.

"He was diagnosed with Bipolar Disorder...and BPD." Bipolar, I understood. But BPD—? As if reading my thoughts, Kevin turned toward me again.

"Borderline Personality Disorder," he said quietly. "BPD is a condition where a person experiences intense emotions, mood swings, and difficulty with relationships and self-image. They may act impulsively. They're terrified of being abandoned. They don't know how to regulate anything, especially pain. When you mix that with Bipolar Disorder," he went on, "you get someone whose emotions aren't just intense—they're explosive. The highs are manic, the lows unbearable, and there's almost nothing in between. It's a constant ride and up, down, over and over again. Every emotion feels like life or death. For them...and everyone around them."

His voice trailed off, and the silence settled over us like fog. I couldn't tell if I was shaking from anger, heartbreak, fear—maybe all three. I wanted to scream, run, and cry until nothing remained. Instead, I stood there with the truth crawling under my skin, twisting inside me, staring at the man I thought I knew and realizing I never truly did.

"Tara didn't want to do it," Kevin said quietly. "The court stuff. The questions. The retelling. She said it would break Aly again...and break her, too. But Aly's parents wanted punishment. They wanted Ian locked away. For them, it was the only way to make sense of what happened."

He rubbed his hands together like they were cold.

"Tara talked to them—told them everything: about us, about the things no one really understood, about the way Ian changed after our parents died. She told them Ian wasn't evil; he was sick. And somehow, she got through to them. They went to the DA, said if Ian was admitted to a psychiatric facility—really admitted, long-term—they'd drop the charges. Aly got a restraining order. And Tara...she had to sign the papers to commit him, because she was all we had."

Each word dropped like a pebble, rippling through everything I thought I knew.

"He didn't go quietly," Kevin continued, voice tightening. "He said Aly loved him—said she was confused, that she needed time to understand what they had. When he realized she wasn't coming back, he broke. I watched them take him away. I watched them hold him down. And I just stood there."

He swallowed hard, eyes fixed on some invisible spot across the room.

"After that, everything changed. Aly's parents made it clear I was just a reminder of what happened to her—that I was too close to him. Everyone else agreed. I became the other half of a story no one wanted to hear. I was ostracized at school, so I left. Got my GED. Kept my head down. I visited him every weekend," he said, mine far away. "Sat across from him in a room steeped in bleach and fear, so sterile it felt like even hope had been scrubbed out. At first, he wouldn't look at me. He'd just stare past me, like I was a shadow he couldn't reach. Wouldn't speak. Wouldn't blink. It was like watching someone vanish in slow motion."

His throat bobbed.

"But then...after months of trying new combinations—adjusting dosages, switching meds—the doctors found something that worked. The fog started to lift. He began talking. Laughing. The therapy was working. He wasn't just existing; he was trying. After five years, they said he was stable—safe—that it was okay to let him out. I had my brother back," he said softly, almost like he didn't believe it himself. "We moved to California together. I started school. Ian picked up part-time jobs—bookstores, electronics shops, even a smoothie place for a while—but nothing lasted. Stability never lasted." Kevin's voice dropped, heavy with guilt. "He'd start feeling good—too good—and that's when he'd slip. He'd decide he didn't need the meds. Said they made him feel numb. So he'd stop. Skip one dose, then two, and slowly everything would slip. His moods turned like tides—impulsive, paranoid, angry. He'd spiral until there was nothing left to hold on to. Each relapse was like watching him vanish all over again."

He drew a shaky breath.

"Then one day, he was just...gone." The words barely held. "No warning. No note. Bed made, closet half-empty, toothbrush gone—like he meant to disappear. That was five years ago."

Five years ago. The year I left my father's house and vanished without looking back. Blood drained from my face. That's when he began looking for me.

Kevin didn't see it. He kept talking, unraveling. "I searched for him. Called every hospital—anyone who knew my brother. Nothing. He vanished. I didn't know if he was alive or dead. And then, out of nowhere, he came back. Just showed up." Kevin's voice cracked. "He looked healthy. Like...really healthy. Confident. Peaceful. He said he'd found

God. Said he was blessed. That he understood what his second chance meant." Kevin's eyes met mine and the truth hit him like a train.

That's when he'd been with my father. That's when Ian went looking for me.

Kevin's shoulders slumped. "I didn't know," he whispered. "I didn't know what he was doing. I thought he was better. I thought we could start over. I was just so damn happy to have him back." His voice trembled. "I didn't protect you. And I'm so sorry, Bethany. I'm so...so sorry."

I stared at him, but I wasn't in the room anymore. I was outside myself, watching the truth claw its way out of the dark. "He was looking for me," I whispered. "Back then. He disappeared because of me."

Kevin flinched. "I didn't know—"

I cut him off. "And yet here we are."

Silence followed. And then, as if he needed to fill the void, I heard him say, "I love you."

The words came suddenly, like they could erase everything that came before. But they didn't. They couldn't. I stepped forward, and Katie—who I'd forgotten was there—moved aside. My skin flushed, fists clenched, nerves stretched thin. When I spoke, my voice was controlled but laced with fury.

"Don't say that," I snapped.

"I do," he said, firmer this time—like he needed me to believe it. Like saying it louder might make it true.

"Do you know he said that to me? 'I love you,'" I said, mocking his words, letting the bitterness drip from every syllable. "That's why I left with him. I thought it was you. He said that to me, and I believed him. And now—now—you want to say it like it means something? Now?" Kevin flinched, his body reacting before he could hide it. But I wasn't done. Not even close.

"You love me?" I spat. "So much you hid your past—him—from me? You left me completely exposed. Vulnerable. And now I'm supposed to believe this wasn't your fault? What happened to me...it's just as much on you as it is on Ian." I was on a roll and didn't care if I was hurting him. I wanted him to hurt, just as much as I had in that root cellar, in that hospital bed, and every single day inside this apartment. I stepped forward, stopped by the coffee table.

"From the start, you pushed me to drop my walls. Made it your mission to earn my trust, knowing what trust had cost me. You knew my past. You saw the damage, the scars, the way I shrank at closeness. And still...you hid him. The one thing that could've saved me. You never gave us a real chance, Kevin. If you had, you would've told me the truth. But you didn't. You chose you. And in the end, it wasn't just a lie—it was a knife in my back. You say you didn't know. But ignorance isn't innocence, Kevin. It's negligence. It's betrayal with a smile."

He tried to speak, but nothing came out.

"How do I know you didn't plan this with him?" I snapped. "One brother seduces me, the other stalks and kidnaps me—tries to brainwash me? Hmm?" I tilted my head, the words seething out. "How is that not exactly what this looks like?"

His face crumpled. "Bethany, please..."

"You betrayed me with your omission of the truth!" I shouted, each word shaking with fury. "I could never trust you, Kevin. Not now. Not ever. Me trusting you almost cost me my life. And if I can't trust you—if I can't even believe what comes out of your mouth—then how the hell am I supposed to be in a relationship with you?" I stepped back. My voice dropped to a whisper. "And it almost killed me."

Kevin looked like he couldn't breathe.

"You think you love me?" I said. "Then you should've protected me. Told me the truth—no matter how ugly. But you didn't. You stayed quiet. And your silence...nearly destroyed me." I turned toward the hallway and started walking, the ache in my chest unbearable.

"Bethany—" Kevin pleaded.

I stopped, one hand on the doorframe. My voice was quiet. "I thought I loved you too...but it was only the version of you that you let me see." I looked at him one last time, the final thread between us snapping in my chest. "I want nothing to do with you." Then I turned to Katie, my friend, my witness to this relationship's slow death. "Will you let him out? I'm done." And then I walked toward my room. For the first time in two weeks, I closed the door behind me—no longer trapped in his version of the truth.

53

EVERYTHING & NOTHING

BETHANY

I bought blackout curtains, not for sleep, but because I couldn't bear the light. It felt intrusive—like it might reveal the pieces of me I was trying to let disappear. The darkness settled over me like a weighted blanket. In a morbid way, it comforted me. It reminded me of the root cellar, suffocating black, the scent of dirt, cold cement against my skin. Somehow, the panic it stirred was the only thing that made me feel real. That fear...that pain...reminded me I hadn't died down there—even if part of me wanted to. Even if most of me still felt dead.

I sold my car to one of those online places that didn't ask questions. They didn't care about the stains or scratches. I didn't care about the money. I just needed it gone. I pictured myself behind the wheel, Ian in the passenger seat, pretending everything was normal, like he wasn't a stranger. Like I hadn't missed every red flag. The details.

Most days, I didn't want to be here—or anywhere. I didn't cry or scream. I just...stopped. Stopped trying. Stopped feeling. Nights blurred into mornings, then into meaningless afternoons. Sleep came in pieces—two hours, maybe less. Every time I closed my eyes, the same images, the same sounds, the same panic waited for me. And when I couldn't take it anymore, I'd sit up gasping, heart racing, throat tight like I was still trapped.

Katie would come in, wide-eyed and worried, her voice the only thing that reached me. She'd lie beside me, trying to calm me down. I'd count her breaths—not because it soothed me, but because it was something to do. Something real in the fog. When she left, I stayed in bed—barely moved, barely blinked. The mattress held me like quicksand.

Showering felt like a performance I couldn't pull off. I'd manage every other day if I was lucky, dragging myself into the bathroom, peeling off my clothes like they clung to me out of protest.

I stared at the stranger in the mirror. My face was hollow, cheeks sunken, eyes dulled like the light inside me had burned out. The hospital had tried to get my weight back up, feeding me carefully, urging me toward something resembling normal. But once I got home, eating felt like too much. I only ate when dizziness hit—like in the cellar, when Ian decided one peanut butter sandwich a day was enough to keep me alive.

I didn't recognize the girl in the mirror. And honestly, I didn't want to. Time stopped mattering. The clock ticked, the sun rose—none of it touched me. The world kept spinning, and I stayed exactly where I was—drifting, silent, and slowly disappearing. I was lying in bed, flat on my back—just breathing. Just existing. That was my new normal. No plans. No expectations. Just one shallow breath at a time. Then came the knock.

"Bethany, can I come in?" Katie's voice floated through the door—gentle, stripped of its usual sparkle. Even that was enough to make my chest ache.

"Yeah." The door creaked open, and she stepped in. Her eyes met mine, nose scrunching like she'd walked into something sour.

"Okay. Enough is enough." Her hands landed on her hips. She stormed to the window and yanked the blackout curtains open like she was pulling the plug on my isolation. Sunlight stabbed my eyes.

"Why?" I groaned, yanking the blanket over my face. My only shield.

I heard the window slide open. "You—" She grabbed the blanket and ripped it from my hands, tossing it across the room like it had wronged her. "Need to shower. ASAP. And this room stinks like it's been abandoned for weeks." She stood over me, arms crossed, eyes burning with something between frustration and concern. Her expression said everything—disgusted, not with me, but with what I'd become.

"I really don't want to. I'm fine with it."

"Well, I'm not!" This wasn't a nudge. It was an explosion. Before I could react, she grabbed my hand and yanked me off the bed. "I'm not taking no for an answer." She dragged me toward the bathroom. "You're getting in that shower. You're going to scrub every inch of yourself, wash that hair, blow dry it, and then we're going for a drive. I'm done coming home to find you buried in this damn cave." She shoved me into the bathroom, flung open the cabinet, and tossed a towel and washcloth onto the counter. "I'm serious, Bethany. Get to cleaning." The door slammed behind me.

I stood there, stunned. Blinking. My reflection stared back at me in the mirror. My hair was tangled and matted—like it had given up, too. I lifted my shirt to my nose. The smell hit me, and I recoiled. God, I reeked. She wasn't wrong. Maybe I was depressed. Maybe disappearing. But smelling this bad? That was a new low. I stripped out of my clothes and stepped into the shower. The water blasted down, scalding. I didn't move. Cold water reminded me of the cabin, standing under it that last night, washing Ian's blood off. I could control this pain. This heat, at least, was mine.

I tilted my head back, letting water run through the knots, like maybe it could rinse the memories out too. I lathered in the shampoo, my fingers combing through the tangles as best I could. While the conditioner sat, I scrubbed myself down, trying to erase the days I'd rotted in bed. My legs were covered in light blond stubble that had turned into patches of fuzz. I groaned under my breath, grabbed my razor, and took my time. Ten minutes, maybe more, until my skin was smooth again. Until I looked like someone who cared, even if I didn't.

When I stepped out, I wrapped myself in the towel and blow-dried my hair, section by section, until it was dry and less wild. My limbs were heavy, but lighter than before. Then I walked into my bedroom and froze. It was...clean. Not just tidy—transformed. My black bedding was gone, replaced with a sunflower-yellow comforter so bright it almost hurt to look at. The sheets were fresh. The air no longer clung to stale sweat and old food. My cluttered dishes, my food containers, my dirty clothes—gone.

In their place was a version of normal I wasn't ready for. Like someone still believed I was worth cleaning up after. On the bed lay a folded white T-shirt and yoga pants, a pair of socks, underwear, a bra, and my Dr. Martens. Katie's touch was everywhere—quiet, but loud enough to feel. Either I took forever in the shower, or Katie had moved like a damn Tasmanian devil. I closed the door and got dressed slowly, one item at a time, dreading whatever she had planned next.

Katie rolled down the window, wind pushing through like it was trying to wake me up. It didn't work. It just made my skin prickle. It was the first time I'd stepped outside in weeks, and the sunlight felt aggressive—too sharp, too loud. People would probably call it a beautiful day, the kind that belongs on postcards or influencer reels. But to me, it was exhausting. The sky was too blue, too clean. I reached into my purse and pulled out my black sunglasses, sliding them on before the brightness could claw its way any deeper.

Katie tapped her fingers against the steering wheel, humming along to some upbeat song on the radio. It was too cheerful, too disconnected from the fog I'd been stuck in for weeks.

Her voice was light when she spoke. "Doesn't this feel good? Getting out, breathing fresh air, letting the sun warm your face?" She turned toward me, hopeful, like maybe this was the part where I'd smile, say thank you, admit that the wind felt like freedom.

I said nothing.

Her smile vanished. She turned back to the road. The silence that followed said everything she didn't. I could feel her disappointment radiating off her in waves—her knuckles tightening around the steering wheel, her jaw ticking as we cruised past the beach.

We drove for miles down the Pacific Coast Highway, like maybe the ocean could wash something clean in me. I stared out at the waves, watching them crash and pull away again. Over and over. I envied them. Their rhythm. Their ability to disappear and come back whole. I rested my head and drifted into that empty space I'd carved—quiet, gray, numb. Somewhere between sleep and escape. Eventually, the car slowed to a stop. I blinked awake, disoriented.

"We're back?" I rubbed my eyes and looked around. This wasn't home. We were in a deserted parking lot behind a nondescript brick building. The windows were tinted so dark you couldn't see inside.

"Where are we?" I sat up straighter. My heart ticked faster.

Katie didn't answer.

"Katie. What's going on?" She released a slow breath, like she'd been holding it since we left the apartment. Then she turned, eyes somber. "We're at your appointment."

I stared at her. "What appointment? I didn't make an appointment."

"I know." Her voice was calm and firm. "I made it for you. With a therapist. Her name is Dr. Sheila."

I locked eyes with her, the heat rising quickly beneath my skin. I balled my fists to keep from yelling. "Are you serious? You made me a therapy appointment without asking? How dare you. Did I ask for help? No. I'm fine."

"Yeah. You're doing great." She folded her arms. "Smell like you've been buried underground, haven't showered in days, barely eating, sleeping in sweat-soaked sheets, staring at the ceiling like you're waiting for something to take you out of your misery—just thriving, Bethany." Her sarcasm sliced through me. I snapped back before I could stop myself.

"You had no right, Katie. If I want to rot in my room, that's my choice. You don't get to drag me out here and ambush me like this. You don't get to decide what I need or how I should cope. Who the hell do you think you are?" She flinched. Her expression cracked.

"Who do I think I am?" she echoed, voice trembling. "The last time I checked, I was your best friend. Your only friend. I've done everything I could to keep you afloat for the past month. I thought I was family. The only person you let in. And now I'm the villain because I won't sit back and watch you fade into nothing?"

She looked away, trying to pull herself together. When she met my eyes again, hers were glassy—but blazing.

"I've been there every single night," she said. "When you screamed yourself awake. When you couldn't breathe, cooked your meals, cleaned your mess, stayed up half the night with you." She paused, looking at me like she didn't recognize me anymore.

"I have watched you disappear right in front of me. And I kept waiting for the day you'd come back. That maybe you'd laugh again. Or go outside. Or look me in the eye. But every day, you slip further away—and you expect me to just watch it happen and say nothing? I've done everything I could to hold you together, but I'm not enough. You need real help, Bethany."

I looked away, back down at my hands, twisting the hem of my shirt between my fingers.

She wasn't finished. "Everything about you—the way you move, the way you sleep, or don't sleep—it's like you're still down there. You're not healing. You're hiding. You don't talk. Don't try. What you went through was hell, but this isn't surviving. It's giving up. You survived Ian, but you didn't come back. Your body got out of that cellar, but your mind...it's still locked down there. You're still his prisoner. And I'm not letting him win."

I stared at her, swallowing the burn rising in my throat. Her words didn't come like an attack. They came like truths she'd been holding too long.

Katie's voice softened—just enough to break me. "I'm not trying to hurt you. I'm trying to save what's left of you. I'm not equipped for this, Bethany. I'm not a therapist.

And I'm not okay either." Katie inhaled, then spoke the words that hit hardest. "You have two choices. Go talk to Dr. Sheila. Or start looking for a new roommate. Because I can't keep living like this, Bethany. I love you, but I'm falling apart, too. And I won't drown with you."

My mouth opened but no words came.

Tears streamed down her face. "I'll move out. I'll give up our place—our rent-controlled unicorn of an apartment—because my mental health is hanging by a thread. You can afford it without me. But I won't keep watching you disappear."

I couldn't breathe. The idea of Katie leaving...of being alone in that apartment...it gutted me. She was all I had left—my tether. My person. And now she was giving me a choice that didn't feel like a choice at all. I turned my head toward the building. It looked the same—sterile, uninviting. But now it felt like a doorway to something I didn't know how to face. Pain. Shame. Healing. I wasn't sure which was worse. Without a word, Katie started the engine and pulled up to the front. She didn't say anything until we stopped.

"I'll be right here." She placed her hand over mine, thumb brushing my knuckles. "Just talk to her. That's all I ask." She let go, and I stared at the door—terrified of what was inside, but more terrified of losing the only person still fighting for me.

54

QUIET WORK

BETHANY

No one said recovery would be fast or easy—but I wished they'd warned me it would be this loud. Even in silence, it felt like screaming. I kept coming here. Twice a week. Because Katie made me, she sat in the car outside and said I had two options: walk in or watch her walk away. And I believed her. For once, she wasn't bluffing. So, I showed up. Not because I believed in the process, but because losing her would break me beyond repair.

Katie—my bossy friend—had somehow gotten bossier. She basically became my personal assistant, scheduling appointments, coordinating rides, even setting phone reminders, like I couldn't function on my own. And I hated that. I resented how she just took over without asking. But deep down, I knew she was right. It wasn't fair, expecting her to carry my grief like it belonged to her.

Dr. Sheila Mendoza didn't ask me why I was there. She never did. She just made space like she expected me to fill it when I was ready. And I hadn't been. Not really. She didn't dress like a therapist. There was no polished, put-together look meant to say authority. Today, she wore loose linen pants and a top with deep-blue stitching across the collar—it looked delicate and handmade. Her jet-black braid always fell over her right shoulder. Something about how she showed up—calm and unbothered—made it easier to do the same.

Her approach was different. We didn't sit in some sterile room under buzzing lights on a stiff, ugly couch. Our first meeting was an hour of drinking tea and talking about it. She said she wanted her patients to feel safe, that all of us had dealt with trauma in one form or another. Apparently, California covered therapy for victims of violent crimes.

That word—victim—still didn't feel like it fit, but I didn't argue. I just nodded and let her pour the tea.

And the truth? I liked her approach. It didn't feel clinical. It didn't feel heavy. It felt...possible. Like she already knew exactly what I needed and wasn't in a rush to pull it out of me. We always sat at the same round table. She never took notes. She didn't cross her legs or tilt her head like she was waiting to diagnose me. There was only ever tea between us, and a plate of cookies neither of us ever touched. Outside the cracked window, the world moved on, like I hadn't come undone. The tea was almost too hot, but I held the mug anyway—something to do. Something to anchor me. The heat seeped into my skin, and for a second, I focused on it instead of everything else.

"I went to the farmers' market with Katie on Sunday." I traced the rim of the mug. "She bought sunflowers. Said they reminded her of summer mornings." My voice sounded strange, like it had been locked up too long and forgotten how to come out. Dr. Sheila gave the smallest smile.

"Do they remind you of anything?" she replied.

I watched the steam rise, letting it fog my thoughts. "I guess...I used to like them. When I was little." I didn't add that the girl who liked sunflowers didn't live in this body anymore. She didn't push—just let the quiet stretch. For once, it didn't feel like pressure. It felt like...breathing room.

Dr. Sheila shifted a little in her seat, then said, "These last couple of weeks, we've talked about what's kept you here. Katie. Your routines. Tea. Moments." I swallowed. My throat was dry. "I wonder," she continued, her voice calm, "if today might be the day we talk about the thing that tried to take you away."

Something inside me recoiled, bracing for impact. I blinked hard, eyes locked on the cup like it held some kind of answer. She didn't say his name—just watched me. Calm. Present. Like she already knew I was halfway there, even if I didn't know it yet. And then—quietly, like she was setting something fragile down between us—she said, "Ian. The cabin."

It hit like ice. Like she cracked open a door I'd been shoving shut with all my weight. My fingers trembled around the mug, and I set it down slowly. I didn't want to give myself away, but my body already had. She leaned back, not retreating, just making space like she saw it all.

"You don't have to explain everything," she said. "Just...tell me where it started. You can stop anytime."

I nodded, but it was automatic. I wasn't even sure I meant it. My eyes dropped to the tea. The surface shook—maybe from me.

"It was cold," I said, finally. My voice cracked halfway through. "Everything about it was cold." And just like that, I felt it again. The way the walls held their silence like a secret. The way I stopped believing I'd ever be warm again.

I pressed my palms flat against my lap. I wasn't in Dr. Sheila's office anymore. I was back in the root cellar. The air turned colder, thinner. My spine stiffened like I'd hit ice water. I didn't remember slipping under, but I was submerged. My eyes were open, but they weren't seeing this room. They saw stone walls. Darkness. That single flickering bulb reminded me how trapped I'd been. I shivered. I needed out.

Panic welled up in my throat, hot and thick. I thought I'd escaped. I thought this part was over. But the cellar lived in me like a second skin—clinging tighter than ever. My chest tightened, each breath smaller, like oxygen was wrung out of me. A gentle hand rested on my shoulder.

"Bethany," Dr. Sheila said softly. The world snapped back, like someone had shaken the snow globe I'd fallen into. I blinked, startled to find her standing beside me, her eyes searching mine.

"Hm?" I croaked.

She stepped back, giving me room, then slowly lowered herself into the chair next to mine. "Where did you just go?"

I swallowed hard, staring at the tea I hadn't touched.

"I was...back in that room," I said, barely above a whisper. It pressed on my chest.

Dr. Sheila nodded, her expression soft. "Do you go there often?" I couldn't bring myself to say it out loud, but I gave a small nod. Even silently, admitting it cracked open a part of me I'd fought to seal shut. "And when it happens," she asked gently, "how do you bring yourself back?"

I hesitated, staring at the steam that had long since faded from my cup. "When I'm with Katie, her voice usually snaps me out of it. But when I'm by myself..." My voice trailed off, lost in the truth I didn't want to say.

She finished the thought for me. "It's harder to get out." Another nod. This one came slower. Heavier. She gave me a knowing smile—the kind that said I wasn't failing, just struggling. "Bethany, can I ask you something? Tell me five things you can see in this room right now."

Blinking, I said, "Five things? Anything?"

"Anything," she confirmed, her smile widening just a little. "Go ahead." I looked around, still feeling a bit disoriented, but willing to try.

"Okay...I see a mushroom figurine on the bookshelf. A stapler is on your desk. The shortbread cookies. My cup of tea. And...you."

She nodded. "Good. Now tell me four things you can touch." I wasn't sure what game we were playing, but I leaned in anyway.

"I can touch the table. I can feel my shirt. The chair under me. And the breeze on my skin from the window."

"Very good." Her voice was like a hand on a rocking boat. "This one might take more effort. Tell me three things you can hear."

I closed my eyes, tuning in. "The birds outside...the ticking clock...and...my breathing." When I opened my eyes, she was still watching me.

"Two things you can smell."

"That's easy." I smiled. "The peppermint tea. And your perfume—it smells like jasmine and vanilla."

Dr. Sheila chuckled softly. "Good nose." It made me feel safe, like I was allowed to be here, in this body, this moment. "Last one," she said. "Tell me one thing you can taste."

I reached across the table, picking up a shortbread cookie. I took a bite, the buttery crumble melting on my tongue. I swallowed and said, "This cookie. And it's amazing." It was the first genuine smile I'd felt all day.

"How do you feel?" She rose from her seat and walked over to her desk. She grabbed a notepad and pen, scribbling something down before tearing the sheet free. I took a breath and let it fill every inch of me. "Good," I said. "Relaxed."

She handed me the paper. I unfolded it:

Grounding Technique

5 – Acknowledge five things you can see

4 – Acknowledge four things you can touch

3 – Acknowledge three things you can hear

2 – Acknowledge two things you can smell

1 – Acknowledge one thing you can taste

Homework – Do this each time you find yourself fading back to the cabin.

"What we just did," she said, "helped you come back to the present. This technique—the grounding technique—it's a tool, Bethany. Something you can use when you start to drift. I want you to practice it. Every time it happens. Especially when you're alone." I folded the paper and tucked it into my purse. Maybe I couldn't erase the cellar. But maybe—just maybe—I could learn how to come back.

For the rest of the month, Dr. Sheila has helped me untangle the cold that lingered in my body long after the cabin. We talk about the loneliness that crept in during the silence of those days, about the emptiness that stays with me even now. It's not gone. But something's starting to shift—slowly, like water dripping into a glass. I sleep through most nights. The nightmares haven't vanished, but they don't strangle me anymore. Sometimes I wake up, and the darkness doesn't feel so heavy.

Today's session feels different—calmer, softer. Dr. Sheila invites me into the small garden behind her office. A light breeze moves through the trees, sunlight filtering down in shifting patterns across the pavement. She looks up at the sky and smiles. "Isn't it a beautiful day?" I take a slow breath, letting it fill me.

"It is," I say—my voice relaxed for once. We walk quietly until she asks, "Bethany, how was it growing up in Indiana?"

The question lands hard. I tripped, catching my foot on a rock. I'm not ready to go back that far—not today. But I let the answer come anyway.

"Um...Willow Creek? There wasn't a whole lot to do. Mostly church and farmland. In summer, it smelled like cow manure almost every day." I give a short laugh and start walking again.

Dr. Sheila chuckles too. "Well, I think I'll keep that place off my list of vacation spots."

I smile—a real one. "You're not missing anything. I don't plan on going back."

She tilts her head. "Why not?" I shrug, trying to sound casual. "There's no reason to. I sold the house, the business, everything. There's no one there I want to keep in touch with." My voice gives something away I hadn't meant to share. She catches it.

"Why is that?"

I stare at the cracks in the pavement. "They're reminders," I say at last. "Of the girl I used to be. They still call me Bethy." The name feels small in my mouth, like it doesn't belong to me anymore. "I'm not her. I left her there six years ago. I've changed. They wouldn't get that. They wouldn't even try. I want to be somewhere I can just be...me. Not the pastor's daughter." Dr. Sheila nods slowly. We walk in silence again, longer this time.

Finally, she asks, "Back then, when you weren't allowed to be yourself, how did it feel? And how did you start to find your way out?"

This time, the answer rises without thought. "I felt trapped," I say. "Like I couldn't breathe in my own house. My dad had rules for everything. So many rules. No space to mess up. No grace. Constant pressure to be perfect." I pause, memories surfacing in slow motion. "One day, he wasn't home. I was alone. I started singing—not worship music, not hymns. Just...music. What he would've called 'the devil's music.' And it felt..." I let out a soft laugh. "It felt like I had air in my lungs again, like maybe there was a version of me outside his expectations."

Dr. Sheila listens, undisturbed.

"I started doing it more. Singing when he wasn't around. And when I couldn't sing, I'd try to write songs. They were bad," I admit, smiling. "Really bad. But I kept writing. And with every song, I got better. It felt like I was building something no one else could touch." I lower my voice. "When we were packing up the house, I found that old notebook—the one I used to write in."

Her eyes flick to me, curious. "Do you still sing?"

The question touches something tender. "No," I whisper. "Not anymore."

I glance at my hands. "I used to. Katie and I would hit karaoke bars sometimes—just for fun. It was our thing. But after the cabin..." I shake my head. "I can't. He made me sing. Forced me. That song...it still haunts me."

I fold my arms, holding myself together. After a moment, she checks her watch and nods. "It looks like our time is up. I'll see you next week?" I turn to leave, but she calls my name softly. "Bethany?"

"Yeah?"

"Before you go, can I share something I noticed?"

"Sure."

She meets my eyes. "When you spoke about discovering your voice—your real voice—you relaxed. You smiled. That wasn't just a hobby; that was you pushing back against your father's control, finding a piece of yourself." Her words sink in. "I read the report," she continues. "I know Ian forced you to sing that church song. It was his way of controlling you—using your voice against you. And by not singing now, he's still doing it. He's still controlling that part of you." My breath catches.

"Maybe it's time to take that piece back," she says. "Write a new song. Sing something for you. Let your voice belong to you again." She smiles and waves. "Just something to consider. Enjoy the rest of your day." With that, she turns toward the building, leaving me caught between the past I ran from and the voice I silenced, wondering if maybe, just maybe, it's time to let it speak again.

I'm lying in bed later that night, Dr. Sheila's words echoing: He's still controlling that part of you. Maybe it's time to take that piece back. My voice. The words chase sleep away. I kick off the covers and sit up. The room is dim. I don't bother with the lamp. Moving on instinct, I cross to my closet, reaching for the top shelf until my fingers find the old composition book. I hold it close, then switch on the light and crawl back into bed.

The moment I open it, memories rush out. The ink has faded, but the words remain: messy, raw, unapologetic. Songs written when I didn't know who I was, but was desperate to find out. Lyrics about escape, freedom, and the ache of living a life that never felt like mine. I studied on a page where the handwriting slants sideways, rushed, as if I have to get the words down before they vanish. I remember writing it. I remember how bold it felt to believe my voice had power.

55

REVERB

BETHANY

Something happened last night. Not loud or dramatic. After reading that old composition book, I couldn't stop thinking. About what I used to write. About who I used to be. The girl who believed a song could carry her out of anything. I found an empty notebook shoved in the back of a drawer. Sitting cross-legged on the bed, I pulled the pen from the spine and started writing. Not because I had some melody burning in my head. Because I needed to say something.

Tired of you debating if you want to be with me
Because I know about her
And I am quite sure she knows about me

I stared at those lines for a long time. My pen hovered, but I couldn't move past them yet. Danny. God. I hadn't said his name in months. Maybe longer. But it was him. Every word. Every syllable. All the nights I pretended I didn't know what he was doing. All the times I took him back. I loved him so much, I forgot how to love myself. Now? I wouldn't give him five minutes of my time, let alone another chance. I hummed under my breath. The lyrics kept coming, like a faucet left on low. And somewhere in the middle of scribbling the chorus, I realized I had a full song. It wasn't perfect. But every word felt true. It felt like mine. I fell asleep with the notebook still open beside me, with the faintest smile on my lips.

I woke up early, not because of a nightmare. I felt refreshed. The sun was barely up. I walked to the kitchen, made coffee, and pulled out a carton of eggs. By the time I cracked the fourth one into the pan, I was humming again. The same melody looped in my head. Katie wandered out in her ridiculous yellow robe, hair in a wild, half-fallen bun.

"That smells good." She stretched. "What are you making?"

"Omelets," I said, tossing spinach into the pan. She leaned over my shoulder just as I flipped hers onto a plate.

"Look at you, domestic goddess," she teased. I handed her the plate and grabbed my own. We sat at the table together.

"It's good to see you up before me," she said, halfway through her first bite. "Did you actually sleep?"

"I did," I said, sipping my coffee. "Got about six hours."

She smiled like that alone was worth celebrating. "That's so good to hear." We made small talk over breakfast. Nothing deep. Nothing heavy. The tune slipped from my lips as I rinsed the plates, like it had found a home in me. "What are you humming?" Katie asked suddenly from behind me.

I jumped, nearly dropping the fork in the sink. "You scared me!" I laughed, wiping my hands on a towel.

She looked startled. "Sorry," she said quickly. Her smile faltered. I hated that. Hated the way her face changed—like she was afraid she'd broken something in me. Like I was fragile.

"I'm okay." I steadied my voice. "Really. I was just humming a song I wrote last night." Her eyes lit up. "You wrote a song?"

I nodded. "Yeah."

Katie crossed the room and pulled me into a hug. "That's amazing, Bethany." She stepped back, eyes searching mine. "What made you start again?" I told her about the notebook. About the lyrics. About what Dr. Sheila said—the part about reclaiming something that was mine. Her words followed me home, whispering to me all night. *Take your voice back.*

"I think it's good that you're writing." She brushed a stray curl out of my face. "That kind of stuff really helps. Are you going to keep doing it?"

I gave a small shrug. "I don't know. I don't want to put pressure on it. If it comes, it comes."

"You never know." She smiled hopefully. "Maybe you'll have a whole album."

"Maybe," I said quietly. But I didn't believe it. One song didn't mean everything was back.

A few weeks had passed since that first song, and after every session with Dr. Sheila, another poured out. Like clockwork—like therapy left a window cracked just wide enough for the music to creep in. I hadn't even realized how much I'd written until tonight. Katie and I curled up on the couch, a throw blanket tangled around our legs while the last season of Bridgerton played in the background. Apparently, I missed a whole season while my life fell apart. Go figure.

I thumbed through my notebook, flipping past scribbled lyrics and half-finished melodies until I reached the last page. I counted—then counted again. "Twelve," I said aloud, almost in disbelief. "Katie, I've written twelve songs."

Her eyes lit up as she moved closer me, reaching for the notebook like it was a fresh batch of gossip. "Let me see!"

I clutched it to my chest, laughing. "I think not!"

She gasped, offended, and kicked at me. I kicked back, gently, and she retaliated by launching a couch pillow at my face. I ducked just in time; the pillow hit the floor with a soft thud. We erupted into laughter—the kind that felt easy, real, and overdue. Catching my breath, I settled against the cushions.

"I missed this."

"Me too." Her voice softened as she squeezed my hand. I looked at her—really looked—and guilt rose to the surface.

"I'm sorry I disappeared into Kevin. You never disappeared. You always showed up, even when I didn't deserve it. I'm just...I'm really thankful for you." Tears blurred my vision. Katie's eyes shimmered, but her smile held.

"I'm just happy I have my best friend back." Her voice dropped. "I'm happy you came back...and that you're alive."

That part landed harder than I expected. I climbed over to her side of the couch and wrapped my arms around her, holding her like I hadn't in ages, like I finally knew what it meant to be held.

"Thank you," I breathed into her shoulder. She didn't answer right away; she just held me tighter.

When I finally loosened my hold, Katie stood abruptly. "I'll be right back." Drawers opened, a closet creaked, then silence. Her footsteps were soft when she returned, but her energy buzzed. "Okay," she began cautiously, something hidden in her hand. "Please don't be mad." I took it slowly, recognizing the bold name the second I saw it.

Collin Conners.

Shadowplay Records

"Katie...what is this?"

She eased beside me like she was defusing a bomb. "You left his card on the table that night. When you went outside, I-I picked it up." She shrugged, a sheepish smile curling at her lips. "I kept it. Just in case you changed your mind."

I stared at her, then back at the card, turning it over like it might reveal something else. My stomach fluttered with dread.

"I don't know about this," I said slowly. "Yes, Collin works for Shadowplay...but he's Kevin's friend, Katie. That's too close. Too messy. I don't want anything to do with Kevin—or anyone orbiting him."

"I get that," she said gently, "but...hear me out." She leaned in. "After everything at the cabin, Collin reached out to me."

My head snapped up. "Wait—what? How did he even get your number?" A teasing glint slipped into my eyes; I remembered how she looked at him, like a mirage in the desert. Katie rolled her eyes, cheeks flushing. Busted.

"We exchanged numbers, okay? But not for the reason you're thinking," she insisted, nudging my ribs.

"Ow!" I laughed, despite myself.

"He thought it might be smart to stay in touch...you know, in case he needed cybersecurity help." She raised an eyebrow. "Because you told him I studied it, remember?" I did. I hadn't thought twice about it then, but now it knotted my stomach. "Anyway," Katie continued, "he just wanted to check on you. He heard...what happened.

290

From—well, from he-who-shall-not-be-named." Disappointment slipped into her tone. "He only asked how you were doing. I haven't heard from him since."

I curled my fingers around the card. "Do you really think I should call him?"

"I think you'd be foolish if you didn't." Her voice softened. "Bethany...you've been through hell. If one good thing can come out of all this, why not let it be you?"

"I haven't sung them out loud. Not really. Not how they're meant to be heard. I don't even know if I can."

Katie clasped my hand, her eyes fierce with love. "Your voice is your voice. No one can take it now. You're not in that place anymore." She pressed my phone into my palm. I stared at the screen, then at Collin's name on the card. My heart thudded, nerves tangled.

"I'm doing this," I whispered. I walked down the hall and closed the door behind me. My fingers hovered for a breath before I dialed—then I pressed call.

I met Collin at Studio A, tucked away inside a building on Wilshire Boulevard. Before I'd even agreed to see him, I'd made one thing crystal clear—he wasn't to tell Kevin, not about the meeting, not about the music, not about anything. Whatever this was, it had to stay strictly professional. Collin agreed. That was all I needed.

Now we sat in the studio. My new guitar rested against my leg, its strings fresh with possibility. Collin brought a sound engineer named John and a producer named Michael—a man whose presence was impossible to ignore.

"Thanks for booking this session for me. I know your time's valuable." I hoped I didn't sound too nervous.

We were gathered in a circle, all of us sunk into rolling chairs like conspirators in a creative heist. Collin looked over at me with that natural charm; he had the kind of face Katie would be drooling over if she were here.

"When you said you wanted to fund this project—use my ear, my experience—I was grateful you remembered me," he said. "What sound are you going for?" I chewed my bottom lip.

"That I'm not really sure of yet. I think I want to experiment—try on different sounds until something feels like mine. Does that make sense?"

"Totally," he said without missing a beat. "That's why I brought Michael in—musical genius." He patted Michael's shoulder who sat back with easy grace, and—damn—he was good-looking. His skin was the color of deep honey kissed by sunlight, his cheekbones round, his lips full, his eyes flickering with mischief—or maybe curiosity. He wore a cardigan with bright neon colors, yet somehow not overwhelming. A silver chain lay against his chest. Even in stillness, he moved with rhythm.

"Collin said your voice was something out of this world. Since this is our first time meeting and I haven't heard you yet...would you play something for me?" I knew this moment was coming. Told myself it was just another karaoke performance. This was the first time I'd let my voice out since Ian—since the silence that followed. I reached for my guitar, settling it across my lap.

"This one's called 'I Hate You.'"

Collin groaned theatrically. "Oh boy."

"It's not about him." I shot him a playful glare. "It's about someone I used to know." I let the strings hum to life. A beat passed. Then another. And I sang.

"You said you wanted to be with me...but all I can see is you're playing with my emotions..."

The words curled like smoke. A blend of rock, blues, and raw soul. My voice trembled at first, then caught fire. Michael began stomping in time, adding crisp claps beneath the melody—sculpting the song like he saw the finished form buried in marble. I broke into the chorus.

"I hate you. I hate your fucking guts."

When the last chord faded, silence held for a heartbeat. Then all three of them clapped like I'd cracked open the sky. Collin turned to Michael—their eyes met in wordless agreement.

"Well, that settles it," he said, grinning. "I think I just heard my next Grammy."

I blinked. "Seriously? It needs a lot of work."

"Sure." Michael smiled. "It needs some cleaning up, a few background vocals, a kicking drumbeat...but with my touch, it's gonna be a smash." Collin stood. "I'll leave you three to it. Bethany, call if you need me." He waved and slipped out—like his part was done, and the rest was up to me.

56

SOUR GRAPES

BETHANY

Katie and I were slouched on the couch, the light from the TV flickering across our faces while Married at First Sight played in the background. She was fully locked in—gasping, giggling, side-eyeing the screen every few seconds—but my mind was a million miles away. I couldn't stop thinking about Michael's last session.

We'd been working together for two months now, sculpting the pieces of this album into something that felt real—something that finally felt like mine. And just when I thought we were wrapping up, I had started packing my guitar when he hit me with it.

"Overall, this album's pretty good," he said casually, like he wasn't about to wreck my sense of accomplishment. "But it's missing something." I froze mid-motion, my fingers still curled around the strap.

"Missing something?" I tried not to sound defensive. "What do you mean?" I thought the songs we'd built were strong, honest. The production was clean, the melodies haunting, the lyrics vulnerable in all the right places. "It sounds good to me."

"It's good," he repeated, "but I think you need a ballad. Something stripped. Something that pulls people right into the center of you."

I rolled my eyes so hard it hurt. "A love song? Michael, seriously. I am not in a place mentally—or emotionally—to write about love." I tightened the strap across my shoulder. "Heartbreak? Sure. Drama? Always. Maybe something flirty about the hot guy at the bar, but love?" I shook my head. "Not happening." He smiled that annoyingly patient smile—confident, silent, infuriating.

"Just think about it," he called after me. "And figure out what you're naming this album already!"

Now, here I was—half-watching a groom argue about compromise while Katie clutched a throw pillow—thinking about the ballad I didn't want to write and the even more stupid fact I still hadn't named the album. I stood and stretched, trying to shake the creative frustration off my skin.

"You want anything from the kitchen?" I asked.

"Yeah," Katie said, eyes glued to the drama. "Bring out those green grapes I bought last night."

I grabbed a bottle of water, rinsed the grapes under the tap, and dumped them into a ceramic bowl. Back on the couch, I handed the bowl to Katie, who immediately plucked one from the stem and popped it into her mouth like it was her favorite candy.

"Mmm, so good. Bethany, try one!" I paused, then flicked one free and tossed it into my mouth. The first chew was awful—bitter and sharp, the kind of sour that catches you off guard and makes your jaw clench. I winced, swallowing anyway.

"Ugh, how can you eat these? They're so sour."

Katie just grinned and popped another in. "They're refreshing. I love how crisp and tart they are. The perfect balance of tanginess and sweetness." I watched her pluck another grape and let it disappear behind her smile. That same bite had curled my tongue and soured my whole mood. I stared at the bowl between us, the thin green skins catching the light, still dewy from the rinse. They looked harmless. Pretty, even. But to me, they were harsh. Too tart to enjoy.

I settled back, pressing the cold water bottle to my cheek, letting the chill settle me while my thoughts wandered. It wasn't just about the grapes. I thought about Michael's words—you need a ballad. I thought about the sessions, the songs, the way I'd been stitching pieces of myself into every lyric. None of it felt clean or smooth or easy to digest. And then, like a slow unfurling, it began to settle into place.

Maybe the music isn't meant to be sweet—or feel good right away. Maybe it's supposed to sting a little—because that's what life has been: bitter at the beginning, tangy in the middle, and every once in a while, there's a note of sweetness. My fingers drifted toward the bowl. I lifted another grape and rolled it between them, studying its light-catching skin. It looked the same as the others, and it dawned on me—that's what this album is.

Some people will hear it and wince. They'll taste the ache in my voice, the sour notes, the truths that don't go down easily. They won't like it. It'll be too much. But others? They'll get it. They'll feel the fractures, the complexity, the honesty because it's real. I was those things. I like the bitterness of reality. It isn't polished or polite. It's raw. Honest. Unapologetic.

A slow smile tugged at the corner of my mouth as I set the grape back in the bowl.

"I think I just figured out the name of the album," I murmured. Katie tore her eyes from the screen. "Yeah?" I relaxed into the cushions, the name solid on my tongue. "Sour Grapes."

A few days later, I was back in Dr. Sheila's office. Gone was the cozy setup: the little table with tea. Today felt clinical, intentional, and prepared. She sat in a structured blue chair I hadn't seen before, her posture more upright than usual. She motioned to the matching couch across from her, the one that made me feel too exposed.

"What's going on?" I asked, cautiously stepping in. "Why the change?"

Her voice was calm, but there was weight to it, as if she were bracing me for impact. "Good afternoon, Bethany. I wanted to try something different with you today. I want to prepare you. This session is going to be heavy. We've come so far with your progress, but we still need to talk about a sensitive subject."

My stomach turned. I knew what was coming—them. I nodded, but it was a reluctant nod that said okay, even though everything inside me screamed no.

"Take your shoes off," she said softly. "Lay back. Get really comfortable." Comfortable. What a joke. Still, I did as I was told. My shoes hit the floor with a soft thud. I eased onto the couch, feeling anything but comfortable. I sank into the cushions, every nerve braced—spine stiff, throat tight.

"I'm probably going to cry today," I whispered.

"That's okay. Let's start slow." She didn't ask about Ian first—that would've been cruel. She asked about Kevin. "What did he bring into your life?"

I stared at the ceiling, blinking hard. My voice came out thin, like paper soaked in water. "Safety," I said. "At least, it felt like that. He made me feel...chosen. Like, for the first time, someone saw me—really saw me—and didn't retreat. He showed up. He remembered the little things. He made the world quieter. I didn't know love could feel that...still..." I paused. "He made me want to believe in things again."

She waited, letting it sit. "And Ian?" she asked softly.

My heart twisted; my jaw locked. "Ian looked like him," I said. "Exactly like him. But everything about him was wrong. His voice was cold. His eyes didn't see me—they studied me. I was something to claim, not someone to care for." My voice cracked.

"I kept praying he'd go back to being the Kevin I remembered—the one who made me feel safe, who held my hand. I knew something was off, but I clung to the hope it was just a moment, a mood he'd shake off. That any second, he'd soften—he'd see me again. And for a while...I let myself believe that."

Tears spilled without warning—hot and violent.

"I didn't know he had a twin. So when I showed up at the apartment and he invited me to the cabin...I felt safe. That's what hurts the most. My guard was down—I thought I was with someone I loved, who loved me back. And that safety? That comfort I let myself feel? It wasn't real. It was a trap. By the time I realized the difference, it was already too late."

"You're allowed to separate them," she said at last. "One brought you love. The other brought you pain." The part of me that curled in the root cellar, praying into the floorboards just to survive, still saw one face.

"How?" I choked. "How do I separate them when I see his face every time I close my eyes? When I hear Kevin's voice, my stomach drops because I still don't know if it's his or Ian's?"

She lowered her voice. "Because your body remembers what your heart couldn't process. That's trauma confusion. You were lied to—violated—by a mirror image of the man you trusted. That kind of betrayal cuts through logic."

Sobbing now, I nodded. "I keep asking myself why...why didn't Kevin tell me? Why did he keep something that big from me?"

"And why do you think that?" she asked.

"Because he didn't trust me," I snapped. "Or worse—he thought I couldn't handle the truth. Like I was too fragile to know what I was walking into."

"Or," she said gently, "because he was afraid."

"Afraid of what? That I'd leave? That I'd see him differently?" I laughed bitterly. "Well, congratulations. I did."

"Sometimes people hide what they're ashamed of. Sometimes they confuse control with protection."

I shook my head. "It wasn't protection—it was power. He decided what I could know, what I could prepare for. And it almost killed me."

I wiped my face.

"You loved him," she said.

I nodded—hard. "With everything I had. I trusted him. I gave him all of me, and he let me walk into hell blind." My voice broke. "I still miss him." She didn't speak; she let the words sit like salt on a wound. "I miss how he smelled, how his hand fit mine, how he looked at me like I was magical. And I hate myself for that."

"That's the cruelty of trauma," she murmured. "It doesn't wipe out the beautiful things—it leaves them behind, tangled with pain."

"I wake up reaching for him," I said. "And then I remember...it wasn't him. It was Ian. That memory lives inside my head. I don't know how to get it out."

"You're not supposed to remove it," she said. "You're meant to live through it—survive it. And you are."

I couldn't breathe; unsaid truths crushed my chest. "What if I never trust myself? What if I fall for someone, and this happens all over again?"

"Then you'll fall wiser, with boundaries—with self-trust. Your gut wasn't wrong—it was deceived."

I turned my face into the couch, tears endless. "I want to forgive him," I whispered. "But I also want him to hurt. To feel all of this."

"You're allowed to want that," she said. "You're allowed to rage—and to grieve the man you lost, both of them, even if one was never really yours."

I stared at the ceiling, empty and full at the same time. "I'm so tired."

"I know," she said. "But this? This is the work. And you're doing it."

For the first time, I didn't feel like I was coming undone. I was ready to let love and pain in—without drowning. I wasn't swimming against the current anymore; I was moving with it. After my session, I didn't want to go home. I wasn't ready for silence—or walls closing in. I ordered an Uber and asked the driver to take me to the beach. It had been too long since I listened to the ocean instead of the noise in my head.

The sun dipped low, casting warm, golden light that made even sadness look beautiful. I sank down into the sand, my bare feet burrowing beneath the surface. The breeze brushed my skin like an apology. I reached into my bag and pulled out my notebook. It was worn—corners curled, spine soft from being opened so many times.

I stared at the water. The waves moved with their own rhythm. I let my mind drift with them. I thought about Kevin. About the first and second dates, the way we danced like the rest of the world didn't exist. The way he made breakfast on Saturdays—barefoot, shirtless, humming like he was already in love. I smiled, even though it hurt. Those were the good parts—the real ones, untouched by what came after. I looked down at the blank page in my lap, and then, without thinking, I wrote:

When two hearts lose one, and the damage is done

How can we get back to where we were one?

This wasn't a love song about fairytale endings. It wasn't the romance people write about in novels. It was about longing—the kind that sits in your throat and won't move. It was about the soft, golden moments before everything cracked open. The impossible ache of wanting something you know won't return in the same shape. A prayer whispered to the past—and the quiet acceptance that the past no longer lives here.

The words poured out of me as though I were bleeding ink. I didn't stop to think. I couldn't. My hand moved faster than fear, faster than pain. I wrote until my fingers cramped, the wind tugged at the pages, like it could carry the weight away—until the ache in my chest softened into something I could survive.

By the time I was done, I felt emptied—completely. As though I had taken every fragment of love, heartbreak, hope, and confusion—every buried emotion I'd been too afraid to name—and spilled it onto those pages. God, it hurt. But it was a good kind of hurt.

It was beauty and pain, tangled like vines. But most of all...it was love.

57

THE FINAL NOTE

BETHANY

We played the whole album for Collin in the studio—just me and Michael. No distractions. No fancy equipment. Just music, nerves, and the ache in my chest. He stood near the board, arms crossed, eyes narrowed. Every so often, he gave a small nod. His expression stayed unreadable. He was listening, but I couldn't tell if he felt any of it. And that scared me more than I expected. Then we reached the final track—the one I dreaded and clung to.

I stared at the screen, finger hovering above the trackpad. My throat was dry, palms damp.

"This next song..." I started, but the words broke apart halfway through.

Michael stepped in. "I challenged her," he said, glancing at Collin. "Told her the album needed a ballad—something stripped down. Something that made people feel everything she didn't say out loud." He looked at me. "And she delivered more than a love song. She gave us heartbreak." He nodded toward the console. "She named it *Even Now.*"

I nodded once, still unable to speak. I didn't want to explain it. Not this one. It wasn't a story I could narrate—it was one I had to let tell itself. I hit play. The first notes slipped through the speakers—soft, bare, exposed. I kept my eyes down, staring at my notebook, though I wasn't reading it. I couldn't look at Collin—couldn't face disinterest masquerading as praise. My voice came in low, hushed—like I'd crept into a room.

"When two hearts lose one..."

I heard every breath in the room. Every pause in the chord. It all felt louder now. Realer. Like the song had been waiting for this space to fully exist. I risked a glance at Collin.

300

He'd closed his eyes. His face had softened. His fingers moved faintly in rhythm—nothing dramatic, just enough to show me he was in it, that he was letting it in.

When the final line faded, no one moved. Collin didn't open his eyes immediately. I didn't realize how tightly I'd been holding everything until that final note fell away. He finally looked up. His eyes met mine, like someone who'd just returned from someplace unexpected.

"That was…" he started, then stopped. The sentence didn't come. Only the emotion behind it did.

Michael broke the silence for him. "Exactly."

I let out a long breath. My spine relaxed in the seat like my body was just now remembering how to exist again.

Collin blinked, still catching up to the moment. "That song…" he said slowly, "is going to wreck people—in the best possible way. People need to hear this. Not just the song. The whole album. You've got something rare. You need to showcase it."

My lips parted in a half-smile. "That's the plan," I said. "Katie's already booked a venue—the same bar where you first saw me sing. She built a website. Set up all the socials. Apparently, I have a full-blown campaign whether I was ready or not."

Collin nodded, calm slipping back into his voice. "When?"

"Two weeks from today."

"I'll be there," he said, with no hesitation. "What do you need from me?"

Before I could answer, Michael cut in. "I've got the rest lined up. Here's what we need…" Their voices folded into plans I once only dreamed of. It felt surreal. Letting the echo of Even Now settle in my bones. Letting myself believe—really believe—that it was finally happening. And that maybe, just maybe, I was ready.

The night had finally come, and Katie fussed over me, eyeliner poised like a weapon, brow furrowed.

"Will you please be still?" she snapped, leaning in. "I'm trying to make your eyes look like they could seduce the moon." I laughed nervously, but my body kept shifting anyway. I couldn't help it. My hands were clammy, my stomach a mess of knots and flutters. I'd sung in front of people before—plenty of times. Karaoke was easy; I could pretend to be someone else, feel someone else's heartbreak, someone else's fire. But this? These were my words. My wounds. My truth. And asking a crowd to feel it with me? Terrifying.

I let out a shaky sigh, loud enough that Katie paused mid-swipe. She stepped back. I cracked one eye open, expecting an eye roll, but her face had softened.

"What?" I asked, startled by the look in her eyes.

She blinked, pulling herself back into motion. "Nothing's wrong. You look beautiful. You're going to be amazing. There's nothing to be nervous about." Before I could reply, she grabbed my hand and tugged me toward the full-length mirror across the room. "Go look."

I stepped in front of the mirror and froze. "Holy shit," I whispered. "What have you done to me?" Katie's eyes widened.

"Wait, do you hate it? I can start over. We've still got time."

I turned to her, laughing through nerves, and shook my head. "No. That's not what I meant." Awe crept into my voice as I looked again. "You made me look like a goddess—an actual, glowing, can't-be-fucked-with goddess." Katie grinned, shoulders finally relaxing. I hugged her tight, meaning it in every inch of me.

"You know this night—this album—none of it would've happened without you. If you hadn't pushed me to see Dr. Sheila, if you hadn't kept Collin's card…I don't know what I did to deserve you, but I'm so damn lucky to have you in my life."

Katie pulled back, tears shining in her eyes. I brushed one from her cheek.

"Don't cry," I said, the laugh wobbling in my throat. "If you cry, I'll cry, and we'll both look like raccoons in combat boots." We pulled apart, both sniffling and smiling. "Besides," I added with a teasing nudge, "you can't walk into that bar with a blotchy face—not when Collin's going to be there. How else are you supposed to turn on the Katie-charm and finally seduce that man?"

Katie rolled her eyes so hard I thought she might tip over. "I don't know what you're talking about," she huffed, already heading off to get dressed. She disappeared, leaving me alone with my reflection. I studied myself, tilting my head to see it all. Long blonde hair pulled into a high ponytail, a few strands loose around my face—soft, pretty, still me.

A plain black crop top hugged my ribs, layered over a sheer black long-sleeved shirt that clung like a second skin. It wasn't flashy, but it felt like armor—honest, a little battle-worn. The skirt was tight red plaid, snug against my hips. It made me look like a dare someone wouldn't walk away from clean.

Fishnets climbed my legs, knee-high socks layered on top—equal parts rebellious and nostalgic. And the boots—black, thick-soled, heavy—felt like a statement with every step, as if, if I stomped hard enough, I could shatter glass and everything that had once broken me. I looked at myself and felt it—the echo of the girl I used to be layered under who I'd become. Bold. Bruised. Still standing. I smirked at the mirror. She's still in there. And tonight, she was ready.

I stood just offstage, half-shielded by the curtain, the low thrum of the crowd crackled through me like static. I could feel the room before I saw it—voices tangled, glasses clinking, laughter buzzing beneath my skin. The place was packed. Every table taken. People lined the back wall, shoulder to shoulder, leaning in like they were holding their breath. Waiting for me. A cold, electric shiver ran down my spine. They're all here...to see me.

Katie had pulled off the impossible. I don't know how—charm, blackmail, or sorcery—but she filled the room with energy, like something big was coming. Something worth showing up for. Michael appeared beside me.

"Hey," he said. "Being nervous is natural—it means you care. Let it live in your chest, but don't let it steer. Go out there and leave it on the stage. This album is gold. You are, too. Believe in it—and believe in you."

I nodded, breath shallow, hands ice-cold. He gave me a quick hug and walked off, heading toward the front where Katie and Collin sat side by side at a small reserved table. They didn't talk, just watched each other. A quiet current between them. Whether I was curious or just deeply amused, I couldn't decide.

DJ DeWayne's voice thundered over the room. "Aight, aight, y'all settle down a bit," he boomed, grinning into the mic. "We've got a real treat tonight. Some of y'all may remember this voice from karaoke night—yeah, I see you smilin'. You know what I'm talkin' about. But tonight? Nah, tonight's on another level."

Laughter faded into a hush. "Tonight," he continued, "she's not just singin'. She's debuting her first full-length album, Sour Grapes. And you lucky sons of bitches are about to hear it before anyone else does." Cheers erupted—stomps, claps, whistles. The walls vibrated. "I've known her as Bethany," he said, stretching the moment, "but tonight she steps onto this stage with a new name—a name you'll remember. So make some noise for the one, the only...Riley Waters!"

The room exploded. The sound had power—thick, pulsing, rising in waves. I felt it in my ribs, my name crashing through the chaos, layered with claps. My heart slammed.

I closed my eyes and whispered, "It's your time. Your voice. No one's holding you back." Then I stepped out.

Stage lights hit my skin. I walked to the mic, not as someone pretending or afraid, but as me. The crowd quieted, every eye on me.

"Good evening, everybody!" I called. "Are you ready to hear some real music tonight? If you are, let me hear you say yeah!"

"YEAH!" they roared. Grinning, I eased the mic off its stand.

"DeWayne," I said, playful, "can you do me a favor?"

"Anything for you, Suga," he chuckled.

"Before you cue up that first track, I need to say something."

I turned to the crowd—women in heels with drinks raised, guys in hoodies already swaying, couples sharing looks over candlelit tables.

"Ladies," I began, "have you ever been in love with a fuckboy?" The place lost its laughter, cheers, and a confession we all shared. "I don't mean the kind you vent to your group chat about. I mean the kind that leaves a mark—the kind that has you questioning your own damn sanity."

"HELL YES!" someone near the bar shouted. We were connected now—one pulse, one breath.

"Well," I said, pacing the stage, "thinking about him now makes me sick to my fucking stomach." More laughter, a few claps, a chorus of preach from the back. "This first song was inspired by that exact kind of man—the kind who leaves a wound so wide it sings while it heals." I flashed the booth a grin. "It's called I Hate You. DeWayne, baby—go ahead." He laughed and hit play.

When the beat dropped, I didn't walk—I arrived. Every line, every note, every breath. I gave it all. I wasn't hiding anymore. I was here. Alive. Unfiltered. Finally—finally—heard. This feeling...God, this feeling was unlike anything I'd ever known, like flying without wings, like stepping into fire and not getting burned. Each song fed me, filled me, lifted me. And the crowd followed—faces lit, bodies swaying, breaths held. I had them.

Completely. I'd cast the spell. Pulled them under. Every lyric, glance, and beat, I held the thread and watched them unravel. And there was only one song left. Just one. And this one? I didn't want to seduce or sway. I wanted to break them, because I needed to break me.

I turned to the booth. "DeWayne, cut the music." He didn't question it—just hit pause. The speakers fell silent. A hush settled over the bar. Not heavy or tense, just still. A breath held in the dark. And that's when I felt it. The ache, the absence, the longing that came without warning—sharp, familiar, stupid.

Kevin.

My eyes scanned the crowd before my body caught up to what my brain already knew. I looked for him anyway—for the tilt of his head, the quiet smile he wore when he thought no one was watching. He wasn't there. Of course, he wasn't. I'd told Collin not to invite him, not to mention the show. And Collin had listened. He honored what I asked. And now here I was, paying the price for it.

My chest throbbed as I stepped forward, grabbing the mic tight. "The next song," I said, "is the last track on the album. I wrote it from a place of love, of pain—of trying to hold on and learning how to let go." I swept the crowd, heart splitting behind my ribs. "This is me—bare, stripped, no filter. I hope it helps you find your truth." I turned to DeWayne and nodded.

The first chords of Even Now slid through the speakers—low, melodic, mournful. Something in me cracked wide open. The sound unraveled me. Vision blurred, tears rising too fast to stop. My throat tightened around the first line. I tried again. The second line slipped out in a whisper, trembling, still not enough. I lifted a hand toward DeWayne. He cut the track. Silence hit harder the second time. I stepped forward, chest heaving, eyes wet.

"I'm sorry," I said, breath catching. "I just...I need a minute. Could I take five? Just five minutes to gather myself?" I felt like I was bleeding out in front of them.

From the back, a voice called, "It's okay, Riley! Take your time—we're here!" Another shout followed: "Go ahead, girl. We got you!"

Something eased inside me—not all the way, but enough. I managed a small smile.

"Thank you," I whispered. Stepping offstage, adrenaline still buzzing, I saw Katie rise. Concern lit her face, purse in hand like she'd storm heaven or hell. I mouthed that I was okay. She stopped then sat back down. I slipped through the side door and into the night.

Air hit my skin like a balm—cool and necessary. I leaned against the brick wall, pressed my head back, and closed my eyes. Above, clouds drifted, but stars shone between them, tiny sparks cutting through the dark. I felt lost and luminous all at once.

Footsteps crunched on gravel. I opened my eyes. And there he was. Kevin. My breath caught. It was him.

"Kevin," I whispered. His name felt fragile—like if I said it too loud, it might break, or worse, he might disappear. A ghost summoned from the past, standing under the same streetlamp where my world had begun to unravel. Time folded in on itself.

He looked almost the same as the night we met—same jacket, same quiet stance—but his hair had grown longer, curled slightly at the ends, and a full beard now framed his jaw. He looked older. Sadder. Soft in that way, grief leaves on people who've carried it for too long. Kevin froze mid-step, like he couldn't trust what he was seeing.

"Bethany?" His voice cracked like a prayer too painful to finish. That ache in his voice was mine too. He took one step toward me. Then two steps back.

I stared at him, heart pounding, trying to make sense of the moment. Was I hallucinating? Was this what it felt like to finally snap—to lose more than your mind, to lose the space that holds your reality together?

"I...I didn't know you'd be here," he said, voice cracking in the middle. "I should go. I shouldn't be here. I'm sorry." He turned and started to walk away—fast. Something inside me lit on fire. This wasn't a dream. This was him. My Kevin.

"Kevin, stop!" I cried. He froze. Turned slowly.

"What are you doing here?" My voice was rougher—harsher than I meant—but I didn't take it back. He stood under the parking-lot lights, hands shoved in his jacket pockets. His body language screamed nerves—darting eyes, tight jaw, unsure legs. He raked a hand through his hair, the way he always did when his thoughts outpaced his words.

"Um...sometimes I come here," he said, quiet, hesitant, still not meeting my eyes.

"Here?" Disbelief coated my voice. "Why? Why here, of all places?"

Then he met my gaze, those gray eyes that once held every promise I believed. "To remember," he whispered. "To remember you. To remember us." My breath stuck. "I'm sorry. I shouldn't be here. This is your place. I'll go. I won't come back." He turned like he meant it. And that—that broke me, hot and buried, simmering for months beneath the grief and silence.

"This," I snapped, stepping forward, "is your problem." He stopped mid-step. "You always think you know what's best for me, for us. You decide and walk away like no one else gets a say. You're such a fucking coward."

He didn't move. Didn't speak. His silence only made it worse.

"Don't you dare turn your back on me," I yelled. "You don't get to show up and leave before I can speak. You lied to me. You kept things that could've prevented everything. Not because you didn't love me, but because you wanted control. You couldn't stand me seeing the mess. So you gave me a fantasy and let me walk into a nightmare." His head dropped, as if the words hit him physically. I didn't stop. "Do you know what that did to me?" My throat burned. "Do you even fucking realize what I had to crawl out of?" Tears streamed, hot and blinding. "For months, I carried the weight of what you did like it was mine to sort through. You didn't trust me enough to let me in, and that choice shattered something I've spent every day since trying to rebuild. No matter how I tried to live with it. Nothing worked."

He looked up then—eyes red, mouth parting like he wanted to speak. Nothing came.

"And the worst part?" I choked. "It's not what Ian did that stuck with me. It's you. Your surrender. The betrayal. The fact that I still reach for you after nightmares I wouldn't even have if you'd just told me the truth."

Kevin's face collapsed, armor finally pierced. "I never meant to hurt you," he said, voice barely holding. "I didn't know how to say it. I didn't know how to explain the kind of damage Ian was capable of. I thought—if I didn't name it, it wouldn't touch you."

I laughed—dry and bitter. "Well, it touched me. It destroyed me." My whole body trembled—rage and sorrow coiled inside me. I tried to shake off the feelings, I stared up at him. I saw the pain in his face, the guilt that looked like it had eaten him alive in my absence. I saw the man I loved, who broke me, and never stopped aching.

"I hate what you did," I whispered. "I hate that I had to go through all of it without you—because I couldn't trust you to stand beside me. I hate that when everything fell apart, you gave me no choice but to walk away." He opened his mouth, but I lifted a hand. "But I still love you." His breath caught; his eyes filled. "I love you in ways that don't make sense anymore. In ways that hurt. I tried to stop—God, I tried—but I can't."

He stepped closer. "Bethany." And I didn't run. I let him close the distance, and when he pulled me into his arms, I didn't push back. I broke against his chest like I'd been holding myself upright for months and only now remembered what it felt like to collapse in someone else's arms. I clawed at his back, clinging to the one person I swore I'd never need again. But I did. I needed him in this moment—like breath, like mercy.

His lips crashed into mine—not soft, not slow, but frantic, devouring. Everything we hadn't said, everything we'd lost—every lie, every scream, every night spent aching alone—erupted between us. His kiss was ruin, redemption, a war we didn't know how to stop fighting. I kissed him like I hated him. Like I loved him. Like truth lived between our mouths, and I needed to feel it. He groaned into my mouth, and I swallowed the sound like it was mine. Hands. Teeth. Breath. Heat. We weren't gentle—we didn't know how to be.

I pressed my forehead to his, our gasps colliding in the space between. His eyes searched mine like he was afraid I'd disappear. I held his face, trying to memorize every line, every scar, every inch of the man I never stopped loving. When he whispered my name like a vow, a plea, a prayer, I kissed him again, drowning, with him as my only air. I clung to him as if his mouth were the only place I still existed. His fingers tangled in my hair; mine clutched his jacket, unwilling to let him go. God, I missed him.

He backed me into the brick wall, and I didn't care. I needed his weight, his heat, the truth of him pressed against me—something I thought I'd lost. I wrapped my legs around him, kissing like I'd never known another mouth. I kissed him until my lungs burned—and still didn't stop. This wasn't just lust. It was love, and it was ours—twisted, bruised, unforgettable. A siren cut through the night. We stilled, breath the only sound. I looked up, lips swollen, eyes full.

"I don't know how to restart this," I whispered, "but I know I don't want it to be over."

He brushed his thumb across my cheek. "I'll wait. I'll do whatever it takes."

I stared at him, then laced our fingers together. "Come on," I said. "I have one more song to sing."

He blinked. "What do you mean?"

I smiled. "I have to finish what I started." I led him through the doors, past the heads that turned as we walked by, toward the table where Katie and Collin sat frozen mid-conversation.

"Get him a seat," I said. Katie's eyes widened. Collin blinked in surprise. Michael just gave a small, knowing nod. I walked back to the stage, pulse even. The mic waited like it always had. The bar quieted. This time, I wasn't singing alone.

308

I nodded once at DeWayne. He nodded back. The intro of Even Now began to play. The chords rose, slow and tender, like breath from a wound, still learning to close. This time, I didn't feel the urge to run. I didn't clench the mic. I didn't shrink. I let the music bloom—curling around my bones, filling every space I thought I'd lost. I let it hold me. Then I sang. Not as Riley or a girl trying to prove she'd survived, but as me. Bethany. Whole. Healing. Still here. My voice didn't tremble. It held because Kevin was here. Because I was still here.

I sang to the man I loved. To the ache I thought I'd buried, to the pieces of us still scattered across time.

The crowd disappeared. Blurry faces. Dimmed lights. The low hum of the world fell away until all that remained was him. His breath. His stillness. The way his eyes never left mine, not for a second. Each word pressed into the air like it had waited months for me to come back and sing it. The lyrics weren't just sound. They were stitches. Every line sewn from months of forgetting, forgiving, and learning to live with both. This time, they didn't break me. They freed me.

By the time I reached the final note, something in me felt...clearer. Like a window cracked just enough to let the light in. The final note stretched, slow and raw, and I let it go with everything I had. Then silence. Not empty, but held. Like the whole room exhaled and didn't dare breathe in again. No clinking glasses. No shifting chairs. Just stillness. The kind that reached inside and refused to let go. Awestruck. Unspoken. Undeniably felt. And then, Kevin stood. His hands lifted slowly, deliberately. Clap. Clap. Not loud or rushed. Measured. Sure. Like he'd waited for the exact second it felt right to move.

The room followed as if they were all waiting for his cue. Applause burst forward, rippling through the space like a wave. A woman near the front wiped her eyes. Someone at the bar murmured, "Damn." Chairs creaked as more people rose to their feet. I stood there, breathing it in like the first real breath after being underwater too long. I'd done it. I bowed to the audience. Katie was on stage before I could react—she crushed me against her, squeezing with enough force to make me stumble.

"You did it!" she shouted into my ear, half-laugh, half-tears.

I hugged her back. "We did it," I whispered, and meant every syllable. Collin and Michael followed, smiling, proud. Their words blurred, but the warmth didn't. Katie snatched the mic with no hesitation, already flipping into full manager mode.

"If you liked what you heard tonight," she announced, "follow @Songbird_Riley_Waters on all platforms. The album is dropping soon. That was just the beginning." The crowd erupted again. People moved forward. Some asked for selfies. Others held out napkins for autographs. I smiled. Posed. Thanked them. But through all of it, my eyes kept going back to him.

Kevin stood near the back, quiet and still in the noise. He didn't interrupt or try to claim the moment. He just stood there. And I think that's what made it feel even more real. Eventually, the crowd thinned. Drinks refilled. Laughter returned. I stepped offstage, boots hitting the floor with a finality I hadn't expected. I walked straight toward him. He didn't move.

"Are you hungry?" I asked, like it wasn't the most loaded question tonight.

He smiled, small and sure. "I could eat."

"Good," I said. "I need a burger like I need sleep."

We turned toward the others. Katie and Collin were at the door. Michael winked and followed. Kevin moved to go with them. I stopped him, slipped my hand into his, and tugged gently. "I'm glad you're here."

His eyes searched mine like he didn't want to miss a thing. "I'm glad I'm here, too."

We stepped into the night. The street buzzed in that easy Friday-night way—cars rolling past, music pulsing from a bar. Katie turned back to us with a bounce in her step.

"We can walk to the burger place. It's just around the corner."

We started moving. I took a step. Then another. But something stopped me. Something unseen rippled through the quiet—a tingle at my neck, a weight in my thoughts. I stilled. Kevin must've felt it too. I saw the way his body went alert, his fingers tightening around mine.

"What is it?" he asked.

"I don't know," I said. "I just...don't like it. Something's off."

He scanned the sidewalk and alley. His jaw clenched. "It's okay. Whatever it is, we'll face it together."

Then—

A shape moved from the shadows. Tall. Slender. Purposeful. The streetlamp didn't catch his face, not right away. Just the slow, eerie silhouette of someone too confident to be unsure of where he was going. Everyone stopped. Even the laughter faded.

Katie turned, concern painting her face. "Bethany?" she asked gently. "You okay?"

I couldn't speak. Because then, the voice came. Silky. Detached. Almost amused.

"Hello, Bethany."

The temperature dropped. That voice. My whole body locked up, like my bones forgot how to move. My hand slipped from Kevin's. I couldn't breathe. The world went quiet. Too quiet. My lips parted. The name slipped out, barely a whisper. But it hit like a scream.

"Danny."

— • —

THE DEVIL & THE DETAILS – PLAYLIST

Music plays a powerful role in this story, both for Bethany and for me as the writer. The songs mentioned throughout the book aren't just background noise; they carry emotion, memory, and meaning. They helped shape the mood of each scene and brought the characters to life in ways words alone couldn't. I wanted to highlight the songs that are featured in the book and the ones that helped me write The Devil & The Details. I hope you'll listen along and feel everything they made me feel while writing. The playlist can be found on Amazon Music, Apple Music, and Spotify.

1. "The First Cut Is the Deepest" – Sheryl Crow
2. "Ocean Eyes" – Billie Eilish
3. "Sleep to Dream" – Fiona Apple
4. "Sullen Girl" – Fiona Apple
5. "Criminal" – Fiona Apple
6. "Levels" – Avicii
7. "Sandstorm" – Darude
8. "Don't You Worry Child" – Swedish House Mafia
9. "Lose Control" – Meduza
10. "Landslide" – Fleetwood Mac
11. "Alone With You" – Alina Baraz
12. "Dangerous Woman" – Ariana Grande
13. "Linger" – The Cranberries
14. "Glory Box" – Portishead
15. "No Light, No Light" – Florence + The Machine
16. "The Chain" – Fleetwood Mac
17. "Genie in a Bottle" – Christina Aguilera

18. "One Way Street" – Reyna Roberts
19. "Black Velvet" – Alannah Myles

HONORABLE MENTIONS

"Wildflower" – Billie Eilish

"Messy" – Lola Young

"Labour" – Paris Paloma

"Earned It" – The Weeknd

"House of Ballons/Glass Table Girls" – The Weeknd

"Wicked Games" – The Weeknd

— • —

ABOUT THE AUTHOR

Kelly R. Nelson is the author of Sisters, It's Not The Way, and The Devil & The Details, where she writes unapologetically about love, survival, and all the messy emotions in between. Her stories are bold, layered, and never shy away from heat. A proud single Mom, California native, and lifelong writer, Kelly balances storytelling with real life—raising her kids, working full-time, and chasing her dream of being a full-time author. She believes in complex women, and her stories aren't just about surviving—they're about reclaiming power, pleasure, and a whole lot of spice.

For more on Kelly R. Nelson, follow her on social media @kellyrnelsonstoryteller.

www.ingramcontent.com/pod-product-compliance
Lightning Source LLC
Chambersburg PA
CBHW050014120726
47903CB00006B/1760